The

Eternal

Saga

Presents...

THE
IMMORTALS

By
Michael R. Finley

Chapters

PHASE I:

The

Angel

In

The

Disguise

Chapters

Enjoy

Chapter 1

A Birthday and an Engagement

(Adam)

It's my 101st birthday and it feels like another night. A night where my body is filled with its normal toxins; alcohol, tobacco, and utter sadness. I sit on my couch, feet up on my wooden coffee table thinking about my life and other things of personal importance. My condo was warm and dimly lit perfectly. I watched out the window as the snow gently covered all of Chicago. What a magnificent sight indeed. As I watched the snow, I started to think to myself; Another year with no answers on why I'm here, what I'm supposed to do, and what is my purpose. I take another long sip of my vodka and another puff of my cancer stick. The way I indulge myself, my lungs and liver should have given out on me years ago, but since I am incapable of a worldly death, it just makes me feel a little less lonely. It's my birthday anyways, I feel as if I'm entitled to treat myself.

I look around my spacious condo only to truly realize how lonely I really am. I just wish my brothers and sisters would call down to me, even just for a brief conversation. I miss them so very much. I look at my phone to see the time. "12:07." I say to myself calculating how many hours I would stay up tonight. I figured I would take this time to pray to my father like I do every night, even if I was 100 percent sure I wouldn't get response.

"Dear heavenly father, please hear my cry. All I ask for is clarity. Why have you taken my wings from me and punished me so cruelly? As one of your most loyal angels, why have you forsaken me so? If this is a test, what do I need to pass? Please father, answer me!" I prayed. My eyes remained closed when I heard a faint beautiful sound coming from the hall way. I managed to get off my knees almost effortlessly and got to my front door. I could hear a piano playing a beautiful tune, an unfamiliar tune. I slowly opened my door and the music allured me as if my ears just started working properly. I walked down the large hall until I reached the door igniting this amazing sound. I knocked on the door twice, unaware of how late it was. After a moment the door opened, and a tall blond-haired man appeared. I never noticed that anyone lived here. He looked around 30 something, with a powerful beard. That was the first thing I noticed. He opened the door a bit startled.

"Umm, hello, how may I help you?"

I felt the need to introduce myself before he thought was I was a lunatic.

"Hello, my name is Adam Tyler. I couldn't help to notice that beautiful sound coming from this room. I just wanted to admire your work. Is it an original piece?" He smiled as I said this. I assumed he doesn't hear this often.

"Wow, well I appreciate that Adam. I'm Jason House, and yes, it is. It doesn't have a name yet. It's just a melody that came to me a few minutes ago."

I sobered up rather quickly. "Well it sounds delightful." I said. He smiled with approval. "I am glad to satisfy your ears. A lot of this younger generation doesn't appreciate fine music." He laughed, I laughed too, for the simple fact that my baby face makes me look no older than 22. "Hey, wait here..." he said as he disappeared into his home. I nodded as I stood in the empty hallway. He soon returned with a card in his hand. "Here, take my card. I give music classes and piano lessons down on Wabash and Lake, you should come down sometime." He said as he gave me his card. I gazed at the card and sure enough it read Jason's House of Music. "You are a Music teacher?"

"Yup, been doing music since I was 7." I placed the card in my pocket before I misplaced it. "When is your next session? I eagerly asked. "Tuesday. 5:30. Will you attend?"

I thought about it briefly and quickly nodded. "I'll be there at 5." He smiled and shook my hand. "Okay, Adam can't wait to see you, now you have a good night." I smiled as I nodded. He shut the door and I stood there for a moment. "Music lessons?" I said to myself. "How random." As I started to walk back to my room, I could hear the beautiful melody again. I had a feeling in my heart, for the first time since I been on earth, that maybe, just maybe, this was something much more than I anticipated it to be. I quickly forgot about the idea after another couple shots of vodka. Drunk and tired, I flopped on my bed. "Happy Birthday to me..." I said right before I closed my eyes and fell into a deep slumber.

(Melody)

I was exhausted. I usually never stay up this late, but clearly, I had no choice. It was my sister Victoria's bachelorette party and I would not have won sibling of the year award if I missed it. The room was highly decorated and extremely loud. All of our female friends managed to make an appearance. I struggled as I tried to place my long curly dark brown hair over my ear as I took another sip of the random carnation of a drink Victoria handed to me earlier. My hair was much too massive to cooperate with me, so I gave up and just left it alone. I wasn't drunk, but I was feeling something.

"Melody?" Victoria said as she flops on the couch next to me. She is drunk off her ass, like she is supposed to be. Her deep brown hair bounced effortlessly as if she was fresh from a movie scene

"Yes, future Mrs. Levine?" I said as we laughed. She placed her arm around me and placed her head on my shoulder.

"I know right? Mrs. Levine? I can't believe I'm getting married!" She said happily. I was so happy for her, beyond happy. Victoria is my incredible older sister and my very best friend in this world. I was happy she finally found someone to spend her life with. Her fiancé Matthew is a nice guy. I like him with her.

"I know we used to talk about this all the time, and now it's finally here. You know I'm ecstatic about it." I said. She smiled at me and held me as a drunken, loving sister should. For some reason, we both burst into tears. This truly has been something we have talked about since we were little girls playing with our Barbies. Thankfully, the room was so loud nobody noticed us crying like drunk babies. The truth was that no matter how happy I was for Victoria, I couldn't help the feeling of my own loneliness. Love is something that I always wanted; something I always hoped to have, by now at least. I just feel like it's not going to happen for me. The guys in this world have lost all sense of chivalry, all sense of manners and charm seemed to evaporate when the 2000's came. Maybe it's been lost even before that. I am such romantic though. I seek a love so great, that it probably doesn't exist.

So, as I hold Victoria, I think to myself, is there a love out there in the world for me? And if so, where is he?

Chapter 2
Crash

(Adam)

I decided to walk to Jason's studio to get some fresh air. It was only a couple blocks down the street, so I thought it would be good for me. It was beautiful outside, even though it was a little cold out. I was dressed well prepared for this Chicago weather. My North Face coat and Ralph Lauren Boots kept me surprising warm.

Nervousness and excitement was on my mind as I thought about this class; maybe because I haven't done anything productive in years. I walked eagerly to get there but slow enough to not reach my destination so quickly. I turned my iPod on and quickly searched around until I found John Mayer's Neon. I love this song for unknown reasons, but I was big on music, so my iPod was my best friend.

I made my way to Wabash and began to walk slower. I was caught in John Mayer's lyrics when I heard a crash. A car crash exactly. I took my ear plugs out and tried to locate where the car swerved to. People began to panic, and the streets began to crowd with passerby's. The car was upside down when I spotted it.

"Call the ambulance!" I screamed as I ran towards it. "Help me!" I heard a faint voice scream from within the vehicle. "I'm coming!" I answer back. I looked down in the passenger seat and there laid a young woman trying to crawl out the car but was stuck on her seat beat. "It's going to be okay. Give me your hand." I said as I reached out both of mine out to her. She struggled as she attempted to reach me. I grabbed her and pulled her seat beat, tearing it in half. She held on to me tight as if any minute I would change my mind and abandon her, but I wouldn't abandon her, I couldn't abandon her. After several minutes she was in my arms, light and delicate. I carried her to the upcoming ambulance truck, looking at her small face and wild brown hair. She had a gash on the right side of her head. The blood was leaking down on to her eyes, so she kept them closed. I was curious to see those eyes of the delicate girl in my arms. Very curious.

"We can take it from here, sir." a police officer said as I placed her on the ambulance bed. She turned her head and managed to open her eyes. I gazed at them, which felt like an eternity. A magnificent eternity. Her green alluring eyes captivated me so deeply, I felt as if she was looking in the core of my very soul. She was beautiful, beyond beautiful. Her green eyes sparkled as she looked at me briefly until she closed them once again. The door shut, and the truck sped off into the distance. "Umm, sir?" I forgot the officer was still standing there for a minute. "I'm sorry, will she be okay?" I replied still standing there, eager to get my answer. "I'm pretty sure she will come out just fine. We will do all we can to make sure of it. We appreciate your help out there. You saved that young lady's life." He said as he started to walk away, but quickly turned back towards me. "How did you break that seat beat?" He said as he looked at the torn belt still in my hands. I didn't even notice that I was still holding it. "I don't know officer, I must have got lucky." I said. He gave me a weird look and turned around. I was just as stunned as he was. I did in fact break that seatbelt. I haven't had an ounce of power since I landed here on Earth.

I stood there for a minute, still trying to contemplate what just happened. I looked at my phone only to see the time. "5:17." I said to myself as I placed my phone back in my pocket and hurried my way to my music class.

I walk in the beautiful studio just in time, and of course all eyes were on me. "Welcome, welcome, you may sit anywhere you like." Jason said. I looked around the class and I was impressed. Beautiful guitars and pianos were everywhere. The room was full of life and the students all smiled at me with big grins. This was a happy place.

"Okay, we are about to start, just waiting on Melody of course." Jason said as he began taking out his books. I assume this Melody girl must have a habit of arriving late.

After a ten minute of waiting, Jason began the class without her. I had my book open and my pencil sharpened. I was ready. I sat next to this young woman named Victoria. I noticed her name on the sheet of paper that she was writing on. She was quite pretty and knew a lot about music, she was the only one raising her hand and volunteering for everything. "You must be the top student in this class?" I managed to ask her. She laughed. "No, I wish. My sister Melody is usually the one who is always on top of everything. I'm just filling in for her I guess." We both laughed and that's when I noticed a brand-new diamond ring on her wedding finger. "Congrats." I said looking down at her hand. She followed my eyes and smiled. "Well, thank you umm, what was your name again?" She asked. I forgot that I never introduced myself. "Adam." I simply said. She smiled as she turned to put her face back in her book. I did the same.

Minutes turn to hours as I sit in the class. I was really enjoying myself, learning how to read and write music. I pick up things rather quickly so after two hours, I could already play four songs on the guitar. I was impressed with myself. "Alright class, we are almost finished, I promise." Jason said as he picked his up guitar. Victoria's phone began to ring frantically as we started to play a tune I wasn't quite familiar with. "Oh, its Melody." She said to Jason and the rest of the class. "Great. Let's see what was so important for her to do, that made her miss her class." Jason said as he sat on his desk waiting patiently.

"Hey girl, where are you?"
Silence.
"What?!"
Silence.
"Oh my God, I'll be right there."
Victoria said as she hung up the phone.

"What's wrong? Jason asked concerned.

"Melody, she was in a car accident. I'm going to go see her." Everybody started to put on their jackets and coats immediately. "A car accident?" I said out loud. Could this be the same young woman I saved earlier? The same young woman who I thought I would never see again. "Impossible."

"May I ride with you?" I asked Jason. "Sure Adam, I'll be in the red Honda outside." He said as he walked out the building with everyone else. I stood in the studio for a moment thinking to myself. "Could this be her?"

Twenty minutes later we arrive at Rush hospital all anxious to see Melody. I think I was the most anxious of them all. It got a lot colder in the last couple hours I was in class.

The sun has been sleeping for some time now, so the moon light glistened off the shiny hospital building. Victoria was leading us all through the hospital while we followed right behind her. We managed to find our way to the waiting room. It was huge and empty. Everyone crowded the receptionist desk to find the whereabouts of Melody. Overwhelmed, the receptionist finally gave us her room, 345. We rushed through the long hallways and up two flights of stairs until we finally reached her room. A nurse named Ms. Potts walked us in quietly and there laying peacefully in bed was the same girl I saved, Melody. She was wide awake watching a show called One Tree Hill very attentively (Don't ask how I know that show). Her beautiful dark brown hair sat on her pillow so delicately. Her skin looked so soft, so rare. I looked at those eyes again, those beautiful green eyes. Melody was beautiful, remarkable. I never seen anything like her before. I couldn't take my eyes off her.

"Melody?!" Victoria said as she ran towards her. Melody smiled as Victoria and the rest of the class embraced her. "Thank you guys. I'm okay..." she started until she saw me. She stared at me deeply, with those eyes, which I could tell were going to be my weakness. I stared back, none of us uttering a single word. Victoria looked at me then back at Melody. "Umm this is Adam, he is new in our class. Do you two know each other?" She asked. Without looking at Victoria, Melody slowly sat up in her bed and placed her feet on the cold hospital floor. Her eyes were still on mine. She stood up off her bed and started to walk towards me. Everybody watched in astonishment. I couldn't bear to look away from her. She stood right in front of me and smiled. "Thank you." She simply said as she embraced me tightly. She placed her head on my chest and closed her eyes. I placed my arms around her and held her even tighter. The room was quiet, wondering what exactly was going on. Victoria smiled. "This may be the start of something interesting." She said. I smiled and prayed that she was right.

(Melody)

"What the hell?" I said as I woke up in a hospital bed with blue scrubs on. I looked around the room for my clothes only to find them laying across a chair sitting next to my bed. My head was throbbing, hip and back was hurting, but other than that I was okay. I sat there trying to replay everything in my head:
Got in my car.
Headed toward my music class.
Listened to Jhene Aiko.
A dog ran across the street.
I pressed my brake.
My car skid down the street.
My car flipped over.
I was trapped.
I'm being carried away by my savior.

That is all I remember. The face of that man that saved me still was on my mind. He saved my life and I may never see him again to repay him. Life has always worked out like that when it came to me.

I place my head on my pillow and stared at the ceiling, thinking. The room was quite chilly, so I pulled the white blanket up to my neck. Letting my mind wonder random thoughts like who the hell took off all my clothes and changed my unconscious body? Who gave them the authority? The face of my savoir entered my thoughts again. I thought about his curly brown hair and hazel eyes glaring at my bloody forehead and banged up body. How bad could a first encounter be? I notice there was a pain on my side that just starting to catch my attention. Without further hurting myself, I adjusted my body to attempt to decrease this irritating pain, only to find out that I was laying on a television remote control. "Wow." I said out loud, as if the remote control was obviously the reason. I pressed power and browsed through the cable channels until I ran across my favorite show of all time. One Tree Hill has been my obsession since it first aired a few years ago. It was a show about half brothers who hate each other, but they were in love with the same girl, well at least that's how it started. I loved it simply because of the romance, and I am a sucker for the romance.

"How are you feeling Ms. Eve?" The nurse said as she entered the room with some baked chicken and rice. She was an older woman, maybe in her fifties. I smiled as she placed the food on my table. "Yes ma'am, I feel alright, just have a headache." She placed her hand on my head and smiled. "Sleep will fix that child. You will be alright." She said. "Oh, and by the way, I am your nurse this evening. Just call me Ms. Potts. "I smiled as I took out my hand from under the blanket.

"Thank you for taking care of me, I'm Melody Eve." She smiled and shook my hand.

"Pleasure to meet you, Ms. Potts."

"The pleasure is all mine." We both laughed in the blank hospital room. One Tree Hill interrupted any awkward silence in the room which was reassuring. I gazed at the chicken for at least seven minutes before taking my first bite. I never felt comfortable eating around other people, but Ms. Potts seemed sweet so far.

"Your family should be here any moment beautiful." I smiled at the compliment thinking about Victoria driving like a bat out of Hell to get here.

"Knowing them, they are probably on the way." I said as I placed another delicious piece of chicken into mouth. Ms. Potts laughed as she fixed up my blanket.

I spent a lot of time in the hospital throughout my life. Every time I came here, it always reminds me of where my real parents were. My parents were unknown to me. I didn't know what they did, who they were, or even their names. I didn't even know if they were alive. My best friend's mother, Vanessa Maria Eve, adopted me as an infant from this very hospital. I was left in the hospital nursery with no evidence of a mother or father. No birth certificate, Nothing. It was like I just appeared there. Ms. Eve has been the only mother I ever known. She treated me as her true daughter and I was blessed for that very reason. What made it even better is that she had an energetic lovable daughter named Victoria, who was only a year older than me. We grew up together, she was my sister blood or not.

"Okay, my dear, I will let you get some rest. Press that button on your remote if you need assistance." She said as she started to leave the room.

"Yes ma'am." I responded as I smiled and pulled the blanket up to my chin. I turned the television down and attempted to watch some my show until the sudden quietness made my eyes drowsy. I finally closed my eyes and entered a slumber...

"Don't worry, I'm here." An unfamiliar voice whispered in my ear. I looked up to see it was the handsome stranger who saved my life. His face was calm, and his curly brown hair was flowing vividly as the wind ran through it. I didn't respond, I was much to intoxicated in his stare. I noticed my feet wasn't on the ground, but my body was in his arms. He was carrying me to an unknown destination I had no clue. I didn't mind, where ever we were going I knew it would be a place of pure bliss. I looked behind us and I noticed my car upside down on the side walk. "Oh my God!" I said out loud. The enchanting stranger placed me in the back of an ambulance truck and fastened me in.

"I will see you soon, Melody." He said as he closed the door. My mind went to completely darkness, but my heart beat never sounded so beautiful.

I opened my eyes only to find out I was dreaming. I looked at the clock to see how long I been out. "7:58." I said to myself. I felt like I was out for much longer. I began watching the last couple of minutes of One Tree Hill until Ms. Potts entered the room again.

"Sorry to bother you Ms. Eve, but you have some visitors." She said smiling. "Let them in please." I responded smiling back. With that came my sweet Victoria leading a pack of my music classmates. All their faces came appearing in the door and they quickly embraced me. I was talking to Victoria until he walked in. An unfamiliar face walked in the room with eyes I could never forget. An unfamiliar face, yet a very familiar face. Thinking to myself "Could it be him?" I stare at him intensely, although it may be rude to look at a stranger without speaking, but I was compelled to stare. I could hear Victoria say something, but all I got out of it was the name Adam. His name was Adam. I examined him intently to make sure I was correct, I was. I slowly sit up in my bed and place my feet on the floor. I could feel all the eyes in the room were on me. I slowly walked towards him, waving away anyone who dared to help me. I couldn't dare take my eyes off him and to my surprise, he didn't look away from my stare. As I stood right in front of him I finally managed to say something. Something I didn't have a chance to say when he rescued me from my car. Something I didn't manage to say when he saved me in my dream. "Thank You." I embraced him. I could feel the tears roll down my cheek as I held him tight. He held me just as tightly. "You're welcome, Melody." He said so calmly in my ear. His soft voice brought chills to my frail body. We could've held each other for an eternity, but I could feel Victoria and everyone else's confusion in the air. I managed to finally let Adam go and with one more final stare at him I turned to face the family I did have. Victoria smiled at me with a look of gratitude and slight confusion. I decided to give them an explanation.

"This is the man who pulled me out of my car once it flipped over, without him I don't know if I would have made it." I finally announced. Victoria looked stunned. "Really Adam? Wow!" She said as she embraced him as well, then embraced me. "This is crazy." She said. We all look at each other trying to fill in all the pieces. "So how do you all know each other?" I ask in great curiosity. "Well, Adam lives in the same condo as I. He came to my room late one night admiring my music and I invited him to a class." Jason Announced. Adam smiled as Jason patted him on the back. "Yes, I was greatly obliged by the opportunity to learn how to play amazing music like you all. It just so happens as I was on my way to class, I saw a car skid down the road. I ran there to assist, and it turned out to be this beautiful woman standing before me." Adam said as he stared at me once again. His mesmerizing gaze had me. I struggled to look away. "I'm so glad you were there Adam, I couldn't imagine..." Victoria said as she looked down. "It's okay, I'll be fine." I said as I wrapped my arms around her. I looked back at Adam, whose eyes stayed on me. The chemistry between us was filling the room, but no one seemed to notice. No one except Victoria of course.

After a while of chatting Ms. Potts came in to inform us visiting hours was over and everyone had to leave. "Ms. Potts, can my sister stay with me tonight?" I asked. Ms. Potts smiled and nodded, "Of course my dear. Looks like you guys have a lot to talk about!" I smiled as she left the room. I thanked everyone for coming as they left and of course Adam was last. "Thank you again, Adam. When I get out of here, I'd love to repay you." I said as he stood in front of me. He smiled at me. "I feel that won't be necessary, Melody, but I do have a small request." He said. Curiously I braced myself. "Yes, Adam?" His eyes stayed on mine as he gently grabbed my hands. I looked down at them and back to his face. He brought his face closer to mine. His smell was so alluring, this was no average man in my eyes. "Promise me...Promise me that I will see you again? I don't see true beauty like you every day." He simply said. I felt my heart skip a beat. I couldn't say anything at first, until Victoria gently pushed my shoulder to snap me back to reality. "Of course, I just hope in better circumstances." I said. He laughed at me and smiled. "Yes, Of course. Well, it was a pleasure to meet you Victoria, and an even greater pleasure to meet you Melody." He said. "You as well, Adam." I embraced him hoping it could last forever, but it doesn't. I released him, and he embraces Victoria and with another brief gaze at me, he exits the room. I take a deep breath and exhale as I flop back on the bed. Victoria flops right beside me. "You can breathe now Mel." She said. I smile and turn to face her. "Do you believe in love at first sight, be honest?" I asked her. She looks at the ceiling then at me, "Honestly, I didn't...Until I saw how you two looked at each other. I never witnessed anything so beautiful." I looked back up at the ceiling, thinking. Could this be it? Could this be Love? I was excited yet frighten. Excited because I felt this could be the defining moment in my life where everything could fall in place, but I was also frightening because this defining moment also can destroy me and my little world I have been so accustomed to all my life. A love so strong, yet so dangerous. "Victoria, I don't think my heart is strong enough for a love like that" I said as I place my head on her shoulder. She holds me in her arms. "Don't worry Mel, I'll be here to pick up the pieces if it happens to break." We laughed as we laid there on this beautiful winter night. I looked out the window to witness flakes of snow falling gracefully from the sky. A beautiful sight indeed. How everything could change in a blink of an eye, little did I know...

(Adam)

I awoke in the middle of the night once again. This has been the third night in the row that my sleep has been interrupted. Thoughts of Melody has kept me from sleeping. How I long to see her again. Ever since our meeting at the hospital, I have been foolishly keeping my distance from returning for reasons I have not grasped yet. Maybe I was afraid of the feeling I get when I look into those eyes of hers. A feeling that was truly foreign to me. I haven't been back to Jason's Studio either. Mainly because of Victoria. I know I would be asked a million questions, just out of her curiosity. I am a stranger to them, A stranger to their world, yet, how I longed to be part of it.

I sat up in my bed and stared at the darkness around me. A quiet buzz rang on my nightstand. I thought briefly who could be calling me at this time of night. I picked it up and of course, it was Lesley. I have been ducking her ever since Melody's accident. It wasn't intentionally, I just had nothing really to say to her. Nothing important anyways. I hope that eventually she would give up her quest of pursuing me and put her time in a guy that could love her back. A good guy. She was an amazing woman, with a true fire in her. I'm sure there is a man in this world that could make her happy.

I let the phone ring until the room was silent again. I remain in my bed for a few more minutes until I finally decided to get up. Without a true destination I put on my pants, sweater, boots, hat, keys and walked out the door.

"Adam! My good friend..." A familiar voice rang from behind me. I turned to see Jason in the hall way smoking a cigar. I smiled and walked towards him. I was relieved to see him. Maybe he could make sense of my feelings toward Melody.

"Jason, how are you? What are you doing out here?" I asked. It was not like him to be up at this time of night, well, maybe it was.

"Just came to get a smoke, don't want the house smelling like tobacco. Where have you been? You haven't been to class since the first day. You didn't enjoy yourself?" He asked. I felt appalled. Mainly because I loved the class. Is this what everyone is thinking?

"No, no, not at all, it's a bit...complicated. May we step in?" I asked. He smiled as he blows out his cigar.

"Shall we?" he said as he opened his door. I oblige and enter his home. Everything was finely furnished and beautiful. It like the home of an artist. The broad red curtains, the black magnificent rug and its texture. It was surely an amazing setup for a young bachelor. I took a sit on his beautiful sofa as he went to the kitchen. "Would you like wine or vodka?" I hesitated for a brief second by the question. This might very well turn out to be a great night. "Vodka hold the ice." I responded. He laughed as he placed the ice back in the freezer. As I patiently wait, I noticed the music piece on his table. "Is this the piece you were working on that night?" I asked. It took him a few seconds to remember what I was talking about, but soon it clicked.

"Yup, it's finished now. I'm going to debut it in class tomorrow. Hope to see you in there." He laughed as he returned with two identical glasses. He hands me one and places his on the table. He slowly takes a seat on a chair besides me in a position that makes me feel as if he is my shrink.

"So, what's been going on?" he begins. I think to myself the best way to go about this.

"Well, umm, I'm going through something...something I never been through. I am seeking for some advice." I respond. He takes a sip of his glass and continues.

"Is it the music I've been teaching? I could definitely go slower..." He starts but I interrupt.

"...No, it's not the music, I'm learning and catching on fast. It's something else. See...It's about Melody." I finally say. He smiles and takes another sip, I follow up behind him. It's much stronger than I expected.

"Oh, Melody? What about her? Oh, and once again, I'm so happy you were there when you were." He said. I take another sip and I begin again.

"Well, here's the thing...I feel like I'm going crazy. I been thinking about her ever since I first laid eyes on her. I am so confused about everything, and I have the slightest clue on what to do." I confess. Jason takes in every word and takes another sip. He smiles.

"Well, Adam, funny thing is, Melody has been talking about you nonstop ever since you left the hospital. I wasn't supposed to tell you any of this, but I couldn't help myself. I've known Melody for years now and I've never seen her like this. Ever. If I really think about it, I've never seen Melody interested in anybody." He said. I smiled to myself just because she hasn't forgotten about me.

"Wow." Was all I managed to say. Jason smiled, took out his cigar, and lit it. "Fuck it, the house will be okay." He said.

"Why haven't you been back to see her?"

"Honestly, I don't know. I wanted to, I just didn't want to feel like a stalker or a creep. I'm still technically a stranger." I responded.

"Melody is not like most women, well most people. She would've enjoyed seeing her savoir." He said as he took another sip. Jason was almost completely done with his drink. How I love a good drinking partner.

"What do you mean when you say she is not like other people?" I asked curiously. Jason adjusts himself in his chair.

"Well, Melody, I can honestly say that she has a beautiful soul. She is the sweetest person I think I have ever met, but she will fight for the ones she loves. She's lost so much in her life, yet she goes through it with a smile. Melody is an angel in disguise if you asked me." He said. "An angel in disguise...the irony." I thought to myself. Her beauty was not only a physical, but it was skin deep. I need to know this woman. I had to know this woman.

"When does she get released from the hospital?" I asked.

"Tomorrow morning."

"What time?"

"9 o'clock. Victoria, her fiancé, and myself are going to get her, you should meet us there. I'm sure she will be happy to see you." I took another sip and placed it back on the table.

"I'll be there! Thank you, Jason, for everything." I said. He smiles as he shakes my hand. "You are a good dude, Adam. It's nice to see Melody like this. I think this is the start of a good friendship." He said as we toast glasses. I think of Melody laying in the hospital bed, probably sleep at this hour, but I know there is a slight chance that maybe she is thinking about me, just as much as I am thinking about her.

(Melody)

I cannot manage to fall asleep tonight even though this room is warm and cozy. The television is on a random channel that I am not paying attention to. I looked at my phone, three missed calls from Victoria. I promise myself I'll call her in the morning before she comes to pick me up. I have a big painting I must finish by the 20th and I haven't even started on it. I stressed about that briefly and then I think about something much more vivid. The same thing I've been trying not to think about since he walked out that door two days ago. No matter what I thought of, or how intense the thought would be, Adam always made his way in my mind invading my conscious. I didn't mind it, but I didn't want to feel crazy about him. I feel like I've already talked Victoria and Jason's ears off about him. I often wondered why he hasn't come visit me again. Maybe the feeling I was feeling was only on my end. Maybe he already has a wife and children. I don't even know this man! He could be a crazy lunatic or mass murderer! Then I remember those eyes of his. Those eyes told me that he wasn't either of those things. Those eyes were eyes of a man who has mystery. Maybe he is like me. His eyes were beautiful, but they also seemed lonely. Adam seemed like a man who has been abandoned, one who has been through his share of heartache. I don't think a woman was the cause of his scars I see when I look at him, but I know something caused them. Maybe one day he would share with me. A secret boiled within him, A secret I feel that he wants to share. I never met a man with eyes that deep. It is obvious, I want him. My mysterious man, who I know nothing about, but long to know. Fate and destiny has brought me here, but it has also brought him here as well.

"Why hasn't he come?" I finally say to myself. I fluff my pillow and attempt to go to sleep once again. I turn on my iPod and place my earphones in my ears. I turn to track seven and let Michael Buble attempt to sing me to sleep. The orchestra sounds beautiful in my ears. I hold my pillow tight wishing it was Adam I was holding. "I need to get it together!" I laugh to myself as I close my heavy eyes.

Chapter 3
Family Affair

(Adam)

The sky was a remarkable scene this morning as I looked out my bedroom window. This could be a sign. A sign that today was going to be a wonderful day. I walked to my one of my most prized possessions, my stereo, and turned it on. I went through my mass cd collection to find the album that could define this day...The Fray "How to Save A Life." I placed it in and pressed play. "Great choice." I tell myself as I retreat to the shower.

Today would be a wonderful day, solely because I knew today I would see her. I feel like a little school boy who just sent his crush a love letter for the first time. The feeling was rather intense to say the least.

I put on my clothes and boots then left in an orderly fashion. I glanced at Jason's door in remembrance of the great night we had. I figured he must be already on the road towards her.

I went inside the elevator and press L for lobby. I waited patiently as the elevator began to descend from my 23rd floor. A young woman entered at the 15th floor. She looked no older than 16 if I was to guess, but she looked so enchanting and so familiar. She was wearing a long black rain coat with a hoody underneath it. There was something about her that I couldn't explain, including the fact that she continued to stare at me smiling for our entire ride on the elevator.

"Hello." The young woman finally said as she stood next to me. "Um, hello." I said awkwardly. Her voice took me off guard.

She looked me up and down and smiled once again. "She must be special, huh?" He said. Confusion struck my face.

"Excuse me?" I asked.

"The look on your face, you must be on your way to see someone special. Looks like you want to pry open these doors, how romantic." She laughed. I smiled at the thought.

"It that obvious?"

"Yes, but it's okay, love is a beautiful thing." She said. There was a silence until we reached the lobby. I let the young woman exit first. As she stepped out the shaft she turned around to face me.

"It was really nice to see you." She said.

"Yes? It was?" I said confused. She smiled at me as I answered.

"Flowers. Don't forget the flowers." She said as she walked out the elevator. "Flowers! What a great idea that would be. Thank..." Before I could finish my thank you, the woman was gone. It feels like she simply disappeared. I looked around for her briefly as I exited the elevator. "That was interesting." I thought to myself.

I walked through the lobby and out to Chicago's windy weather. I wrapped a scarf around my neck and headed to my car. My Dodge Challenger was surrounded by snow, which was far from unusual. It was a lot, but I knew my Dodge could make it out. I go through my pockets trying to feel for my keys when I feel a presence behind me.

"Adam?" a very familiar and beautiful voice rang in my ear. I stopped my search for my keys and tried to remember who this voice belongs to.

"Adam?" She repeated. The voice finally came to me. In complete shock and nervousness, I turned around to witness if my prediction was correct. To my utterly surprise, it was. In front of me, stood a beautiful woman with long curly black hair, with a smile that could brighten anyone's day. Her skin was so vibrating and golden. Just like mine. She tilted her head and smiled at me. "My Adam, My sweet Adam." She said as she embraced me. Still in utter shock, I manage to embrace her back.

"Gabriel. Could it be?" I finally say after taking in the moment. She steps back to look at me and smiles.

"My dear brother, it is so wonderful to see you again. One hundred years has been far too long."

Gabriel was indeed my sister, therefore making her an angel like myself. After all this time, someone has finally found me. I had a million questions. A million things I long to know. My excitement was unmatched.

"Yes, it has! I have so many questions." I said.

"And I will answer them to the fullest of my abilities, can we go to a more secluded or warm place? I had no idea it got so cold in this area. It is much colder than I anticipated." She said. I looked at my phone to see the time.

"Shit." I said as I pulled out my keys. "What is it brother?" Gabriel asked.

"I been waiting one hundred years to have this conversation with you, but can it wait a couple more hours, I have something important I must do first." I said as I started the car. She smiled. "Of course, Adam, I'll be here." She said.

"It's so good to see you sister. I really hope you stay a while." She smiled and kissed me on the cheek. "We came for you brother, we are not going anywhere."

"Umm, We?" I asked. Gabriel laughed. "Well of course, You thought I would make this trip alone? All of your sisters are here!" The happiness in my heart couldn't be explained so I simply said, "I cannot wait to see you all!" I begin to drive through the thick layer of snow to the hospital. I attempt to wave at Gabriel, but she has disappeared just as quickly as she came. I began to think of what exactly just happened. Gabriel and my sisters are here on earth. My prayers have finally been answered. The timing was just a little weird to me, but it was too much to think about right now.

I rushed through the hospital doors and stomped the snow off my boots. The building was warm and brightly lit. Without hesitation, I walked straight to Melody's room hoping I wasn't too late. The hallway was long and dreadful. I could feel myself starting to become nervous as I reached closer to her room. My palms were sweating, and my nerves got worse as I took each step. The young woman's voice rang in my ear. "Flowers! How could I forget?" I said to myself. It was far too late for that now, I could hear her beautiful voice ringing down the hall at this point.

She was talking to Victoria about life and times and I could hear the laughter echo. I took a deep breath and walked in her room. Victoria's eyes caught me first and then went instantly to Melody's to see her response. I looked at Melody and she was just as beautiful as I left her. She was wearing a red sweater that showed her left shoulder, her hair was flowing delicately down her back and her leggings portrayed her frame perfectly. She was truly a work of art.

"Good morning." I finally said. Victoria smiled, and Melody's eyes remained on mine. "Hello Adam, it's nice to see you again." Melody said as she smiled. I laughed as I walked deeper in the room. I found an abandoned chair and made it my temporary home.

"I would've came to visit you more, but I didn't want to feel like a creep." I admitted. Victoria busted into laugher and so did Melody. I smiled and thought that maybe Jason was right. "Why would I think you were a creep? You saved my little life and I will forever be grateful." She said. Her voice was so soothing to my ears. "Okay, I promise you will see more of me." I said. "You already made that promise, remember?" She said as smiled and looked down. I could see her blood rushing to her cheeks.

"I'm here!" Jason said as he walked in the room. "Hey Jason, bout time you showed up; you are missing the magic that is happening here." Victoria said as she smiles at Melody and I. Jason smiled as he looked around the room. "Where is Mathew? I thought he was coming?" He asked Victoria. "He wanted too, but he had to work this morning." She responded. Jason nodded as he found a seat next to me.

"Happy you finally came!" He said as he patted me on the back. "Of course, I wouldn't miss it." I said as I caught Melody's eyes once again lingering on mine. We looked at each other with such intensity that the room starred in awe at the awesome event. Victoria finally broke the silence.

"Adam we are throwing Melody a welcome home party tonight, it would mean a lot if you would join us." I smiled as I stood up from my seat. "Of course. Where and what time?" I asked. "2361 W. Monroe Street and at 8:30." Victoria said. "I'll be there." Melody stood up to face me. "So, I will see you tonight then." I smiled and took her hand. "Of course, Melody. I'll be there at 8:29." I said. She blushed as she put her head down and slowly released my hand.

"Alright guys, you ready?" Jason said as he walked towards the exit. Victoria walked toward me and gave me hug.

"I like you Adam, so please don't mess this up." She whispered in my ear. I smiled as I hugged her back.

"Don't worry I'm one of the good guys." I responded. She laughed at my response and slowly walked out the room. Melody began to follow her until she reached the door. So elegant and graceful, she turned to face me and smiled.

"I don't know what's going here between us, but I like it." She said.

"Yes, whatever it is, I feel it too. I owe you a beautiful conversation." She laughed as she leaned on the door.

"That you do. I'll be looking forward to it." Everyone in the room smiled at the sheer connection we shared, though we were still strangers amongst each other.

"Me as well." I said. She smiled at me as she disappeared out the door. My body wanted to jump up with joy, but instead I stood there smiling to myself. Tonight, would be a great night for me and I was beyond excited. As I left the building I instantly thought of my sisters and their presence on the Earth. I had to come to them, not only for answers, but simply because I missed them more than they could ever know.

(Melody)

        My body was still full of anxiousness as I sat in my comfortable love seat Victoria gave me for my birthday a couple years back. Adam, this mysterious man who came literally out of nowhere, runs through my mind. The very thought of me seeing him tonight is terrifying to say the very least. As my mind wondered, I was interrupted with a pile of clothes thrown on me.

        "Girl stop daydreaming! You need to find something to wear." Victoria yelled at me. She was right, I been in scrubs all day and the clothes I was wearing had faded blood stains on them from the accident. I was exhausted, maybe a little bit too exhausted to take a shower. I kicked off my shoes, took off my semi-bloody attire, and flopped down on the bed. I felt free in just my t-shirt and underwear. Victoria shook her head and sat down on my love seat.

        "I forgot, the doctor did tell me to make sure you get your rest." She announced right before I almost went into a deep slumber.

        "I'll be up in a minute, let me take a quick nap." I said as I closed my eyes and thought of pure blankness. My mind went from one sequence to another. That's when I knew I was dreaming. As my mind began to wonder I could see darkness starting to cover up my very vivid dreams. The darkness continued to form until darkness was all I could see. A figure began to form in the darkness. It was too unclear to make of what it was, but I could feel my muscles starting to get tense, tense as if I needed to run or retreat. The dark entity eventually revealed himself to me. He was tall with short black hair. He smiled at me as if he knew me. It's because he did know me, and I knew him. When I was a little girl, I used to have nightmares about him. My mom read me a story one night and I never saw the man again. That was about 20 years ago. Why was he back in my dreams? I glared into his eyes intently, afraid, but standing my ground. I couldn't run or move. My body was paralyzed. He smiled at me and simply said. "I found you."

        I woke up screaming.

        "Melody!" I heard her say as I fought whatever I was seeing. I felt her arms grabbing me, trying to console me, but there was no consoling. There was no peace at this time. It was official, my nightmares have started again. Victoria was fully aware of my night terrors, but we both thought they were gone for good.

I finally managed to open my eyes as I sat up on my bed. Victoria stared at me intently, waiting for a response. I gave her none.

"Melody what's wrong? I haven't heard you scream like that since..." She stopped and placed her hand on my head. "The nightmares? They are back? "She asked. I just put my face in my hands. "I don't know why. What could have triggered it?" I asked myself. Victoria immediately picked up the phone and started dialing a number. "What are you doing?" I asked. "Calling Mom." She said briefly before putting the phone to her ear. I sat there in silence.

"Hey mom, how are you?"
Silence.
"It's Melody."
Silence.
"We are on the way."

Victoria hung up the phone and started getting dressed. "How does she always know?" I asked as I started putting on clothes. "I don't know, but the moment I picked up the phone she knew something was wrong." Our mom always knew when something was wrong. She had a sixth sense to it.

We jumped in the car and sped to our mom's house. Victoria drove as if we were in emergency. Her love for me was evident. After a quick drive, we were in front of our childhood home. Mom was already on the porch. To be almost 50 she looked as if she was our age, no seriously, she really did. People would often mistake her for our sister. When mom use to visit our high school all the boys, and even the teachers lusted after her.

She stood on the porch with a worrisome look on her face. Her beautiful long brown curly hair breezed as the wind ran through it. She stood there smiling at us as we left the car. "Hey Mom, I've missed you." Victoria said as she ran to her. I wasn't too far behind her. "My beautiful girls, I missed you both. Come in the house. It's so cold out here." She said as she kissed us on our cheeks.

"Mom, it's happened again." I said as we walked in the house together. She looked at me and smiled. "I know, we will take care of it." Victoria went to the kitchen while Mom and I went to her living room. It was filled with books of all shapes and sizes. "Take a seat Melody." She asked as she searched for a book. Victoria returned with three cups of tea and handed them to us. "Mommy, so what is it? Why are the dreams resurfacing?" Victoria asked. Mom grabbed a book and sat down in between us. "Well, I think something good or divine has entered your life. I believe this is what triggered the nightmares. You see the light and dark are in constant war for souls. The more good that comes in your life, the more the darkness will try to intervene." She said. My mom is very spiritual, I used to believe she was a witch or a shaman when I was younger. All the old books, the fact that she doesn't have one gray hair, and the fact that she always knows everything could be giveaway. Yet over the years I kind of abandoned that idea.

"Something good? What do you mean?" Victoria asked. "I don't know exactly sweetheart, but something has entered your life that has ignited the interest of an evil entity. Something I haven't seen before. Where have you been the last few days?" She asked. I looked at Victoria then back at my mother. Victoria opened her mouth first.

"Mom, Melody got into a car accident a few days ago. We have been in the hospital. We didn't tell you because you didn't want you to worry." I could see my mom's face quickly change for the worst. "What do you mean you were at the hospital! And you decided to not inform me that your sister was in a car accident!" She said furiously. "We both mutually decided to not tell you, we know your heart is weak Ma. A scare like that could have sent you to the hospital with me. I didn't want that." I said. She calmed down and looked at us both. "Now listen girls, you are all I have. I am strong enough to take some unwelcome news but not strong enough to be lied too." She said. Victoria and I nodded as we hugged her. "We are sorry ma." I said. "Now looking at you, I could tell that something was off." She said as she placed her hand on the bruise on my head. "My poor baby, I'm so happy you are okay." I smiled as I placed my head on her lap. "Well, you probably ran into an angel in the hospital. There are plenty of them surrounding places of birth and death." She said. "I think she might have met one before that." Victoria said jokingly. I slapped Victoria's arm. "What does your sister mean, Melody?" She asked me. I instantly thought of Adam. "My car flipped over in the accident. I was bleeding out and I couldn't get out. A young man came out of nowhere and pulled me out. He saved my life. What makes it even stranger is that Jason invited him to our music class that day. He literally saved my life on his way to our class. I thought I would never see him again until he walked in the hospital with Victoria and the rest of my class." I said. My mom stood up and walked to her old treasure box. "Is that so?" She simply said. "How does he make you feel." I started to blush as I looked around. "You don't even have to say anything, I could see it on your face." She said smiling. "I would like you to bring him over for dinner. I would like to thank him for saving my daughter's life." I looked at Victoria as she laughed. "I will bring Matthew." She said to me. I smiled as I thought about what he would say. "Okay mom, I will see him tonight. Victoria invited him to the house for a party she is throwing for me. I will be sure I ask him." I said. "Oh, you girls don't have a chill button, do you? A party already, you are fresh out of the hospital." She said jokingly. We all laughed as mom tried to talk about our young lifestyle. "It's a Christmas party too ma." Victoria said laughing. "Well make sure you two don't drink too much, well, actually I'm only talking to Victoria." She said as she kissed her. "Yes Mom." She replied as if she was 8 years old again. Mom pulled a beautiful necklace out her a treasure box and handed it to me. "Wear this. It will protect you from evil entities. This should cure you of your nightmares." She said as she handed me a gorgeous gold necklace with a small ring band connected to it. "Thank you, mommy," I said as I put it around my neck.

"Quick question though?" I asked. "Yes, what is it?" I looked at the necklace then back at her. "What did you do the first time I had nightmares. How did you make them disappear all those years ago?" I asked. Victoria got up and looked at mom as well, curious about the answer as well. "Well your aunt Catherine sent me a spell to protect you both when you were little." She said. Victoria and I laughed as we started placing on our coats to leave. "Okay Mom, whatever you say. Well, we should be going, we have a party to host and I'm sure Melody wants to shower." Victoria said as she walked toward the front door. Witchcraft stuff always made Victoria feel uneasy. "Okay my loves, we need to set up that dinner. Don't forget." She said as we walk out the house. "Yes mom, I will call you with more details. I love you." I said as I kiss her on the cheek. "I love you too my love. Please take care of yourself." She asked. "Yes ma'am." We said our goodbyes and headed back home. I looked at my necklace hoping it would protect me from nightmares...

(Adam)

My mind was thinking of many things as I pulled up to my home: Melody, this party, and of course my darling sisters; which was still a mystery to where they could be right now. As I walk toward the door to my home, I could hear the television on. I smiled to myself as I opened the door. An elegant fragrance ran wild through the rooms as I entered. A fragrance that I remember so well. I walk down the hall into my living room and there they were, my three beautiful sisters waiting patiently for my arrival. Gabriel stood there with a smile so vibrate, it would bring anyone to tears.

"Adam, finally!" she said as she embraced me once more. Right behind her was the fiery, edgy Natalia. Her beautiful red hair could be visible from the heavens.

"I've missed you so much." Natalia said as she embraced me as well. Right after her was the shy, timid, Lyla. Her elegance and clumsy ways was just one of the many reasons why I loved her.

"Adam!" Lyla said as she ran up to me and jumped on all of us, causing us to all fumble to the ground. We all laughed at each other as we laid scattered across the floor. Now my three sisters were completely different in their own rights. Gabriel was the oldest between them. She was the mothering sister who took care of whatever needed to be taken of. Then there was Natalia. Now she was the fearless sister who did whatever she wanted. She was never afraid of a challenge and was a fierce fighter. Finally, we have Lyla. She was the loving caring one of the bunch. Her patience was unlimited, and her heart was full.

"My dear sisters, I am so glad to see you all. I missed all of you so much." I finally uttered out. We all started to get to our feet and walked over to my couch. "I have so many questions to ask, I don't even know where to begin." I announced. Natalia looked at me, then to Gabriel.

"Adam, what happened to you? How did you get down here? What do you remember?" Natalia said. I looked at her intently.

"Honestly, I don't know. The last thing I remember was the fall here and waking up in a field completely naked. I noticed I no longer had my angelic powers when I landed here, so I took it upon myself to just blend in with the humans. I picked up their ways and lived amongst them for the last 101 years." I said looking at all three of them. Gabriel looked at Natalia then back at me. "What is it?" I asked. "That could explain why it took us so long to find you. We looked all over this world for you since you disappeared." Natalia said. "We have been here looking for you since you fell Adam." Lyla chimed in. I went to the kitchen and opened my wine cabinet. The wine was aged and only should be used for a special occasion. This was a special occasion.

"So how did you guys find me?" I said as I poured three glasses of wine and gave them to my sisters. "Well, that's the difficult part to explain. After years of living on earth we managed to blend in with the humans and start lives as well. Now in our time here, we have seen some amazing things and beings. We figured being here, we would eventually run into you. A few days ago, Lyla, Natalia, and myself felt something, here, in Chicago. We felt something angelic that reminded me of you, so we flew here in search and came to the source of what we felt. It was a young woman lying in a hospital bed. We saw you enter the room that first night you two met. We saw the energy between you two. Who is this young woman?" Gabriel asked as she took a sip of her wine. Lyla and Natalia seemed to be just as interested by the question. "Wait, why didn't you come to me that night? Why did you wait until now?" I asked. "We were curious about your relationship between the woman. We are here now, so tell us." Natalia asked. I took a long breath. "Well, her name is Melody. I saved her life a few days ago in a car accident; but I'm confused. You say you felt something in her?" I asked. Lyla smiled at the comment. "I felt great power in her. Something I never felt in a human before. I think you entering her life, could be what triggered it." Natalia said. I wish I could feel what they were feeling. I thought to myself. "That kind of power, could be dangerous for her. Especially now that she has angels hovering around her. It could make her a target, could make us a target." Natalia said to Gabriel. "Wait, a target? What do you mean?" I asked. They both looked at me with wide eyes. "I forgot, you have no idea what's going on." Gabriel said as she took my hand. I shook my head as I prepared myself. "The last couple of years, more and more demons have escaped hell, over 4 angels have died, which is unheard of because there is no such being on Earth that I know of that could kill an angel, besides another angel of course." Gabriel said. I looked at her in awe not believing what she was telling me   .

"So, there is an angel or an entity killing other angels and freeing demons from hell? Who could have the power to do such a thing?" I asked in confusion. "I don't know, but whoever it is, they have a sinister plan. If they found Melody, the pure interest of her unknown gifts would make her a target. They would want to manipulate her or destroy her. My only question is, why did it erupt once she met you?" Natalia asked. I looked out the window, thinking about her once again. A woman who truly stayed on my mind. "I don't know. I wish I did." I said. Lyla moved in closer to me and examined me.

"You like her, don't you?" She asked looking at me right in the face. I could feel my face begin to turn red. "Umm, I just think we should keep an eye on her. I wouldn't want anything to happen to her." I said getting around the question. "So, you do like her?" She continued with a giggle. I could never hide anything from them. They were too skilled at getting whatever they wanted out of me.   .

"Alright you got me...I am interested. I am actually going to see her tonight. Her sister is throwing her a 'welcome home party." I said. Lyla's grin got even bigger.

"Adam, you must want us to come with you. I think it is exactly what we need to celebrate us all being together as one again." Lyla said. I smiled and took another sip of my wine.

"Of course, all of you can come! Maybe we can find out more information." I said. My sisters all smiled as they sat across the room. I wondered about Melody, and this mysterious power my sisters speak of. What could it be? Who could she really be? My sisters were right about one thing; if my sisters were able to feel it, I know other angels and entities would have felt it too. If this is true, it would be a matter of time...

Chapter 4
Revelations

(Melody)

       As I finished my last touches of my make up, I took a glance in the mirror to preview my outfit knowing it would disappoint me. It did. "Victoria!" I yell down stairs to her. The music was already playing, and a few people have already started to arrive, so the party was well under way. Victoria and I decorated the house in a Christmas theme since Christmas was right around the corner anyways. I could hear Victoria's frustrated footsteps coming towards me.

       "Yes, my lovely?" she said as she sat on the toilet seat.

       "I know this is like the 5th time I asked you, but do you think I look alright?" I asked with a straight face. She smiled as she moved my body towards the mirror.

       "You didn't look this good for my bachelorette party. "You look gorgeous. I'm positive Adam will love it." She said. I smiled and gave her a hug.

       "I love you Victoria, I really do." I said as I released her. "Is he here yet?" Victoria smiled.

       "No Melody, not yet. Just calm down. Have a drink." She said as she handed me one of her famous random carnations. I took a few sips and gave it back to her.   "No sis, keep it. You are going to need it" She said. We both laugh and sit in the bathroom for long moment.

       "Do you hear that? It sounds like a lot more people have arrived." Victoria said as she stood up. She was right, it sounded like a full-blown party downstairs.
"You ready Melody?" she asked me. I took one more shot of her carnation and reached for the door.

       "I'm ready." I said as I exited the bathroom. I looked in the mirror once again and Victoria was right, I looked rather nice. My red dress and black pumps went together well. I did my hair more curly than usual. I felt pretty for once.

We walked to the balcony to oversee the party and it was quite a lot of people here. I searched the crowd to find Adam. Nothing.

"Don't worry, the way he was looking at you, he will be here." Victoria said. I smiled and started my way down the stairs. Everyone was so happy to see that that I was okay, and I was very appreciative. I sat at the kitchen counter, talking conversing, being a good host, anxiously waiting for Adam to walk through my door.

"You okay?" I turn to my left and there sat Matthew, Victoria's fiancé. I laugh to myself.

"I must look like a fool?" I said foolishly. He smiled as he looked at Victoria dancing in the crowd.

"No, you just look like you're in love." He replied. I smile and look at Victoria as she embraces herself to Black Eye Peas. "Going off the description Victoria gave me, I think that's your guy." He said as he points to the door. I look in the direction he points, and I could feel my heart begin to melt. There he was, Adam, my Adam. He was wearing a tailored tux with a silk red tie, and casual black shoes. He looked like a model straight out of an Express store. He was holding a special bottle of campaign and bouquet of roses. His curly hair was vibrant, and his smile showed all his white teeth. A beautiful man indeed. Victoria ran towards me when she spotted him.

"There's your man, but who are those strikingly beautiful women with him though?" she asked. I was so wrapped up in admiring Adam I didn't even notice the three Victoria's Secret models behind him. One had beautiful long black hair and enchanting gray eyes. She was the tallest of the three and the closest to Adam. Her green apple Versace dress and elegant black heels were to die for. The next one had fiery red hair flowing down her back. Her walk was fierce, as well as her gold shimmery dress, but her smile was intoxicating. And the last one had short black curls to die for wide big beautiful eyes. She was the smallest of them all but just as beautiful in an elegant black dress. All four of them looked as if their skin was glowing. Everyone stared at these four beautiful strangers as they made their way through the crowd.

Every guy awed at Adam's mysterious friends, but no one dared to approach them. Not because of Adam, but simply because of their beauty. I didn't blame them, it was quite intimidating, maybe even a little scary.

Adam caught my eye contact and began making his way towards me.

"Here they come." Victoria said. I could feel my stomach begin to turn.

"What I miss?" Jason said as he came from the patio.

"Nothing yet, Melody's date has just arrived, and he brought three women with him." Matthew said. Jason looks and their direction and then looks at me.

"Wow, they are gorgeous! Are those his dates?" Jason asked. Victoria reached for three beers and opened them.

"Let's hope not." She said as she takes a large gulp of her Corona. Adam smiles at me, a reassuring smile that made me feel at ease. After a long day of waiting, here he was, right in front of me. I just stared at him... I couldn't produce a word.

"How are you guys? Sorry I was late, A wise woman told me never to forget flowers." Adam said with such charm, I forgot he was even late.

"It's no problem, I'm just glad you made it." I managed to say. He smiled as he gazed into my eyes, melting my already melted heart.

"These are for you." He said as he handed me a lovely bouquet of flowers. "And this is for you two." He said as he handed a bottle of campaign to Victoria and Matthew. It was a bottle of Ace of Spades, a very expensive bottle of campaign to be exact. Matthew glowed as he received it. "An Engagement gift, congratulations."

"Thank you, Adam, you didn't have to do that." I said.

"Yes, Adam, you really didn't. This is amazing." Victoria said. He just smiled and looked at me.

"It my pleasure guys, don't worry. "He said.

"Oh Adam, this is my fiancé, Matthew." Victoria said as Matthew reached out his hand.

"It's a pleasure to meet you Matthew, I've heard nothing but good things about you." Adam said as he shook his hand.

"Hopefully good things." Matthew laughs.

"Of course, my good friend." Adam said laughing.

"But on another note, we are so grateful for you saving our Melody. She means the world to our little gang." He said as everybody looks at me. I can certainly feel the love now.

"I'm just glad I was there." He responds while he looks at me with those dreamy eyes I could not resist. The tall girl with him pulls his arm, and Adam eyes turn to her.

"How rude of me, I would like to introduce you all to Gabriel, Natalia, and Lyla. My Sisters." He said. The three beautiful women took the center stage.

"Nice to finally meet you Melody, my brother can't stop taking about you, and I can see why. You are beautiful." Gabriel said as she hugged me. She felt warm and divine. I could feel my face blushing.

"So, he has, has he?" I said raising my eye brow. Adam turns away to hide his red face. Lyla begins to laugh.

"So, these are your sisters?" Jason asked. Adam smirks as he turns to face him.

"Yes, they came to visit me for the holidays." He said. I don't know why I didn't think of that before. They all have remarkable similar features. I bet their parents were a sight to see.

"Well okay, it's time for me to get drunk and dance the night away." Victoria said as she stood up.

"May I come with you?" Gabriel said smiling. Victoria laughed and wrapped her arm around her.

"I love you already." Victoria said as she walked away. "Have fun Mel." She said as they disappeared in the crowd.

"We will be outside if you need us." Jason said as he signaled Matthew to follow him.

"Alright, you guys." I said as I hugged them. Jason panted Adam on the back and Matthew shook his hand again then they were gone.

"Come on Lyla, let's let these two have some time..." Natalia said. Lyla shock her head and kissed Adam on the cheek.

"It was a pleasure to meet you Melody." Lyla said as she kissed me on the cheek.

"No, it was pleasure to meet you two." I said. Lyla and Natalia smiled and disappeared into the crowd. At last, we were alone.

"Why are your sisters so beautiful?" I asked as I saw them disappear into the crowd. He smiled and leaned against the counter next to me. His fragrance was more than intoxicating.

"Why are you so beautiful?" He asked. I looked down before I answered.

"I could ask you the same thing..." I managed to say. We both laugh as we glanced at Victoria and Gabriel dancing. As beautiful as Gabriel is, it looks like she has never danced in her life.

"I told my mom about the man who saved my life, she would love to meet you." I said. "I would love too, just tell me when and I'll be there." He said with a beautiful smile. Then he looked at me so calmly. "

Can I be completely honest with you right now?" He asked.

"Of course, what is it?" He hesitated as he was looking for the proper words.

"Melody, ever since I looked in your eyes, I haven't been able to see anything else. You have been on my mind every hour, every minute, every second of the day and to be completely honest, I like it." I paused my thought to catch every word that uttered from his perfect lips. Was this really happening right now? Was I dreaming a dream of pure bliss? I was speechless for more than a moment before I finally thought of words to say.

"Well Adam, what would you say if I told you I felt the same way?" I managed to choke out. He smiled and stood up.

"Take my hand." He said. I looked around, and without hesitating I took it.

"Follow me." He said as he led me through the crowd and out the front door.   "Where are we going?" I asked. He stopped and looked at me. He took my other hand and smiled.

"When was the last time you did something without thinking about it?" He asked. I laughed and really thought to myself.

"Just now, when I took your hand." I replied. He smiled.

"Come with me, I want to show you something." He said. I looked back towards the house.

"We can't just leave, I have a whole party going on, and what about your sisters?" I asked. He looks at the house then back to me.

"My sisters are there, nothing will go wrong. Victoria won't even know you are missing." He said so calmly.

"What does your sisters being there have to do with anything?" I asked and once again he smiled.

"My sisters are a lot stronger than you think. Your home will be protected." He said. I didn't know what he was trying to get at, but for some reason I believed him. Every word he said felt so right. My heart believed him therefore my mind had to agree.

"Okay, Adam. I believe you. Let's go." I finally said. He just smiled and carried me to this black challenger at the end of the block. I was beyond appreciative of him because he carried me through the snow and I was definitely wearing heels. He opened the door and sat me down like a perfect gentleman.

Even his vehicle smelt enchanted. This guy was just to perfect. He could be a serial killer or anything, and I'm just in the car with him, alone. He was an absolute stranger to me, a beautiful stranger, but still a stranger. I saw all of that, but nothing could shake me from this undeniable feeling I had for him. I was drawn to him, and I could tell he was drawn to me. Even when he saved my life, I knew this man would be something special to me. There were no words to describe what I was feeling, or have been feeling since I met him, so I won't try to make one up. I just know I wanted to be around him, to breathe his air, to feel his skin. So, as I wonder what our destination was, a part of me was hoping we never return.

(Adam)

          The night was cold, but full of life as Melody and I drove through the Chicago streets. It was a beautiful night, but nothing was more beautiful than the woman sitting next to me. Melody was absolutely gorgeous tonight. Her dazzling red dress and accessories instantly caught my eye. She was a work of art, a masterpiece.

          "Adam, please, the anticipation is killing me." She said as she looked at me. I threw her a smile back and grabbed her delicate hand. Her skin was so soft, I couldn't bear to let go.

          "Trust me." I simply said. She smiled and placed her head on my shoulder.

          "Have I thanked you for saving my life?" she asked as she started playing with the radio.

          "You have, many times." I said laughing. She laughed as she looked up at me.

          "Oh, I just don't think you truly know how appreciative I am. If it wasn't for you, I'll probably wouldn't be alive." She confessed. I looked at those mesmerizing eyes. So much I wanted to say to her, but her beauty had me frozen.

          "We are here." I said as I parked in my parking lot. Melody's eyes started scanning the area.

          "Where are we?" She asked. I opened my door and smiled.

          "My home. Just follow me." I said as I reached out my hand. She raised her eye brow and took my hand. Swiftly, I scooped her off the icy ground and carried her in my arms.

          "Oh my..." Melody uttered as I began carrying up the stairway that led to the lobby.

          "Thank you, Adam." She said as she wraps her arms around me. We took the elevator up to my home and eagerly opened the door. Melody eyes widen as we enter.

          "You have a beautiful place Adam." She said as marveled around. I sat her on my love seat and went to the kitchen for some drinks.

          "Oh, it's nothing, really." I said modestly. Her eyes wondered around the house. I quickly returned with two holiday cocktails for us. Melody took a sip and placed the glass on the table.

"You are such a mystery to me Adam. I want to know everything about you." She said as she folded her legs. Those beautiful legs. How I dared to touch them. Her eyes looked at me with sincere curiosity. It was as if she wanted to see my soul.

"I'm an open book." I replied as I took another sip. She smiled as she took sip out of her glass as well. The air in the room was so very calm. Melody examined me. She started twisting her hair as she thought of questions.

"Well, Adam, where are you from? Who are your parents?" She asked patiently. I hesitated and thought about the usual lies I have been telling the world for years. The truth, I feared was far too extreme. I took a long sip of my cocktail before answering.

"Well Melody, I'm from right here, right up north around Wrigley Field. My parents passed when I was young. So, it's just been my sisters and I." I said as I take another sip out of my glass. Melody's face was filled with even more curiosity.

"Wow, I'm so sorry…You have done so well for yourself. That story sounds similar to mine actually." She said. I began to become even more curious than her.

"How so? Tell me about your family?" I asked. She hesitated briefly.

"Well, my parents abandoned me as an infant at the hospital. Victoria's mom took me in and she has been the only mother I've ever known." She said. I took in every word thinking to myself, who would abandon such a beautiful woman?

"Victoria must be a great sister! I see how you two are." I said. She smiled. "Yes! She is my best friend. She has been taking care of me since my whole life." I looked at her as she spoke. I could feel the emotion.

"So, besides music what do you do?" I asked trying to find out everything about my new shy mysterious lady friend. Her eyes looked like they had a story to tell.

"I'm finishing my music major in school right now. I'm on my last year! I love to paint as well. I sell my painting on eBay. I'm currently working at the Hilton Hotel until I get done with school. What about you?" She asked. Her passion of music fell from her lips the moment she parted them.

"Well I do real estate. I sell people houses for a living." She looked around my place once more. "I see you kept one house for yourself." Her humor was delightful, and her company was soothing to me. I never wanted her to leave.

"Hey Adam, I have a question?" She asked as she moved closer to me.

"Yes, anything."

"Okay this might sound a bit crazy...?

"Trust me, I know crazy." I said thinking about my life.

"Okay, so here's the thing. I don't really believe in coincidences, so I know it was fate that brought you to save my life. It was fate that brought you back to me in the hospital. I also believe that it was fate that has us here together now." I listened to every word she uttered. "I will have to agree with you." I said. She grabbed my hand and ran her fingers up my arm, eyes completely locked on me.

"Fate explains that you were meant to enter my life, but it doesn't explain how you effortlessly pulled me out of the car." She said her eyes focused on mine. "What do you mean?" I said defensively. She smiled and took a sip of her cup.

"My seat belt was broken, it wouldn't unbuckle. I didn't remember this at first, but over time, things start coming back to me. I saw you pull it off with one hand." She said as she started investigating me. I felt totally surprised at her remembering that minor detail.

"Well my adrenaline must have helped." I try to respond vaguely, but she was not buying it. She grabbed my hands and looked me in the eyes.

"No man could have pulled that belt apart the way you did. Just be honest with me. Are you a vampire or something? That could explain the charming personality and good looks. I read a lot." She said as laughed. I laughed with her at the thought. "No, I'm not a vampire..." I said as I contemplated as if I should tell her the truth.

"Well I'm not leaving until you tell me what you are Adam." She said as she started getting comfortable. I hesitated briefly and took a sip of my cup. "Are you sure you are ready for this? I asked.

"I'm ready."

I took a deep breath and said something I've never told anyone on this earth...

"Okay, Melody. I am an Angel. Well, a fallen angel." I said willingly. She looked at me with those eyes. Eyes I couldn't read.

" An angel? Like a real angel?" She said in amazement.

"Yes, like the real angel." I said, she looked at me with astonishment.

"So, your sisters are too?"

"Yes, they are. They came after me after I fell." I tried to explain. She walked around the room in deep thought, contemplating what I just said. She flopped back on the couch with a huge grin on her face.

"Would you believe me if I already knew that?" She said as she took another sip of her glass. I didn't know what to say.

"Well I thought you were angel when you saved my life. I was so afraid that I wasn't ever going to see you again, but when you walked in my hospital room with my sister, I knew this had to be a dream. When I first looked in your eyes, I knew there was something about you. Something I couldn't explain. But if you are what you say you are, I have a silly question? Where are your wings?" She asked. I took in her words slowly, but surely.

"I lost them when I fell. You see, every angel has this thing called a Divine. It gives us our power, but mine was lost when I fell here" I responded. Her focus on me sharpened intensely.

"You fell from Heaven? Why?" She asked.

"Yes, I fell from Heaven. And honestly, I don't know why."

"Maybe you fell for me?" She said hopefully. The idea didn't sound too farfetched at this point. "That would explain a few things actually. It would finally give me a purpose." She smiled at my comment and we just sat for a moment.

"How was it up there, in Heaven? I always wondered about it. Wondered if my parents were up there." She said as she put her head down in thought.

"Everyone's Heaven is different, but it is eternal bliss. I can ask Gabriel about your parents if you like. I know it is a burden not knowing." I said. Her head instantly picked up as she smiled at me. "That would be amazing." She came closer to me and placed her head on my shoulder.

She took another sip of her glass and laughed at herself.

"You must think I'm crazy for believing all of this, huh? I promise you that I am sober; For the most part." She asked.

"I don't know, I never told another human being before. So, honestly, I didn't know what to expect. I just know I couldn't lie to you about this." She smiled at me.

"And why is that? What if I reacted the complete opposite?" she asked.

"I haven't told anyone the truth about me because I haven't met anyone who I think should know. I thought remaining invisible was the smartest choice. Especially, if I had no idea on how long I would be here. Your reaction is quite calm. A lot calmer than I ever would've expected. A different reaction would have made more sense." I said as I took a sip of my glass. I could tell she was intrigued at this point.

"How long have you been here, on Earth I mean? I don't want to bombard you with a thousand questions, I'm just so curious about you!" She pleaded. I smiled at her and nodded.

"It's no problem, I'm actually just relieved that you don't think I'm crazy. But I've been here for 101 years. Actually, my birthday just passed on the 3rd of December." Her eyes widened as I spoke.

"Wait, you have been here for 101 years? That's insane! You don't look a year pass 23! And Happy belated birthday. It's not too late to celebrate it is it? She asked. I laugh as I finish my glass.

"Well, after my first decade here, I recognized my body has not aged a bit. So, I came up with the conclusion that maybe my body wont. And I think it's too late for my birthday. When is yours?" I asked.

"Wow, that's amazing! Totally amazing! And it's April 23rd, nothing special. I always thought it was weird that my last name was Eve, but I wasn't born on an 'eve' day, you know?" She said completely confusing all my thoughts. "What do mean?" I asked as I laughed. "Don't laugh at me, I'm just saying I wish I was born on a 'eve' day. Like a day before something great." She said as she smiled. "I think the day you were born should be a holiday. What's funnier is that my name is Adam and your last name is Eve. Maybe we are supposed to repopulate the earth." I said laughing. "I'll be fine with that." She replied laughing with me.

The night was getting darker and the cold was getting colder, but none of that mattered at this point. As curious as she was about me, I was just as curious about her.

"Melody, as I sit here and gaze upon you, my mind continues to wonder...I really want to know everything about you." I said with sincerity. Her radiant smile took hold of the entire room. I could feel her mind beginning...

"Well, what do you want to know about me angel man?" She said in her beautiful voice.

"Whatever you want to tell me." I replied. She closed her eyes to gather her thoughts.

"Well, I feel like I've always been lost in this world. Things never quite happen the way I imagine them too. All I know is my music and my family." She started to begin. "It's crazy because my mother always believed that the world is filled with angels. We just can't see them. Is that true?" She asked me with a look of true curiosity. "Your mother is quite informed. There are angels all around us. They are known as guardian angels, created to protect you. I'm what is known as Heaven's Angel. I'm supposed to spend most of my existence in heaven, but I was chosen to fall down to earth for reasons that are still unknown to me. My sisters are Heaven's Angels as well. They fell to earth in hopes of finding me, which they succeeded." I explained. She was mesmerized by the sheer thought of it. She didn't speak, she just looked at me. A look that could break even the strongest of men.

"You are beautiful Adam." Melody said out of the blue. I could feel my face turning red. "I know that was random, but I just had to say it. I mean you are an angel for God's sake. An Angel! You can't tell me you been on this Earth for one hundred years and never fell for someone before. I mean you could have anyone. What makes me so special? I am a mess. My life is all over the place." She confessed. I smirked and took her delicate hand.

"Melody?" I simply said.

Yes Adam?"

"You and I are more alike than you know. See, I've spent my entire life wondering...wondering about this world and the next. I've always longed for purpose. Purpose for my life and the point of it all. I would drink myself to sleep pondering the many thoughts in my head. The many unanswered questions that lurked in my conscious eat me up every day. The day I pulled you out that car is the day I honestly felt like I could finally see my purpose. I find you remarkably beautiful and soothing to my soul. Looking at you is the closest resemblance to Heaven that I have found here on Earth. I was drawn to you the first time I laid eyes on you. I've never felt this way before, ever, in my entire existence and you made me feel this way. That is why you are special." I said. She looked at me with the biggest smile I've ever seen.

"Wow."

"I know. Wow." I agreed. She looked at me and, in her eyes, I could see that she was still processing every word that I said. She had a million thoughts in her head, but instead of acting on them, she remained quiet.

"No one has ever said anything remotely close to that to me. Thank you. Thank you for being so kind and sweet." She said sincerely as she held my hand tighter.

"You deserve it. You really do." I replied. We sat there briefly without a word. Both of us decided to take in this moment silently, and so we did. She laid her head of my shoulder effortlessly and turned to face me.

"Now, I'm curious..." she said breaking the silence.

"Curious about what? Me being an Angel? I know how it sounds but I promise you it's the truth—" I started to begin.

"No, it's not that. I accepted that the moment it came from your lips." She said smiling.

"Oh, then what is it you are curious about?" I asked.

"You said you brought me here to show me something, remember?" she said as she got up on her feet.

"Oh, you're right. I do want to show you something and I think you'll like it!"

"Well, I'm waiting." She said as she stuck out her hand. I smiled as I took it and began leading her to my balcony.

(Melody)

Adam led me to his balcony and all I could see was beauty at its absolute form. The city skyline at this view was immaculate. Truly magnificent. The moon was even full tonight.

"Oh my God." I managed to finally get out. He pulled out a chair for me so that I could sit and I gladly obliged. Something about him just made me smile. I think my jaws were swollen from smiling so much. How I wish that this night would never end.

I sat still staring at the skyline in a complete daze. My mind was still comprehending the reality of Adam's true being. I wasn't battling it, like any normal person would do because I had dreams about him being my angel in the Hospital, but to know my dreams were reality was just so rewarding. I've been asking God to bring a love so real and genuine to me, but I never thought it would come like this. I smiled to myself.

"Are you happy?" Adam said as he came out with a big blanket and a bottle of wine. I smiled at him.

"Are you kidding this is one of the happiest day of my little life." I said as he put the blanket over me. The moon was beaming an aura that just made this such a romantic setting. I wondered how his lips would feel to mine. I knew we were moving too fast already, but I didn't care. I wanted to be here. I wanted to be here forever.

"Adam?" I said. He turned at me as he started pouring two glasses of wine.

"Yes, Melody?" I hesitated briefly.

"Your existence. Should I keep this a secret?" It was a random question, but I needed to know if this was something I should guard with my life.

"I would like that you did. I wasn't even supposed to tell you. You are the only human that knows." He said calmly. I remained silent. He walked over to me and placed his hand on my cheek. It was soft and comforting.

"It could be dangerous for you to know. There are dark times ahead in my world." He said as he looked into my eyes. I could feel the sadness in his voice.

"Please share with me." I asked patiently. He smiled and looked at the sky.

"Well, there is an angel who has been murdering other angels for unknown reasons. I think there is something sinister happening and we don't understand it yet, but once we do, we might be in for a fight. My sisters feel that it has something to do with you." He said. I couldn't think of the words or thoughts. My reality was not my reality anymore.

"What do mean something to do with me?" I asked frantically. He placed his head down before answering.

"Well, Melody this is going to be hard to understand because we quite don't understand it, but there is a power within you. Me saving your life triggered something inside of you. I don't know much on this, but my sisters feel you may be gifted." I just stared at him. "After everything I've heard you say today, this was by far the only thing I don't believe. I know myself, and I can assure you that they are mistaken. I feel the same as I always felt." I ran my hand through his soft hair.

"This is too much..." I said. He held me in his arms.

"I know this is a lot to handle. About myself, you, my sisters, my life, but I feel compelled to tell you. I am sorry. I should have waited or told you in increments. It wasn't very wise to tell you all this at once." He said. I could feel his compassion. He must have thought that I would assume he was a mad man. Crazy. One who has lost all his sense of reality. But something in my heart believed every word he uttered from his lips. It was unbelievable. I was still technically a stranger to him, yet he has opened to me in ways I never thought were possible. I held him closely to me, not planning on letting him go.

"I knew you had a pain in your heart. I could see it in those brown eyes of yours. I know because I felt the same way, until I met you. I've been waiting for you just as long as you have been waiting for me. Don't worry Adam, I won't let anything happen to you. Your secret is safe with me. And if you say I have this power, maybe I can use it to save you, save everyone" I comforted him.

"Melody, you are a dream." He said. I smiled to myself.

"No, you are the dream. The dream I have been waiting to come true." I responded. It was silence for a moment until a shooting star appeared in the sky. It reminded me of something.

He placed his soft hands on my face and he slowly press his lips against mine. The feeling was more than intoxicating, more than exhilarating. It was magical. It was divine.

"I think I'm in love with you Melody." He said as he parted from my lips. I looked him and that's when I knew my life would change forever. At that exact moment I knew nothing would ever be the same. In that final moment I knew I was in love with one of God's greatest creations.

"I love you too Adam." I said as I pressed my lips back against his. We remained like that until the moon started to disappear. I placed my head against his warm chest and I reluctantly started to close my eyes hopping that when I wake he would still be here holding me endlessly.

I woke up that morning, feeling angelic myself. It was a wonderful night and one I would never forget. Adam drove me home and together we both walked through the door.

We entered the Kitchen and I ended up right into Victoria's arms. She surprisingly managed to catch and hold me. "Woah. Someone is happy to see you." Matthew said as I held her. Victoria held me back to look at me.

"Hey girl, everything alright?" She said. I smiled. "Everything is fantastic! We had a great night. How was the party?" I engage as Adam walked toward the guys.

"I love you Adam! No one has ever made my sister smile like this." She said making a scene. "She must be still a little drunk. Women and their alcohol." Jason said as stared at Natalia. "Umm, it was so nice to meet you girls. Especially you Natalia. What happened to you guys though? You guys just disappeared." Jason said as he turned his attention to Adam and I. Natalia smiled at him and looked at Lyla. Lyla looked back at her, then they both looked at me.

"Adam kidnapped me. I went unwillingly." I said as I wrapped my arms around him. Jason looked at Matthew then at me.

"Oh…well, good for you." Jason said.

"You all were having such an enjoyable time, it seemed you didn't need us." Adam said smiling. Everyone laughed and that's when I knew this would be the beginning of a beautiful future…and it sure would be…

Chapter 5
Angels and Demons

(Adam)

Our next four months were glorious. We spent every day together learning more and more about each other. Melody, my sisters, Victoria, and I became a family. She knew everything, and we protected her with our lives. Victoria even got married, which was a fun experience in itself. The longer we were together the stronger I became.

The life that I knew was long gone. I haven't been to work in months; I don't even know where my cell phone is located. I know my boss, Mr. Newson, is having a field day with all my absences. I feel as if life for me has just begun.

I look at the morning sun shine brightly in the horizon. I couldn't help to admire the amazing scene. Melody was sleeping so peacefully, she didn't move once. Her elegance was present even in her slumber.

Last night was like any night of ours. As I look at her, I knew that I could never leave her side. She was my eternity, and she knew it.

The candles were still burning from the night before and my sisters were nowhere to be found. I figured they were enjoying the nice weather that has been hitting us the last couple of days. I know Lyla enjoys being at the lake. Even when it is extremely cold. Melody usually goes with her, but since she was sleep, I guess Natalia and Gabriel had to replace her. I kissed Melody on the cheek and I as I headed toward the kitchen, I could feel we were no longer alone.

"Hello, old friend." A vaguely familiar voice rang in my ear. I turned around to face whomever entered my home uninvited.

"Ariel?" I said in confusion. Ariel was an angel that I knew back before I fell. He was a friend. It was good to see him, but I felt his presence here was questionable.

"Yes, my friend. It's been a long time." He said with a crooked smirk. I played along.

"It has. It's good to see you, it has been a long time."

"Why my friend, I haven't seen you in centuries. You disappeared without a trace. What happened to you Adam?" He asked. His concern seemed genuine.

"I truly don't know. But I feel it is becoming clearer as the days go by. Do you have any news for me? You must, if you come this far.

"I wish I had better news, but I don't. I am in awe of how you got here as well. No one knew anything or where you were, but your sisters were diligent in finding you." He said. "So, what do I owe this visit? I know you must have some sort of information." I said as I poured me a glass of wine. "Well, I…" He started until a sleepy Melody walked in the room.

.   "Adam?" she said as she stood in the door way. Her eyes slowly opened with surprise as she aimed them at Ariel, who was a stranger to her. Ariel's eyes looked at Melody in utter amazement. "Is everything okay? I heard a noise." She said worried. I turned to face her.

"Everything is fine my love. I would like to introduce you to a longtime friend of mine." I said as I took her hand. She took her eyes off Ariel and placed them on mine. "This is Ariel, Ariel this is Melody Marie Eve."

"Nice to meet you." She said as she stuck out her hand, still skeptical. Ariel looked at her still in surprise

"Nice to meet you Melody." He said. Then he turned to me. "We have to talk in private, when is an appropriate time for me to return?" He said. I looked at him then at Melody. She gave me a worrisome look. I placed my hand on her cheek and kissed her forehead. She wrapped her arms around me and closed her eyes. Taking every moment in. I focused back on Ariel.

"She knows Ariel." I simply said. Ariel's face was unreadable.

"Knows what? He asked. I smiled at him.

"Everything. She knows everything."
Ariel looked at me in astonishment then at Melody. Her eyes focused on him unaware of the situation at hand.

"Amazing." Ariel said. He paced around the room before returning to face us. Melody released me and met him Ariel face to face.

"Ariel, I know Adam wasn't supposed to tell me, but I promise I will keep this a secret for the rest of my life, please don't hurt him." She pleaded. I wondered how she guessed he was an Angel. Maybe it was his silky blond hair and the fact that his angelic radiance was too much to ignore. Ariel smiled and placed his hand on her shoulder.

"My dear Melody, no one is here to hurt Adam. As a matter of fact, I don't think anyone could if they tried." He said. She looked at him in confusion.

"I know he doesn't have his power, so his powerless against you all, but I will fight long side him." She said as she clinched her little fist. Ariel smiled at her.

"She is a feisty one. I like her." He said. I smiled as I grabbed her and held her in my arms.

"I promise you Melody, I am a friend." Ariel announced "I kissed Melody's forehead again to reassure her.

"I'm actually here because we need to find your Divine, Adam. Two more angels have died. The first in last couple of months." Ariel said sadly. I looked at Melody and she looked at me.

"We still have no idea who is responsible?"

"No, not a clue. We need to find your Divine. We could really use your strength right now." He said as he looked at me. "I know." I simply said as I thought about where it could be. I had no idea. I doubted if I would ever return to my old self. Melody placed her head on my chest. "Don't worry, we will find it baby." She reassured me. I smiled to myself. I could feel Ariel observe us.

"Love...what a beautiful thing." Ariel asked. I looked at her and smiled. "I loved her the moment I laid eyes on her." I said. Melody smiled and held me tighter.

"God truly works in mysterious ways. I feel this is one of his miracles." Ariel said. We all started smiling and laughing in joy. At that moment, I had a dark eerie feeling about my sisters. "What is it Adam?" Melody said as she immediately noticed a change in me. "My sisters…They are in danger? Ariel, you must take me to them." I asked. Ariel looked at me with haste. "Of course." He said as he began to focus. "Wait, I'm coming too!" Melody announced as she began to put on her shoes. "No, my love, it could be dangerous. I don't know what I feel exactly. I just want to make sure they are okay." I said. She gave me a look that I have grown to know and love. "Gabriel, Natalia, and Lyla are just as much as my sisters than they are yours. If they are in trouble, I'm going as well." She demanded. I had nothing to say. Their woman bond was strong to argue with. "Okay, but you have to stand right by me." I said. She nodded as she pulled a butcher knife out of the drawer. "Okay, now I'm ready." She said. I looked at Ariel to see was he ready. "Okay, let's go." He said as he ejected his wings and flew us to our destination.

(Gabriel)

"What are we doing here?" Lyla said as we walked in our fifth store in the mall. "Seeing if we could find something in here." Natalia said as her eyes gazed amongst the aisles of clothes. "I know that, but what are we doing in here? I don't think Melody will like any of this stuff." Lyla said as she folded her arms. "Excuse me ladies, can I help you with something." An employee said as he walked towards us. "Umm, yes it's our little sister's birthday tomorrow and we are trying to find something for her. Now, I know its last minute, but you don't understand my sister. She is the hardest person to give gifts too!" Victoria announced. The man looked nervous as we all stood and looked at him. "Umm, I can see what I can do." He said as he walked away as fast as he could. "Victoria, you did it again. You ran away another employee." I said as I laughed. "It's not my fault. I swear. I'm just very vocal at times. You guys know that!" Victoria said as she laughed with us. "Let's check out the store we just passed, I think I saw a great gift. We should've just went with Adam when he went shopping." Victoria said as we walked out of the store. I noticed three strange men standing in the middle of the walk way. I looked at them briefly, just to come to the conclusion that they were not men at all.

"Natalia, Lyla, do you see what I see?" I asked them as they braced themselves. "Who are they and why are they just staring at us?" Victoria asked. One of the men began walking towards us. "I can smell what they are." Natalia said. I could feel her rage begin to build within her body. Flame began ejecting from her hair as she grew more impatient with our demonic guest. "Natalia, control yourself." I said. Natalia has the ability to project and manipulate fire from within her body. She used these special abilities when she attacked, but her flames were uncontrollable when she was angered. We have been working with her for centuries to help her control her power.

"What are they doing here?" Lyla asked. "Stay here and protect Victoria. Natalia come with me." I instructed. "Gabriel what's happening? Natalia you are on fire!" Victoria cried as she ran towards her only to be stopped by Lyla. She pressed her index finger on Victoria's neck, causing her to pass out. Lyla instantly picked her up before she touched the ground. Melody knew who we really were, but not Victoria. We all decided that Melody would be the one to tell her once the time was right.

"Thanks Lyla." Natalia said as we walk toward the three demons. "The one in the middle was obviously their leader so I would address him first." I said to Natalia as we walked towards them. She nodded without even looking at me. Her eyes were focused on them. Natalia lived for a fight.

We stopped a few feet from them and they continued to stare until the one in the middle step in front of the others. Unfortunately, the middle demon looked very familiar.

"Tell me, why would a trio of angels be protecting one little girl?" The man asked. "What is your business here demon!?" I simply said. He smiled a devilish smile before talking again. "I have come along way and waited a long time for this day and I have to say I'm a little disappointed. I thought the birthday girl would be here." He said looking around. His words created a curiosity that I was not ready for. "Melody? What do you want with her." I asked. The man stepped closer until we were face to face. "You see, my name is Damon and Melody happens to be my daughter. I have been looking and searching for her for some time now, but I haven't had any luck. I heard some angels were in the city and of course you would be the reason why I can't wish my daughter a happy birthday." He said. I looked at him in disgust. "Melody…is your daughter? That cannot be!" I yell at him in anger. "I'm sorry Gabriel to upset you, but it is the truth…and yes I know who you are. I know who all of you are, including your powerless Adam. Now you know who I am and know that I will stop at nothing to get back my daughter." He said as he and his two other demons disappeared within the crowd.

"Where did he go?" Natalia asked. I looked around only to find out his true motives. "He didn't come here to fight…" I said. Adam, Melody, and an unlikely angel appeared next to us. "Hey, are you all okay? I had a feeling." Adam said as he looked at all of us. "Victoria? What happened to Victoria?" Melody said as she ran to her side. "She will be fine, I had to put her on sleep. I didn't want her getting hurt." Lyla said. "Hurt by who?" Melody asked. I looked at Adam with bold eyes. "Trouble." I simply said. Adam looked at me with eyes I have only seen once. Eyes of anger.

(Adam)

"Okay, can someone please explain to me what has happened." Melody said as we return to my home. Lyla placed Victoria on the couch and placed a thin blanket over her body. I looked at Gabriel only to see an expression of worry. I noticed that all their faces were in distraught. Something horrible happened. Lyla walked over to me and wrapped her arms around me. "Gabriel?" I said calmly. Melody eyes wondered around the room in confusion. Ariel's eyes looked just as confused as hers.

"We have a problem brother." Gabriel said. I could feel the rage boil in Gabriel as I looked at her. I knew that times of peace were officially over.

"Gabriel. What happened?" I asked. She looked at me and then she glanced at Melody.

"Can I talk to you on the balcony?" Gabriel asked. I nodded as I led the way. The morning sun was a sight to see. "Adam?" Melody said. "It's alright. I will tell you everything. Watch over Victoria, she should be waking up soon." I said as I kissed her and walked to the balcony. I closed the door behind me.

"Now, talk to me." I asked. She took my hand and looked back at Melody.

"I don't know where to start." She asked.

"Just start from the beginning." She hesitated.

"Gabriel." I continued. She turns to face me. I prepare myself.

"A demon came looking for Melody. His name is Damon. He is a high-ranking demon who managed to find his way on Earth." I felt my fist clinch. "Why would he be looking for Melody?" I asked. "Well you are not going to believe this but, he claims to be Melody's biological father." She said. I just stood there stunned for a while. I was in a trance of disbelief. "Adam?" Gabriel said trying to gain back my focus. "How could this be? How could we not detect it?" I asked as I paced around. "I do not know, But I do know one thing, we have to act fast. Damon will find her, and we must be ready." She said. "I also believe he is involved with the killing of the angels. He has a plan, and I expect that his plan includes Melody in some way."

I looked back at Melody, completely unaware of what is going on. "Whatever happens, we must not tell Melody. We must figure this out between us." I said as I continued to look at Melody. "I have to disagree with you brother. I think Melody deserves the right to know. I'm sure she has been curious about her parents. She needs to know the truth. All of it." She said. I thought about her words and saw some truth in them. But I also saw the pain that Melody would feel after learning the truth. "Okay, she does deserve to know. I will tell her myself when the time is right." I said. Gabriel nodded. "Of course, but what can we do? Without your power, they will kill you. I will never let that happen. We need you ready." She responded.

"I'm sure we will find a way. I must find a way. Protecting Melody and you guys is all I care about." I said as I stared at the glimmering sun. "We need to come up with a plan." She said as she started pacing around.

"I agree, and I know someone who could help." Ariel said as he opened the balcony door. "How did you find my brother?" Gabriel asked as she looked at him suspiciously. "The same way you did." Ariel responded. Gabriel gave him a look before turning her face back to me.

"Everything that is happening is far to strange. Protecting the girl should be our main priority. Melody is special, but all of this is putting her in grave danger. They will stop at nothing until they find her. That is the characteristics of demon. The most alarming question of them all is, if Damon is her father, who is her mother? This could change everything." I listened to Ariel's words as I looked at Melody. Her innocent face had no clue of the dangers that await us.

"I know Ariel, but who could help us? Not only am I putting Melody in danger, all her friends could possibly be targets. Damon could possibly know where Melody lives. We need to act now." I said. Gabriel nodded and grabbed my hand.

"Adam, whatever we need to do, we will do. Ariel who is this someone you speak off?" She asked. Ariel smiled as he looked at the clouds.

"It has been said that God spoke to one angel that he sent to earth to protect his words and gospels. This particular angel is the divine bridge to God himself and I feel that he will tell us our next step." He said.

Gabriel eyes began to widen.

"Zachariah!" she said in shock. Ariel smiled and nodded. "But where could we find him? If he were here, we would have felt his presence by now." Gabriel debated.

"You would have felt his presence...if he were still an angel." Ariel protested.

"What are you saying?"

"I'm saying that when God sent him on earth, Zachariah chose to live a human life." Ariel said. Gabriel continued.

"His body would have aged, and he would've been dead some time, ago right?" she said.

Ariel looked at me and smiled.

"Has your brother's body showed any indications of aging? He has been on earth for 101 years!" he announced. Ariel had a point. Gabriel smiled and shook her head.

"It's a long shot, but we have nothing to lose. How do we find him?" She asked. I looked at Ariel, anxious to see what he will say.

"Give me a few hours, I will have additional information. But until then, stay safe." He said as he disappeared in the wind.

Gabriel stared at me with eyes of worry. I held her effortlessly. "Everything will be alright my love, I promise you." I reassured her. She smiled and took my hand. "It's something about Ariel that I don't trust." She said as she looked away from me. "You never liked him." I said as I placed my arm around her. "We will find away. WE will find a way." I comforted her

"I know Adam, we will be fine." I looked at her then at Melody. She stared at me with those beautiful eyes, eyes of concern. Eyes of worry. "You ready?" Gabriel said disrupting my focus on Melody.

"Yes, Its time." I responded as I took her hand. We walked back into my home with patient eyes staring at us. Melody walked over and held me with an embrace she wasn't prepared to let go. Natalia and Lyla just looked at us. They were already aware of what was going on since they heard everything fluently while we were outside. Melody was the only one left in the dark.

"Melody." I said as I looked into her eyes.

"Yes Adam, I am here." She responded so gracefully.

"I know I have opened up to you and flooded you with so many things in these past months, but there is more you should know." I said. She prepared herself for the worst.

"Tell me." She said unafraid of what it might be. I took a deep breath.

"There is something happening, something that we don't understand yet, but we need to get you home to make sure your friends and family are safe." I said. She looked at Gabriel then back at me.

"I am not following, what has happened Adam?" She said in confusion. Lyla grabbed her hand, focusing Melody's attention on her.

"We have to move Melody, I promise we will explain everything." Lyla explained. Melody took a step back.

"You guys are hiding something. Tell me what happened!?" She said as her voice got louder. I hated lying to her, but I couldn't dare tell her the truth. Not now at least.

"In this world that you live in, there are things humans are blind of. For one, us. Before meeting me, you probably didn't even truly know of our existence. For every angel in creation, there is a dark evil entity called a 'Demon' and they are the epitome of evil. One of these creatures came looking for you today. Remember when I told you that you were special, well, it turns out that you are far more special than any of us could imagine. So, we must go to your house to check on your friends. Are they still at your home?" I asked. She took every word in and didn't respond right away. The room was quiet for a moment before anyone uttered another word.

"We have to go." Melody said as she ran towards the front door.

She put on her jacket and she disappeared in the hall way. I placed on my boats and jacket and followed behind her.

"I'll get Victoria." Natalia whispered in my ear as we reached the elevator. I nodded as all of us exited my home.

"I can only imagine what she is thinking right now" I say to myself as I look upon a suddenly worried and focused Melody.

As we exited the elevator, I bumped hard into an unexpected person. "I'm so sorry." I said as I helped the young woman up.

"Don't worry about it." She said as she got up smiling. I immediately remember the familiar face. It was the young woman who I met four months ago. She insisted that I give Melody flowers on that amazing day. I haven't seen her since then actually, now that I think about it. "Hey, it's you?" I said as I look at her. For some reason seeing her was quite soothing. I felt like I knew her. "Yup, it's me! Did you get the flowers?" She asked.

"Why yes, I did. She loved them. Thank you for that." I said. She smiled at me with a glance that was all so familiar.

"Brazil, he's in Brazil." She said as she exited the elevator. I looked at Melody and my sisters as they exited the building.

"Who's in Brazil?" I said as I tried to put my attention back on her, but she was nowhere to be found. I looked around the lobby and there was no sight of her anywhere. "Brazil?" I repeated to myself as I headed toward the exit.

(Melody)

Today has been a crazy day and just like that it became the scariest. I sat in the car waiting for Adam to start it. Gabriel sat in the back seat without uttering a single word. Adam finally managed to get inside and started the ignition. I wondered what took him so long? He was right behind us. I thought to myself, but didn't say anything about it. He also didn't say a single word either. I knew last night Victoria and Matthew was having a get together at the house and I would die if any of my family and friends got hurt because of me. I looked at Victoria, still asleep on my shoulder. I wondered what really happened and who was this 'demon.' Maybe he was the one who has been haunting me for all these years...

"We pulled up to my home and I ran out before the car came to a stop. I entered the house and started scanning the area. "Melody? What's wrong?" Jason said as he stood up off the couch and approached us. "Victoria?" Matthew said as he ran to his new wife." Adam placed her on the couch. "She fainted while she was shopping for a birthday present for Melody." Gabriel said as he looked at him intently. Matthew placed his hand on her face as he looked at her worried. "I checked her pulse. She will be just fine." Gabriel continued.

Gabriel has informed everyone in my life that she was indeed a doctor (something to cover her angelic background), so this coming from her was reassuring for Matthew to hear. "Thank you so much guys. Let me get her to bed," He said as he carried her up to her room. As I looked around I noticed that there were party balloons and confetti everywhere. They were preparing a surprise birthday party for me.

"It looks like everything is just fine here." Adam said as he looked around with a smile. "What are you smiling about?" I asked as I placed my hand on his face. "I guess the surprise is over." He said as he looked at his sisters. I smiled to myself. "I already knew...Lyla cannot hold a secret to save her life." I said as I kissed Adam on the cheek. He looked at Lyla as she simply shrugged and walked away.

"Melody. V wants to talk to you. She woke up before I could even tuck her in." Matthew said from the top of the stair case. Well, that was quick. Typical Victoria. Nothing could put her out for long. Not even angelic powers.

"Okay, tell her I'll be right up." I said as gazed at Adam once more before heading towards the stairs. "I'll be right back Adam. Don't go anywhere." I said. He kissed my lips briefly, but it was enough to give me chills.

"I don't plan on it." He said as he smiled. I blushed and headed up the stairs.

"Melody?" I heard him say as I reached the top. I looked down at him and he answered before I could say anything. "Be honest." I smiled at him thinking to myself this is his way of telling me to "Tell her the truth" which I knew he really wanted me to do for quite a while. I was reluctant to do so because I didn't want her involved in this world. I didn't want any of my family involved. As much as I would love them too, I felt it was for their own safety.

I walked to our room and I plopped on the bed next to her, exhausted from the long morning I've had. Victoria sat up and gave me a stern look.

"I know there is something going on Melody. I have the weirdest feeling...And how did I get home? Last thing I remember, I was in the mall..."

She was so confused. I had no choice but to finally tell her. She deserved to know more than anyone, but before I could say anything she continued to ramble.

"Is Adam everything you dreamed of? I only ask because I feel he may be a little too perfect. These past couple months, I been really thinking he might be a vampire or something." Victoria said. I smiled as I thought the same thing when I first met him.

"Victoria, you have no idea." I simply said as I laid my head on her stomach.

"He is amazing. Nothing I ever experienced." Victoria smiled as she played in my wild hair. "I'm so happy for you Melody. Beyond happy. You deserve this." She said. I looked at the ceiling thinking about Adam and how happy I really was despite all the dangers that laid ahead.

"Thank you so much sis, I really appreciate it." I said before hesitating. Victoria gave me a look of concern.

"What's wrong girl, you know I know you to well." She said. I sat up and finally gave her eye contact.

"I guess you do know me." I said. She continued to look at me with her all-knowing look, waiting on me to respond. I took a deep breath.

"Okay, so what I'm about to tell you is going to sound...well, rather crazy at first, but you know me more than anyone." I said firmly. She grabbed my hand as she continued to glare at me.

"Melody tell me." I took another deep breath once again.

"Do you believe in Angels and Demons?" I asked. Victoria look didn't change.

"I don't know, why?" She said.

"Well what if I told you Adam was indeed too good to be true...Because he was an angel. And that a demon is after me. I think it must be the guy I seen in my dreams. It has to be!" I said looking away from her. The room was quiet for a brief time before I managed to look at Victoria again. Her face was unreadable.

"Melody, you are scaring me, what's really going on? You sound like mom..." Victoria started before she was interrupted.

"It's true Victoria." Gabriel said as appeared behind us. Victoria turned around in shock. I smiled at Gabriel, happy to use her assistance.

"Gabriel, how did you get in here? The door was closed. We would have seen you come in." She said in confusion.

"We are Angels, Melody was telling you the truth. I know this is hard to take in right now, but you are in danger." Gabriel said as she sat on the bed with us. Victoria was at a loss for words. "Lyla, Natalia, and I came to Earth to look for our fallen brother. You see he's been here on Earth for 100 years. We don't know how he fell, but I feel Melody has something to do with it." Gabriel said. I looked at Victoria as she looked me.

Victoria took everything in and stood up off the bed. "I need a little space. Excuse me." She said as she left the room.

"Victoria?" I called to her, but she didn't stop. Gabriel grabbed my hand.

"She will be alright, it's just a lot to take in right now, but Melody I heard you mention about seeing someone in your dreams?" Gabriel said as Victoria continued to walk away. "Yes, ever since I was a little, I would have these horrible nightmares of this mysterious man. My mom would say a demon was trying to find me through my dreams. So, she told me that she read me a spell or something and for the last 20 years, I have been nightmare free. Around the time I met Adam, my nightmares returned. I know it's no coincidence. My mom gave me a necklace to protect me." I said. Gabriel looked at my necklace and examined it. "This is some powerful magic, where did you say you got this from? She asked. "My mother got it from my aunt Catherine. Did you say magic?" I said as I looked at it. Gabriel didn't answer, she just continued to look at the necklace. "This world is going to get a lot bigger for you Melody, and I'm sorry about that." She simply said. I couldn't say anything back. I was worried, truly worried. Adam and his world were beyond dangerous, and I wouldn't forgive myself if anything happened to my family and friends. What world did I truly enter?

"Let's go back down stairs. Victoria will be fine, she just needs some time." Gabriel said as she wrapped her arm around me and lead me down stairs. Adam's gaze assured me that things were going to be alright, but I wasn't exactly sure how.

"How did it go?" He asked me in the gentlest of voices. I simply placed my head on his chest and wrapped my arms around him. "That bad huh?" He whispered in my ear. "Don't worry, she will come around."

We all sat on the couch, all except Victoria, who was still locked upstairs. "Hey, where's Victoria? Is she okay?" Matthew finally asked after ten minutes of her absence. "Yeah, she told me she wasn't feeling good, so she decided to try and go back to sleep." I quickly responded. He nodded as he disappeared to the kitchen.

After an hour, I decided to check on my dear sister. "I'm going to go check on V." I said as started up the stairs. Adam nodded as he sat down and began talking with his sisters. Victoria's door was closed which was such a rare sight. "Victoria?" I said as I knocked softly. "Come in." She responded sharply. She was sitting in her bed with our picture book in her hands flipping through pages. I quietly sat right next to her and began looking over her shoulder.

"Remember this one?" She said as she pointed at a picture. It was when we were seven years old. The first time we went to six flags great America. "That was such a good day." I responded. Victoria closed the book and looked at me. "What's wrong V?" I ask her. She looks down at the closed book then back to me with the most serious look I have ever seen her give me.

"I'm afraid. I'm afraid to lose you. This angel and demon talk is terrifying. I don't want you apart of it." She said. I could see the emotion in her face. "But I know you Melody. You will be a part of it, because that's who you are. Mom always said something like this would happen. You are special, you have always been special." She said with a smile. "Who knew the first guy you decide to really like turns out to be an angel. You sure know how to pick them." We both laugh at the reality. "He is amazing. But I feel this is much bigger than me V. We are talking about the world. So much is going on right now, it's crazy." I said as I thought about everything. "Tell me about the man in your dream? He is a real thing?" She asked. I hesitate briefly before answering. "I'm pretty sure. Yes. All this time he was a real being and now he is here. I know he is the one that Adam was telling me about. It may sound crazy, but I can actually feel his presence." I stood up as I started pacing around the room. "He is after me for reasons I cannot explain." I said as I plopped on her bed and burrowed my head under her pillow. Victoria snuggled up right under me as she consoled me.

"Adam will protect you. I can see it in his eyes." I also saw this passion in his eyes as well. "Oh, and it looks like we were right about mom after all this time." I said. Victoria looked at me in confusion. "What do you mean?" She asked. "Well, the necklace mom gave me actually did protect me from demons because it is magic! Mom may actually be a witch like we thought." I said. Victoria shook her head. "As much as I feared it, I always knew that she was. Aunt Catherine too. Maybe there is a way I could help you. Adam and his angel sisters may have your back, But I'm your sister. I will not let you go through this alone. She said as she got up and grabbed her car keys. "I'm going to talk to mom. She might come clean and maybe even teach me a few things. Maybe I could be of use." She said. I was astounded. "V, you don't have to do that. It's going to be okay. And I doubt mom is actually a witch. Maybe she just knows a few old things, you know?" I said trying to convince her. "No, Melody, I've seen her in action. I never told you because I was too afraid to bring it up, she has power I can't explain. Maybe she could teach me some of her abilities. I feel like she always knew I would come seeking her. I feel this is the best time." She said as she gave me a kiss on the cheek. "I will be back soon sis." She said as she opened the window and began climbing out.

"Why are you leaving out the window?" I asked.

"I'm not a good liar, and I don't want to lie to Matthew, He doesn't need to be a part of this. Tell him that I love him and that I will return in a few days." She said as she climbed out the window and disappeared from my view. I sat on the bed alone; which reminded me it has been my first time I've been alone since all of this began. "I hope I am strong enough for this."

Chapter 6
Amora's Proposal

(Adam)

    "What are we going to do?" Natalia said as we all sat down in the living room. We all patiently waited for Matthew to leave before we conducted in any angel-demon conversation. I looked at Gabriel with a look of concern. "I don't know yet, but we have to move fast. We don't know when Damon will return. Melody is not safe here." I said. I know Damon will not return like he did before, he will have a more sinister plan. "I think we should wait for Ariel to return with good news." Lyla said as she got up to lean against the stair rails. "I don't think we have that much time. I think Melody knows this demon. She told me a demon has been invading her dreams. It has to be Damon, right?" Gabriel responded.

    "Wait, what?" I said as I placed all my focus on Gabriel.

    "Yes, I believe Damon has been trying to locate her for a while."

    I could feel myself becoming enraged. How could this be? How could I not have known?

    I sat in silence as I thought about Melody, Damon, and everything that was going on. The reality of it all was overwhelming. Damon, a demon, was after the woman who I love and so happens to be her father. What was his plan? If only we could find Zachariah, maybe we would have a chance. All the sudden it hit me.

    "Brazil." I uttered under my breath. My sisters all stopped their conversations and looked at me. "What's wrong Adam?" Natalia asked. "Zachariah is in Brazil!" I said as I stood up. My sisters looked at me in confusion. "What are you talking about Adam?" Gabriel asked as she stood up too. "I can't explain it, but I KNOW that we will find him there. Trust me!" I said. They all looked at each other and nodded. "Well let's go! We have no time to waste." Lyla said. I looked up stairs and then back down. "I'm going to need you to stay here and watch over Melody, Victoria and the house. Natalia, I'm going to need you to watch over

Jason and Matthew. Gabriel, you come with me. That way everybody here is protected." I announced.

"I'm coming with you." Melody's voice rang from the top of the stairs. "Melody, I…" I started to say before she continued. "I am a part of this Adam. I am no longer a normal girl lost in this world with more questions than answers, I am much more than that. I never fitted in and I always felt that my purpose was on a bigger scale. You saved my life when you pulled me out of that car, but you also saved my life when let me in your world. Now I don't know what I was created on this earth to do, but I know that I was created to do it with you. I will fight alongside you." She said as she came down the stairs. Gabriel and Natalia smiled at her while Lyla grabbed her hand and brought her in our circle. It took me a moment to find the proper words to say.

"It will be dangerous my love." I said. She took my hand and smiled. "I'm coming with you and that's the end. Now, where are your car keys? I'm driving to the airport." She said as she dug in my pocket and took the keys. Gabriel couldn't help to laugh. "Where is Victoria?" I asked. She's gone. She has her own mission she wants to do and once she has her mind on something, there is no stopping her." Melody said. "Yes, my brother. It seems Victoria has finally decided to tap into her purpose as well." Gabriel said as she walked out the front door. I was confused. "What are you two talking about?" I finally ask. "I'll tell you on the way to the airport." Gabriel said.

Melody was on the front porch ready to leave. I noticed her determination that I didn't notice before. She was motivated. "You know it's okay if you just want to fly there by yourself, these airplanes are slow. The flight will be at least 12 hours. You could get there in minutes." I told Gabriel as we walked to the car. "I think I would like to have the airplane experience." She said as she entered the car. Melody ran and gave my sisters a big hug and ran back to the car to escape the Chicago trick spring weather. I look at Gabriel and then to Melody and smile to myself. Melody smiled at me as she held my hand.

"We will be fine." She assured me. I believed in her words more than she knew. I started to think about the woman I've continued to bump into and wondered who exactly she was. Why was I so firm on going to Brazil after I merely heard her utter the words? My intuition assures me that this is a great move. The only move.

The airport was crowded which was nothing unusual. Melody and Gabriel hung to my arm as I navigated to obtain our boarding passes. After about an hour of dealing with airport foolishness we finally make it to the section where we waited to be boarded. Melody was beyond quiet since we got here.

"What's wrong Melody?" I finally ask as we sit down. Gabriel looked up to see what she would say. I guess she was just as curious as I was. She hesitated briefly before she answered. "Something is wrong." She said as she looked through the crowded hall way. I grabbed her hand and looked at her intently. "What do you mean?" I asked. "I can't explain it, but I just feel something is wrong." Gabriel looked at her than back to me in concern. "I do feel something as well." Gabriel said. Melody's eyes widen as a loud commotion started down the west wing. "What in the hell?" I said to myself as I listen to the women and men screaming rushing towards us. "Stay behind me." I said to Melody as she quickly hid behind right shoulder. Gabriel stood up right beside me, ready for what was to come. Behind all the screaming people I finally saw the menace who was causing the spectacle. He walked with a grin I knew so very well. A grin of pure malice. "It's him, It's the demon." Gabriel simply said as he began to approach us. Melody grabbed my hand in worry. "Brother remember you don't have your power. I will take care of this!" Gabriel said as she began to walk toward him. I stopped her. Melody held me even tighter as he got closer. Her eyes looked at Damon in pure hatred as well as fear. "I have my power right here." I said as I kissed Melody on the forehead. "Don't you worry." I assured them both.

Damon stopped about twenty feet away us and just looked at as for a moment. My eyes fueled with rage as I gazed upon him. He was wearing all black just as my sisters described him. Everyone remained still as civilians continued to attempt to leave the building while some were brave enough to watch this altercation.

"Melody! My beautiful daughter! I have been searching for you for quite some time. You have grown into an exceptional woman. How long has it been? About 22 years since I last saw you." Damon began as he started walking toward us again.

"Daughter? What is he talking about Adam?" I couldn't manage to say anything. "Oh, your angel boyfriend didn't tell you? Yes, it's true...I know you have been wondering who your parents are right? Well, I am your father. You are a princess my love. Now come dear, we have a lot of work to do." He said as he held his hands out towards her. "You are not my father. I don't have one. You will never be my father!" She screamed. Damon's face quickly changed to anger. "Listen, your ungrateful little maggot! I have bestowed a lot of power within you for a purpose that you will fulfill regardless if you cooperate or not. This is bigger than you my love." He said. The intercom finally said that our flight was ready to board. "Take Melody with you on the plane. I'll handle him." I said without turning around. Gabriel gave Damon a look of hatred and took Melody's hand as she tried to resist. "I can't leave you with this thing. It's my fault he is here. It is my fight." Melody said. "It's going to be okay. I promise. Now go. I will see you soon." I said as I smiled at her. Gabriel nodded, and they entered the plane. I put all my focus back on Damon who stood there patiently for me to return the conversation.

"That will be the last time you see her." I said as I began walking towards him. He looked down as he smiled at the situation.

"This had nothing to do with you or your sisters, but being what you are you just had to get involved." He said as his smile quickly began to fade.

"I don't think I gave you my blessings to be with my daughter." Damon said as he started walking closer to me." I laughed instantly. "I don't need your 'blessing' beast. I will kill you myself." I started closing the distance between us only to be interrupted by oncoming police and airport security.

"Freeze!" police officers yell as the pointed their guns at us. "I'm sorry officers, I'm kind of in the middle of something." He flicked his hands and all the officers flung to the wall. "I am going to enjoy killing you." He said as he attempted to attack. A dark smoke cloud started to appear from beneath the ground changing both our attention. People began to panic even more as the cloud started to form something. Damon continued to gaze upon me as something began to be seen from inside the cloud: A person and two smaller beings. Damon began to back up slowly and the dark cloud started to expand to the ceiling. A large black Jackal appeared first growling ferocious at me. His eyes were pitch black, something not of this world. Behind the Jackal, A large black dog or Hyena appeared more vicious than the Jackal. Both growled but didn't move. Their eyes focused on me, but I didn't budge. Fear has never been an option for me and it wasn't going to be an option today.

    "My Damon, what a wonderful surprise." A sinister but seductive voice echoed from the dark cloud. "No, what are you doing here?" He said annoyed. "I'm here for my daughter. Now, I recommend you leave this place." She said. I stood motionless, curious to see who she was. The wild dogs stopped growling and sat completely still. A beautiful woman appeared from the black smoke completely naked. Her long black hair fell down her back as she stood there gazing upon this world. She was truly the mother of Melody, the similarities were evident. Her hair covered most of body figure and her eyes were enchanting as looked around the airport. She stood about 5'7 and looked no more than 130 pounds maybe. She was remarkable, but also very familiar.

    "Amora! I have finally found her! I have finally found our daughter!" He said placing his eyes on her. "Thank you for tracking her down. I always knew you would do it." She said as she kissed him on the cheek. Damon smiled as he turned his focus on me. "Now, let me finish off this angel!" He said as he began to approach me only to be stopped by one of Amora's arms. "No. I want him to myself. Go wait for me dear. I want be long." She said as she glared at me. Damon nodded. "Of course." He gave me one final look before walking into her smoke cloud. She watched patiently as the smoke evaporated then she turned her sights on me.

    "Let's talk." She said as she snapped her fingers. With the snap of her fingers she sent us to a familiar pasture in the middle of a forest. I looked around only to see trees that looked over 100 years old along with beautiful plants and flowers. Standing in the pasture was the mysterious naked woman staring at me intently. I stood there, amazed in her power. Who was she? Why did she remind me of someone I once knew?

    "Adam, it's nice to see you again. It's been lifetimes. "She said as she began walking towards me. I looked at her in bewilderment, but I did not move. Not because of fear, but because of sheer interest.

"I'm not sure we ever met before. Who are you?" I finally asked. She stopped walking and looked upon me as if I offended her. "Are you serious?" She asked as she looked at me. From the moment I saw her, she felt familiar, but I didn't know who she was.

"I'm sorry, I don't know who you are." She tilted her head as she continued to walk towards me. "Think long and hard. You remember your sisters, but you don't remember me?" She said as she stood directly in front of me. I looked at her again, but this time, I started to notice trivial things about her that I did recognize. "Amora?" I said as memories began flooding back. I glanced at her nude body briefly as she looked upon me. "Don't be ashamed, you can look, touch, feel my body." She took my hand and placed it on her soft breast. They were warm on my hand. I pulled back and regained my composure.

"Amora! Amora, is it really you? I remember everything now."

"Yes, it is me. It's been a long time Adam." I heard her velvet voice ring in my ear. A voice that I truly missed.

"Yes, it has." I said as I stood my ground. Amora and I have a vast history. She was my partner in battle and a longtime friend to me. I didn't recognize her initially because something was different about her. All her power has blinded me from the angel who was so dear to me. She looked at me with those eyes that I remembered so well. "Now, we can talk." I said as I began looking around the pasture. "This is where I fell!" I said surprised.

"It is. I brought you here to give you something. I been taking care of it since you lost it." She said as she placed her hand on my head. I could feel my body began to tremble as I fell on the ground. Slowly, my eyes opened, and I could notice that I was different. "My Divine! You had it all this time? How?" I asked in amazement. She smiled before answering. When you fell, I fell shortly after you. I followed you, but when you landed, your divine left you. It happens sometimes. I found it, but I didn't find you. I just kept it in hopes of this day." She said laughing. I could feel all my power returning. It was good to be back.

"Thank you Amora. I can't believe you held on to my Divine for so long." I said as I continued to look upon her, trying to figure out what was different about her. "Of course," She said as she smiled. "It is so good to see you." She said as she kisses my lips and put my hands on her body. I fall into her world for merely a moment before I push away from her. "I had to see was it true." Amora said as she examines me. "What?"

"That you are in love with my daughter." I stand there observing her, realizing that his is not the Amora I remember and loved. This was someone else. I woke up from what I thought would be a happy reunion.

"What have you done? Why would you do this? You and a demon? I don't understand." I said. Amora smiled. "Nephilim, the child of an angel and a demon. A power that cannot be matched. The ultimate power. It was perfect. On another note, I am happy, seriously. You may be just what she needs to prepare her." She said.

"Prepare her for what?"

"There is a war coming. Lilith's war, and Melody has the power to be the one to lead it." She said as she walked away. I looked at her in awe. I couldn't believe what she was saying.

"What are you talking about? What war? Let me guest, you are the one that's responsible for the death of the angels and the releasing of the demons, right?" I asked. She smiled at me as she picked up a violet. "The war against humanity. The war to rebuild the world. The war to destroy all life. And I need all the souls I can get for this…" She said as she placed her hand on a black stone around her neck. "This little rock is called 'The Black Supreme.' Once this little baby is full, it will release enough energy to release Lilith. Human souls are so weak you know? Angels souls really pack the power. So, killing a few of them for a greater cause seemed to make sense to me. It also gives me the power to free demons from Hell as long as their allegiance is to me" She said happily. "Amora? What has happen to you?" I asked. "Power. I have found a new leader. A new god to serve in Lilith. Oh, excuse me, I keep rambling on. I'm sure you have heard of her right?" She said as she smiled at me. "Of course. Who doesn't know her story of betrayal. I fought her once before. Many years ago." I responded.

Lilith was the original woman created from the same substance of Adam, before Eve, in the beginning of this world. She refused to be Adam's partner in life and refused God's love. She abandoned the Garden of Eden and disappeared, gaining power and knowledge among all beings in creation. Her power is considered limitless in myth. They say that she is imprisoned in this place called 'The Darkness.' Once she is free, she will rage war against this world. Destroying all of God's creation and rebuilding a new.

"You can't be serious?" I ask. "I am. I am tired of your God and his antics. I figured you of all people would be the first to join my quest of freeing Lilith. That's why I kept your Divine for all this time." I couldn't believe what I was hearing. Amora, a woman who I had so much love for was telling me her faith in our father has diminished and that she was planning on bringing in a war controlled by a monster.

"I will not join you in this crusade Amora, and neither will Melody. Her soul is pure. She would never fight with you, let along lead your army. Is this really your plan?" I asked. "Melody was created for this moment. Lilith needs a Nephilim to lead her army, and I created her one. Her power will be immense, something that this world has never seen." She gloried.

The legend behind the Nephilim was quite an interesting one. It has been said that a Nephilim is the perfect balance between good and evil. Their power has always been known to be overwhelming. As powerful as the Nephilim are, no one has seen one in thousands of years. Melody was the first in a long time, and I knew this would change everything.

"Melody is your daughter! How could you use her as a weapon!" She held the violet to be to me as she engulfed it in flames. "She is not a weapon, she is my daughter. I have given her this power so that she could use it. I will not let her potential go to waste. It is her destiny." She said. "And this is all for Lilith?" "Yes, Adam. Don't you see? Lilith has a plan for us. All of us." She announced.

"No, Amora. You are wrong. Lilith is evil!" I pleaded. "She has given me powers and abilities that you could never imagine. Powers that could be used to free her from The Darkness to the physical world, which I plan to do. Doesn't it sound magical?" She asked.

"Amora…" I said as I glared at her. "I know, it is quite alluring isn't it? I went through quite a lot to get to this point, but now is the time. Somehow, Once Melody met you, you have unlocked her potential. I thank you for that."

"Amora, this is madness!" I yelled. She looked at me in a dazed look as if I said something crazy. "What are you talking about? Why are you making this so complicated? Your God abandoned you for 101 years with no explanation. He left you here, powerless and weak with the pathetic human race. This is our chance to finally oppose him and win. With you and my beautiful daughter, no one could or would oppose us."

I began to think about Melody and why she was chosen for this path. A path I could never see her take. "This can't be." I simply said. Amora walked towards me. "I know you Adam. I know you don't want to believe, but this is what you have been praying for. Your purpose. Lilith can save us all Adam. Everything that has happened, has happened for a reason." She said.

I looked at the sun, gazing at its glory. "Amora, Our God has his reasons, but killing all the angels and destroying this world is not the answer. Why would you follow behind Lilith? Why are you fighting? Why are YOU doing this? Me falling from Heaven had nothing to do with you. Tell me Now!" I demanded as I looked directly in her eyes. She hesitated briefly and then turned around. "I have never seen your God ever in my existence. He simply put these humans in front of us and pushed us to the side. Our lives are dedicated to these weak creatures filled with sin and hate for one another. I'm tired of following orders. I'm tired of following behind a father I don't even know. If he cares so much, why doesn't he speak to us? Why doesn't he show himself? So, I took it upon myself to make my own choices. The first choice I decided to do, was fall after you. You did nothing to deserve what happened to you Adam, and I couldn't let that stand. I spent years on this horrible planet searching for something, a purpose of my own. That when I came across a demon named Damon. He showed me how power was the most important thing. During our time together, we fell in love which is a decision I do not regret. We created two children together, twins actually. a beautiful baby girl and boy. I finally managed to find my little girl after all this years. She took the last name of her adopted mother which I found extremely ironic, but it all just made it make more sense to Damon that we gave birth to a God of our own. A full-blooded Nephilim. Our daughter would be a queen. Our son is out there somewhere, but now that we found Melody, his whereabouts is not of my concern, plus Lilith would be more pleased with a woman leading her army. Lilith was a woman who decided to follow her own course and it's given her powers paralleled to your God. She has seen and written out the future. More than your God has done in the last million years. I have learned so much. I have learned how to use the souls of the angels I kill to fuel my ever-growing power." She said. I didn't say anything. "You see I've been waiting for this moment for quite some time. Damon, no matter how much I attempted to control him, he is still a demon, filled with anger and rage. He sees Melody as nothing more than a war tool and that's why I had to let go of him and continue my quest on my own. I see her as a daughter, and I do plan on putting our power together to create something better than what your God has done. Once we unleash Lilith, you we see the glory. I promise." She continued. She was passionate in every word. "Amora, what about faith? You must not give in to this. I cannot let you manipulate Melody. We could leave here right now. Put all this behind us. All of us could live in harmony on Earth. Please. Lilith is evil, can't you see that?" I begged. She turned back around and held my hands. "Faith? I have faith, just in a more promising leader. And Lilith is not evil Adam. She is one thing we always wanted to be...Free. She has a view of a better world." She continued. I released her hands from me. "There was another who wanted a new world too..." I mentioned as I continued to look for a thought of clarity within her. I saw nothing. "Lilith is nothing like Lucifer. Lucifer was selfish and only cared for himself. Lilith cares for all, except for mankind of course." She was fully convinced. I felt as if I was talking to a soulless being. "I am sorry Amora, But I do not share your same believes as you do. If you cannot see that this is wrong, then I have truly lost you." I said as I looked down at the violets. She gave me a weak smile and turned around with her back facing me.

"Finding you was an amazing feeling, but finding you protecting my daughter was among the biggest surprises. I bet you never knew I was deeply in love with you before the fall. Before Damon, before Melody. You will always have a special place in my heart." She said as she continued to look away. I was stunned by her words.

"I know Amora, I've always known." I said. She smiled. "I know where your heart lies. As a mother, I feel Melody is perfect for you and you perfect for her." She said as she kissed me on my cheek and began to walk away.

"Amora?" I said. She stopped and answered without turning around. "I love you Adam and I respect your decision to not join me, but you will due time. I will not back down from my plans. I thought discussing this alone with no other opinions might have been a better idea, but Lilith will come, and Melody will lead this war." She said. "Amora, I'm sorry, but that will never happen. I will never allow it." I responded. Amora was quiet. "In seven days from today, I will come for my daughter, and she will live out her purpose and if any one opposes me, I will kill them." She said still not facing me. "I guess I will see you in seven days." I responded. She turned her head briefly for one last view of eye contact. I noticed a little tear falling down her eye. "Prepare yourself my love, for you too, will live out your purpose." She said as she snapped her fingers instantly placing me back in the airport. I looked around only to notice police tape was everywhere.

"Excuse me sir, you can't be here. There was a terrorist attack here earlier. Please exit the building swiftly. He said as he escorted me towards the exit. All I could think about was Melody and what Amora said before she vanished to live out whatever plan she had. Amora may have lost elements of herself, which hurt me, but I know I had to eventually stop her. But there was still evidence in my heart that the darkness hasn't fully taken over her.

(Melody)

     I couldn't stop thinking about my father, the demon. How fucked up could my life truly be? All this time, my father was the one stalking my dreams. I think I was still numb about everything because I didn't speak once we got on the plane. I could tell Gabriel was beyond worried because she kept looking at me hopping I would say something.

     "I apologize for not telling you about Damon sooner. Adam and I was waiting on the right time and the right way to tell you." Gabriel said. "I understand. How do you tell someone that your dad happens to be a demon from hell?" I responded. My life literally made no sense, and it just gets more unbelievable every hour. I was starting to think that maybe this was a dream. A very long, grueling dream that I cannot wake up from.

     I missed my Adam. My mind has been racing ever since I left him. "How could we leave him Gabriel?" I finally asked. She looked at me and held my hands. "I have known my brother all my life. I know that he will be okay. He is probably in Brazil waiting for us right now. Don't worry Melody, it's not good for you."

     Most of the plane was sleep. It just felt like Gabriel and I were the only people on here. I looked out the window only to see darkness. "Gabriel?" I said as I continued to look out the window. "Talk to me." She said. I figured I was ready to talk her head off.

     "Why are you guys putting your lives on the line for me? I'm just a girl, that's all. I don't understand what Adam truly sees in me. I mean you are angels! Divine beings! I hate putting you guys through this." I said as I continued to look at the dark night sky. There was a brief silence before Gabriel spoke. "I know all of this is a lot to take in, but one thing I need you to understand is the love Adam, Me, and the rest of my sisters have for you. Adam chose you, no one else. You are a part of our family now. We would die for you if it came down to it." She said as calm as she could. I looked in her eyes to see her intensity. "Times are going to get hard in the next couple of days. With all this demon and angel business, I'm going to need to ask something of you." She said looking at me intently. "Whatever it is, I'll do it." I responded. She took my hand once again. "I'm going you to need you to trust me. Trust Natalia. Trust Lyla. And most importantly, trust Adam. We are going to need you more than you know." She said as she smiled at me. Gabriel's voice was so soothing, it reassured all my worries. We were in this together, even if I was powerless. "Okay Gabriel, I will." I took a drink of my Sprite and closed my eyes. I thought about the future; my future. I thought about Adam and Gabriel words. I thought about Victoria as well as Jason and Matthew and how I put all their lives in danger. Then I thought about Heaven and God and all the unanswered questions mankind has come with.

"Heaven. Tell me about it." I asked. Gabriel smiled before answering. "Wouldn't you like to wait for the surprise like every other human being?" She responded. "Um, no, I think I'm alright." I said as I laughed. "Okay Melody, I will tell you, but you cannot tell anyone okay?" She said to my surprise. "Okay, okay. I promise." I responded excited. "Melody, this is serious. You cannot tell Victoria, or any of your friends." She said with a firm face. I felt that this must be a serious manner because her face did not change until I nodded my silence to the world. "I promise Gabriel. Trust me." I said seriously. "Okay I believe you. Well Heaven is everything you could never imagine and everything you can imagine." I looked at her in a puzzling manner. "Well that sounds exciting." I said. Gabriel looked at me and smiled. "Well, there are three sections of Heaven. The first section is where every living creature goes when they die, well every living creature that has their name in the Book of Heaven." She said. I was beyond intrigued. "What is the Book of Heaven?" I asked. "It is the book that has every name of every chosen creature that has a designed spot in Heaven. Everyone has an open canvas, the opportunity to create your own heaven. Anything you want, desire, your imagination is your Heaven. That is the first section." I was amazed. "That sounds amazing!" I said. Gabriel smiled at my excitement. "It is quite lovely. You lose human emotions like pain, sorrow, sadness, elements that you know all too familiar on earth. It is truly an eternal paradise." She said. I didn't say anything. I was blown away by the new-found knowledge. "The second section of Heaven consists of us Angels. This is where the we live and watch over you. The third and final section is where God is." She said. I sat and thought about everything. Gabriel noticed my silence and placed her hand on my head.

"Are you okay?" She asked. "Yes. I was just thinking. Everything that the rest of the world doesn't know. So much information. Are you able to go to other people's Heavens?" I asked. Gabriel smiled. "Absolutely. Enjoy this life though. Trust me, I'm taking in every moment I spend on Earth. That parties you and your sister throw are so much fun. I never had so much fun in my life. Us angels spend our entire existence watching over and protecting you all. There is no time for fun." Gabriel looked a little sad as she explained this. I couldn't imagine a life like that, but this has been her life before she came here. I thought about that as I placed my hand on hers. "I'm blessed to have you in my life. I hope you could just stay here with me." I said. Gabriel smiled. "I will be here for you Melody. Always. You are my family." She said. I didn't know how all of this would end, but I was optimistic about it all. Adam just came in my life and the thought of losing him was too much to bear. My body suddenly felt a jolt of pain go through my entire body. I grabbed my chest in agony as I fell to the floor. Gabriel immediately came to my side by the time I landed on the ground. "What is it Melody?" She asked as she examined me. "I don't know!" I could barely get the words out as I clinch my heart. "Excuse me miss, is everything alright?" I could hear the flight attendant ask. Gabriel placed her hand on my body and closed her eyes. She opened them with a surge of surprise. "Adam. He has his power back." She said as she looked at me. My pain slowly began to stop the just as fast as it came. "Yes, we are alright ma'am." Gabriel said as she picked me up and helped me back in my seat. "What are you talking about? What does that have to do with my body?" I asked as I unclenched my hand off my chest. Gabriel stood still, deep in thought before answering. "Well, I'm not completely sure. I never experienced anything like this before. Maybe that potential we spoke about inside of you has finally awoke." She said as she reached for her water. "Drink this." She handed me the bottle of water and without hesitation I began gulping it down as if I haven't drunk anything for days. "Okay, so why did my body suddenly feel like that? It felt like I was imploding." I asked. Gabriel looked at me as if she could see right through me. Her beauty was far more captivating than I remembered. I glanced around the plane just to notice that everything looked a little different. It looked as if everything was in high definition. As if I had a new pair of eyes or something. I looked at my hands only to notice them in a new light. "What is happening?" I asked. Gabriel continued to examine me thoroughly. "You are changing." She said with her eyes wide open. I looked at her in confusion, but something about her words caused me to notice that I did feel different. "I can feel Adam flow through you, you two have bonded in some way." She said. I sat in wonder as I could feel Adam throughout me. His mind, body and soul were mine to examine. I could even see through his eyes when I closed my own. These new-found gifts were beyond me to understand, but I wasn't objective to it. "Adam's in Brazil already. He is waiting for us." I said. Whatever has happened to me, it has brought me closer to him.

Was our love powerful enough to change everything? That was the question, but one of the questions. My one true question was why did I feel Adam was in pain? Not physical, thank God, but emotionally. I closed my eyes and I ventured deeper into my thoughts that ultimately gained me sight into his. "Who is Amora?" I asked as I opened my eyes. Gabriel's face went from confusion to horror. It felt like the name set a chill through her body. "How do you know that name?" She said. "I don't know, but he is thinking about her right now."

Chapter 7
Angels in Disguise

(Adam)

I hesitated to leave the Rio De Janeiro airport about four hours ago, but my excitement to see Melody was stronger than my will to go find Zachariah at this point. I was familiar with the area since I spent some time here a few years back. Being on earth for 101 years, there's not too many places I haven't been. Thirteen hours felt entirely too long as I sat in the lobby watching all the passerby's walk by. Even as a full fledge angel, I felt nothing has truly changed, except the fact that I could finally protect my family. As much as I thought about Melody, I couldn't help but to think about Amora. She was so different, so dark. I couldn't understand her motives. Why would she go through this significant effort to destroy such a wonderful world? As I looked in her eyes, I could see the passion in which the words she spoke. Even after everything she said, I still have compassion for her; maybe even love. Our history was rich, full of joy. It was hard to dispose of that, but it wasn't impossible. My love for Amora was evident, but my love for Melody was also evident. I knew I would have to come with terms that Amora is not the Amora I once cared for. My mind scrambled as I thought of her words over and over in my head. I knew I had to stop her, but how? I thought about Lilith and how did she come to follow her? I fought Lilith thousands of years ago. At the time, I didn't see this over-powerful God, I saw a conflicted soul. I couldn't understand it. I witnessed the power the Lilith has given her, but I wasn't afraid.

"Adam?" An unknown voice said from behind me, breaking me out of my random thoughts. I looked to notice a young man, probably in his earlier 20's. He was smiling at me as he had his hand out for me to shake. "I looked around him to see was anybody else with him.

"Umm, yes, I'm Adam, who are you?" I asked. "You are looking for Zachariah, right?" He asked. "Yes, how did you know that? Who are you?" I asked again. "Too many questions, let's go he is ready to see you." He said as his hand remained out. I took it has he led me out the airport.

"I can't leave yet, I'm waiting for..."

"I know, you are waiting for Gabriel and Melody. They will be here in about two hours. I will be back to pick them up. Zachariah wanted to talk to you before their arrival." He said before I could finish my sentence. This man knew his stuff. I nodded as he led me to a red jeep parked right outside. "Hang on." He said as we drove off into the Brazil streets. We passed the beautiful city of Rio and into a quieter area of the magical place. We began to slow down as we got to a nice size house on the edge of the city. "Right this way." The young man directed me into the house where I was greeted by a woman. "It's a pleasure to finally meet you Adam, my name is Jade. My husband has been waiting for you, so have I." She said so lovely. Her short brown hair blew effortlessly in the wind. "Wow, thank you so much. I didn't know Zachariah was married." I said looking at her. I could feel she was human, but something was different in her. I felt a great power in her. I felt a divine inside of her.

"Most angels wouldn't know and yes what you are feeling is true. Hello Adam." A man said as he came to appearance. He looked about 30 something in great shape. He smiled at me as he came to embrace me. "Look at you, you look great son." He said as he looked at me. "I been waiting for you since you for the last hundred years. I knew you would eventually find yourself here." He said smiling. "It is a pleasure to finally meet you Zachariah. I have so many questions for you." I said. "I'll get started on lunch." Jade said as she kissed him and disappeared into the kitchen. "Okay honey. Come on Adam lets go to the patio." He said as he led me to the back of the house. "I'm going to go back in town for Gabriel and Melody dad." The young man who drove me here said as he disappeared out the front door. "You have a son!? You can have kids?" I asked in awe. He laughed as he took a seat on his love chair on his patio. I took a seat on the first available chair. "There is a lot you don't know son." He said. The air was so calm and soothing. He took out two beers and threw my one. "Okay, I wanted to talk to you alone because what you and I have to discuss is more on a personal level." He said as he took a swig of his corona. I took a swig as well. "Months ago, I would have asked you even more questions, why am I here? What is my purpose? Things of that nature, but after everything that has transpired lately, I just want to know is what I'm thinking is true?" I asked. He looked at me deeply before answering. "Adam, the reason you were sent here on Earth is because you have a mission in this life like every other man, woman, angel, whatever. Now your mission will never be revealed to you how you would want to perceive it, but you will know in your heart." He asked. "Melody." I simply said. He took another swig of his beer and smiled. "She is quite special isn't she, but I sense fear in your heart Adam." I looked down, surprised at his abilities. "I am afraid. Afraid to lose her." He looked at me intently. "Why would you lose her?" He asked. "Because dark times are coming Zachariah, and I don't know if I am ready for them." It was quite for a while. The beautiful South American animals were all we could hear in the silence.

Zachariah stood up and looked at the distant city. "Adam, you didn't fall to earth for no reason. You fell for a reason. You fell because you were meant to save the world; to save Melody. She is your light. No matter what happens, you will stand tall at the end of it all. You will save her son…but what do I know, I'm just an old soul" He said. I didn't know how he knew all of this, but there was such certainty in his voice, that there was no need to question him. "I think you are right." I responded. "I know it's a lot going through your mind, but I need you to know that everything will be okay. I know Amora is the one killing angels and freeing demons from hell. I know she believes that Melody will be the one to lead Lilith's army. Melody is a Nephilim and her very own parents want to use her true power to destroy everything. All of this is a lot, but you must keep the faith son." He said. I looked at him shockingly. "How could you possible know this?" I asked in amazement. He sat back down in his lounge chair and took a nice long swing of his Corona. "I'm old Adam. There are not many things I don't know. Now, do I understand? Not really." He said looking at me to further explain. "Well, Amora fell right after me upset that our God sent me out in the first place. I think she just wanted the freedom she longed for. When we spoke, I could feel the anger within her. She believes that Lilith wants to create a better world." I said. Zachariah looked at me in awe. "Her power is unmatched because she has spent an eternity gaining power with nowhere to release it. She would destroy this world in her rage guaranteed. Amora is blind in that aspect." He said. I thought about Amora's words again trying to make sense of her decision to follow a being capable of such malice. "Is there any way to save Amora too?" I asked. Zachariah took his final sip of his Corona. "There is always a way, but she must want to be saved. I feel it is far too late for your old friend, but I have seen many miracles in my day." He responded. "But she fell for me, and she held on to my divine for all these years. She waited for me. There has to be something in her that is still...pure." I said. Zachariah looked at the sky before answering. "She loves you Adam. She always has. You were blind to that until you saw her again. I know how you feel, but she must be stopped. She has already murdered enough angels in her wake. She will kill your sisters and anyone who stands in her way. Your compassion for her maybe the only thing that is holding you back." He was right. Maybe the Amora I knew was gone and maybe I needed to focus more on a plan to defeat her, rather than trying to save her. "Well, it is said that Lilith has the power to see the future, but it's her future that she sees. Not yours or Melody's. Only you two have the power to detest it." I thought about his words of wisdom and I couldn't lie, I was highly impressed. His knowledge was certainly staggering.

"Melody is going to need you now more than ever. Especially now since she is beginning to tap into her power. You must stay focus. Amora will stop at nothing to get to her daughter." He said. "Absolutely, I can feel her getting stronger ever since I got my power back." I responded. "Well I say that because the power of a Nephilim is strange. Her demonic energy is in a constant battle for dominance with her angelic energy. Since she is pure, the angelic energy has already claimed dominance within her body, but the demonic energy still lingers and will always linger waiting for a moment of anger or rage. An anger strong enough could ignite her demonic energy and take over her body and once that happens it will be almost impossible to bring her back to the light." His words brought me great concern. "She is going to need you Adam. Teach her how to maintain her power. I think it's time that she knows the truth." He was right. Melody deserved the right to know who she was, who her parents are, and her importance in this. Just a few days ago, she was just a young girl in this world. I think this may be too big of a burden for her. I can only imagine what she was going through right now. How I missed her. "I need some air." I said as I walked off his back patio into an open patch of trees. I began walking without a destination, letting my mind lead me. So much was weighing on my shoulders. I had no idea that this planet was in my hands. I'm a struggling alcoholic angel who just regained my abilities. I prayed that I was ready for this. I only had seven days to prepare, which wasn't a lot of time. I began to look over the horizon and prepare myself for flight, until I heard a familiar voice rang in my head.

"What are you doing my love?" Melody said in my head. I looked around to make sure I wasn't losing my mind. "Melody?" I said out loud. "I am here. What are you doing my love?" she repeated. I closed my eyes, and only then could I see her. We were truly bonded. "I miss you." I said. "What is troubling you?" She asked so concerning. "I found Zachariah, and the news he has told me is troubling." I said. There was a silence before she spoke again. "I can see only what you allow me to see. There are still elements in your thoughts that you keep hidden from me. Let me help you Adam." She asked. I sat down against a tree and ran my hands through my hair. "Melody, I love you. I need to talk to you in person. This is merely just a tease. I need you as a whole." I said. I could see her beautiful smile in my head. Her smile made me feel better, like it always did. "Yes, my love, I'll be there shortly. We will fight whatever comes our way, together. I love you." She said as she disappeared from my thoughts. Melody was such an amazing woman, but to tell her that she was something else completely would be difficult. I was curious to see how powerful she could really be. Could she be powerful enough to fight Amora head on? I would never allow that to happen. I could never put Melody in that kind of danger. This was my mess and I had to fix it one way or another. I heard Zachariah walk up behind me.

"She is incredible, isn't she?" He said referring to Melody's gifts. "She is amazing." I responded looking at the clouds. "My wife has the same gifts. You see, you and I have so much in common. Two fallen angels who fell for love among other things. Its enchanting." We both laughed together as we both walked back in the house. In the house, I was surprised to find Ariel sitting down talking to Jade.

"I made turkey sandwiches for you, your sister, and your mate for when they arrive." Jade said as she smiled. "Thank you Jade." I said as I took the sandwich. She smiled and placed her hand on my shoulder. "Everything will be okay Adam. Do not stress yourself about things out of your control." She said as she disappeared back in the kitchen. I nodded to myself and took a bite of my sandwich.

"How did you find Zachariah before me?" Ariel asked as he shook my hand. "I can't really recall...Wait now that I think of it, an young women told me to go to Brazil." I said not truly believing what I'm saying myself. "An young woman, huh. How did she look?" Zachariah asked. "Well, she was young, as in a teenager. She is quite a sight to see actually. She reminds me of someone, but I just can't quite get it." Zachariah smiled as I described her. Maybe he knew who this mysterious woman was.

"Did you find out any information?" Ariel said. "Too much, turns out Amora is responsible for all of this." I responded.

"Adam!" Melody called from the front door as she entered the house. Before I could answer, she was already in arms. "Oh, how I missed you like crazy So glad you are okay." She said as she burrowed her head in my chest. I held her close in my arms no prepared to release her. "I missed you more." I said as I kissed her fore head. I could tell that her body went through angelic changes. She was even more beautiful than I remembered. I could see through her mind that she was focused on me, trying to find out what I was hiding. I couldn't let her in just yet. Gabriel walked in with Jade smiling at the commotion. "Gabriel, it's been ages!" Zachariah said as he hugged her. "Yes, it has old friend. Your wife is remarkable." She responded as she held Jade's hand. Jade smiled as she took a seat near Zachariah. Their son also entered the patio and shook hands with Ariel and Gabriel. Melody was still hanging on to me as the full room continued to fill.

"Oh, I'm so sorry. Let me introduce myself, I am Melody. I'm so sorry to just barge in your beautiful household without introducing myself." She said as she released herself from me. "It's alright Melody, I figured you were be excited to see Adam. Especially with all that's been happening with you." Zachariah said as he took her hand. "Yeah, I'm still trying to cope with everything. I really don't know what's really happening to me." She said. Gabriel walk towards me and squeezed me. "I see that you found you divine. Congrats on that. Melody has been getting stronger and stronger at a remarkable pace. She has powers I can't even explain." Gabriel said. Melody turned to me. "Why am I changing?" She said as she came back in my arms. "Like I told Adam, You and he are one. His power and abilities are yours as well. He is your soul mate and you are his." Zachariah said. Melody looked at Zachariah then at me. "Is this true?" She asked me. "Yes, my love, that's why you can enter my mind as you please." I said calmly. "May I talk to you Adam?" Gabriel said as she walked off the patio. "Sure, I will be right back Melody. Don't you go flying anywhere okay?" I said to Melody. She laughed as she kissed my lips. "I will try not to." She said smiling.

Gabriel and I walk toward the trees about 20 feet from the house until she suddenly stops. She looks at me with great concern. "Amora...she is here." She said as she continues to look at me. "You knew this." I look at her not knowing what to say. "Yes, I know. She appeared at the airport. Damon is actually her mate." I said. Gabriel face was appalled. "Her mate? If that is true, then Amora is Melody's mother? Why would she do this?" She responded. "Amora is not the same as we remember." I said looking away. "She is responsible of the angel killings. She is responsible for everything." Gabriel looked at me intently. "How could she achieve that much power?" She asked. "Believe it or not, she obtained The Black Supreme. A dark amulet with powerful abilities. It has given her power unimaginable. She plans on freeing Lilith using Melody to lead an her supposed army. Lilith will destroy everything. We have seven days to prepare. This was my warning." She sat down where she stood and placed her head in her lap. "What are we going to do Adam?" She asked as she looked defeated. I got down with her to console her. I felt exactly how she felt. "We will overcome this Gabriel. I think there may be some good left in Amora." Gabriel stood up and held my hand. "Amora is evil Adam, there is nothing more inside of her." She simply said. "But Gabriel, she fell after me, like you did. She even held on to my divine. She held on to it for all this years. There must be good in her." Gabriel shook her head in disapproval. "There is much more to the story than she told you." She began. "Amora came down to earth, but she didn't leave on her own free will. She was casted out." Gabriel said. I looked at her intently. "What are you talking about?" I asked. Gabriel began walking closer towards me. "I know this is going to hurt you, but Amora deceived us all. She was casted out because she had evil intentions Adam. She longed to leave Heaven and start her own world on Earth. She searched for a being with her same goal, thus finding Lilith. I mean, she even created a child solely for a weapon. How can you be so blind?" She said. The words she spoke were truths. She was evil, but why did I still feel she could be helped? "She loves you Adam. That is why she held on to your divine. That is why she didn't kill you. Therefore, she gave you time. You must not let her manipulate your decisions." She said. I hesitated before answering. "I love Melody. I would do whatever it takes to keep her safe." I said. Gabriel placed her hand on my heart. "You seem conflicted my brother. Melody loves you blindly. You entered this girl's life and changed everything about it. You have even changed her very core. We can clearly see that Melody is the one for you. Why are you still holding on to Amora, after all that she has done?" She asked. "Yes, Gabriel. I understand. I will take care of Amora myself. I promise." I said as I walked back towards the house. "You need to talk to Melody. She is the one who asked me about Amora." She said. I stopped in my steps. How could she know about her, but then I figured she must have been going thru my mind. She began walking towards the house until she stopped to face me once more. "I didn't give her much information I figured that would be a conversation you would want to have." She said as she entered the house.

There standing on the stairs was Melody. The look in her eyes were unreadable, but I could tell she wanted answers. "What is wrong Adam?" She asked. I took her hand and led her outside. "Let's get away for a few days? It is still your birthday, technically. Would you like that?" I asked. She smiled as she looked at me then back to the house. "I would love that, but what about what's going on?" She said. "Don't worry about that right now...I think we need to get away for a while. I know a nice little spot not too far from here." I said. I could feel her beginning to blush. "Okay Adam, I'll go anywhere with you."

I kissed her lips and ran back in the house. "Gabriel, I'm going to need you to watch over things for a few days." I said. Gabriel smiled at me as she held Jade's hand. "Absolutely, You two be safe and I'll contact you if anything happens." She said. I nodded as I reached for Zachariah's hand. "It was such a pleasure to finally meet you." I said as I shook his hand. "No, the pleasure was all mine." I said my good byes as I exited the house. I ran to Melody with open arms and scooped her up. I was running with her in my arms at a great speed. "I haven't done this in a while so bear with me." I said as I carried her through the wood line. "Should I be worried?" she said as she held me closer. I ejected my large white wings from my back and with one large flap, we were in the air. Melody's eyes widen as we flew above the clouds.

(Victoria)

I waited in my mother's living room for what seemed like forever and a half. I was starting to regret even coming over here in the first place, but after seeing Gabriel just appear in my room; I became a believer.

"Sorry honey, I was just finishing up some chores. Now tell me what's going on? Why are you over here before 2 o'clock? I know you are not a morning person." She said as she laughed. I poured us a cup of tea only wishing it was some vodka, some strong vodka. I had to mentally prepare myself for what I was about to ask her. I felt like I was 7 years old again.

"Well, this is going to be hard for me to say…so give me some time to come up with the words." I began. My mother didn't say anything, instead she just looked aat me with wide eyes. "Damn, I wish I would've got a drink before this." I said to myself. "Victoria. Talk to me." I placed my face in my hands and took a deep breath.

"Melody is in trouble and I want to help." She immediately got up from love chair. "Where is she?"
"Calm down. She's safe."
"How do you know?"
"She is with Adam and his sisters."
"How does that justify her being safe?"

Now I knew I would have to talk. "Because Adam is…special. Long story short, I came to you because I am ready. I am finally ready…" I said. She gave me a peculiar look. "Ready for what?" She folded my arms. "Mom, I know you and Aunt Cat are witches and I am ready to learn the family business." I blurted out without looking at her. "Honey? What are you talking about?" She responded. "I know mom. I've known for quite for a while, now are you going to help me? Melody needs me." She looked at me briefly with an unreadable face before walking away. "Geez." I sighed as she disappeared behind the corner. She returned with a brown box with a huge lock on it. "It's that demon isn't it? That damn demon is after her again?" I looked at her in bewilderment. "So, you knew all along?"
"Of course. This evil entity has been trying to reach her since she was born. It was a blessing that I was the one who adopted her." She

said as she opened her mystery box. "I knew this day would come, but I would never think you would come to me solely to protect your sister. It brings tears to my eyes when I see you two together. I was blessed with two angels." She continued. "Okay mom, don't make me start crying. I would do anything for my sister, even if that means I have to become Hermione Granger." I said as I began to laugh. My mother just looked at me. "Hermione…from the Harry Potter books. She was a witch too. Please don't tell me you don't know what I am talking about?" I asked. "Sorry sweetheart, I don't." I placed my head in my hands again. "So, my joke meant nothing to you?" I said disappointed. She pulled out a huge old looking book and dropped it on the coffee table. "Okay, time to get serious. This is real magic. It could become very dangerous if used incorrectly. You have the power within you to become a very powerful witch, but you must learn to focus. We can start with some of these protective spells. Where is your sister? She is safest with us." She said. "Mom, another thing…Adam and his beautiful sisters are angels, so I am pretty sure they can protect her for the time being." I blurted out once more. This day continued to get longer and longer for me.

"Excuse me?" She asked.

"Believe me, I looked the exact same way when Mel first told me; until Gabriel just appeared out of nowhere in my locked room. Now that I think about it, it all makes perfect sense. No man was good enough to catch Melody's attention, it just had to be an angel." I said. My mother smiled as she looked at me. "That girl is something isn't she?" My mother said. "She is. She really is."

She turned to a page in her huge book and pointed at it. "Okay, we will start here." She said. I wasn't ready to be a witch, but I was ready to protect my sister by any means necessary. "Okay, I'm ready…"

(Melody)

　　I've had beautiful moments in my life time, but when Adam lifted me up and literally flew me to this hidden cottage right outside of town; I have to say that was the most amazing, spectacular moment of my existence. His beautiful wings were magnificent. I can remember the way he looked at me were we in the air. My body was still trembling, even as I sat here waiting for him to get out the shower. How I longed to join him...but I could feel my shyness building up again. I felt exactly how I felt when I waited for him to walk through the door at my party.

　　I sat on the bed that could fit at least three more of me. It was massive. The room looked as if no one has entered in years, but it was a good thing. It was beautiful. The windows brought in so much natural light that there was no need for electric lights. The room must have gotten pitch black at night. I didn't mind, I was excited. The floors were hardwood, but soft to my bare feet as I walked around. There were hundreds of books on the shelf, with at least a hundred vinyl's next to them. I immediately went through his vast music section. "Maxwell, huh?" I said to myself. His collection was quite impressive. I felt I was falling in love with him all over again as I flip through his music. I suddenly felt my longing for my own music.

　　"I have something you might like." Adam said as he came behind me. The fragrance that lingered off his body was more than invigorating. I closed my eyes and let his smell enter my body. His body was still wet on my back which felt soothing to my skin.

　　"How would you know what I like?" I joked. He kissed my neck and turned me around. He looked at me like he always did. The look that always made me melt into his world. His eyes on mine were too much to bare so I just did what I could to escape his enchanting stare. My lips instantly connected with his, bringing a chill down my spine. I could feel my body getting weaker as I felt his tongue massage mine. I wrapped my arms around him, not to pull him closer, but because I felt my knees start to buckle. He wrapped one arm around me and placed his other hand on my ass. I could feel his chest against mine and the only thing between our bare bodies was a tank top and some joggers I had on and his towel. I could feel him carry me to a room I haven't explored yet, but my eyes were still closed, still enthralled by his kiss. He sat me on top of a foreign object and released his lips from mine.

"Open your eyes." He said as he parted from my grip. I looked at him and then around the room. I was mesmerized. It was a room filled with CDs and vinyl records. There had to be thousands and thousands of hours of music in this room. "I would come out here just to get away from the world and listen to music. One of the best things humanity offered me. No one has ever been here before...I'm happy I waited for you. I had another birthday present for you back at home, but I feel this is a tad bit better. Happy birthday Melody." He said. I couldn't utter a word. Music meant so much to me. It had to be more than a coincidence that I was named Melody. "Say something." He said as he waited for a response. "I must be dreaming. Wait, what exactly are you giving me?" I asked as I looked around. "This whole cottage, and everything in here. Especially this..." He took my hand and placed it on the object I forgot I was sitting on. I ran my hand on the wooden top and instantly hopped off. "Oh My?" I said as I examined it. It was a beautiful piano that looked as if was crafted just for me. "I know how much music means to you, and if I can recall, I never heard you play." He said with a smile. I ran my fingers along the keys to see was it in tune. It was. It sounded delightful. "Well, you could've heard me if I would made it to Jason's class that day you saved my life." I said as I held him. He pulled a chair up by just looking at it and sat down. "Well, here is your opportunity to redeem yourself." He said as he folded his legs. I instantly got nervous, which was unusual for me since nerves were something I didn't get when it came to the music. "Okay mister, what would you like to hear?" I said with confidence. No matter how nervous I felt, I couldn't let my nerves best me this time. He makes me nervous with everything, I couldn't give him this. "Surprise me?" He asked. I sat down on the piano seat and noticed a pen and paper. "Give me a minute." I asked as I wrote the first thing that came to my head.

"Oh, an original piece?" He asked. I nodded trying to concentrate. After about 7 minutes, I had something. "Okay, don't laugh. I just wrote this." I said happily. "You could just write a song that fast? That's impressive." He said. "Well, it's kind of a gift. Whatever I'm thinking, I could just write it up...Most of my songs are about what is touching my heart at the time." I said as I looked at him. "Well, tell me what is touching your heart now?" He asked. I smiled and kissed his lips. Without a word, I turned around and began playing the keys I thought would go great with the song...I played for a while and suddenly my mouth opened with the lyrics:

I never thought that I would find you
Now that I have, there's nothing I won't do
You own my heart, my sweet angel
Now I know I was strictly made for you
No more of being lonely
I found my one and only
And nothing seems to matter anymore...

Adam suddenly came in to my surprise with lyrics of his own. I continued to play the piano, mesmerized by his voice...

I never thought that I could find you
Now that I have, can't live without you
No one compares, you are my angel
This love we have, I never want to lose
This world so cold, and all I need is you
only you
only you, you, you. you...

"Baby, that was so good...I think we got something." I said smiling. "I got some skill." He said with that confidence that I loved. I continued to play and thought of more lyrics to the song... I opened my mouth and sang what was in my heart...

Share my life
I really need you boy.

Adam came right behind me...
I want to be
the center of your world...

I followed his voice...
I love you so

and nothing matters anymore...

I was so in love with this man, the words were just spilling from my lips...

This has to be a fantasy
cause I have never felt the way I feel
I will never leave your side
till the day I die
I got to be in Love
In Love with you
I got to be in love
in love
in love with you
I ain't never felt it.

I stopped the piano and closed my eyes. I could feel a tear coming down my face as I sang the last words. Adam caught it before it fell of my face. "What's wrong my love?" Adam said as he held me. My emotions were running wild at this point. I was a little embarrassed by the whole thing. "I just feel so in love. Like I never felt this way. It's the scariest thing to me. Adam, I just love you so much. I love you to the point where it hurts...the words of this song define exactly how I feel and the fact that you came with your own lyrics just made this even more special." I just let the words fly out of my mouth without out thinking. Adam just smiled at me. I knew I looked like a fool, but in his eyes, I felt like a queen. "Melody, words can't explain how I feel about you, so I always let my actions speak for me. I could spend every day with you like this..." He said. His words were alluring. I truly loved this man more than I could ever love anyone. It was dangerous. But I didn't care. All I cared about was him. Even before myself. I know I was crazy, but I would just be crazy. "Just hold me. Don't ever let me go." I simply said as I buried my tears in his chest. I could feel tears running down my neck. I looked up to see a sight I thought I would never see. Adam's eyes were red with the prettiest tears running down his face. "I'm so happy...finally." He said. I wiped his face and kissed his precious lips. "When I first saw you, I knew what you were. But you were in disguise, trying to fool me. I know an angel when I see one, and you were one to me; wings or no wings." I said. He smiled at me intently. I tried to read his mine only to find out we were thinking the exact thing. I kissed him passionately and held his body close to mine. I pulled my tank top over my head and as he softly unbuttoned my bra. I watched as he examined my breast and the rest of my body. He looked upon me as a gift from God. I took off my joggers as thoroughly as I could. He took off his towel and I gazed upon his beautiful manhood. I could feel the heat between my thighs increase to a boiling point. My hands ran across his perfect body, my nails dug in to his soft skin. He picked me up and laid me across the grand piano with the full intention of taking me. My body wanted him. My mind wanted him. My soul longed for him. He grabbed my leg and ran his hands down my body. I couldn't control my myself as he got closer to my garden. "I want you to have me..." I whispered. He looked at me with look of longing. I could tell he wanted me more than I could imagine. My toes were in his mouth as he pulled of my already soaked panties. He ran his tongue down my leg till he reached the center of thighs. My moans were uncontrollable as I felt is tongue go in and out of my paradise. I tried to grab hold of something as my body trembled in pleasure. No matter how much I moved, he kept me in one place. His strength was impressive. I could feel my body about to explode as he continued to please every one of my senses. I never felt an orgasm of this intensity. I never had an orgasm at all. I didn't know this type of pleasure was even possible for a human being to experience. He lifted me up of the piano only to have me in his arms. "I love You Melody." He whispered in my ear. "I love you too Adam!" I said as I pulled him closer. I could feel him slowly go inside me which made my body quiver in the ultimate form of love. He thrusted slowly as my juices began to fountain out of my rainforest. I thought the first orgasm was heavenly, the second felt holy, as if these feeling was not made for man. It probably wasn't. Adam and I were not having sex, or even making love, this was at act of Divine matters. I felt as I wasn't a woman, but an enchanted being, and with my dad being a demon, maybe that was exactly what I was. Every thrust of him made me more and more inhuman. It was beautiful, it was passionate, it was Divine. I prayed that this moment would never end. If Heaven was something we created, then this would be it. This would be my Heaven. Adam and I connected like this for an eternity. My body belonged to him and his belonged to me. He turned me around and bended me over the piano. I arched my back and looked at him, ready for him. "Take me Adam! I need you!" I screamed as I prepared the position. Without hesitation he entered me once again and I felt every inch go inside of me. Instead of screaming out, I dung my head in the piano; enjoying every stroke. I was addicted to him. I called out his name as I heard him grunt; The sexiest sound I think I ever heard in this world. The third orgasm was even more intense. I could feel my body being lifted, even though he wasn't lifting me. I turned around and pushed him as hard as I could. My new abilities gave me the strength I needed to cause him to fly across to the bedroom. He spread his beautiful wings to stop his fall. I immediately jump on top of him and placed his beautiful penis inside of me. I rode him as he his wings kept us in the air. I could see the sweat dripping off his face down to the floor. He placed his hands on my breast as I pleased him. He flipped us around and placed my back on the bed while he still stroked me. He was quite an artist. I could feel his heart begin to pound heavy as he continued to please me. I felt a fourth orgasm coming as I held him closer. I cried out in pleasure as I felt him ejaculating inside of me. I held him as tight as I could to make sure every drop entered my body. He didn't move and neither did I. we were in total bliss. He looked at me and kissed my sweaty lips. I could feel my tangled hair and trembling legs, but I didn't care. He flipped me over, so I could lay on top of him while his wings covered me up like a blanket. Pure bliss as we both slept for the first time in days.

***

Chapter 8
Truth

(Melody)

Adam's fragrance and alluring smell of seasoned ground beef woke me as I sat up in our ruined bed. The clock read 10:32 pm, which tells me I have been sleep for majority of the day. I ran my hands through my tangled locks as I got out of bed to find my missing lover. I followed the smells and it ultimately lead me to the kitchen. I grabbed one of his T-shirts on the way, placing it on my nude body. I pranced in the kitchen only to be picked up off the air.

"Look who decided to finally join me?" Adam said as he placed me back on solid ground. I ran my hand through his perfect hair as I kissed his lips. "I know, I know...It's all your fault." I said as I thought about this morning. "This morning was...incredible. I feel like a new woman." I said as I held him. He simply kissed my forehead. "Taste this." He said as he held a spoon to my mouth. Without looking at it, I opened my mouth gladly. "Oh my God, what did you season this with?" I asked as my fat girl became to come out. "It's a secret. You like?" He asked as he took my hand. "I love it! What did you cook?" I asked as I started looking for the food. He led me to a patio and on a large table sat a taco buffet filled with bowls of lettuce, diced tomatoes, onions, shredded cheese, salsa, sour cream, flour tortillas, a bottle of red wine, and a big bowl of ground meat that smelt heavenly. "I just fell in love all over again. You have to let me catch my breath." I said as I jumped in his arms once again. I loved his smile, it just made me want to rip his clothes off again. I struggled to reframe myself. "I figured you were going to be hungry when you woke. And I don't know too many people who could deny a taco. "He said laughing. "He knew me so well." I thought to myself. "Baby, tacos are the food to my soul!" I said as I ran to the table. I could hear him laughing as I ran, but I suddenly stopped in my tracks and turned to face my love. "I really appreciate what you do for me, everything you do. What would you want on your taco?" I asked. He smiled as he walked towards me. "I love you Melody. Eternally. And everything except tomatoes." He said as he kissed me.

I made us both three tacos each with mine filled with everything on the table. Adam poured us some wine and lit more candles to an already candle lit dinner. It was about 1 O'clock and here we were eating tacos talking about everything under the moonlight. Our lives might be in danger, but none of that mattered at this moment.

"I could be here with you forever." He said as he looked at me intently. I grabbed his hand. "After all this angel demon mess we are in, we can be like this forever." I said. I saw his face suddenly change as he looked down. "What is it Adam?" I asked worried. "I have something to tell you Melody." He simply said as his eyes met mine. I instantly could feel in his heart where this conversation was going. I took a big swig of my wine stood up from the table. "Amora." I simply said. I didn't even have to go in his mind. "Yes, Amora." He said. This conversation has been dwelling in my mind since I first felt her inside of him on the plane. I didn't know how to bring it up, but I guess this was better than any time. "Who is she Adam? I want to know everything. Do not keep me in the dark anymore." I said. He stood up as well but didn't move. I stared at him waiting for him answer. "I know so much has changed for you since we met. I know it's a lot, but there are still things you must know." He said. I took in his words and prepared myself. "I'm ready Adam." I lied. He looked at the moon for a while. It was a full moon tonight, which looked spectacular. "Before we talk about Amora, let's catch up on everything that has transpired already." I began to think about my so-called demon father. "My father is a demon. I'm still don't know where to begin with that. I'm a little worried, and a little scared. What does that mean? Does that mean I'm a demon? What will happen with me? You know me Adam, I am not a monster. I don't want to be a monster." I said. I could feel the emotion spill out as I thought about the haunting truth. Adam quickly turned around and held my little hands. His eyes were locked on mine. "Melody, you are not a monster. Don't you ever think that." He said. I struggled to unlock my gaze upon him. I pulled my hands back. "Then what am I? You are an angel Adam, an angel. I am a demon! A horrible demon. There is no Heaven for a creature like me. I can feel the power inside of me. It gets stronger as the time passes. I don't know how to stop it." I cried out. Adam placed his hand on my cheek. It was warm and soothing to my face.

"You may have a demon as a father, and you may have demonic blood running through your veins; but you are far from a demon my love. I can see your soul and it is beautiful. You will never become a monster. You are what they call a Nephilim. It's a very rare and special being that possess extraordinary gifts. You will be more powerful than all of us all, even myself." His words scared me more. "A Nephilim? You have to explain that to me." I asked. "A Nephilim is a child born from a demon and an angel. Your father may be a demon, but your mother, your mother is an angel." He said. I felt as if I was going to faint. "Are you telling me that demon father had sex with my angel mother, and that's how I came to be?" I asked trying to take all of it in. "Well that sums it up. I know how this must sound, but if you look into my mind, you know it to be true." I didn't have to read his mind to know the truth. Adam's face assured me. I sat back down in my seat, locked in my own thoughts. "So, I'm not even human if that's the case." I said to myself as I paced back and forth. "Remember when you told me that you always felt different, like you didn't belong? That's because you didn't. Melody you are special. You must know that. There is a Heaven for you. I will be here with you always. Whatever it is, I am here for you." He said as he watched me pace back in forth. I could feel that he was hurting watching me like this. "I need to find my mother. Why would she sleep with a demon and then abandon me? Why would she even be with a demon? I'm confused about all of this Adam." I ranted. I was in a place of limbo, confusion, anger, and a bit of sadness. Finding out that your whole life has been a lie is much too difficult to bare. "Please calm down Melody, you are at a very vulnerable stage right now. Your demonic and angelic blood is at a constant battle to control your body. You anger could ignite the demon within you. We can't let this happen." He said as he tried to console me. I could feel the evil inside of me, which angered me more. "I need to find my mother! I need answers from her." I said as I pushed Adam off me. My emotions were getting the best of me. "Melody." Adam simply said. I looked at him and I could see there was more he wanted to say. I didn't bother to wait as I went inside his mind only to be more horrified. "Amora! She is my mother!?" I said as I looked at him. He said nothing, nor did he block his thoughts from me. His mind was as open to me, every conversation, every detail was mine to observe. Amora was my mother. She wants me to join her in destroying the world. I was created solely for this. I wasn't special, I was a weapon. I was created to be a weapon. My tears began to fall from my eyes as I fell to my knees. Was this my life? Was this my purpose? How could Adam ever love a creation like me? I was created to destroy the world and in seven days, my parents will come for me and possibly kill everyone I love to get to me. She would kill everyone, but I could see she wouldn't kill Adam. Why was that? I continued to search his mind as I sobbed only to find an even more shocking truth. "She loves you." I said as I looked upon him. "Melody. Please..." I didn't let him finish. "And you love her too, don't you?" I asked scared of the answer. "Melody.... I can't lie to you..."

"You can't." I responded. Adam hesitated before he answered. "I love you, Melody. That is all." He said. I felt my heart drop from out of my chest. "What are you saying to me right now? That didn't answer my question." I responded. "I'm not in love with her Melody, I am and always will be in love with you, can't you see that?" He pleaded. I knew he was telling the truth, but my emotions were too wild at this point. I had to get out of here. I slowly got up and began walking in a direction unknown to me. "Melody?" He called to me in agony. I didn't turn around, I couldn't bear to look at Adam in my currently state. "This is just too much Adam. My life is in shambles. Amora is coming in seven days and I will not let her hurt the people I love. This no longer concerns you. I know she needs me to free Lilith, I won't let her get to me." He looked at me intently. I could see how hurt he was. "It's not your fault, stop blaming yourself. This is between my parents and me. I will end this myself." I said as I closed my eyes and let my new abilities guide me. I could feel my wings begin to appear on my back. Adam looked at awe, unable to speak. "I will return to you as soon as I take care of this. I love you Adam." I flew as fast as I could, ignoring my emotions.

I gazed upon the clouds, mesmerized by how beautiful they were. The darkness surrounded me, but I wasn't afraid. My anger clouded all my other senses. I thought about what Adam said. How not to let my anger take over so I tried my best to calm down. The winds were strong as my wings flapped among the clouds. I gazed at them in amazement, still in awe about having wings in the first place. I thought about Adam, and how I left him so broken. I could feel his pain and worry for me, but I needed to do this. I began flying east with no intentions of stopping. I just had to get away and clear my head. I flew until the sun appeared over the horizon.

***

The morning breeze felt wonderful on my skin as I sat in the silky sand on an empty beach in Mexico. I spent hours just thinking and watching the water, trying to figure out what to do next. My body was tired, but I wasn't sleepy. I had no idea what I was doing or what I was going to do. "I need to see my mom and sister." I said out loud as I got up from the sand. My body was tired and I had no idea how to get back to Chicago.

"Excuse me sir, but where is the closest airport?" I asked a random stranger as he walked pass. He smiled at me and pointed north. "It's right down the road ma'am." He said. With Adam on my mind, and hope in my heart, I headed towards the airport. Before I could find Amora. I had to see my family. Just in case I didn't survive these next six days.

(Adam)

I stood in the very spot Melody left me in; hurt, sad, and depressed. She was gone, and I didn't even have the courage to stop her. Why should I? I felt that I was responsible for everything that has transpired. Me entering her life has caused so much turmoil that maybe it would have been better if I never entered at all. I could've saved her life and ignored my inter-intentions. I knew that she owed my heart, all of it. I sat down and just watched the sun and clouds coexist feeling sorry for myself. Out of rage, I kicked the table filled with our taco buffet to the floor. "Damn!" I scream as I get up and enter the house. Her perfume still lingered throughout the room. How I missed her dearly. I immediately open the fridge and pull out an old bottle of cognac and down it as if it was water. The taste of hard alcohol refreshed my sleep taste buds. A bottle that probably would have killed a man just made all my worldly functions disappear. I found myself sitting on the floor looking at nothing. I pulled out another bottle and began to down that one as quick as the first. I decided to lay my head down only to come to complete darkness and the scent of my precious Melody...

(Gabriel))

       The sun was so bright today, it looked as if it was meant to be a perfect day. I took a sip of my ice-cold lemonade as I help cook with Jade. The simplicity of it all was absolutely refreshing. I learned so much from Zachariah since I been here. From chess to UNO, I was enjoying my time, but I always kept in mind the threat that was coming.

       "Gabriel!" I heard Adam scream as he entered the house. I instantly became worried.

"Adam? What is it? Where is Melody?" I asked frantically. Jade, Ariel, and Zachariah examined an angry post drunken Adam. "What has happened to you son?" Zachariah asked concerned. "I looked at him as I embraced him. "You told her the truth." I simply said. He looked at me. I could feel his pain. "She left." He said. Everyone looked in amazement. "She flew away to find Amora." He said. We looked at him in awe. "She did what! And you let her go!" Ariel said with anger. I examined my brother, he was broken. Whatever transpired has left a mark. "Adam, come with me." I said as I pulled him into the bathroom. He reluctantly followed me as I grabbed his arm. "I have to find her Gabriel. We can't let her fight Amora." He murmured. I sat him down on the toilet seat. "I know you are going through a lot right now, but you need to get yourself together. Why didn't you stop her?" I asked as I looked into his drunken eyes. "I couldn't...I ruined her life Gabriel; can't you see that? If she never met me, she would still be a normal woman living her normal life. This was truth that was better hidden." He said. I looked at him in confusion. "Are you serious right now? If you never entered her life, she would be dead. You do remember you saved her life? And even if you didn't, Amora would have found her anyways. You were right to tell her who she was, who her parents were. She needed to know Adam." I said. He looked at me but didn't say anything. "Drinking will not solve anything. The woman you love is somewhere out in the world attempting to battle a being she is not ready for. Sober up and get ready. We are going to find her." I continued. Adam got up from the toilet seat and looked in the mirror. "Thank you, Gabriel, but how can we find her? She has blocked me from her mind so finding her will be a challenge." He said. "Melody is a woman, right now she is hurt, confused. She would go somewhere that is familiar to her." I said as I thought of one place. "Home." Adam said. "Absolutely, we will try there first. I've been talking to Lyla and Natalia too, we need to all come together and finish formulating a plan for Amora and Damon." I said. He nodded as he washed his face, trying to get out his drunken state. "We have to find her Gabriel." I held him in my arms. "We will brother. Let's go get her."

Adam and I walked out the bathroom together eager to get home. Adam looked sober and focus. I knew he loved Melody, but to see him like this meant that he loved her in ways I never thought. She was truly his heart. I never imagined that a love could be so powerful. His eyes were bent on finding her.

"It was great seeing you again Zachariah, and it was such a delight meeting you Jade, but we have to get home." I said I held them both in my arms. "Of course, my dear, get out of here and save us all." Zachariah said. "I promise, we will return soon. Thank you for everything." I responded. Jade held Adam's hand as he said his goodbyes. "Find you love Adam. She needs you more than you could possibly know." She said to him. Adam smiled. "I will, thank you so much for your hospitality. We will return." He simply said. Jade smiled as she hugged him and wished him luck. "I want you two to know that I believe in you. Love conquers all, even the darkest of entities. Amora may be powerful, but you are more powerful. Believe that." He said as he looked at us. I took in his words deeply and nodded. "Love conquers all." Adam repeated as he looked at me. "Let's do this brother." I said looking back at him. "Ariel, Gabriel and I are going to find Melody, I need you find out where Amora is. We are not going to wait for her to come for us, we are going to bring the fight to her. That way none of Melody's family and friends will be involved." Adam directed. Ariel nodded without hesitation. We said our final goodbyes as we left Zachariah's house. "Adam, wait!" Zachariah yelled as he ran to him with a wooden box. "I want you to take this with you. It has gotten me through many battles and I am sure it will assist you as well." Adam opened the box to see a magnificently crafted sword. "An Angel crest sword." He said as he took it out of the box. "The weapon links to its owner's soul, and now it belongs to you. It will appear when you call upon it." He said. Adam held the weapon in my hand as he gazed upon it. "Thank you for this." Adam said as I embraced him. He simply smiled and nodded.

I was ready to end this, just so we could finally live in bliss, I just hoped we wasn't to late...

Chapter 9
A Mother's Undying Love...

(Melody)

I stood outside my mother's house for at least an hour now, hesitating if I should even enter. I couldn't lie to her, so I was more than afraid to tell her the truth about myself. Rain clouds were hovering over me omitting most of my actions. I took a deep breath and walked towards the front door.

"Mom! It's me!" I yelled as I entered the dimly lit house. I felt an uneasy feeling upon entering, like something wasn't right. "Mom? Are you home?" I called out again. "I'm here my dear." A voice that I never heard before echoed from the kitchen. I immediately followed it only to find a woman who certainly was not my mother. Standing in the kitchen was a beautiful woman with alluring green eyes and long dark hair. "My beautiful Melody. Look at the woman you have become." She said. "Who are you?! And where is my mother?" I demanded. "She smiled at me as she walked closer. "You know who I am." She simply said. I did know, I knew the moment I heard her voice. "Amora." I responded. She examined me as a mother would examine a child they haven't seen in 23 years. "You have my eyes." She said still at awe at the sight of me. "Where is my mother and sister?"

"You mean your foster mother and sister? They are safe, don't worry about them. I just wanted an opportunity to finally meet my daughter." She said as she began touching my hair. I brushed her hand away. "You may have birthed me, but you are not my mother. Now, I demand you tell me where they are!" I said. She looked at me in confusion. "You are not happy to see me?" She asked sincerely. "How did you find me?"

She walked to the refrigerator and pulled out a pitcher of lemonade. She gently poured two glasses and handed me one. "A little birdy told me where you were headed so I figured I would meet you here. I think I owe you an explanation." She said as she took a sip. I placed my lemonade down on the table. "I don't want to hear what you have to say. Adam has already told me more than enough about who you are, what you are. You are a monster! You created me to be your special weapon to destroy my world. I don't know what your plan is to get me to join you, but I'm telling you that it will never NEVER happen. I'm relieved that you are here. I can end this right here and now." I said as I prepared myself. She took another sip of her lemonade and placed the cup next to mine. "A monster? I think that's taking it a little too far." She said as she laughed. I could feel my rage beginning to build. The house began to shake as I felt my power. She looked at me in wonder. "Incredible." She said as she sat down. "I know you have power. Power that can't be matched, but you don't have the power nor skill to defeat me, not yet. I need you, Melody. Now here's what is going to happen; first, you are going to calm down before you destroy your foster's mother beautiful home. Second, you are going to leave with me now, so we can free our goddess, Lililth, from her entrapment. And lastly, you are going to respect me as the being who gave your life and all the power you wield." She simply said as she focused on me. "You are crazy! Didn't you hear what I just said! I will never join you nor respect you EVER!" I screamed. "She stood up and pulled out one of my mother's necklaces. Her favorite necklace. A necklace that she would never take off. "My mother's necklace! What have you done!" I demanded as I reached for it. She waved her hand and I flew to living room and landed on a table, destroying it. "Now, you listen to me my beautiful daughter. You will do whatever I say because if you don't you little foster mother will be the one to suffer, and your father is a master at making these humans suffer. Is that what you want?" I couldn't say anything. My mother was all I could think about. I was such a fool for leaving Adam. I couldn't do this alone. I was powerless when it came to the protection of my family. "Do we have an understanding?" She asked. I hesitated before answering. "Yes. We have an understanding." I responded unwilling. "What about my sister?" I asked. She smiled as she started walking towards the front door. "Killing her is out the question. Did you know your foster mother comes from a long bloodline of witches? Going through this house, I found all kinds of hexes and spell books; it explains why you were so difficult to find after all these years. Your sister will be a prodigy once we unlock her potential. She may be of use to Lililth." She said as she waited at the door for me, expecting me to follow her to where ever our next destination was. I struggle to get to my feet. "I am going to kill you." I said as I glared at her. She smiled. "You will learn to love me Melody. One day you will be more powerful than me and this world will be yours once you let go of your emotions. Now come along we have a lot of work to do before your Adam comes and tries to save the day." She said. "Adam, where are you?" I said to myself as I followed her into the clouds; and at that moment, the rain began to pour. A storm was brewing.

(Adam)

"Adam, where are you." I could hear Melody's voice crying out in my mind as I stood in front of her home only to find it empty. "What is it?" Gabriel said as she watched my face quickly change into anger.

The rain began falling among my sister and I as we stood on her front stairs. "Amora has Melody and her family." I said as I immediately exited the premises. "What do you mean? How do you know?" Gabriel asked frantically. "Melody told me. She was never here. She was at her mother's house. We have to go." I said. Gabriel looked at me in confusion. "How did Amora find her?" She asked. I began searching Melody's mind for clues only to find something more surprising. "Someone informed her." I said surprised by my own words. "Who could have told Amora something that was so fresh. That information was only known to us." I said as I looked up at the sky. "Where is Lyla and Natalia? They were supposed to be here by now." I announced. "We are here." I turn to see Natalia carrying a wounded Lyla in her arms. Her clothes were battered and torn, and she was bleeding from her arm. "Oh my God!" Gabriel screamed as we ran to her aid. "My dearest sister, what has happened?" I said as I held her in my arms. "Demons. Hordes of them. They attacked her and took Victoria and her mother." Natalia said with such anger. I examined Lyla and her wounds as I held her. She was unconscious, but alive.

Melody's home became our homes as we entered the empty house. I placed Lyla upstairs in Melody's bed as I attended to her wounds. "Will she be alright Adam?" Natalia asked in a voice I never heard from her. A voice of worry. As hard as her exterior is, her family in danger could always bring her true emotion out. "Yes, she will be okay. She just needs to rest." I responded. "I can't believe it! This war is really happening. We need to stop this now brother. Now that you have your power back, we must fight. Fight for our lives and this world." Natalia said. She was right. Amora has Melody. The time of action was now. I entered Melody's mind once more to find where Amora has taken her. "I am coming for you." I said to Melody. "Please, come Adam. There isn't much time left." She responded.

"Rest my sister, we will return to you" I said as I kissed Lyla on the forehead. "Amora is headed to Sudan. We must go now." I said as I began exiting the house. "This isn't a normal storm. This is the work of Amora. Will we be able to cross it?" Gabriel asked. I looked at her as I grabbed her hand. "We don't have a choice." She nodded as we walked back into the rain.

"Adam!" A familiar voice resonated from my side. "Melody? "I said in astonishment only to see the young woman I saw in the elevator on that special day. "Take this. Don't read it until the time is right. You will understand it then." She simply said as she started to walk away. I looked in my hand only to see a piece of paper folded up quite a few times. "Who are you? How did you know I would be here?" I said in confusion. She smiled at me. "I was just in the neighborhood." She simply said as she continued to walk in the distance. I looked at my hand in confusion as the rain continued to pour. "What is it?" Gabriel asked as she starred at the whole ordeal. "I don't know." I said as I continued to look confused. "Hey, how did you know my name?" I called out towards the mysterious girl's location only to see that she was no longer visible. "Where did she go?" I asked myself.

"We have to go!" Gabriel said breaking my puzzling train of thought. "Yes, of course." I placed the folded paper in my pocket as I took to the sky effortless and unafraid. Finding Melody and killing Amora was all my mind could fathom, but this mysterious girl was also a mystery I wanted to solve.

(Melody)

"Why do you look so upset my love?" Amora said as she glanced upon me. I wiped the sweat from my face and said nothing. I knew Adam would come for me, but I didn't want him too. I put many people in danger already and now their lives would hang in the balance. "Where is my mother?" I responded. Amora's face quickly turned to disgust as I asked my question. "Damon, bring her precious mother and sister out here." She said as she waved her hands. Damon smiled as he disappeared into a tiny hut. We were in an empty field that plants and trees used to live before they were destroyed for the space; possibly done by Amora herself. I glanced upon her in rage, trying not to trigger my demonic abilities, but I believed that might be the only way to defeat her. Despite how much I hated her very core, she did look quite like myself. Same delicate eyes, Same body complexion, Same long hair; even though hers was jet black. We even shared the same smile. She was like a clone of myself, just more beautiful and full. Her breast and thighs were to die for. She would have been amongst the most beautiful beings on this planet. It didn't help that we looked about the same age as well.

Damon returns with my sister and mother and I couldn't be more excited to see them. I ran to them unafraid of what Amora might do and held them in my arms. "I am so sorry! I am sorry for all of this!" I said as the tears ran down my face. My mother ran her hand through my hair as she examined me. "It's okay baby, It's okay. Are you alright?" She asked, still thinking about my well-being over her own. "I'm fine mom, don't worry about me." Victoria held on to me even longer. "Mel, what's happening. Who are these people? Where is Adam?" She asked. I looked at Amora as she started her way towards us.

"I am Amora. Melody's true mother." She started. Damon began to walk towards us as well. "This is Damon, Melody's true father. We have brought you here because I want you to witness the beginning of a new world." Victoria looked at her in confusion. "What is she talking about Melody?" She asked. I held Victoria's and my mother's hand. "She is telling the truth. They are my parents." I reassured them. Amora's smile grew wider as I spoke. She reminded me of a proud parent when their kid wins an award.

My mother walked in front of us confronting an amused Amora. "What are you?" She asked as if she knew she wasn't human. Amora walked closer to my mother so that they were face to face. "I am what you humans call an Angel. Therefore, Melody needs to be with her own kind. She is my daughter, not yours." She said. "You are no angel. Angels are meant to protect us. What you plan to do is crazy, unholy." My mother responded. Amora looked around the area then back to us. "What do you think I'm doing? You are here for your protection. Once we free Lilith, you will be the first humans she has seen since her inprisonment. I hope she will be merciful and spare you and your witch daughter. Your powers could be used to our advantage." She said as she began to walk away.

"I can assume your lover is a demon. I could smell his horrible stench ever since he came to my home." My mother responded. Damon began to approach my mother until Amora stopped him. "The disrespect." Damon said as he kissed Amora's shoulder. "Don't worry about her, Judgment will be casted upon her soon enough." Damon smiled and disappeared into an old cave that sat in the middle of the field. "They say that life started right here in this very spot. The first human took his first steps here. That cave that you see is not just a cave. It is where our new God will rise. This is where Lilith lies, and this is where she will return. The time is now." She said as she began walking towards the cave. "Lilith? She's trying to resurrect Lilith? We can't let her do this." My mother whispered. "Who is this Lilith mom? What does this mean?" Victoria asked. "What do you know about her?" I also asked, intrigued by my mother's knowledge. "Well, you read about Lilith in your first years of witch hood. Lilith is the woman created for Adam in the Garden of Eden. She refused to live side by side by man, so it was said that she created her own wings and flew away from God and his kingdom. If she is released, she will certainly destroy this world simply because God created it." She said. Her eyes focused in on me. "Melody, I am so sorry about keeping you in the dark like this. I should have told the both of you the truth about me. I did it to keep you two safe. It turns out that it didn't turn out that way." She said with tears coming down her face. "It's okay mom, Victoria and

I had an idea years ago. It's not your fault we are here, It is mine. They want my power." I responded. She looked at me and smiled. "My beautiful daughter. I've always known you would be special. Your auntie Catherine has always said that you would grow into something magnificent and here you are. I am so proud of you." She said as she held me. I could feel the tears coming down my face as I felt the looming truth.

A familiar angel landed down in the ground which made me feel hopeful. "Ariel!" I called out to him. "You know him?" My mother whispered. "Yes, he is one of Adam's friends." Ariel glanced at me briefly then began walking towards Amora. "Wait don't fight her alone, let me help you I said as I begin running towards them. Ariel smiled as he bowed down to her. I stopped dead in my tracks. "Adam and his sister are just over the horizon, my queen." He said to my surprise. "What? What are you doing?" I screamed at him. His face remained looking at the ground as I spoke. Amora just laughed at the whole fiasco. "Oh, you didn't know? Ariel is my information. I spared his life, in return, he gives me information on you and your precious Adam. You see, I'm always two steps ahead. I know Adam is your soulmate, so you two can communicate via mind waves, I guess. I knew you would bring him to me, just so I can kill him in front of you." She said. "Wait, what? I don't understand. You love him!" I argued as I felt my anger begin to build. She and Damon both laughed at that comment. "I gave Adam an opportunity to join me and he refused. He chose you. A fatal mistake!" She said as she continued to laughed. I wanted to slap that smile from her face. "I was a little bitter after I found out that he loved another, but the fact that he loves YOU more than me bothered me more than I anticipated. You see Melody, love would make you do some crazy things and I rather kill him, than kill you. For what it's worth, I like you two together, but you don't deserve to have him to yourself; and if I can't have him, no one will." She stated. Damon looked at her in confusion. "What are you saying? I thought we had a deal? I surrendered Melody to you. I did all of this just so you could love me. Again! I have changed Amora. I want what you want." He cried. She kissed him passionately and ran her hand through his hair. "I'm sorry my love." She said as she ran a long black stake through his stomach. Damon screamed in agony. This was the man responsible for all my nightmares, yet, I felt great sorrow for him.

"Why?" He said as he fell to his knees. "You are a monster. You are unable to change. I have my daughter back. That is all that matters. I am sorry." She said as she pulled the stake out of him. We all watched in horror as Damon's body lost all trances of life. Only one single tear ran from Amora's cold face.

"You are a Monster!" I called out. She smiled at me as she wiped the blood off her stake on Damon's shirt. "I'm not a monster. I am a mother. I did what was best for you and your future. Now come a long, we must get started." She said. I refused to move. "Stay behind me." I tell my sister and mother. "I'm not going anywhere with you." I announced. Amora turned around to face me. "Excuse me?" She asked in confusion. "You heard me, you horrible bitch! I'm not going anywhere with you." I repeated. She stood there, and I could feel her anger build. The winds began to pick up as we stood in the empty field. Demons began to enter the field through the trees, ultimately surrounding My family and me. "Now look your ungrateful little shit. All of this is for us. Everything I did is for you. Either you come with me willingly, or I let them kill your mother and your sister in front of you, and then you come with me. Either way you are coming." She said. I clinched my fist in horror as my options seemed to dwindle. I turned to face my mom and sister, prepared to make the ultimate sacrifice. If I had to die, I wanted to go with my family. That way we could all go together. No one would mourn anyone. I just wish I could've told Adam one more time that I love him. That would be my only regret. I thought to myself.

"You won't have to." A familiar voice in my head rang out causing me to look around. "Melody!" Look!" Victoria screamed pointing in the sky. There he was, and I could see in his face that his anger easily subdued mine. Adam, Natalia, and Gabriel landed right in front of us causing the demons surrounding us to become rowdier. He turned and looked at me with those eyes that I loved and missed. "I cannot tell you how happy I am that you are here." I said as he looked me in my eyes. "Melody, I'm sorry for everything. I should've let you leave." He said as he kissed me on the forehead.

"It's so good for you to finally make it." Amora said as the demons let her get in their circle surrounding us. Adam turned around to face her. "Of course. I knew you didn't have the patience to wait seven days nor did you have the honor to tell me the truth of your plans. It's nice to see you too Ariel. I knew you couldn't be trusted my old friend." He said staring at them both. "I'm sorry Adam, I want to live through this. Amora was the only way." Ariel responded. Adam smiled as his beautifully crafted sword appeared out of nowhere in his hands. "No, I'm sorry brother." He said as he threw the sword right through Ariel's chest killing him instantly. The sword flew right back into his hands. I was amazed. "An Angel crest sword. I can tell that beautiful weapon anywhere. How did you get your hands on it?" Amora asked in excitement. "An old friend." He responded. "Melody, watch over your family. Mrs. Eve and Victoria, we could really use your abilities." Gabriel said. She nodded and turned to my sister. "Now, stay close to me and remember what I taught you." She said to Victoria. She braced herself. "My demons, kill them all, but spare Melody for she is for me." Amora said. The demons began to close the gap between us. "I will take care of her Melody. I love you!" He said. "Right after this, we are going back to Rio. We never finished our taco date." I said as tears began running down my eyes. He smiled as he passionately kissed my lips. I didn't want him to go, but I had to let him save the world. Adam ran towards Amora ejecting his wings to give him more speed. Amora placed her hand on the ground and from the earth crafted a beautiful sword of her own. They both smashed each other weapons together as they took the sky.

   "Everyone stay close!" Natalia said as her hair began to ignite flames. She placed her hands out and ejected powerful hot blasts of fire, engulfing every demon in her sight. I ejected my wings and flew through as many demons as I could, slashing through them with my powerful wings. Gabriel threw me a sword of my own, which I used to my best ability. My mom and sister were back to back flinging demons with spells I couldn't see or hear. It felt like a war, a battle that seemed like everything was at stake. We all were fighting for our lives, but as I looked around, I saw how outnumbered we really were. No matter how many demons we slay, more and more seemed to come. My mom and Victoria were doing great, I was so proud of them. Natalia and Gabriel were both giving their all. I couldn't believe what warriors they were. We fought our way back into a circle as they began to overpower us.

"What do we do!" Victoria asked as the demons surrounded us. At that very moment, Adam came crashing down to the ground. "Adam!" I screamed at the top of my lungs. Amora followed him and landed on top of him. I fought my way through to get to Adam only to walk in a face-off between them. "Adam!" I screamed as I ran to him. He was wounded and hurt as I held him in my arms. "There is a necklace that Amora has. That is what she needs to release Lilith. We have to destroy it." He said in my head so only I can hear it. "Where is it? I don't see it on her." I responded. "I believe it is in the cave. It's the only place she would keep it if that's where Lilith is going to rise." He responded. "What are you two talking about?" Amora said as she began to walk towards us. "Go now! I'll stall her." He demanded. I glanced at Amora with pure hate as I flew toward the cave.

"Where do you think you are going?" She said as she tried to grab me only to be tackled by Adam. "Go!" Adam screamed. Without hesitating I flew as fast as I can through the cave searching for the necklace, only to find it laying near a body of water. I picked it up and placed my sword towards it. "Wait!" Amora said as she appeared from the opening. "I need that! My precious daughter. Listen to me! I demand you!" She screamed. I throw the necklace up in the air and with one slash with my sword, I cut the emblem in half. A large powerful bright light comes from the charm, causing us to fly to cave's hard rocky walls "You foolish girl, look what you have done!" She screamed. Adam flew in the cave just as he get our feet. "I will punish you my daughter!" She said as she flew towards me. Adam came charging after her, saving me the blow. "Stay back Melody." He said in my head. I refused to listen as I got my sword and came charging towards her. Adam smiled as we both began to attack her together, as a team, like we should have in the beginning. I could feel us starting to overpower her as we corner her against the cave's wall. "I tried to save you my daughter, I tried but you have chosen your path. And I have chosen mine." She said as she kicked Adam in the chest. She grabbed my throat and lifted me off the ground. "Sorry my love." She said as she drove her sword right through my stomach. She pulled the sword out just as fast as she drove it inside of me and tossed it the body of water. "Destroying The Black Supreme was smart, but unnecessary. I have gained more than enough energy to resurrect Lilith. All I needed now was a single drop of your blood. I hope you survive long enough to see our new God." She said as she dropped me on the hard ground. I screamed in agony as I witnessed my blood pour out of me. "Melody!" I could hear Adam scream as he ran to my side. I could see Amora smile at my pain as I laid there dying. Adam held me in his arms saying things I couldn't hear as I began to drift away. The cave began to shake as the water began to rise. "Prepare yourselves!" Amora screamed as she laughed at the spectacle. "Let me help you." A familiar voice said in my thoughts, but to my dismay, it wasn't Adam. "Let me save you." The voice repeated. I held Adam as tight as I could until I couldn't anymore. I closed my eyes and entered an immediate darkness.

I managed to open my eyes again, only to see I'm not only in the cave anymore, I'm standing in a park. A very familiar park. When I was a little girl my mom would take my sister and I here. "I must be in Heaven?" I asked myself. "No, not yet. I refuse to let you die. I just thought being here would settle your mind." I turn to the voice only to witness a reflection of myself. Standing in front of me was a woman who looked exactly like me, except the fact that her hair pitch black and she had one large beautiful black wing. "Who are you?" I finally asked after staring at her for a while. She smiled at me but didn't move. "I am you. You see you have three sides of you. Your demonic, your angelic, and the normal boring weak you. I brought you here to save your life. You should let me take over for a while, your demonic side of course. You are hurt and injured, and I can't let you die on me." She said. "I don't know what this is but..." I started but was quickly interrupted. "Look we are running out of time!" She demanded. "You are a demon! I rather die than trust you with my body!" I screamed. "Fine, have it your way. But Adam will live the rest of his life in regret knowing he couldn't save you! You really want to do that to him, your family?" She asked. I couldn't do that. "Where is my other side? Where is she?" I asked about my angelic side. "Not here. Make a decision now!" She said. I screamed at the top of my lungs as I fell to my knees. "Yes! Okay!" I screamed. She smiled as winked at me. "Open your eyes." She said. I entered a stage of darkness once again.

Chapter 10
The Darkness

(Adam)

The water was beginning to flood the cave as I held on to Melody's dying body. I refused to let her die. "Bring her back to me!" I screamed at the top of my lungs. The cave suddenly stopped shaking as a being arose from the water. She had beautiful pale skin with long jet black hair. Her eyes were eyes I have never seen before in anyone. She remained floating in the air until she slowly placed her feet on the surface of the water. The water became her floor as she began walking on it towards Amora. "My queen! You have returned to us!" She said as she bowed. Lilith continued to walk towards her without saying a word until she saw me. Her eye contact was piercing. "You!" She said as if she has had anger built in for me for thousands of years. I know she did. She then took her eyes off me and on to Melody. She tilt her head at her and in a blink of an eye, she appeared right by our side. "Who did this to you child?" She said with sorrow. Amora picked her head up to witness. Lilith placed her hand on top of Melody's head. I looked at Lilith in disgust as I placed my sword to her neck. "Do not touch her." I said. She smiled as she got up and looked down upon us. "The prodigy child is dead. What a waste." She said as she walked away. I didn't believe her. I wouldn't. I knew my Melody was far from dead. I closed my eyes buried my tears in her shirt.

"I'm here my love!" I could hear Melody speak inside my head. I smiled as I looked at her. She slowly opened her eyes and smiled at me. "I love you too much to leave you already." She said. I instantly kissed her lips as if I would never have a chance to again. "I got this Adam." She said as I looked at her in confusion. "Amora!" She screamed as she got to her feet. Amora and Lilith both gazed at her in amazement. "You have tried to take everything from me! And now I think it's time to end this." She said as the caves begin to shake once again. "What? How is she still alive? Amora asked. Lilith remained silent as she laid witnessed to Melody's power. Suddenly, Melody's wings began to turn complete black. "What is this trick!" Amora said in frustration. "Finally, a power that could shadow mine." Lilith said as she stepped in front of Amora. "I am the supreme ruler of this planet. Fight me for it!" She demanded. Melody smiled and suddenly disappeared. "Where did she go?" Amora called out. Melody appeared right behind her and thrusted her with her sword. Lilith laughed at the attempt. "Silly girl, your weapons will not harm me." She said as she pulled it out. "Melody!" I yell at her as I throw another sword at her. She smiles as she reads my mind. "Another sword? I told you your weapons have no effect on me." She said. "It's not for you." She said as she spins around and slashes an upcoming Amora taking her head right off. Without the power of The Black Supreme, she was very capable of death. Amora didn't have the time to even whisper her last words. "No!" Lilith screamed as she looked upon a lifeless and headless Amora. "I shall destroy this world, but you will not live to witness it." She said as she came for Melody. They began to fight in the air at a level that was too fast, even for me. I began to wonder, this must be the power Zachariah was referring to. I watched in awe as Melody went blow to blow with a so-called God. They managed to land on the ground. "Are you okay my love?" She asked me. I nodded at her with the little strength I had left. "Love. This love you have will never last. It is why you will never defeat me. Your love will hold you back! Love is for the foolish. It will be the first thing I destroy." She said as she put her focus on me. She began to fly towards me until Melody grabbed her by her hair and tossed her against the cave walls. "Let's go." She said as she lifted my arm over her head. "I am not strong enough to kill her, and she isn't strong enough to kill me. I have to get you out of here." She said as she flew me out the cave.

She laid me down near a tree and searched for my wounds. The fighting was still ongoing, but it seems as if a lot more angels joined the fight. Gabriel saw me and instantly ran to my side. "Are you two okay?" She asked. "Yes, I'm fine. Where did we get all this help?" I asked. "Lyla. She called reinforcements." I looked up to see my fellow angels, Victoria, and Melody's mom all working together. I haven't noticed how powerful Melody's mom was. Her and Victoria were truly impressive. "Melody? Are you okay?" She said as Melody looked at the cave. "Lilith."

Suddenly the cave exploded throwing rubble and debris everywhere. Lilith rised among the destruction gaining the attention of everyone fighting.

"This world will be mine! "She screamed. Melody and I just looked at her. Lilith raised her hands holding the two halves of The Black Supreme and said some words that I've never heard before. "I thought I destroyed that charm. What could she possibly do with them now?" Melody asked. "That is The Black Supreme! Cutting them in half will not destroy them, but it will stop the bond that Amora created with them. We need to stop her!" Gabriel screamed. "All of you attack!" Gabriel screamed as she began to fly towards her. Amora's demons began trying to intervene only to be cut through. Gabriel was not going to let her do whatever she had planned.

The clouds suddenly began to turn dark. Unreasonably dark. "What is happening?" I asked myself. Melody held me close as I rested. My body was worn out, damaged. "It's going to be okay." She said as kissed my forehead. The dark cloud began to grow, swallowing the entire sky, only to disappear just as fast as it came. Lilith smiled at as she disappeared with the cloud. "No!" Gabriel yelled as she threw her sword to the ground. "She got away." Melody said as she looked up in the sky. I slowly got to my feet as Gabriel came back down to the ground. "I'm sorry." Gabriel said putting her head down. I managed to get to her only to hug her. "She is weak now, she knows we have the potential to kill her, so she will go into hiding until she finds a new course of actions." I said. She throws me a weak smile as she looked among the warzone. "Lyla!" She said as she rushes to her side. Lyla was wounded as well, but her smile would have told you otherwise. "I'm okay Gabriel. Check on the others." She said pointing to other angels.

"What happened to the clouds? What did she do?" I asked Natalia as she walked towards us with Victoria and her mother. "I have no idea. I know Gabriel knows and by the way she responded, it's nothing good." I looked at Gabriel thinking about the possible dangers that we awaited. I took my attention off Gabriel and put all my focus in someone I have yet introduced myself too.

"I know this has to be the worst impression in history, but I'm Adam. These are my sisters, Natalia, Lyla and Gabriel. It's more than a pleasure to finally meet you." I said as my sisters finally reached us. "Well, I have to say, this is definitely the most memorable. It's not every day you save the world. My name is Karen. The pleasure is all mine." She said as she opened her arms for me to enter. Melody's smile couldn't be any bigger. "I thought you had this under control Adam! What the hell?" Victoria said as she got in between us. I looked at Melody then back to Victoria. "I know, I am responsible for everything that has transpired here." I said as I waited for a vicious respond. Before Victoria could respond, Karen stepped in. "It's not your fault my dear. This was her fate. This would have happened if you were here or not. I'm just blessed that she found you when she did. You have saved all of our lives. All of you." Karen said as she held her two girls. I nodded as I looked back at Victoria. "Okay. I'll give you one more chance." She said as smiled at me. A reassuring smile.

"So, you guys are really witches? How did learn so much in that small amount of time? You guys were crazy out there. I couldn't believe what I was seeing." Melody asked. I was also curious about this new-found talent. "Mama taught me a few easy defensive spells. It's like I always knew, but knowing you would be in danger just made me go over the edge. Losing you was not an option." She responded. "This is not the end is it?" Karen asked me. "I'm afraid it's just the beginning. Lilith is still alive, and she will return." I said as I looked at Karen with eyes of hope. "We have bigger things to deal with other than Lilith." Gabriel said as she looked in the sky. "Lilith released The Darkness among this world. We must prepare." She said. "The Darkness?" Melody asked. Gabriel looked at her and then to all of us. "The Darkness is the home of the most powerful evil entities. It was Lilith's home before she was released. It is a place that holds beings that are too powerful for Hell." Everybody remained silent, just taking in her words. "How many beings are we talking about." I asked. "I don't know how many exactly, but there were four beings with immense power, one including Lilith. We would have to research as much as we can." She responded. Four powerful beings, Lilith being one of them, was a disturbing thought. Was Lilith the strongest among them, was the most important question? Was she the weakest? Even though Amora had help from her special necklace, she still overpowered me. I would have to get stronger if I had any chance of saving my family. Melody caught my eyes as I thought to myself.

Melody gave me that look that I loved as she walked in my arms. "Mom. V. I don't want you involved in this. You gave your lives for me and that is something I could never ask you to do again. This is my fight. I want you to disappear until this is all over. I know Aunt Catherine has spells that could do just that." Melody demanded. "Yeah, mom I don't want you part of this either." Victoria said. Melody looked at her in confusion. "I meant you as well V. I thought I lost you guys, I don't want you involved in this." Victoria stepped closer to Melody. "Now look, you are my sister and I would lay down my life for you any day. I'm going to Aunt Catherine's, so I can become more of use in this cosmic shit-storm. Ma says that she has a school in her massive home, kind of like Hogwarts." She said as she laughed. Everyone remained silent. Victoria looked around in awe. "You know, like Harry Potter?" She continued. Silence once again. "Damn, does anyone read around here!" She yelled. Everyone bursted into laughter. "Of course we know of Mr. Potter! You can be like Ms. Granger!" Lyla said as she wrapped her arm around her. "Thank you! Someone gets my jokes! Plus, if the people we are fighting are that powerful, you guys are going to need all the help we can get." She said immediately turning back towards her mom. "She is right Mel. We need all the help would could get. I'm much too old to battle, those days are much behind me." Karen said as she looked at me and my sisters. Right when she said that, I remembered about the note the mysterious young woman gave me. Without hesitation, I went in my pocket and pulled the note out and opened it:

Dear Adam,
I know this might sound strange, but I promise it will all make sense to you one day. There is something coming. If you are reading this, then I'm sure you are already aware. Melody is going to need you, but you are right in thinking that you need to leave to train. Do this! I promise everything will be alright once you return. I am about to give you names of people that are going to fight with you. Send your sisters and Melody to retrieve them. Once again, I know how this sounds, but I promise I'm here to help. The names are mostly friends of yours:

Joshua Wolf

Ruin & Alexandria
*And for the one you don't know, Adrian Locke. You need to find him
as soon as possible.*

I know you will succeed.

I remained looking at the letter even after I have read it several times. Who was this woman and how did she have so much knowledge? I couldn't put my finger on it, but I trusted her words. I longed to see her again, just so I could get my answers, but for now I just smiled and placed the note back in my pocket. Maybe I had my own personal guardian angel.

"Let's get home. I think we all need a rest." I said as I entered myself back in the conversation. I felt Melody's pretty eyes glaring at me, wanting answers. She walked towards me and stared at me so calmly. I kissed her forehead and wrapped my arm around Karen.

"Wait. I have someone I want you all to meet." Lyla said as she came back with an unfamiliar angel. "This is Roy. He is the captain of the angels that came to our rescue. He is the only one that responded to my distress call. He was tall and bald with battle scars all over his arms from previous battles. He looked as if war was all he knew. "Thank you so much for saving my family." I said as put out my hand. He smiled as he shook it. "I've been waiting for what seems like a life time for this. This world doesn't deserve to parish. My soldiers and myself are here for the next battle, which I assume isn't that far away." He said as he turned away. "Thank you again Roy." Lyla said. He smiled as he and his fellow angels disappeared in the sky. We all looked at the sky, speechless, at the sheer beauty of the world. They say that we seem to take for granted the things that are always in front of us. Knowing that this world hangs in the balance is enough for us to appreciate its beauty. I gazed at Melody knowing what I must do.

"Go without us. Make sure my mother and sister get home for me?" Melody whispered to Gabriel. "Of course, Melody. Oh, and by the way, you fought like a warrior today." She said as she hugged her. Melody smiled but didn't respond. I can tell that she was exhausted, but she managed to keep it together.

Melody and I said our goodbyes until we were alone in the empty field. She walked up to me and placed her head on my chest. I ran my hands through her hair wishing we could just stand here together forever.

"Being able to read your mind is a gift and a curse. You do know, that right?" She said without moving. "I think it's more of a curse." I said. She laughed as she leaned her head up to look at me. "You know I'm not letting you go anywhere right?" She said. I smiled as I placed my hand on her face. "I need to get stronger Melody. These new threats could have powers we could never imagine. Gabriel, Lyla, Natalia, Victoria, and Karen are my family. I need to be ready." I said. Melody looked at the ground. "So, you are leaving?" I kissed the top of her head.
"I will return my love, swiftly." I said reassuring. The thought of being apart from Melody once again was something I didn't long for, but I know once I returned, I would be strong enough to keep us safe forever.

Melody took a few steps back to look at me. "I refuse to lose you again, so I suggest that you come back exactly how you intend." She said laughing trying to hold back upcoming tears. My hand caught them before they fell off her face. "I'm just going to miss you so much." She continued. "Just come back to me." I kissed her lips softly. "Always." I said as I began to take a few steps back. "There is something that I need you to do for me?" I asked. "Anything." I smiled as I thought of four names in my head. "I need you to find these four people for me? They may serve to be an immense help to us for the upcoming times." Melody as I handed her the note. She looked at it an instantly noticed, that it wasn't my hand writing. "Who gave you this? Who are these people? She asked.

"Most of them are old friends that I haven't seen in a while. I know that they will help with anything that I ask. That last name is the only one I am unfamiliar with. I'm sure he is special for my guardian angel to request him." I said. She smiled as I said this. "Your guardian angel?"
"Yes, a mysterious woman has been helping me along the way. Ever since I met you, she has been giving my clues to what I need to do. I believe she must be something of that nature." I simply said. She continued to look at the note, examining it thoroughly. "Adrian, this is who we need to find first right?" She asked. "That is what it says.

I am curious to meet him. I think you should be the one to retrieve him." She nodded again. "Okay, I got the names. we will start searching for them." She responded. "Take Gabriel with you, she is great at finding people. She found me." I said. She smiled at me. "Of course, Adam. Just know that I love you." I smiled at her, knowing I felt the same. "I know." She said reading my mind. I smiled once more before lifting my body and disappearing into the clouds with Melody living in my mind. She knew where I was going, she wouldn't be able to reach me or vice versa. That was the thing that worried me the most, but I placed my faith in front of my fears. I placed Melody above all.

(Melody)

As I stood there motionless in an empty field, all I could think about was Adam. I didn't know where he would be at or if he would be safe. My old life was over. I could feel the demonic power inside my body. It kept me alive, so a part of my felt gracious that I had it. I thought of the names Adam gave to me wondering who these mysterious people could be. I was curious about them all, but more curious about the last name he gave me. "Who was this Adrian?" I said to myself.

As I prepared myself to go home, I felt a pain that I have never encountered in my new or old life. "What in the world?!" I screamed as I held to my stomach. The pain was so unimaginable, I couldn't even stand up. I instantly felt to my knees and held my stomach. My mind couldn't think of anything clear, it only saw red. The pain was unbearable. "Adam!" I screamed in the middle of the African Congo only to be met by silence and more unforgiving pain. I closed my eyes and awaited an end. An end that felt like an eternity…

■■

Epilogue

(Lililth)

"Remarkable." I said as I sat thinking about the prodigy child's power in my new crafted throne. I was now the queen of the prison that held me captive for so long. Revenge was all I could think about as I glanced out of my tower's window. Now that The Darkness was open, my worries were small, but my curiosity was massive. I needed to know more about Adam and this Nephilim they called, Melody.

"My queen, thank you for freeing us. I promise that I fulfill my duties and rage against this world." I glanced to see Demitri, the demon king, kneeling before me. "Rise." I simply said as I walk next to him. "This world will burn and the Heavens shall fall and kneel to us. I am grateful that you have come to me." I said as I placed my hand on his face. "I am forever in debt to you. I will find and kill this Nephilim myself if you demand it." I smiled at his gesture until I had a thought of my own.

"No, I will handle her. There is something else I would like you to do for me." I walked back to my throne and obtained a dark red chest underneath it. I opened it and retrieved something that I knew he would like out of it."I need you to find a man. A man who may be of use to me one day. Use this to find him." I handled him one of the two pieces of The Black Supreme I retrieved from the cave's floors back in Africa. "Use its power as you wish to get the job done. Find him and make him embrace the darkness within him. His sister has failed me, but there is still hope for him." Demitri smiled as he held The Black Supreme, knowing it's abilities. I had no doubt that he would use it to it upmost power.

"As you wish." He said as he began to turn around. "Wait, my queen, what is this man's name?" He finally asked. "His name is Adrian. The brother of the Nephilim we failed to claim. Now go and do not disappoint me." Demitri smiled as walked away with his infamous daughter and disappeared into the world.

"Do you think it was foolish to give a demon that much power?" A recognizable voice said from behind me. "No Morgana. If he fails, or if he succeeds, it doesn't matter to me. His job is to only stir them up. I want to see what power we are up against." Morgana walks to my side and leans on my throne. "Interesting. So, shall I get started?" She asked. I stood up and walked to my large window. "Yes. The war has already begun, and I need soldiers. Take this and use all its power to create me an army like none other. I trust with your abilities, this can be done?" I asked as I handed her the other half of The Black Supreme. "Yes, I will create you an immortal army, filled with monsters that cannot die. In honor of our new goddess. In honor of our new world." I smiled at her words with gratitude. "Will you have me create a leader as well?" She asked. I crafted a crown with my endless power and placed it on my head. "No, I have someone in mind for that position. Now go and create my army." Morgana bowed her head and left my chambers. I sat in darkness with a smile on my face. "This is only the beginning…" I said to myself as I closed my eyes and thought of nothing but my plans and what I was willing to do to make them reality…

PHASE

II:

The

KING

Of

The Darkness

Chapters

The King of The Darkness

Chapter 12
Adrian and Scarlett

(Adrian)

I stood there motionlessly at my mother's funeral, thinking about the last talk we ever had. I remember it being as intimate and as personal as any of our many conversations, but for some reason, I knew it would be our last. She told me that she would love me and that she was proud of me no matter what happens or transpired in my life. Those things were not hard to believe coming from her. If those words came from anybody else's lips besides her, or Scarlett's, I would've never believed it. My life has been a constant fight, a fight that I have never backed down from. If you asked me, I wouldn't label myself as one who causes trouble, but one who truly doesn't give a fuck about anything or anyone; except the ones I do care about. That list was extremely small.

I was angry. I was pissed. These are not foreign emotions to me, but at this moment, I was angrier than I ever been. My anger pumped through my body so viciously, I could feel my body truly vibrating. The day was dark and gloomy which fit the occasion perfectly. The clouds simmered over me as if darkness prepared itself to descend. I felt compelled to look around to see if anyone was paying attention to me. My eyes met no one, which isn't a surprise. This was a funeral filled with people who more or likely despised me. Mr. Omaha glanced at me briefly, but immediately went back to the service. He claimed I broke into his convenient store a couple weeks ago, but charges were dropped on the lack of evidence and because no one dared to make my mother upset. She was the most loved person on the east side of Los Angeles. It was a crime I didn't even commit. People just see me and see a tattooed up, black leather jacket wearing bad boy. The nerve that people have is annoying to say the least. I already don't like people, but they continue to give me more reasons. Being judged and seen as a criminal was the summary of my twenty-five years on earth so far.

My mother was a goddess in my eyes; the sweetest woman to ever walk this earth. She was a marvel among mankind. She had the biggest heart and ironically, that's what gave out on her. She died in her sleep from sudden heart attack, which was unheard of, because she was only forty-five years old. The doctors didn't know what to make out of it, and neither did I. My father passed when I was three, so I barely remember anything about him. I was too young to curse God then, but I'm fully able and capable to curse him now.

I looked at the sky with anger in my heart questioning God and his motives or purpose for his course of action in this situation. What was the point of taking away my father before I got the chance or opportunity to know him and taking away my mother entirely too soon? Why do you enjoy talking away everything that means something to me? These were my unanswered questions. Dark clouds started to hover over our horizon. I guess rain was his answer.

I zoned out the pastor, as he prayed over my mother's casket. I felt my anger build up into a rage. I clinched up my fist and prepared to hit something, anything; until I felt a gentle hand held on to me. It was only be one person that knew how to calm me down. I opened my hand reluctantly and held hers.

"It's going to be alright Adrian. I'm right here." She said as she held my hand tighter. I turned to look at her only to see fresh tears running down her face. She threw me a weak smile with all the energy she had. It was obvious that she was hurting too. I immediately grab her little body and held and her in my arms. At this moment, I didn't care about anybody else that may have been observing us. This moment was about me and the only person I have left.

Scarlett Dawson and I have been friends since we were babies. If you want to be technical, since birth to be exact. My mother and her mother were best friends since elementary school and coincidently got pregnant around the same time. Scarlett's birthday happened to fall on the 23th of April, while my birthday was literally the next day. We did everything together, and I mean everything. She was the most important thing to me in this world. She loved my mother just as much as she loved her own, so today was just as hard for her as it was for me.

As I held her in my arms, I could only think about the last time I held her like this. It was sixteen years ago, at her parent's funeral. They both passed in a plane crash while celebrating their anniversary. Scarlett took it hard, but I was there for her every day. She has been living with my mom and I ever since. We were a family, who would do whatever for one another. My mom always wanted a little girl, and when Scarlett was born, that's exactly what she got. My mother adored Scarlett and always told me that she would be the woman I would spend the rest of my life with. I never disagreed.

Scarlett and I looked with heavy eyes as the casket descended into the ground. "I love you mom. Always and forever." I said. Scarlett grabbed my arm and placed her head on me. "Let's get out of here." I whispered in her ear. She wiped the one tear from my eye that refused to fall. "You don't want to talk to anyone before leaving?" She asked. I looked around to see no one worth talking too. "The last of my family is standing in front of me." I replied. She kissed me on the cheek and led me through the crowd of people to the parking lot. Scarlett was just like me in many ways. She brushed through everyone without giving anyone the satisfaction of eye contact.

"Pop the trunk, I got something for you." Scarlett said as she ran to the trunk of my car. One thing my dad did leave behind for me was a clean black 1970 Charger he had rebuilt. My mom would always tell me stories about my dad and his love for cars. She said he rebuilt it just for me to have. My mom never drove it since he passed because it was supposed to be my sixteen-birthday present. She hid it at a storage garage for years and had the manager keep up with it until she finally gave it to me. That's the kind of things my mother would do. Scarlett knew about it years ago before I even had a clue.

"Oh really? I wonder what it could be." I said smiling at her. I popped the trunk and she began going through the endless amount of junk that was back there.

"Okay, found it. Now close your eyes." She said as she pranced around with excitement. "Okay." I said. I closed my eyes eagerly wondering what she could possibly have.

"Adrian?" She said in a concerning voice. I opened my eyes and noticed her looking behind me. I turned to notice an unknown woman walking towards us. She was wearing the appropriate funeral attire, but I would have noticed the dark red hair.

"Who is she?" Scarlett asked. "I never saw her before." I glanced back at Scarlett. "Neither have I. Let me see what the hell she wants." I started to meet the mysterious woman half way as she certainly had her sights on us. She approached me with a friendly face, another unusual thing I noticed.

"Hello, my name is Evelyn Rogers. I was a friend of your mothers. I'm so sorry for your lost." She said. "Umm, thank you." I said while I examined her. "How did you know my mother?" I asked waiting to hear this response. "I worked with her. She was so kind to me. I knew you were her son, you are two are identical." She said with a smile. I threw a light smile back at her to be kind. "Everything okay baby?" Scarlett asked as she begins to walk up to the conversation. Throughout my entire life, Scarlett has always been very protective over me. So, this was her going into natural instincts.

"Yeah Scar, this is Evelyn Rogers. She said she worked with mom." I said. Scarlett examined her too before saying anything. "Oh, okay nice to meet you Ms. Rogers; I'm Scarlett, Adrian's girlfriend." She said in her professional voice. Evelyn looked at Scarlett in a weird way before responding. "Nice to meet you. Well I must be getting off. I just wanted to catch you, Adrian, before you left." She said. "Thank you. I appreciate that." She nodded and gave Scarlett one more look then turned around and walked away. "What the hell was that about? Why was she looking at me all crazy?" Scarlett asked. "I noticed that too, something was off about her." I said as I turned back to look at Scarlett. Her long black curly hair was covering her face from the powerful Los Angeles wind. I stood there for a moment, just to admire her sheer beauty. Scarlett was truly a work of art. From her size four and half feet to those perfect eyes to all that hair she could never take care of, she was the most beautiful thing to me.

"You know I hate when you stare at me like that. It makes my face turn red and you know I'm too bright for all that." She said as she started walking towards me. Her head rested on my chest as if it belonged there. I wrapped my arms around her only to see a fifth of Hennessy behind her back. "Oh, so that was your surprise!?" I said as I grabbed the bottle. "Well I know how you handle things like this and I feel the best thing to do is get fucked up and worry about everything tomorrow." She knew me so well it was scary sometimes. "I love you Scarlett." I simply said. She placed her hand on my cheek and grabbed my face. She pulled it closer to hers and placed her lips on mine. "I love you too crazy, now let's get out of here, it's getting cold." She said. I nodded and released her from my arms. I watched her get in the car then I looked up at the sky. "I'll see you soon Mom. I love you." I said to myself. I get into the car and start it up. Scarlett instantly starts to play with the radio until she found a song she liked then goes in the back seat to look for cups. I light up a black and mild I left in the ashtray as Scarlett pours up two cups Hennessy. "I make this a toast to mom." Scarlett said as she raised her cup. "A toast to mom, we love you." I replied. We click our cups together and take big gulps. "Okay let's get out of here." I put the car in gear and drive out the parking lot without even glancing in my rearview mirror.

We drive with just the music playing in the background. Scarlett has her hand on my neck and her other hand on her drink. We both know that we are numb to the fact that my mom is not going to be at the house when we get home, because Scarlett and I process things the same. The realization will hit us, but we are going to do whatever it takes so it won't hit us today.

"You said you were my girlfriend back there." I said as I remembered. "What?" I could tell that I broke her concentration. "You called me your boyfriend to that red hair woman. You never called me that before." I noticed. She smiled "I don't know why. Technically, we have been dating since I was old enough to talk. We never gave each other a title. I think that now is the best time to do that. I think your mom would love that." She said as she ran her fingers through my hair. She was right. Everybody who knows me knows that Scarlett was my absolute better half. Guys wouldn't even waste their time or energy trying to get her attention, not because I would probably kill them, but because She might kill them. No matter how much trouble I would get into in school or in life, Scarlett always would get me out. She got straight A's throughout her entire high school career, while I barely graduated. She would never let me fail though, even if she had to walk me through every assignment. My mother truly believed that I was the luckiest boy in the world because I found my soul mate when I was an infant. I truly did.

"To me you were always mine. Title or no title you will always be mine." I simply said. You are my soul mate Scarlett, at least that's what mom always said." She smiled at me and placed her head on my shoulder.

We pulled in our driveway and noticed mom's 2003 Pontiac Grand Prix parked outside the house. "Hey Baby, I'm going to go park mom's car in the back. Take the keys." I tossed them to her, so she could get in the house. She looked at me worried. "Are you hungry? I'm about to order some pizza for us, okay?" She said. I nodded as I got into mom's car and start it up. The engine instantly woke up. "Okay, that's fine." I said. She gave me one more look and turned around and went to the house. I drove around to the back of the house and parked it in the garage. I turn the engine off and sat in darkness. No matter how hard I tried to hold back my tears, grief soon overwhelmed me. All the tears I been holding back since the funeral began flooding out uncontrollably. I bury my head in the steering wheel, ashamed and angry that I let myself get to this point. The car became my opponent as I started punching the dashboard, blooding up my fist. I hear the garage door open which brought in a small light to my darkness. Scarlett Immediate gets in the passenger seat without a word and places my head on her chest. I continue to cry as she consoles me. She knew I needed her, and I did. I needed her more than she knew. She examined my bloody fist and held them. "Oh my God Adrian, they are bleeding horribly." She began to take off her white tee shirt she just placed on and wrapped my hands in it. "This should stop the bleeding, at least until we get in the house." I looked at her eyes and I could see she was about to cry too, but not because of my mother's passing, but because she knew I was hurt. She felt that same pain I felt. I looked at her body as she sat next to me with just a bra and a pair of my basketball shorts. She looked at me intently as she held my bloody hands. I placed my hand on her face gently, as if she was made of gold. I leaned forward slowly and placed my lips on hers. It was a passionate kiss, the type of kiss that took years to develop. A type of kiss that felt like nothing else mattered in the world. She pulled back and looked at me as if she could see right through my soul.

"Don't you ever hide from me!" she said as she stared me down with eyes full of tears.
"I don't like you seeing me like this." I replied ashamed. She pulled my head up to get my eye contact. "Do you not love me? Have I not seen you at your absolute worst? Have I not been here for you? Am I

not going to spend the rest of my life with you? Don't do that. Don't you ever do that! All we have is each other. Me and you. You and me. I love you more than I could ever love anyone. Don't hide from me, ever!" She demanded as she started to cry. I held her and started kissing her neck and her shoulders. "I'm sorry baby." I said repeatedly. I felt her hands run through my shirt as she lifted it over my head. I pulled her on top of me as I pushed the seat back to give us more room. My hands ran across her back, exploring the vases of her perfect body. I unhooked her bra and watched as her flawless breast fall right into place. I quickly began to use my tongue to place her nipple in my mouth. She pulled me closer as and I began to suck them. I could hear her moaning in my ear which only intensified our situation. I placed her legs up and took off her basketball shorts and boy shorts that she was wearing. I placed two fingers in my mouth for saliva and I placed them inside of her. "I love you Adrian." She whispered in my ear. I stuck my tongue in her mouth and held her even closer. "I love you too Scar." I said as I removed my fingers, unzipped my dress pants, and slowly went inside her. "Oh, Shit Adrian!" She said as I went deeper inside of her. Scarlett and I have never had "sex" in our lives. Every time we get intimate is something completely different. Our mind, body, and souls are completely one during these moments. It was something I could never truly explain. Nothing else matters but us.

She slept on top of me as we lay in the car. I ran my hand through her hair and I continued to kiss her softly. Scarlett slept like a bear, so I know waking her up would be pointless. I gently placed her basketball shorts on her and found her one of my jackets in the back seat and put that on her. I picked her up as a new born which was easy since I was 6'2 and she was 5'4. I carried her into the house and placed her in the bed. She was all I truly had at this point. My whole life. I kissed her on the forehead. "I love you, goodnight." She smiled and turned her head. That was her letting me know that she heard me.

(Scarlett)

The sun glimmered through my window, blinding me from seeing anything. I figured Adrian put me to bed last night as usual. I was such a baby, falling asleep so early. I know Adrian probably killed the bottle in my absence. I finally roll out of bed and slip on my Winnie the Poo house shoes. The house was semi-clean, there was just our clothes we wore to the funeral on the floor. I walked down stairs and turned on the television and poured me a bowl of cereal. Adrian worked out every morning, so I knew I would have the house to myself for a few hours.

I sat on the couch with my cereal and started watching an old episode of Hey Arnold. This was Adrian's and I favorite show when we were younger. Before we found out the difficulties of the real word. I could remember Aurora always finding the time to watch it with us. I missed Adrian's mother so much. How I wish I could just hold her again. I know Adrian's taking it a lot harder than he is letting me see, but that man can't fool me. Last night, when I caught him breaking down in the car, that was one of the first times I ever seen him cry. I hated seeing him hurt like this.

I stepped outside to check the weather and to my surprise, it was nice out. "Maybe I should go for a jog." I said to myself knowing that wasn't likely. Adrian pulled up seconds after I came out. I shake my head and look up at the sky. "Magic." Watching him exit the car only reminded me how much I missed him. His face was plain, until he met my eyes. He smiled with that same rare smile. A smile only I really saw. I couldn't help but to blush foolishly.

"The dead has awoken. I can't believe you right now." He said mentioning the fact that I fell asleep on him last night. "I knew you were going to say that. I'm Sorry I'm sorry." I reply as I jump in his arms. "Baby, you know I'm all sweaty right?" he said laughing. I kissed him on his chest before replying. "That's when I like you the most." He smiled and carried me inside. Our lips couldn't find a way off one another as we stumbled in the house. "I got a surprise for you." He said as he pulled away from me. I raised my eyebrows. "Let me guess, two tickets to Vegas, we are getting married." I said hoping that was the surprise. He smiled at me as he dug in his pocket and got on one knee. I was beyond speechless.

"Scarlett, you know I love you right?" He asked so intensely. I was stunned. "Of course, Adrian, more than anything." He finally pulled a small red box out of his pocket and opened it. It was a beautiful diamond ring that was also very familiar. "Oh my God Adrian." I simply said. It looked exactly like his mother, Aurora's, wedding ring. I always told Adrian I wanted a ring just like his moms and he listened. "Is it...?" I started, but Adrian immediately took the words from my mouth. "Is it my mother's ring? Yes Scar, it is. She gave it to me about three years ago. The day I told her I was going to spend the rest of my life with you." He said. I couldn't help to look at him and cry. How could a love be so strong? I don't know, but this was the ultimate form of it. "Adrian." I said trying to figure out more to say.

"Scarlett, will you have me as you husband, so I can have you as my wife; because living without you is not possible. I knew that then, and I know that now. Marry me?" I picked him up off his knee and placed my lips to his. "I been waiting on you to ask me that since I was seven years old. Of course, baby!" I really have been waiting on this day for a long time and now that it's here, I'm the happiest woman on this earth.

As I held my future husband in my arms, I heard something faint in the back room. I quietly let go of Adrian and reach for the pistol underneath the seat of the couch. "Scar, what...?" I instantly hush him and walk toward the back door. I grab a clip from the kitchen and load it thinking whoever this is who decided to break in our house at the moment my best friend asked me to marry him is about to get three holes in them. Everybody thinks that Adrian is the bad one, but behind closed doors, I am the one you should be worried about. I am a rider! Adrian taught me how to shoot years ago and he has a great shot. He could hit anything. He is beyond dangerous with a pistol. I'm right behind him.

"Baby, wait!" I hear Adrian in the back ground. I hear steps coming from around the corner, so I know I wasn't hearing things. "Scarlett has a gun." He said as he laughed. "What?" I said in confusion as I look back at him. "You think I wasn't going to invite your best friend for this occasion?" He simply said as he pointed toward the back. I follow his finger only to see my good friend

Carmen Greyson smiling as she approached me. I could feel my cheeks turning red as Adrian came behind me and took the gun from my hands.

"Congratulations baby girl! He called me and told me to come by! I wanted to surprise you, but of course you had to get a gun." Carmen said as she held me. Carmen has been my best friend for years, so I knew she would be excited to hear the news. I just never thought Adrian would ever arrange something like this. Carmen was my ride or die, anything that would happen or anything I ever needed, she was there. She was also one of my only friends who really accepted Adrian and who he is. She knows exactly what he means to me. She thought we were meant to be the first time she saw us interact. "All I can say is that it is about time! We been waiting on this thing forever." She continued. "Girl, I still can't believe it. So glad that you are here!" I said emotionally. Carmen looked at me and then looked at Adrian. "Come here brother, you finally did right." She said as she embraced him. He just simply smiled. "I know, couldn't have done this without you." I look at him then her. "Yes girl, we been planning this moment. We figured you would feel more comfortable here than anywhere else. You know you are a home body. I'm just upset I missed it. You told me that you were going to wait until we got here, sir?" Carmen said as she went off. "I know Carmen, she was on to me." He laughed as he picked up his car keys.

"Where are you going baby?" I asked. I had no intentions of him leaving this house for at least three to four days. I had to thank him for finally proposing. "I'm going to step out, I know you need your girl time. I'll come back with a bottle. We can celebrate when I get back okay?" I walked over to him and gave him a nice long kiss. "Promise?" I said in my young girl voice. He smiled as he kissed me on my forehead. "I promise." He looked at me with those eyes, so I didn't question him. I hated when Adrian would leave me, but I knew he would always come back. I knew he would always find a way back to me. "See you later Adrian. We gone talk later. Congratulations. I love you guys." Carmen said as she gave him another hug. "I'll see you guys, bye baby. See you later Carmen." Adrian said as he exited the house. I smiled at him once more and turned my attention towards Carmen. "Oh, I love that man." I said to myself. Carmen laughed as she walked passed me to sit on the couch. "Come on girl, sit down. Let me see the ring." My excitement was evident. Happiness wasn't even the appropriate word to use to explain my feelings right now. "Okay girl here I come." I picked up the pistol Adrian left on the kitchen counter and placed it under the couch seat. Carmen grabbed my hand and sat me down, so she could examine my engagement ring. It had one nice size diamond with two smaller diamonds on the side. It was very traditional, with just a tad of flash. The ring fit Aurora's personality perfect. I was beyond thrilled to wear it.

"This is so pretty!" Carmen said as she awed at my finger. "I know, it's so beautiful. It was his mother's." Carmen looked at me then back at the ring. "Are you excited?" She asked. My eyes simply just looked at her. "Okay, dumb question. Well, are you ready? Marriage is a big deal?" She lets go of my hand as she waited for a response. "Adrian is my everything. I love him Carmen. I would do anything for that boy. In my opinion, it took him to long to propose." I confessed. Carmen could do nothing more but smile at me. "You guys are crazy, but I believe in you two. There is no doubt in my mind that you two truly belong together." She said. "How is he doing with his mom?" I hesitated before answering. "Not good. He is a mess, but he is trying to put on his normal manly exterior." Carmen looked at me worried, then she held my hands. "How are you doing?" She asked. I hesitated once again. "I'm alright, I have to stay strong for him." There was a brief silence in the room, which reminded me Hey Arnold was still playing in the back ground. The morning was still quite young. It could be no later than ten o'clock. It felt like it should have been much later

"Let's turn up! We need to celebrate! We can't feel all gloomy, you are getting married!" Carmen said as she got up in search for something. "What are you looking for?" I said laughing at her attempt. She searched the kitchen cabinets and then the refrigerator. "Found you!" She said with such excitement, I felt the need to get up to see what she had got her hands on. It was the bottle of Hennessy from last night. "I thought Adrian would have drunk all of that?" I asked myself. The bottle was more than half full, which lets me know that he didn't drink any of it after I fell asleep. That was not like him at all.

Carmen took out two shot glasses and filled them to the top. "Here you go, sis." She handed me the glass as she sat right next to me. "Cheers." She simply said as she downed her shot. Carmen could drink Adrian and I under the table easily. Some night Adrian and Carmen would stay up all night drinking, playing cards betting who would pass out first. "Cheers." I down my drink and smack it on the table. The doorbell rings immediately after I finish the shot of Hennessey. The taste still was very evident in my chest. "Who the hell could that be this early?" I asked as I pull the pistol from under the couch pillow once again. "You and this gun girl, I don't think you are going need that." Carmen said as she walked toward the door. "You never know girl. This is LA." I simply said. Carmen looked through the peek hole to see who the mystery person was. "I never seen this red hair girl before." She said. "Red hair?" I repeated as I got up to see for myself. Carmen moved out the way as I opened the door without looking through the peep hole. Standing there was Evelyn Rogers, the red hair woman from the funeral. What was she doing here? "Can I help you?" I asked still thinking about the way she looked at me strange yesterday. She smiled with a sinister grin. "Actually, you can." Her eyes go completely black like in a horror movie. Before I could respond, she kicked me hard in the chest, flying me across the house into the kitchen. On my hands and knees, I cough out blood and wipe my mouth. Holding my chest, I manage to stand up on my feet and grab my pistol off the kitchen floor. "Carmen get down and call Adrian." I simply said as I stare down Evelyn. Carmen nods as she pulls out her phone and began dialing numbers. "You think your boyfriend is going to rescue you?" Evelyn said as she stood in the doorway. I spit out another mouthful of blood and smile. "No, I'm going to need his help to carry you out of here after I get done killing your ass." I said as I raise the pistol and pull the trigger. Confusion appeared on my face as I look at Evelyn. I fired three shots, all aimed at her chest. I can see blood pouring from her. Her blood appeared to be black, pitch black; and she looked unharmed. She smiled at me. "What the hell?" I said as I started to walk backward. "You shouldn't have done that." Evelyn said. She began approaching me. "What are you? You must be on some P.C.P. or drug. You shouldn't be alive right now." I said as I continued to walk backwards. "Silly girl, the things you don't know. Too bad you will never know." She grabbed my throat making it extremely hard to breath. "Scarlett!" I hear Carmen yelling in the background. I struggle to fight back, but I could feel my body slowly falling into a nothing. My body became numb and all I was aware of was Carmen's screams and Evelyn dark eyes looking down on me. My arms finally fell toward the ground and my eyes slowly closed. I was surrounded by darkness hopping and wishing that Adrian would pull me out of it. I waited in the darkness for his arms. They never came.

Chapter 13
The Chosen One

(Adrian)

Today was the happiest day of my life. I knew this without a shadow of a doubt. I finally managed to propose and finally give Scar the ring that's been in my possession for so long now. Keeping it a secret from her was among the hardest shit I think I ever had to do.

I pulled in Walgreen's parking lot and backed in the first available spot I could find. It was a lot of cars here, so I assumed it was packed, but to my surprise it was damn near empty. "What's up with all the cars?" I ask the cashier. "Church service across the street." Right out the window was the service. How could I have missed that? I thought. My brain was focused on other things at this point and the church was never something I looked for. My mother used to beg me to go with her when I was younger. I guess back then it wasn't that bad. I noticed the cashier gazing at me as I daydreamed about flashbacks. I nodded at him and continued my way down aisle eight straight toward the liquor. I picked up a bottle of you guessed it, Hennessy and returned to the cashier. "Let me get a box of blacks too, wine plastic tip." I said as I took out my money. I know it's still a whole bottle at the house, but it wouldn't hurt to get another one. "40.23 sir." The cashier said. I counted the money and glanced at the church again. "Let me get this too." I picked up a carnation of flowers sitting on display next to the register. "Must be a special occasion?" the cashier said trying to be friendly. I looked at him and tossed him a fifty as I grabbed the items and headed to the exit. "Keep the change." That was me being nice.

I drove pass the house and parked at the graveyard where my mother laid peacefully. Walking to her grave was just as hard as it was yesterday, but I just had to see her. "Hey ma." I started as I took one knee on her grave. The place was empty. I was probably the only person here this early. It was peaceful and serene. The birds and the animals, all with their distinctive sounds filled up the vacant area. I placed the carnation on her grave and sat there. "I finally did it ma. I finally proposed. Just how you always wanted me too." I said. The wind was light and perfect. "I wish you were here ma. I wish you could have been there. We are going to need you. I'm going to need you." I looked up at the sky and closed my eyes hoping that I could get some response from her. "Adrian. It's nice to see you again." A voice said from behind me. Without turning around or standing up, I respond. "I knew all my mother's friends. All of them. You are not one of them. Now I'm only going to ask you this one time. Who are you and what are you doing here?" She begins to move closer and stands right beside me. "Bravo, bravo! You got me. I didn't work with your mother, but I did know her. She's begging me to spare your life right now." She said with a hint of amusement. At this point, she caught my attention. "What did you just say to me?" I asked as I stood up and looked at her in her face. I was trying to understand what was happening. Does this woman want to intentionally piss me off right in front of my mother's grave? I thought to myself. "I said your mother is begging me not to kill you right now. Tell her that's not why I'm here. She's on the right of you." I look to my right only to see nothing. I didn't know what game she was playing here, but I was far from amused. The only thing keeping her safe now is the fact that I am at my mother's grave. "You have five seconds to leave here." I said as I felt my fist start to clinch. "Listen, we have a proposition for you" I look at her as if she is crazy. I immediately realize this Evelyn Rogers is a lunatic. "Get out of here, before you get hurt." I said as I begin to walk towards my car. I take three or four stops before my body goes numb and unable to move. "What the fuck?" I said as I struggle to move forward. "You see, I wasn't done with you." Evelyn said as she walks in front of me. "As much as I would love to tear you apart, I can't. Like I said we have a proposition for you and it's something you cannot refuse." I continue to struggle but to no avail. I am stuck to listen to whatever she has to say. "What did you do to me?" I ask in confusion. "It doesn't matter, just know you aren't going anywhere until you agree to our proposal." Her eyes turned completely black. I've seen these eyes before. "What are you?" I simply ask. She smiled at me. Sinister yes, but I wasn't afraid. I was just ready to kill whatever she was. "You know what I am, don't you?" I did, but the reality of it was far to unreal. "You seen us before. When you were younger, lurking around. You always been special. Now it's the time to fulfill your destiny." She said as she released me from her hold. "What the fuck do you want?" To come face to face with pure evil was not how I intended this day would go, but I was unafraid. Her red beautiful hair was flowing in the wind as she stood motionless. Her golden skin and body motion was beyond human, the only thing that gives her away were those pitch-black eyes. "Like I said, we have a proposition for you." She said. I tilt my head. "You have to be shitting me?" I said as my anger continued to build. She walks closer to me smiling. "There is something we need you to do." I instantly started for her, prepared to knock her head off, only to be stopped again.

"Wow, you are consistent." She said as she began to laugh at my current state. "Why would I do a damn thing for you?" I screamed. "Because you love your precious Scarlett correct?" My mind suddenly went dark. I turned my body towards Evelyn, breaking her hold on me. "What did you just say?" I demand. She looked at me in awe. "How did you break out of my hold?" She asked confused. I began to walk towards her with the full intention of killing her. "What did you just say?" I repeated myself. She began to walk backwards away from me. "Remarkable." She said as she looked at me as if I was a lab rat that just did an impossible feat. On a scale from one to ten of being pissed, I was at a thirteen. I didn't know what was happening or who she really was or what she even wanted from me, and honestly, I truly didn't give a fuck. The fact that she even brought up Scarlett was more than enough to end this conversation personally. I began to run towards her with my fist ready to strike. Evelyn didn't even try to dodge or block. My fist landed hard against her nose causing her to hit the ground. I stood, looking down at her making sure she was out; a punch that could have probably killed a normal person, but I knew she wasn't normal.

"Fuck you and whoever you work for. You can tell whoever you work for I said the shit." I said as I stick up my middle finger I turn back around towards my car. As I look up, Evelyn appears next to me. Her calmness has turned to anger. "Nice hit, I actually felt that. Don't worry Adrian, you will pay for your disrespect in blood."

I open the door and take out my two pistols from under the seat. "Okay bitch, this ends now." I said as I point the guns in her face. "Who said anything about your blood?" she said as she disappeared. "What the fuck could she mean...?" I immediately began to think about Scarlett. As I started the car and began my drive home, my phone rings. Carmen answers the phone screaming about a red head bitch until I hear gunshots. My blood started boiling as my heart dropped to my stomach and anger started to take over. I immediately put my foot on the gas and floored it until I got home thinking if she touched one hair on Scarlett...

I drove like a maniac, passing every car that I could. My stomach began to drop the closer I got to my destination. "I'm going to kill them." I said to myself as I pressed harder on the gas. I stopped the car in front of the house without turning it off. My two pistols were loaded and aimed at the entrance. "Adrian?" familiar voices called my name outside. My eyes were glued to the already open door of my home.

"Scarlett!" I scream as I walk in the house. Furniture was turned over and the door seemed to be off the hinges. Broken glass was all I heard as I entered deeper into my destroyed house. "Adrian!" Carmen screams from behind the kitchen table. In her arms she was holding Scarlett, who seemed lifeless. My pistols dropped to the floor along with my knees. My heart seemed to fall on the floor as well. I crawled to her and held her in my arms. Without noticing, my tears began falling on Scarlett's delicate face. I didn't say anything. I couldn't say anything. What was there to say? I thought about my mother and what she would do. Carmen was crying hysterically, and I said nothing. Hey Arnold, was still playing in the background as this horrible event was taking place. I didn't even know what happened and honestly it didn't matter at this time. All that mattered was Scarlett and I had to wake myself out of this trance I seemed to be in as I held her body. I placed my fingers on her neck to try to find a pulse. I did. "She is still alive." I said to myself. "Oh my God! We have to go to a hospital!" Carmen said. I gave her the keys as I picked up Scarlett. Tears still falling down my face as I carry Scarlett in my arms, all I could think about was that this was my fault. Her life was fading, and she might not even make it to the hospital, but I tried not to think about that. "Drive, I'll be in the back seat with her." I simply said. Carmen ran to the car and I followed behind her with Scarlett in my arms. "You are going to be okay Scar." I whisper to her. Eyes watch us as we exited outside. People who live in the neighborhood and familiar passersby gazed at the spectacle, but none dared to say anything. They could probably see the fire in my eyes.

I placed Scarlett's body in the back seat of the car. I ignored at all the lingering eyes on us before I followed behind her. Carmen immediately sped off to the nearest hospital. I sat in the back seat holding Scarlett, stroking her beautiful hair. "What happened Carmen?" I said surprisingly calm. I knew what happened, I just needed clarity. "This woman with red hair came and knocked down the door. She choked Scar. This bitch was on some type drugs or something because she was invincible, like she didn't feel any pain. I hit her in the head with a frying pan and she just looked at me. She was also strong as hell. She choked Scar with one hand and had her in the air. who was she?" She sounded as if she didn't believe what she was saying herself. "You believe me, right?" She asked. "I do. This is my second run in with her. The next will be our last." I gazed at Scar once more before I picked up one my pistol. "Who is she Adrian? What is she?" she asked unprepared for an answer. "Carmen, I don't want you apart of this." I said trying to control my emotions. "I need to know, look what she did to my best friend? I must know." She asked. She stops in the front of the hospital and turns around for me to give her an answer. "Another time Carmen." I exit the car and carry Scarlett in the building. Nurses and doctors immediately take her from me. They began asking me hundreds of questions, but I hear nothing. My mind is elsewhere, somewhere dark. I could see Scarlett being carried away on a stretcher, that image alone was too much for me to handle. "Adrian!" I heard Carmen from some distance behind me. I couldn't open my mouth to response, I could move. I felt my body slowly began to shut down. I fell to my knees and my eyes closed before the rest of my body hit the floor…I was surrounded by darkness, a feeling a knew far too well…

I awoke to an unfamiliar bridge structure. It was dark, and snow was falling and sticking to the ground. I looked behind only to see more bitter darkness. There was no sound and only one source of light, A brightly lit street light at the end of the bridge. As I looked closer, I noticed a person standing underneath it. The snow soon started to cover the edges of my boots, so I began my way towards the person in the light. The cold was durable, but unwanted. How did I get out here? I asked myself. I immediately started thinking about Scarlett and wondered how I was going to get back to her. As I got closer to the light I could see that this was a woman. A woman I knew. "Scarlett?" I asked myself as I began to run towards her. She didn't move or speak she just looked. The closer I got the more snow began to fall. She held out her arms to me as I reached her. "Help me…" she said as she vanished behind the darkness and snowfall. "Scarlett!" I screamed in frustration. "I told you." Evelyn said from behind me. I punched the ground as I heard her. "She is going to die, and it's all your fault." Evelyn said in a pleasing matter. Without hesitation, I turn around and charge at her to the ground. I began punching her as hard and as viciously as I could. After a few hits, she grabs my fist and headbutts me off her. "What a waste you are." She said as she back hands me causing me to fly a few feet away. I landed in a pile of snow that braced my landing. "All you had to do was listen!" she said as she kicked me in the stomach causing me to once again fly in the air and land hard. I turned around on my back to see her as she walked toward me. I could see her vividly, and I could also see her black wings as they fluttered. She smiled at me as I screamed in pain. "Okay, I've had my fun." She said as she grabbed my leg and tossed me again. As I hit the ground I notice that there was no more snow, I realized I wasn't even in the same place. Gold was surrounding me. Gold swords, jewelry, artifacts, bones, skulls were in the thousands in huge piles. I stood to my feet to notice I was in some type of castle or dungeon of some sort. I looked behind me to see Evelyn bowing down to something or someone. I turn around to see a huge golden throne with a man sitting there. The first thing I noticed about him was that his eyes couldn't be seen. He wore some sort of band around his head covering his eyes. I also noticed that there was a large scar down his face. Even though I couldn't see them, I felt his eyes were peering at me. He had curly black hair and wore an all-black robe with gold rings almost on every finger. He had large black wings on his back, much bigger than Evelyn's. He smiled at me before he spoke. "Leave us." The mysterious man said. Evelyn stood on her feet and walked out the huge palace. I stood there motionless, waiting for whatever was bound to happen. "I've been waiting for this moment for quite a while, Adrian." He said. I didn't move or say anything. His presence was a little intimidating which was unusual for me. He stood up from the gold throne and started approaching me.

"Don't be afraid, I am your friend." He said as he smiled. "I don't know where I am at, or what is happening, but I can tell you I'm officially pissed." I said as I attempt to strike the man. My fist seemed to freeze before I could connect with his face. "So much rage. I love it. I could see why she would be interested in you." He said. I struggled to move my fist, but it was freezing in the angle I left it. What was going on? I started to think to myself. "Let me introduce myself...I am Demetri. I've been keeping my eyes on you and I have to say, I am impressed to say the least." He simply said. "Why? Who are you? What the fuck do you people want from ME?" I screamed. "All your life you have been surrounded by darkness. That is because you are the darkness. The truth is that your life is a lie. Your loving father and caring mother that raised you are not your real parents. Your real father was a demon who was murdered by your angelic mother." He said. "What are you talking about?" I responded. "Don't worry, you will find out soon enough. I want to show you your true power. Your true potential. Your inner demonic power. That's all I want Adrian." He said. "I don't know what you are talking about." I said as I tried to look away. "Sure, you do. I know you have always felt it inside of you. The anger, the rage. You possess a power that has yet been untapped. I want to show you how to use it." I just looked at him. "I don't believe you and I don't care. Now get me out of here!" I stood my ground. Demetri pointed behind me causing me to look to turn around. "Scarlett!?" I yelled. She just stood there in a white gown emotionless. "She is going to die, but you can save her." Demetri said as he stood beside me. "Why did you do this? Why me?" I asked as I fell to my knees. "I know how much you care about her. Are you willing to give your life for hers?" He asked. I looked at him filled with hatred. "Of course." I simply said defeated. "What do you want me to do?" I asked. He smiled as he took out a gold dagger. "This knife was created by Lucifer when he was casted out of Heaven." He said as he swiped his hand with it. The blood from his hand began to drip on the golden floor. "Give me your right hand." Reluctantly, I did what he asked. He swiped it just as he did his own. "Once we shake hands, our agreement will be final." He said. I felt so helpless. The only thing I could think about was Scarlett and the fact that I was going to kill whatever this devil was.

He stuck out his hand waiting for me to shake it. I looked at him and then his hand as I prepared to make whatever agreement we had final. Just as I raised my hand something unexpected happened...

"Adrian..." I heard a faint voice call my name from a distance. Demetri's eyes began to wonder around trying to locate the voice. "Adrian..." The voice repeated itself, but this time it was louder and clearer. "Scarlett?" I said as I began to look around. "Adrian! Wake up!" Scarlett said from an unknown place. I slowly began to walk backwards from Demetri, wiping the blood from my open cut on my hand. "What are you doing?" He asked as he stood there motionless. "I'm here!" Scarlett said. She sounded even closer than before. I could feel my environment began to change. "No!" Demetri said as he began walking towards me. The room went dark as if my eyes were closed. There was silence.

"Adrian?" I opened my eyes to see my beloved Scarlett's face looking down upon me. I was laying exactly where I fell. "Scarlett, what happened? Are you okay?" I said as I looked at her. All her bruises were gone. "I am fine now. This one girl placed her fingers on my head, and I was healed. What the fuck, right?" She said. "A lot of shit that I can't explain has been going on. Where is this woman?" I asked only to be tapped on the shoulder from behind. Without hesitation, I turned to face two enchanting looking women standing staring at me. One was a tall black haired beauty who may have been a model and the other had beautiful brown curly hair with pretty eyes, same color as mine. They both looked at me without saying anything.

"Hello Adrian, my name is Gabriel, and this is Melody. We don't have a lot of time to explain, but I need you guys to come with us." I looked at Scarlett and Carmen after they spoke. Scarlett shrugged as I looked at her for approval. "Do you promise to explain everything?" Scarlett said to Gabriel. Melody continued to look at me as if she knew me. I felt the same, but I couldn't put a name on her. "I promise, but we must go, now." Just as she said that, Melody ran into the hallway. "We have company." She said as she ran back to us. I grabbed Scarlett's hand as we followed Gabriel and Melody to the hallway. At the end of the hallway stood four men with pitch black eyes. Evelyn came in between them smiling toward us. "That bitch!" Scarlett said as she began to walk towards her. I grabbed her hand stopping her. The hospital alarm began to ring as police started running up the stairs. "Melody, you lead them outside, I'll stall them." Gabriel said as her beautiful wings began to spread from her back. "Oh my God!" Scarlett said in awe at the spectacular event. "Go!" Gabriel demanded. I nodded as we followed Melody to our destination.

(Melody)

"Melody?" Gabriel called my name from the other room. I took one last bite of my delicious pancakes Jade had made for us this morning before getting up. It's been two months since our fight in Africa and there have been no traces of Lilith or any of the monsters she unleashed upon this world. Also, I haven't heard from my beloved Adam either. I knew communication would be scarce, but this was unbearable. I missed him just as much as I knew I would. Natalia and Lyla went on separate missions to find the people Adam instructed me to search for. I missed them as well. Victoria left for New Orleans to train with our powerful witch auntie, Catherine (It still sounds unreal every time I say it). Everybody was preparing themselves for what was to happen, but I was worried. I couldn't stop thinking about everything that has transpired already.

I walked in the living room to see Gabriel getting ready to leave. Zachariah and his son went to the market earlier, so it was just us girls at the house. I was bent on returning to Rio after we left Africa for personal reasons and Gabriel wouldn't dare leave my side, especially since Adam wasn't present. "What is it Gabriel?" I asked. "I found him. I finally found Adrian and he is in trouble. We have to get to him now." She said as she tied up her boots. Adrian was one of the people Adam wanted us to find. There was something special about him, since Adam insisted we found him before anyone else. Jade gave me a worrisome look as Gabriel spoke. "Where is he?" I asked. "Los Angeles." Jade got up and went to the kitchen expecting me to follow her. "Okay Gabriel, I'll meet you outside. Let me get dressed." I said. She nodded as she quickly left the house. I smiled at her as she disappeared and immediately turned toward the kitchen. Jade stood there with a cup of water. "Drink this." She said. I took the glass and took a huge swig. "I don't think you should go Melody. It's too dangerous for you now." She said as she looked at me worried. I took another swig of water and placed the glass down. "I have too, Gabriel needs me." Jade walked towards me and placed her hands on my belly. "If Gabriel knew you were pregnant, she wouldn't think of letting you go. When are you going to tell her, or your family?" She asked. I placed my hands on my belly. "We are in the middle of a war Jade. Gabriel needs me, my mother and sister needs me, Adam needs me. This is much bigger than me. I know if I

told Gabriel, she would never let me fight. I want to fight. I need to."
Jade smiled at me as she hugged me tight. "I know you are a fighter,
Melody. Just promise me that you will be careful?" she whispered in
my ear. I nodded as she released me.

When I was in Africa, I had the most unimaginable pain in
my life. Eventually the pain subsided and the first person I went to
was Jade. I figured she would know what to do more than my
angelic sisters and telling my mom and sister would be a horrible
idea. I didn't need a test or confirmation to know I was pregnant, I
felt it. I felt the life inside of me. How I got pregnant so fast is
beyond me. Jade informed me that the rules of a normal pregnancy
doesn't apply to me since neither Adam or myself were not human to
begin with, so I didn't know what to really expect. She also told me
pregnancy within angels happened much swiftly than natural human
births, but pregnancy within Nephilim's was something I still knew
nothing about. I couldn't understand why Gabriel hasn't been able to
detect it. I figured maybe because she was so focused on finding
Adrian; either way, I needed the extra time. I was scared, but I had to
hope for the best. How I wish Adam was here.

Gabriel and I flew to Los Angeles as fast as we could and
winded up at a hospital. "He is here." Gabriel simply said. I looked
up at the hospital only to find out that I could feel him too. I got
chills at his presence. It seemed so familiar, like I knew him. I also
felt an evil presence as well. In these last two months, my abilities
have improved, and Gabriel has helped me a lot.

"Do you feel that?" I asked. Gabriel continued to look at the
building. "Yes, I do...this is bad. Let's go find him." Gabriel said as
she started to enter the building.

The hospital was busy. We walked passed hundreds of
people until we came across a young man fainted on the floor. "Oh
my God, I don't know what happened! Can you please help?" A
young lady said as she approached us. I looked around the room and
noticed another young woman lying on the hospital bed. She looked
as if she was attacked by something. Her life was fading fast.
"Adrian?" Gabriel said as she looked at him. "How did you know his
name?" The young lady asked as she looked at us suspiciously.
"Gabriel, this woman needs our help." I said holding her hand.
"What happened to her?" I asked the young lady. "She was attacked
by this extremely strong woman with black eyes. I don't know

what's going on anymore." I looked at Gabriel as she looked at me. "A demon did this." Gabriel said. The young lady's face quickly changed. "A demon?" She asked. Gabriel placed her hand on the woman lying on the bed. "She is dying." Gabriel said as she closed her eyes and began healing her. The young lady just looked in astonishment at the miracle that was transpiring. The woman opened her eyes only to look for someone. "Where's Adrian?" She asked immediately. Her compassion reminded me of myself when I thought of Adam. Adrian must be her lover. "Scarlett are you alright?" She asked her. Scarlett eyes wondered around the room until she saw a fallen Adrian on the floor. "Adrian!" She screamed as she ran to his aid. Her beautiful hair just flew right behind her as if were flying to him. She placed her hand on his head and looked at me. "Can you fix him, like you fixed me? I don't know who you people are, but WE need your help. Please!" Scarlett begged.

Just like Natalia, Gabriel had abilities as well. She had healing abilities that I recently found out during our time together. She could heal human beings easily, but it took much focus and power to heal any other beings, including myself. This means that I couldn't afford to be reckless.

I could see her compassion in Scarlett's eyes as she looked at Gabriel for help. "Of course, Scarlett, don't worry." I said reassuring her. Gabriel placed her hand on his head and closed her eyes. "Adrian." Scarlett said as she looked down at him. "He's not in this world..." Gabriel said so lightly that only I could hear. "What do you mean?" I responded. "Something has him...something powerful." I looked at Scarlett as she continued to call his name. "I can't reach him...I need you." Gabriel said as she started to look at Scarlett. "Place your hand on his head and call out to him." Gabriel asked. Scarlett nodded as she listened to Gabriel. "Adrian, wake up!" She called out to him. His eyes started to open and to my surprise they were the same color as mine. He gazed into Scarlett's eyes as if time didn't exist around them.

"Something is wrong." I said to myself. I ran in the hallway only to see a group of demons at the end of the hallway. They had blank faces as they stood there motionless. "This isn't good." I told myself.

(Adrian)

I ran through the hallway as fast as I could pulling Scarlett by her delicate hands. Melody led the way as we brush past hundreds of people. "Angels and Demons exist." I simply said as we got outside, still trying to process everything. Melody looked at me and then at Scarlett. Carmen put her face in her hands. "The world is much bigger than you know. I'm sorry to enter your lives like this, I promise it wasn't our intentions. This world is relatively new to me as well..." Melody said. I let go of Scarlett's hand. "Well, please, tell me what are your intentions? A demon attacked me and my fiancé. I just saw your friend fly down the hallway. What the fuck is happening. I need answers!" I demanded. "Calm down. Remember, they just saved our lives!" Scarlett said. "I never got the chance to thank you and your friend." She said to Melody. Every time I looked at her, she reminded me of someone I knew. I couldn't shake the feeling. "I think I know you...you seem so familiar." I said to Melody before she could respond. She looked at me as if she was going to agree, but instead she looked up towards the hospital. "Everybody moves!" She said pushing us out the way. Gabriel came flying out the window a few stories above us with demons falling hitting the ground. "Do you guys have a car?" Melody asked.

"Yeah, come on Scarlett!" I ran to the car and quickly entered it. "Start the car! follow us!" Melody said as she took to the sky to aid Gabriel. "I can't believe what I'm seeing." Carmen said as she looked at the angels in the sky. I looked at Scarlett only to see a calm face. She wasn't losing her mind during any of this. "Let's go baby." She said to me as she took my hand.

"Baby pop the trunk so I can get that shot gun. We might be in for a fight." Scarlett said as she exited the car. I popped it and pulled out my two pistols and ammo. Gabriel landed right next to the car and looked inside. "Hand me your weapons. That ammo you have will not suffice." Gabriel asked. Scarlett handed her the shotgun and with a simple touch, the weapon glowed briefly. "I blessed the weapon...they should be able to hurt or even kill them." She said as she looked at me. I held on to my guns refusing to let them go. "Adrian, if we are going to survive this, you have to trust me. The demon that is after you, he will stop at nothing until he has you. Now give me your weapons." I looked at her, not knowing how she knew what she knew. "Baby, what demon? That Evelyn chick?" Scarlett asked. "No, Evelyn is just a pawn. The real threat is much more powerful, much more terrifying. You seen him Adrian. We need to trust in one another." Gabriel asked. Scarlett held my hands. "It's okay. Adrian, it's okay." Scarlett said smoothly. I didn't want to be believe her. I didn't want to listen, but I knew she was right. As stubborn as I wanted to be, I had no choice to agree. Scarlett always knew how to get in my head.

"Okay." I simply said as I handed over my guns to Gabriel. She held them and did the same thing she did to the shotgun before handing them back to me. "Follow me." She said as she took to the sky.

Police cruisers began crowding the area as we pulled out the parking lot. The ground suddenly started to shake underneath us. "Great. An earthquake. What perfect timing." Carmen said. Scarlett and I both looked at each other. "That's no earthquake." I said as I put the car in drive. "Go!" Scarlett screamed as we drove off. "Oh my God! Look behind us." Carmen yelled. I looked in the rearview mirror to see a sight I never thought was possible. Demons were coming up from the rumble from the earthquake. They didn't look like the human-like demons we seen earlier. These were winged creatures who were hideous in the face. Gabriel and Melody flew past the car which I took as a hint to start following them. The demons were on our trail, torching everything in their wake. "Take the wheel." I said to Carmen. She was scared, but she nodded and climbed in the front seat while I took the back. "You ready?" I asked Scarlett as I placed clips in my guns. "Of course, my love." She said as she gave me a faint smile. I never been afraid of anything in my life but seeing the fear in Scarlett put fear in me. "I love you Scar." I said as if this was our last moments. She leaned over and kissed me passionately. "I love you too...WE are not going to die on the day you propose to me Adrian, okay?" She announced. "Okay I can promise that." I said as I kissed her one more time.

I rolled down the back window and wrapped my leg around the seat beat as I sat on the edge of the window seal. I aimed at all the demons close by and started shooting their heads off. Scarlett was on the opposite side blasting them with her shotgun, while Carmen drove through the earthquake. "What the hell!" Carmen said, and she started swerving. I looked a head only to see a man standing in the middle of the road. The closer we got, the more I noticed that it wasn't a man at all, but it was the demon who caused all of this in the first place. "Fuck." I said as I began shooting at him. He smiled at me as began running towards me. "Run him over Carmen!" I screamed. She floored it with the full intention of smashing right in to him. He stopped and smiled. I pulled Scarlett in the car just as we impacted with him. Demetri didn't move, instead, he simply wacked the car off the road causing us to flip over a few times before coming to stop.

***

I kicked open the door with the little strength I had left and fell to the ground. "Scarlett! Carmen! Are you guys alright?" I asked as I crawled to the driver's side only to see that Carmen wasn't there. I noticed a big hole in the front window. "Carmen!" I screamed when I saw her lifeless body 12 feet away from the car. Gabriel flew to the aid of Carmen as soon as I laid eyes on her. "Scarlett!" I screamed as I crawled to her side of the car only to see that she was not there either. "Such a fragile thing, isn't she?" I turn around to see Demetri holding her in his arms. "Adrian!" She screamed. "Let her go!" I screamed at him. He smiled at me. "Did you really think you could run from me? You remind me so much of your father, He was a warrior! A demon king. My King! He made a mistake going after Melody. I knew you would have the real power. He was foolish for falling for your angelic mother. That same angelic mother who killed him. That is what love will do to you Adrian don't you see?" He said. I managed to get to my feet as he spoke. "You don't know anything about me! Put Scarlett down now!" I demanded. He smiled as he dropped her on the floor. Scarlett crawled to my arms immediately.

"I don't want to kill you Adrian. I just want you to understand who you are. You are a king!" Demetri simply said. "Who are you and what do you want?" Melody said as she landed in front of us. Demetri began walking towards us. Melody stood her ground. She was not intimidated in any fashion. "Melody! It's a pleasure to finally meet you. I am Demetri, the demon king. I wanted to thank you for releasing The Darkness. I been locked up for so long, it feels good to be free again." He said. Melody's face changed by his words. What was this darkness place he was talking about? "You came from the Darkness? How many of you are there?" She asked. "Four. Your God put four of his greatest creations in The Darkness because our power is too great for this world." He simply said. "Who am I?" I asked interrupting their conversation. Melody looked at me, so did Demetri. "You are the son of Damon and Amora. Those are your real parents. You are what is called Nephilim. A powerful being, with angelic and demonic traits. The most powerful beings in existence. Your power has been dormant because you have yet to release it. I just want to help you do just that." He said. I couldn't think or say anything. Scarlett held on to me even tighter. "Impossible. He is lying to you Adrian." Melody said as she looked at me. I could see in her eyes that, she didn't know what the truth really was. Gabriel flew to us carrying Carmen in her arms. "Oh my God, Carmen!" Scarlett ran to her side. "There's much your angels friends don't know. Every Nephilim comes in twos. One represents the light, while the other represents the dark. Once Amora and Damon found Melody, they didn't bother looking for you. Why would they? One Nephilim was enough for their blood-thirsty quest." He said. I couldn't believe what was being said. It was all too crazy to believe. Melody didn't say anything, neither did Gabriel. "I bet Gabriel didn't know even know you had a little one on the way. I'm sensing your about 2 months pregnant at this point, right?" He snarled. I looked at Melody with eyes wide open while her eyes never met mine since they were glued to Demetri's words.

Despite what he has said or weather I thought they were true or not, the look in Melody's eyes seemed to tell a different story. Her eyes looked as if truth were being told in its purest form. That indeed Melody was pregnant, that I was this this 'Nephilim' that he spoke of, and finally, that Melody was indeed my sister. All my life I felt as if I was different, as if my life was meant for something more. My rage never truly made sense to me, not until now. Demons were something I believed in, even before this chain of events even happened.

When I was younger, I used to see dark figures shadowing me. They never spoke or approached me, but they were always there. As I got older, the figures began to disappear, but I never spoke about them, not even to Scarlett. As I listened to Demetri, a full fledge demon, my eyes were open. Nothing in this world scared me, but this truth was horrifying. I thought of my mother, not my angel mom, but my mom of flesh and blood. Why didn't she tell me the truth? Did she even know the truth? I had questions, and maybe Demetri was the only one who could answer them.

"Melody?" Gabriel said with her velvet voice. Melody said nothing. "You son of a bitch!" Scarlett screamed at the top of her lungs. I grabbed her as she tried to attack Demetri. With everything going on, I glanced at Carmen, hoping she was sill alive. I would have to live with that for the rest of my life if she wasn't, and that would be a pain I couldn't take.

Evelyn landed right next to her demon king, proud of the destruction and mayhem that they caused on this day. Her smile made my stomach turn. I never hated two beings more than I hated anyone. I looked up to see the thousands of demons hovering above us, covering the sky. We were outnumbered and out matched, and we knew this. Demetri smiled as he turned his back on us. "Your world will soon be mine, and so will your soul." He said as he looked at me intently. His voice was calm and confident. I spat at him, for that was all the energy I could possess at the time. He grinned as he took one final look at us and took to the sky. "I'll see you soon." Evelyn said as she looked at me then glanced at the rest of us before she took to the sky following Demetri. The sky cleared, erasing all evidence except for the rumble they left behind. I fell to my knees only to be held by Scarlett. We both ran to Carmen. "Please tell me she is okay!?" Scarlett said as she held her head. "She is in critical health, but she is alive. I will do all I can, but we would need to get out of here." Gabriel said. "Thank God! And of course. We can go to our home. Follow us?" Scarlett said. The reality of it all was too much to deal. "Yes, lets go." Melody said as the police sirens began holler from the distance.

I just looked and said nothing. I felt nothing. I walked to abandoned car and jump started since my beautiful car was totaled. "Come on let's go home." I said to Scarlett. Adrian took Carmen's unconscious body in the car. Before pulling off, I glanced at Melody. "You guys a re coming right?" I simply said. Melody nodded without a word. I placed the car in gear and sped off away from the destruction.

Chapter 15
Witches, Vampires, and Werewolves

(Victoria) New Orleans)

The rain began to pour tremendously as I stood outside of our massive school. The school was my great auntie's Catherine mansion that was at least 100 years old. It was a beautiful Victorian home with too many rooms to count.

I've been here for about two months, and I have to say, I'm learning at a much faster pace than I or anymore else expected. Miss Catherine is as elegant and as powerful as my mom said. I know that here, I would be able to truly help my sister. It still baffles me that after all these years growing up, I never been here. I can definitely understand now.

I looked at my phone only to see two missed calls from Matthew, my husband. That was by far the hardest thing about this whole ordeal...the fact that I had to be away from him; to protect him. Telling him I was in training to be a witch to save the world sounded a little farfetched, so of course I lied, unwillingly. I remember how that conversation went so vividly:

"Baby, where have you been?" Matthew said the moment I walked in the door from our little trip from Africa. He was pacing back and forward with a cup of vodka in his hand. Jason was also there, looking just as worried. "Look at your clothes!" He said as he walked towards me. Jason followed just to be as shocked as he my husband. "Oh my God, what has happened?" Jason asked. They had questions, but I had no answers. No truthful answers.

"Listen, you just have to trust me, okay?" I said as I walked passed them to my room. Matthew followed me without hesitation. "What are you talking about, trust you? You have been gone for days without a single phone call. Then you come in the house with your clothes all battered with no explanation. Talk to me!" He demanded. His voice was stern and serious, A side I never seen before in our five years of knowing him. It kind of aroused me a bit to be honest. I turned to face him only to see a serious yet worried man. I didn't blame him. If the roles were reversed, I probably would have put him in the hospital; but here he stood in front of me, trying to talk, trying mend our relationship that was never broken to me. I just knew I couldn't tell him about this, about me.

"Listen Matthew, I love you. I love you so much. You are my best friend. My husband. I can't tell you what is going on in any detail, but I promise you it is for the best. One day I will, but for now, I'm just going to need you to trust me. Can you do that?" I asked. He just looked at me. A look I never saw before. "Can I at least know where you are going? He asked. I hesitated before answering. "New Orleans." I said as I started packing clothes. "When will I see my wife again?" He also asked. I zipped up my suitcase and placed it on the floor. "Soon, I promise." I said. He just looked at me again, making it harder to walk away from him. I truly did love him more than anything. This was much harder that anything I've ever done. I kissed him on the lips, as if I was never going to see him again. "I will see you soon." I said sincerely as I attempted to walk away, only to have my arm grabbed as I touched the door knob. He lifted me up without a word and placed me on the bed. He climbed on top of me and whispered something tasteful in my ear. "Come back to me." I nodded as I escaped into his love...

I let my thoughts run wild until they were interrupted by no one else other than the one person who seemed created to give me a tough time here. "What are you doing out here in the rain? Finally decided to go back home?" She said laughing. "No Dawn, I just like the rain. What do you want?" I snapped back.

Dawn was the youngest daughter of the DeLorean's, a rich and powerful family who owned damn near half of everything in New Orleans. She was the youngest of four children, but the only one to inherit her father's witch blood. She began noticing her powers at the early age of 8 and ever since then she has been one of the leading witches here. She was a prodigy among the world of the witches. Despite her power and her potential, her arrogance and nasty attitude left her with more enemies than friends. At the tender age of 24, she was supposed to graduate into a Enchantress; the final level of any female witch's destiny. But "The Enlighten Ones" refuse to give their graces. The Enlighten ones are a group of the most powerful and oldest witches in the world of the living. They decide the fate of all the young witches and if you have any ounce of darkness in your soul, you would not be granted Enchantress. This is Dawn's problem.

Dawn walked closer towards me standing side by side. We have been going at it ever since I got down here. She is mean to everybody, but particularly mean to me. I really don't care, it's just that I don't want to hit her and feel bad about it afterwards. I really think she is jealous of my relationship with Miss Catherine. I can't help that the most powerful witch in existence happens to be my favorite aunt.

"You think you are so good, don't you?" She said looking at the rain pour. I sighed. "You just can't help yourself, can you?" She walked in front of me smiling menacingly. Her curly brown hair and beautiful golden brown skin made her a sight to see. She looked like a character from the movie "The Craft," except the movie was released today. For a mean bitch, she was beautiful. I couldn't lie about that.

"I hear Miss Catherine and the others talk about your potential, but I have failed to see anything impressive." She said. I could feel her getting under my skin once again. I tried to annoy her advances.

"You are intimidated by me aren't you. Your years of work only to be overshadowed by my two months...must be sad?" I said arrogantly. I could see me getting under her skin as well. She lifted her arms and the rain instantly paused as if she pressed pause on a television screen.

"You could never overshadow me! Once I become a part of The Enlighten Ones, I wouldn't have to deal with the likes of you. I could mentor you though. Be your teacher. You would like that right?" She said sarcastically. I lifted my hand only to dissipate the rain all together. The sun instantly came out as I cleared the skies. "Maybe I could be your mentor or teacher? You would like that...*right?*" I said in the same notion as she did. Her face was red with disgust, not capable of saying anything.

"Hey guys, you have to come see this!" One of the witches from the house said as she ran outside. The panic in her voice seemed urgent. Dawn and I both look at each other as we race into the house. "Turn it up." Dawn demanded. The girls quickly grabbed the remote as they turned up the volume of the television.

"What you are about to see will disturb you." The news anchorman said as it switched to live footage of a scene happening right now in Los Angeles. "As you can see, there are what appears to be winged creatures coming up from what seems like the ground. There is also two winged women hovering above them in what looks like a fight of biblical proportions. At this point we have no news of what's happening or what will happen, but I can assure the American people of the world that this footage is one hundred percent real." The reporter said before the network completely went off air. "Melody!" I screamed still focused on a blank screen. "What the hell is going on?" Dawn said as she too looked at a blank screen. The room suddenly went into commotion as the news hit the minds and hearts of everyone in the room.

"Melody." I repeated as I began to drift away from the crowd. "Where are you going and who is Melody?" Dawn said as she followed me. "Please Dawn, not right now." I said as I ran upstairs to my room to gather up some clothes. Dawn grabbed my arm stopping me in my tracks. "I'm serious. I know I give you a lot of shit, but I saw in your eyes..." She said with real sincerity, which is a side I never saw before. "What did you see?" she looked at me briefly before answering. "I saw destruction. I saw pain." She said. I grabbed my bag filled with clothes and looked her in her eyes. I'm going to Los Angeles; my sister needs me." I said as I started toward to door. "She was the one with the gray wings, wasn't she?" She said stopping me once again with her words. "How did you know that?" I asked turning around. "I saw your face when they showed her. I felt your energy. You are a witch now, you can't hide your feelings from your coven." She explained. I listened to her every word truly realizing her true intentions. "I always wondered why you came here. Why are you now just deciding to become what you were meant to be? And now I know. Those demons that arose from ground, you know what's happening, don't you?" She asked. I could feel her trying to pick through my soul. "I don't know exactly, but I know where it spawned from. I have to go." I said finally leaving the room. "I'm coming with you."

"What?" I said turning to look at her.

"Look, I know how it sounds, but I want to come with you. You are going to need my help." I looked at her, trying to figure her out.

"What do you want from me! You are a bitch to me for two months and now you want to be my best friend?" I snapped in frustration. "Listen, I'm a bitch. That's who I am, but I'm also the same witch who knows a spell to get us in Los Angeles in three minutes." She said as she walked pass me. "Wait, what?" I said following her.

"So, you were going to leave without a word?" Catherine said to us as we opened the front door. "I'm sorry Madame, I have to go..." I said. Catherine smiled at me, her words were so soothing that anything she said seemed right. "I know you have to go, I'm not stopping you, but I do feel you are not ready to face whatever forces come your way alone, so I want Dawn to come with you. Now Dawn, your father will be against it, but you are old enough to make your own decisions." She said to the both of us. "Of course, Miss Catherine." Dawn said. "Now this journey you are about to face is not going to be easy, but you two are sisters because of this coven. Work together and you will survive...divide and you both may parish. Now get out of here. You have no time to waste." She said as she hugged both of us. Dawn and I both looked at each other as we prepared to embark on our mission. "Close your eyes." Dawn said as she held my hand. I obeyed as my eyes closed. "Uforica!" She announces. and what felt like seconds, we appeared in the middle of a damaged street in Los Angeles. "Now let's find your sister."

(Natalia) Paris, France

I stood in front of the enormous castle for hours, mentally preparing myself for this encounter. Lyla and I went on separate missions to find separate people off Adams list. How I missed my brother and sisters, but I knew this was bigger than us.

It didn't take me long to find the ever-elusive castle of "Les plus beaux," but once I found it I stayed clear of it for months. I didn't feel the need to approach it until this morning after the events in Los Angeles. I know now that the beings from The Darkness are starting to show. It was still a disbelief that all of this was happening, but fighting was something that I loved so this was just the beginning. I couldn't wait to finally get my hands dirty again.

Looking at the castle only reminded me of my last time I was here. I couldn't resist a second coming. About 60 years ago, while my sisters and I searched for our precious brother, I traveled to Paris on my own. I figured Adam would love it here, so I explored it. While in Paris I ran across a man, or that's what I thought at first. His skin was cold as snow. his eyes were golden brown, and his body was chiseled like a statue. He was gorgeous. Somehow, he seduced me into bed with him, which was unusual since humans didn't attract me. He was so soft with me, which is probably why I was drawn to him because I'm so *not*. I remember waking up in his enormous castle naked in his bed alone. I searched for him only to find the disturbing truth. I found him in a dungeon biting a chained-up prisoner. There was blood all over his flesh as if he ripped through him. My first sexual encounter was with a Vampire.

Now, in my defense, I knew the existence of vampires, but never encountered one. The way pop culture depicts them are almost completely false. The only thing they got right is their obsession with blood. Sunlight doesn't kill them, doesn't even hurt them. Crosses and garlic are useless, and A dagger to the heart would probably just piss them off. Their power is great, some of the stronger ones could even fight an angel head first. Not too many other beings could say that. The only sure-fire way to kill one is to cut off its head, which is hard to do. Vampires are strong, fast, skilled killers, which makes sense of why Adam would send us here. The million-dollar question is how did he know of these Vampires? That was the question I needed to know.

I was particularly interested if I would run into my mystery vampire while I was here, since I never got his name, but there would be no time to look for him.

I finally began walking to the castle, which had a long path between the rest of Paris and its own sanctuary. The castle was isolated, a least one mile away from anything. There was a small forest surrounding it, which possibly kept visitors out.

I reached a large black gate that was guarded by two humans to my surprise. They looked at me as if I was the first person to ever walk up here.

"Excuse me miss, I think you are lost. The road is back that way." One of the guards said. I pulled out a piece of paper that read the names of the people I came to see. "I'm here for Ruin and Alexandria. It is urgent." I said as I stood before them. "Impossible, No one sees the prince or the princess without proper invitation. I'm going to have to ask you to leave." The guard announced. "Prince and princess?" I said to myself. I looked at my watch just to realized that I wasted enough time dealing with these humans. "I'm sorry." I said as I kicked one on the guards into a tree and the other into the iron gates. I checked their pulse to make sure they were still alive, they were. "Gabriel would kill me if I killed you guys." I said looking at them. I examined the gate and prepared to kick it open until I heard multiple footsteps stomping towards me from a distance. I look up at the gate only to see it start opening. twelve guards came running down from the castle and stopped once they reached my presence. These were in fact vampires. I prepared myself for a fight until one of the guards took of his helmet. He had piercing blue eyes with long black hair. "The Princess and Prince invite you inside for brunch Madame." He said as he held out his hand. I looked around before I hesitantly took it. I was alert, but more curious than anything.

The guards escorted me into the beautiful and luxurious castle. It was more amazing than I remembered. The large ballroom had hundreds of portraits all over the walls. The marble floors and amazing architecture of the building was incredible.

"Wait here Madame, they will be with you shortly." He said as he and the other guards disappeared into another room. I stood there patiently waiting for royalty, praying in the back of my mind that I didn't have to kill anyone today.

"That was impressive what you did to my guards. Welcome." A soft velvet voice echoed from the top of a beautifully crafted staircase. I turned to face the voice only to be stunned by her mere beauty. Standing on the top of the stair case was a small woman. She couldn't be any taller than 5'2, but she was magnificent. Her breast and hips were perfect on her as she wore this gorgeous but revealing write dress that showed off her legs, stomach, and cleavage. She was as pale as my one-night stand and her hair was long, lavish, and dark blond. She looked like royalty. She smiled at the fact that I didn't say anything. She must be used to people staring at all at her sheer beauty. "I am Alexandria, Princess of King Devours of the original vampire clan. The first of our kind." She said as she glided down the stairs. "I am Natalia, I'm here representing my brother, Adam. Sorry about your guards." I said. I could see her face instantly changed once I spoke of my brother's name. "Did you say Adam?" She said as she looked at me intently. "Yes Adam." I instantly interested about their relationship.

She smiled as she looked at me. "I don't meet a lot of people, and I only know of one Adam. Tall, handsome, curly hair. Is this who you speak of?" She asked. "That described him perfectly." She smiled as stood before me. "Oh Adam, he came to me many years ago. He said that he lost his angelic divine. We tried to help him find it, but to no prevail. He claimed he was an angel. The way he looked, he might have been one." She said laughing. "Well, he has found it now. Thank you for your help. I didn't know my brother knew any vampires, especially royal ones your highness." I said trying to be formal. She looked at me and began to laugh again. "I only helped him because I thought he was mad, and quite cute actually. And what do you mean, 'he's found it?' There is no such thing as angels. Now demons, I believe in. It's a mess what has happened in Los Angeles. I knew it would be a matter of time before this world began unfolding." She said as she began walking pass me hinting I should follow. "Well I can assure you my brother wasn't 'mad' when he came to you. Angels do exist, and we are here on earth. Which is why I have come to you..." I began but was quickly interrupted. "Did you say brother?" She said stopping in her tracks. "Yes, Adam is my brother and he needs your help." She looked at me briefly. "Now I've seen a lot of different beings in my 375 years of living, but I've never seen anything close to an angel. Show me and I'll shall listen to your plea." She said as grabbed a chair to seat down and observe. "Okay, very well." I took a few steps back and spread my wings. I could feel the flames on my hair start to glow as I increased my power. Alexandria eyes were wide with awe. I let my wings take me off the ground and around her spacious ball room. "Magnificent." She said as I landed in front her. "I never thought I would see the day."

I have so many questions." She said as she examined my wings. "And I would love to answer them all on the way to America." She looked at me confusingly. "America? Why would I go to that dirty place?" She said. "Because we need your help. Have you ever heard of The Darkness?" I asked. "Of course, is that why you have come?" A manly but yet charming voice replied from behind me. The voice I have been dying to hear. I turned around to see the mysterious vampire smiling at me. He wasn't wearing a shirt, but he was wearing his crown.

"Happy for you to join us. Natalia, this is my brother and the prince, Ruin. Ruin, this is the angel, Natalia. You knew of their kind?" She asked him. "Of course. Just as I know of The Darkness." He said as he walked closer to me. "Why haven't I been informed of any of this! I have a right to know! What is The Darkness?" She demanded. "These things don't concern you my darling. You weren't informed because it's nothing you needed to know." He said so calm. "I am tired of being lied too. Being trapped in this Castle! The events in America, that's why she has come. She needs our help brother." She cried. "I will talk to her, alone." He said turning his sights on me. "But brother..." She protested only to be given a stern look. She threw him a look of disgust and she stormed away. "Don't mind her, she will be alright." He stated as he examined me. "It's good to see you again." He simply said. "I should kill you. The last time I saw you, you were feeding on an innocent man." I denounced. "Oh really, that's all you remember from our night." He said smiling. I tried my hardest to resist his charming efforts. "You are a murderer. How many innocent lives that you and your sister take every year, huh?" I asked trying my hardest to be a bitch. He began walking outside without saying anything. "Hey! I'm talking to you!" I called out following him. He picked up a beautiful rose and handed it to me. "For you." He simply said. I took it reluctantly. "Well, thank you, but it still doesn't take away all the murders you have committed." I said. "Wait, I thought you needed our help. Why would you come to murderers for help in the first-place beautiful?" He asked. He was right. Why would Adam send me here to recruit murdering vampires to help us? He wouldn't do that. "I don't know why Adam sent me here. Maybe he is desperate, but I'm not." I shouted as I started walking away. He quickly appeared in front of me with that smile as if this whole ordeal was amusing. "Get out of my way. I rather leave than to kill you." I said. "Adam was a joy to have around when he was here. I knew of his true nature and I'm the one that told him to go to the states." He said. I remained quiet. "And as for being a murderer, I am. But since the death of our father, which was over 200 years ago, my sister and I only feed on condemned murders, rapist, men who have done unspeakable crimes. Never the innocent." He explained. I looked at him instantly believing him, but still wanted to be a bitch anyways...I couldn't. "Oh… well, I'm sorry, or whatever." I said looking at the rose. "And the rose is beautiful." He smiled as he sat down on a wooden bench. I followed behind him.

"Now, I need you to tell me what is happening. I know Adam wouldn't send you if it wasn't important." He said. "Well, long story short; Adam's mate's mother released Lilith and Lilith released The Darkness upon the world. Adam sent us to find individuals that he thought would fight alongside us and you two were among the first." I said. He looked down as he grabbed every word I said. "So, The Darkness has been released? That's not good at all. Who is Adam's mate? Who is her mother?" He asked. "Her name is Melody. Her mother was an angel named Amora and her father was a demon named Damon." I responded. He looked at me in awe. "She is a Nephilim? I didn't know that they actually existed?" He asked. "We all didn't either, but she is real, and her power is limitless, but she is still learning. It's a new world for my newest sister and protecting her and destroying Lilith is our main objective." I said. "I didn't take you as the 'caring' type." I gave him an annoyed look. "I'm not. But the way Adam looks at her, it made me a believer…" I said caught in my own thoughts. "A believer in what?" The way he looked at me, I almost lost myself in his stare. "Nothing, anyways are you going to help us or not?" He smiled as he got up from his seat. "I will go to Los Angeles to help, but Alexandria must stay here. I will bring my strongest allies with me." He said. I looked at him confused by his words. "Why are you going to leave her?" I finally asked. "To protect her. There are things she is not ready for. It would be best if she stayed here in the castle." He said. I looked up at the sky and then back to Ruin. "Look, I know you are protecting her, but I remember her saying you two are the descendants from the very first vampire in creation. That makes you two pure bloods, right? I may not know everything about Vampire lore, but I know that pure blood vampires are the strongest of your kind. I knew killing you would not be an easy feat." I said smiling. "So, what is your point?" He asked. "My point is this is a battle that will decide the fate of this world. We need the absolute strongest to face the beings we must face. Your sister's power is immense. I felt it right after I awed at her beauty. I know she is well trained. We need her." I said. Ruin began pacing around. "Her strength and abilities are not an issue. Some would say she could even best me in a challenge. The issue is our father." He said. "Devorus? What about him?" I asked. He looked at the ground briefly before responding. "The reason vampires get such a bad name is because of him. He would slaughter anyone, for food, or for the sheer fun of it. He would make my sister and I do the same. He started infecting as many humans as he could, so he could have an army of his own. After the years, thousands of humans were now vampires. I couldn't let this stand, so I went looking for answers. I found a powerful Witch named Fredrick and together we banished him into the dark abyss which is known as The Darkness. If what you say is true, then Devorus is released. My sister couldn't handle seeing let along fighting him. She loved him, and he loved her dearly. After finding out what I did, she killed Fredrick and refused to talk to me for 67 years. She would never be able to face him." He said. "I will be brother." Alexandria beautiful voice cried from behind us. "I did not know the horrible things he was doing at the time. I know now, and I will be ready." She announced. Ruin smiled as they hugged one another. "Wait, if he is free, why hasn't he come here yet. It's been 2 months since The Darkness was released." Right as I said that the clouds started the turn dark. Flames instantly began to sprout from hair as I prepared myself. "You just had to say it, didn't you?" Ruin said.

"Hello Children. I missed you." The alluring voice ran a chill through my body as I turned around to face our impossible foe. His hair was jet black and his skin was pale but not as pale as all the other vampires I've met so far. There were hundreds of scars across his entire body, except on his face. He looked like Ruin but was much bigger. He was at least 7 feet with powerful bat like wings on his back. He smiled at us with a smile that assured me, He was pissed. Lucky for him, I was ready for a fight.

(Lyla) Montreal, Canada

I flew through the white clouds over the ongoing snow storm, freely enjoying myself. While my sisters got relatively harder goals, mines was on more an interesting journey. I rarely spent time alone since my time here on earth, and this was my first time, so I took the time to explore. Canada was always a place I was interested in, and ironically, this is the place where I was meant to be. My loving brother said that a man named Joshua Wolfe was here and that he could help us.

Contacting Roy and saving the day in Africa assured my sisters that I was ready for this. They were extremely overprotective over me, which mad sense since I was the youngest of us four. Adam was the most protective and would probably be highly upset if he heard I was doing this mission on my own.

I was curious about this Joshua fellow. I never heard of him, and I can only imagine what he could do for us. But if my brother believed, I certainly did.

As I landed in an abandon alley unseen by anyone, I noticed a sense of panic in the streets. People were running, and cars were going way past their speed limits as the flew to their destination. I could only imagine the worst.

"Excuse me sir, what has transpired?" I asked a passerby. He would've ignored me if I was a human, but it's something about us angels that no matter what, humans always seem to drop everything to talk to us.

"Umm, there's been an attack in America. It's the end of the world. Excuse me." He said as he blew right past me. I could only think of my sisters and Melody at this point. I know it had something to do with them. I ran to a nearby Best Buy, so I could look at the televisions. I figured what ever happened, had to be playing on every single one. I was correct. "Oh my!" I said to myself as I looked in horror. Thousands of demons flooding the streets in broad daylight. Gabriel and Melody in full view of it all. So, wonder the humans think it's the end of the world. It would be soon if we didn't stop it. I figured now was the best time to find this mystery man.

Lucky enough, Joshua was the only one on Adams list that had an address, so finding him shouldn't be difficult. I flew to 3701 W. Hirshall street only to find an old beat up trailer with a broken mailbox that read the exact address. It looks like mail hasn't come here in years by the cobwebs present in it. I walked up to the door and took a deep breath trying to get all my words right. I knocked on the door lightly, hoping I wouldn't have to knock again. I waited for what seems like days...silence. I peeked through the window only to see a man laid out on the couch sleep. "I don't have time for this." I said as I knocked on his door louder, trying my hardest not to break it. "Okay, okay, I'm coming!" I could hear him say. "Who are you little girl?" I heard a female voice come from behind me. I turned to face her only to see a guy standing beside her. They both looked dingy and dirty as if they been in the woods all night. The girl had short black hair, wide eyes and an unreadable face. She was wearing a dirty tank top, some black shorts and boots. The guy with her had light brown hair, little eyes, and a goatee. He wasn't wearing any shirt, but he had torn up style jeans and black boots as well. I found both of their outfits odd since it was at least 35 degrees outside.

"Aren't you guys cold?" I couldn't help myself to ask. They both looked at each other and laughed. awkwardly, I giggled with them. They saw this and immediately stopped.

"Woah, I didn't order any hookers today but, damn, they never look this good. What are we talking two hundred?" The loud drunk man from inside the trailer said as he opened the door. I was so positive that he was not talking to me.

"Excuse me?" I said trying to keep calm. He smiled at me with an inviting grin. He was tall, at least 6'5. He was also in shape, but not gym shape. It looks like he got his muscles from lifting logs up and down. He had a head filled with short black curly hair and he had a beautiful beard that took up most of his face. He had no shirt on or no pants. He came to the door with only his boxer briefs. "You are one fine piece of ass! Who sent you here, Monty? Oh. tell that son of a bitch thank you!" He said as he smacked my ass. My face turn red. "How dare you!" I said as I pulled my hand back and drove my hand across his face. I didn't know how mad I was or how hard I hit him until he flew through right through his trailer, creating a large hole that I felt couldn't be repaired. The man and the woman behind me began to walk towards me but with a quick glance, they instead went to the aid to their jerk of a friend. I slapped him at least 30 feet. He probably would have gone further if he didn't land on a tree in the woods.

"Is he dead?" I asked. as I finally approached him. He opened his eyes and smiled. "Well, I got to say...you have one hell of a slap." He said as he spat out blood and wiped his face. "That's impossible, how did she do that to you Jay?" The man asked him. He looked at me as he got up. "That's a damn good question. Who are you?" He finally asked. I looked at all three of them before answering. "My name is Lyla. Can we sit down?" I asked. He looked at me then back to his trailer. "Well, I would ask you to come inside, but you knocked a huge hole in my trailer!" He screamed. "Well you should learn to keep your hands to yourself!" I screamed back. He cracked his neck and walked back in his trailer only to come out fully dressed. "Did you drive?" He asked me. "No, I flew." I instantly replied. He looked at me as if he wanted to say something then changed his thoughts. "Right, well I've seen stranger things happen today." He said as he walked to this old red pickup truck. "Get in." He instructed me. His demeanor was beyond rude and arrogant. "Excuse me?" I said standing my ground. "Stop being complicated and just get in. We can go somewhere in town and talk." He said as he held the door open for me. I stood there for a few seconds before surrendering. "Okay fine." I entered the truck. "I'll be back before dinner." he called out the window as he drove away.

The ride was quiet. I caught him looking at me a few times, but he didn't say anything. "What the fuck is going on out here!" He said as he maneuvered pass cars driving wild. "Haven't you seen the news?" I asked. He throws me a glance of disgust. "I don't watch T.V." He simply said. I looked at him in confusion. "What do you mean, *you don't watch T.V.?* What do you do then?" I asked sincerely curious. "None of your business. I should kill you for slapping me in the first place. I'm wondering in my head what the hell you are. I know you are not of my kind...I would've smelled you a mile away." He said. "So, he wasn't human?" I thought to myself. "So, what exactly is your kind." I asked. He stopped the trunk. "We are here." He said as he got out. I looked up to see a place called "Whiskey Business." I tried my hardest to keep my composure. "Really? A bar? You take me to bar?" I said. He walked to the entrance and opened the door. "What? You are too good for this place? Well I don't care! I just got slapped through my trailer. I need a drink." He replied as he disappeared into the building. I stomped my feet in frustration before following him inside.

The place was dimly lit. I could tell it wasn't the most popular in Canada by the cheap barstools and grimy appearance. "Four shots of jack, Tim." He said as he sat down. I remained standing. "Sit down, let's get this over it." He said inviting me to sit down. I reluctantly sat down and watched him drink all four shots. "You want something?" He asked me surprisingly. "No, I'm fine." I replied. He smiled and called the bar tender back over. "Give this young lady a shot too." He asked. The bartender smiled and poured another glass and slide it in front of me. "Drink, or I'm not talking to you about anything." He said. I could feel my face getting red again. How dare he try to trick me into drinking with him. "Oh my God, you are such a ... such a ...JERK!" I said as I took the awful shot. I didn't know how Adam drank this stuff. "A jerk, really? That's all you got?" He laughed. I was pissed, I wanted to slap him again. The day was still young.

"Okay, who are you? What are you? And what do you want from me." He asked frankly. "Well like I said earlier, my name is Lyla. I'm an angel sent here by my brother Adam to ask for your help to save the world." He looked at me. "Okay I'll bite, so you are an angel. That could explain why you hit so hard. I'm not the brightest man in the world, but I know angels are supposed to have wings, right?" He said in his usual asshole matter. "I do have wings, I can choose when I want to show them." I said. The news was showing the footage from Los Angeles, which managed to catch his eye. "Holy shit! Is this real!?" He screamed as he turned up the volume. "Yes, that's where we should be right now!" I said. He looked at me as if I was crazy. "Are you serious? Look at those things! And plus, I can't go to America. I don't have a passport. And another thing, Who the hell is Adam?" He went on. I could feel my patience running thin with this idiot. Where did my brother find him? "What do you mean you don't have a passport? Forget the passport, the entire world may not be here tomorrow! And this is Adam..." I said as I showed him a picture on my phone. He looked at it and then smiled. "Wow, it's been years since the last time we bumped heads. No one could out drink me. No body but him; that sorry son of a bitch." He said as he thought about old memories. "Believe it or not, he was an angel too. And he has asked me to ask you to fight with us. So, could you please? We don't have a lot of time left." He stood up and dug in his pocket. "Adam was a great friend of mine. He helped me a lot through the years. I just need to know what we are fighting and how do we kill them." He said. I stood up as I watched the television. "Well, those are demons that you see on T.V., and killing them is easy. Rip them apart. But I need to know, what exactly are you? Why would my brother want to recruit you? From all I see, you are just big jerk who could take a punch from an angel and not die." I said as I walked out the bar. He ran up to my side smiling. "Oh really? Well your brother knows me. He knows what I'm capable of, and he knows not a lot of things can stand toe to toe with me. And just for that I'm going to show you little girl a sample." He said as he took off his clothes. I looked at him in confusion. "What are you doing?" I bluntly ask. He was a huge jerk and buffoon, but I couldn't deny his body. "Shut up and just watch." I felt like slapping him again. He stood there briefly then suddenly, he transformed into a giant black wolf in broad daylight. He stood on his hind legs which took him to a height of at least 10 feet. He was huge and intimidating. He just looked at me as he walked closer to me. Without knowing it, I was backed into a corner. He growled at me, which caused me to jump. "Get back before I hurt you for real this time." I warned. He growled at me again, but this time he attempted to pounce on me. I instantly spread my wings and flew out of the corner and behind him.

"What the hell?!" I screamed. He stood there and just like that, turned back to himself. "What were you trying to do!? I screamed at him. He stood there completely naked as he laughed at me. He took a cigarette out his pockets and placed his clothes back on back on. "I wanted to see your wings. Now that I know you are what you say you are, we should be hitting the road. We got a long drive ahead of us." He said as he got in the car. I looked at him baffled once again. "What do you mean, ride? You are taking a plane." I announced. "Umm no, I can't fly, it makes me sick to my stomach. And I'm not driving all alone, so WE are driving." He demanded. "No, no, no... I am not going to sit in a car with you for 2 days straight. It's not going to happen. Take one of your werewolf buddies." I demanded. "No! Then I'm not going...That's the only way." I wanted to kill him, I really did. "Don't talk to me, don't even look at me okay?" I demanded as I got in the truck. "Yeah yeah, whatever." He said as he attempted to start the truck. "And I'm driving." I said as I took the keys out the ignition. "Okay, whatever!"

I started the truck and we were off on a long grueling trip to Los Angeles. "My name is Joshua by the way. For future reference." He said holding out his hand. "Didn't I tell you not to talk to me." I repeated. He smiled and shook his head. "Who's the jerk now...?" he uttered. I turned my head, so he couldn't see a glimpse of my smile. I wanted to remain hating him until this ride was over; an impossible feat indeed.

Chapter 16
Destiny

(Melody)

I could feel Gabriel's eyes on me as we flew to Adrian and Scarlett's home. Eyes of worry. My body was tired and needed to rest so I figured it would be best to relax and calculate a plan of some sort. I thought about everything as I flew through the skies. I never thought this would be my life, but I wasn't afraid as I once was. I have family and friends to protect, but most importantly, my child.

I was still being tormented by the words of Demetri, still trying to grasp what he implied. That Adrian was my brother; twin brother to be exact. When I looked at him, I saw myself, but I couldn't put into reality. I know he probably hates me right now, and I wouldn't blame him if he did. We just came and destroyed his life, and got his friend seriously hurt. I know how it feels to have your life twisted upside down. I still remember the moment Adam came in my life. Ironically, if he didn't come in when he did, I would probably be dead. When Gabriel and I found Adrian, he was in a demonic war with a demon and his girlfriend was in a coma. Maybe us coming wasn't such a burden.

"Wait Melody." Gabriel said as we landed in front of Adrian and Scarlett's home. I looked at her with wide eyes knowing exactly what she was going to say. She walked up closer to me and looked at my stomach as she places a hand on it. "How could I not have known that you were pregnant? How could I not know about your twin? I am so useless." She said as she looked down in shame. "Gabriel, no, you are amazing. There was too much going on, and you been so busy...I was going to tell you when it was all done." I said. She looked at me as if my words carried no value. I felt bad not telling her. "We have to get you back to Zachariah's. There you would be safe." She said. "No Gabriel, that's why I didn't want to tell you. This is my fight. I can't sit on the sidelines." She gave me a stern look. "Does Adam know?" I looked at her without speaking. "You haven't spoken to him about it?" She asked. "I can't.

Wherever he is at, I can't reach him. Plus, he is busy working hard, I don't want to bother him in his training." I said as I began to walk in the house before Gabriel grabbed my arm. "Melody, my dear sister. I can't, or I won't let anything happen to you or the child." She said sincerely. I loved Gabriel. Her words were so real. "I know Gabriel, I love you too. But please don't tell anybody. Not Natalie, not Lyla, and definitely not Adam. Just let me do it okay?" I asked. She nodded unwillingly.

I noticed that the front door was off the hinges as I entered. The living room looks as a fight was present earlier. "Please come in. I have a bed upstairs for Carmen. Please help her!" Scarlett implored. Adrian carried an unconscious Carmen in the house. Gabriel grabbed her body from him effortlessly.

"Of course, Scarlett. You friend will survive, but she will need a lot of rest." Gabriel declared. Scarlett nodded as she showed us where to lay her down. I loved when Gabriel used her amazing gifts. She placed her hand on Carmen for a moment, then she stood up and observe her. "Yes. she will be fine." Scarlett smiled as she held Carmen's hand. "I told you girl. You are going to be just fine. Now stay up here and rest. When you wake up, all of this craziness will be over." Scarlett said to a sleeping Carmen. Gabriel and I smiled to one another, satisfied that we saved her life. "Thank you. Thank you for everything." She said with such emotion, that I knew Carmen meant a lot to her. "It our pleasure, it's the very least we can do. I know this must all be so strange for you. I am sorry." I respond. Scarlett looks back at her friend. "I have a million questions, but my mind is a blank. I'm just glad Carmen is going to be okay." She said. "You guys are good people with good hearts. When you have lived a life like Adrian and I, you can tell the good ones immediately." She said as she turned her attention towards the doorway.

Adrian walked in the room with his two pistols. "Melody, can I talk to you in private?" He asked. I looked at Scarlett as her eyes went to Adrian. "I need to talk to her baby, give me a few minutes." He said to Scarlett as he walked out the room and out the front door. "I gave him a 'you better behave' look, so you will be fine." Scarlett said as she smiled at me. "Is he always this tense?" I asked. Scarlett laughed instantly. "He will lighten up. Oh, and Melody?"
"Yes?"

"I hope you and Adrian are brother and sister. He could use some family other than me. We both could." Scarlett said as she sat down next to Carmen. I smiled at her words, hoping that maybe it could be true. "Gabriel, let me know our next move. We won't be able to rest for long." I said. "Of course." I walked downstairs and followed an awaiting Adrian on his front porch.

Adrian sat at the end of his stair way and just looked up at the sky. "I never thought in my life that I would be standing here really thinking about demons, angels, and a sister I never thought existed. Help me understand what is happening with me." He asked calmly. I was stunned at his vulnerability, for the simple fact that ever since I met him, he has been the complete opposite. I took a seat at the bottom of his steps right next to him. "Almost a year ago, I was a normal girl with a normal life. I got into a car accident and almost died, until a stranger rescued me. My soulmate rescued me. Turns out that stranger turned out to be an angel. Meeting him and entering his life ultimately awoken my true self. I was afraid, I was angry, and I was forced to be a part of this war because I ultimately started it. I know exactly how you feel, but looking at you, I can see that you have a lot more fight in you. A lot more acceptance of what's going on. How long have you known Scarlett?" I asked curious. He smiled, the first smile I seen him do. "I've known Scarlett for my whole life. Our parents were best friends and got pregnant at the same time, or so that was the story. Now I feel my life is a lie." He said not looking at me. I placed my hand on my brother's shoulder. "Trust me Adrian, I know. Our birth parents were monsters. I'm so glad that you didn't get a chance to meet them; but our real parents are the ones who took care of us. How are your parents? I have a few more sisters and a mother I want you to meet."

Adrian gave me a weak smile before answering. "My parents are dead. I just buried my mother yesterday." He said. His eyes were just like mine, but with so much pain. "I'm so sorry Adrian." I said as I consoled him. Scarlett walked out and sat down with us. I could see the love between them. It was beautiful.

"Now, it's just Scar and I." He said as he kissed her forehead. I smiled at them and grabbed both of their hands. "No, you have us now." I said smiling. We sat on the stairs for a while just in thought. I thought a lot. I thought about how much Adrian has already lost. I thought about the fact that I had a brother. I thought about Adam and how much I truly missed him. Then I thought about something that I should have asked to myself...How did Adam's mysterious and so-called guardian angel know about Adrian, and did she know he was my brother? I couldn't wait to see this person just to grill her with questions.

We sat outside for a long period in silence, just thinking to ourselves. I knew Adrian would need time to process the changes of his life and future just as I did. Gabriel finally made her way outside and sat with us. "I just got off the phone with Natalia and Lyla. They both found who they were looking for and will be in route as soon as possible." Gabriel said. I nodded at her.

The beautiful blue sky caught my attention. There were so many clouds. My mother used to tell me that cloudy days meant good luck. I sure wished that she was right today.

"Demetri, what does he want? I don't understand his motives completely." Scarlett asked. I stood up trying to think of a great answer. "I feel he wants to do what they tried to do with me; turn Adrian into a weapon. Utilize his power for whatever they planned." I responded. "But why would I ever fight for a demon? I know I'm fucked up, but I would never stoop that low." Adrian interrupted. "True, but what is the most important thing to you in this world? They will take Scarlett and force you to do whatever they tell you too. This is how demons work." Gabriel said. Scarlett moved closer to Adrian, holding him tighter. "Maybe we should take her to Zachariah's? She would be safe there." I offered. Adrian's face quickly changed. "I can't leave her." Adrian simply said. "It's dangerous for Scarlett. They will come after her above everything." I said. Scarlett looked at us then to Adrian. "I will go, but only if Melody comes with me." She said as she placed her hand on my stomach. "Your baby needs just as much protection as I do." She said. I couldn't say anything. If this was the only way to keep Scarlett safe, then I had no choice. "Okay. We will go together." I said. Adrian stood up to look at us all. "And are you all sure that is a safe place?" Adrian asked. "Zachariah has a hideaway in Brazil, no demon could ever find it." I assured him. Zachariah's hideout was our best bet, but I soon began to think about Ariel and his all the information that he knew about us. He could have easily told Lilith about Brazil, but if that was the case, they would have come months ago. I may be with child, but I had plenty of enough power if they ever did decide to come after Scarlett.

"Then it is done." Adrian said as he kissed Scarlett on her forehead. Gabriel smiled at the two and then walked toward me. "They remind me so much of you and Adam. I miss him dearly. Have you heard from him?" She asked me as I gazed upon Adrian and Scarlett's union as well, thinking solely of the fact I would do whatever it took to keep them safe. My very own lost brother and his beautiful girlfriend were my family, and I was blessed for that.

"Melody!?" A surprising voice interrupted my thoughts from behind me. "Victoria? How? What are you doing here?" I asked shocked by her presence. "I saw what happened on the news, I wanted to make sure you were okay. It looked really bad." She said. "Yeah, it was pretty intense...oh hello?" I said shifting my focus to her friend I haven't got a chance to meet. She looked at all of us and stared in amazement. "Only one of you is a human being, I think." She said looking at all of us. She then came to me. "I'm sorry, I never been around real angels before. I'm a little clustered for words, I'm Dawn DeLorean. Pleasure to meet you." She said as she took out her hand. I smiled as I shook her hand. "Pleasure to meet you too." I said looking at Victoria. "I couldn't stop her. She was advent of coming."

Victoria said changing her sights on everyone else. "Hey Gabriel? Have you been talking care of my sister while Adam's away?" She said as she held her. "Of course, How has your training been going? Gabriel asked. "Great, I have been learning quite quickly." She said but I could see her eyes lock on Adrian and Scarlett. "I don't think we have had the chance to meet. I'm Victoria, Melody's older sister." Adrian's face quickly looked at mine then back to Victoria. "I'm Adrian, and this is my fiancé, Scarlett. Apparently, Melody is my twin sister. Small world huh?" Adrian announced. Victoria examined him then fixed her eyes on me. I smiled as I saw her face. "It is true. Amora, the woman who wanted to kill us all, had twins. Adrian is my brother." Victoria was amazed. "Oh my God! Our family just keeps getting bigger! Hey, my new brother!" These were the things Victoria loved. I knew she would embrace him the moment she sat eyes on him. He was one of us. A survivor.

Scarlett smiled at the beautiful scene. Adrian was speechless. I could tell he wasn't good at accepting love, but he would learn too dealing with us. We are too lovey dovey. "Come here girl, you are part of this too!" Victoria said as she pulled Scarlett into her arms as well. "Oh, wow! Thank you!" Scarlett said barely getting her words out. I wrapped my arms around Gabriel as we witnessed the moment. Finally, something to smile about.

Dawn walked up to Adrian and just stared as if she was trying to figure him out. "Umm, excuse me?" Scarlett said as Dawn continued to examine him. "Why are you concealing your power?" Dawn simply said. "What?" He said as he began to look around. Dawn closed her eyes and held one of Adrian's hands. We all looked at her in awe, unaware of what would happen next. The sky suddenly got black and a large thunderbolt hit the ground. Dawn opened her eyes and the sky turned back to normal. "What the fuck was that?!" Adrian said as he opened his eyes in what looked like a state of panic and maybe even fear. "That is your fate if you decide to not embrace your power..." Dawn said as she walked away from him. Adrian jumped up and ran in the house. Scarlett looked puzzled for I think she has never seen Adrian like this. "What did you do? What are you?" She asked. Dawn turned around and faced Scarlett. "I used my power to help him unleash his true potential. I gave him a glimpse of his upcoming future if he doesn't use it." She said looking unbothered. "What an interesting first impression." I said to Gabriel as she just looked among us. Scarlett was furious as she reached for one of her pistols. "Wait Scarlett!" Victoria cried as she jumped in between them. "They are witches. Dawn used her power to nelp unlock Adrian's untapped power. She could have warned us first though." Gabriel said, finally stepping in. "Dawn, if you are going to be here, you need to control yourself. Your self-esteem and ego will certainly get you killed in this battle." I said as I stood side by side by Gabriel.

We all entered the house together. All eyes were turned on an Adrian. Something was certainly different about him, but his posture was normal. "Adrian!" Scarlett said as she ran in his arms. "I'm okay Scar." he said as he kissed her forehead. He released her and walked toward Dawn. We all stood in silence, even Scarlett, she didn't even try to stop him. Dawn stood still, unaware of what was about to happen. "I don't know what you did but thank you." He said. Dawn looked at him, shocked at his response...I'm sure everyone thought the same thing. "Just trying to help." Dawn said as she kept her composure. Adrian smiled and turned back to face the group. "So... what is the plan?"

Chapter 16
Mission: Impossible

(Natalia)

I stared at Devorus, unafraid. My fist was clinched, and my legs were ready to charge after him, but as I stood there, I noticed Ruin and Alexandria were not on my left or right. I turn around to witness them behind me, looking at their awaken father in awe. Ruin's eyes looked as if he was looking at a ghost.

"It's good to see you Ruin." He crudely said as he stood there emotionless. I was unable to read his face, nor was I able to read his motive. He spoke so calmly, as if he wasn't a prisoner for hundreds of years.

Ruin said nothing, but he did move to my side as if talking was not an option between them. I could see the utter rage and hate within his eyes. "Alexandria, my love. Look at you. Just as beautiful as I remembered. Your mother would be so proud." Devorus said as he began to walk closer to us. To my surprise, Alexandria began to walk ahead of us towards him. "Alexandria!" Ruin called out only to be dismissed by her hand. "I knew you were still my little girl." He said as he opened his arms for her.

"Mother would be proud...If she was still alive." Alexandria said as Devorus held her in his arms. Ruin and I looked at her in awe. "She must have a plan, right?" I whispered in Ruin's ear. "If I know my sister, she definitely does." He assured me. Looking at them I wasn't fully convinced.

"I miss your mother too, my love." He said. Alexandria smiled. "You murdered her. father. You murdered thousands. All for your own sick pleasure. I once believed in the things you told me because I loved you. I even killed for you. You have deceived me for the last time." Alexandria said as she kissed her father on the cheek. "Alexandria?" Devorus said confused. Alexandria drove her fangs into the neck of Devorus causing him to wail in agony. I watched in amazement as the powerful Devorus fell to his knees as Alexandria continued to rip through his flesh with her teeth. Devorus face turned from pain to anger as he flung her towards us. His blood was still evident on her mouth as Ruin lifted her up.

"Foolish girl. Your brother was too weak to live out his destiny, but I had high hopes for you. How disappointing." He said as his wounded neck began to heal instantly. "You are the disappointment my dear father." Alexandria said as she spit out parts of his flesh. He smiled at us briefly before charging at us. I grounded myself as I flew to the sky dodging his attack. The air was cold and unviting as I looked down upon them. I could feel the flames erupting down my hair as I flew at a remarkable speed towards our common enemy. Ruin and Alexandria were amazed as my flames became evident throughout our battlefield. "Get out the way!" I screamed to Ruin and Alexandria as I set my sights on Devorus. Ruin smiled as he kicked Devorus away from Alexandria and himself, positioning Devorus right where I wanted him. Without a single word, I ejected as many flames as I could, fully engulfing his body and everything around him. The flames were so hot, Ruin and Alexandria retreated towards me to stay away from the crossfire. I could hear Devorus wailing and screaming as the flames devoured his skin. "Look." Ruin said as he pointed at the no longer visible Devorus. I stopped my onslaught only to see the burned rumble of my attack, but no Devorus. I smiled at my success as I flew down to join Ruin and Alexandria.

"I'm sorry. I got carried away." I said as I continued to look at the damage I created. They remained quite as they too examined the torched area. "It looks like I burned him to ashes. No way he could regenerate after all that." I said as I turned and began walking back to the castle. "We need to get to America immediately, there are other enemies that we must kill, and we lack time." I continued only to realize that Ruin or Alexandria wasn't following me. "What is it?" I asked turning to face them. Ruin looked at Alexandria and then to me.

"He escaped. He is still alive." Ruin said as he walked towards me. Alexandria dropped a piece of rumble she was holding and followed her brother. "Wait, how is that possible? I torched him until there was nothing left. Where could he have escaped too?" I asked in confusion. "He has powers that even we don't understand. I can still feel his pulse. He far away from here now. I have no idea how, but he is still very much alive." Alexandria said sadly. "How could he survive that, let alone escape from it?" I wondered to myself. I should've known a vampire king would be entirely more difficult to kill.

We entered their castle only to be greeted by at least 50 guards. "Sir, Madame, I have gathered our strongest vampires..." One of the guards said. Ruin nodded as he walked passed them. "Do you know any of the other beings released from The Darkness besides Lilith and my father?" Ruin asked as we continued to walk through the castle. "The demon that destroyed parts of Los Angeles. I don't really know too much information on him." I said as we reached a large door. "I asked because Devorus is hurt, he is going to seek refuge. He knows that he cannot defeat us on his own..." He said. "So, what are you saying?" I asked. "I'm saying we need to find this demon before he does." Ruin said as he opened a giant door leading to a walkway on the roof. "Wait a minute, You guys have a private jet?" I said as stared at the beautiful plane sitting on their roof. Alexandria laughed as she brushed pass me. "We are royalty, remember? We have an abundance of money." She said as she entered the plane. "We must be quick about this. You are coming right?" Ruin asked me as he stuck out his hand. "I think I could fly faster than your beautiful jet sir." I said jokingly. He smiled as he grabbed my hand so softly. I could feel my face begin to blush, which I hated. "You want to make a bet? Just come with us. I would love your company." He said smiling. "Okay, you convinced me. I'll go...but just because I need to make sure you guys get there." I said as I entered the plane.

"We should be there in a few hours, the engine on this thing is fantastic. Ruin said as he patted the pilot on the back signaling him to take off. The plane was even more beautiful inside. Alexandria sat next to me while Ruin sat in the seat across from us. "Here." Alexandria said as she handed me a glass of red wine. I took a sip only to notice I was being spied on by Ruin. I continued to ignore his beautiful stare.

The plane took off quickly and within minutes we were in the air. I couldn't help to think about my dear sisters, including Melody. I had no idea what type of trouble they were in. I knew Ruin and Alexandria would be great assets to our 'supergroup' of beings to help us fight. I also wondered about Adam and his whereabouts. He always made great decisions, so I knew he would return when we really need him. As I focused on my thoughts, I could see Ruin getting up from his seat and moving towards me.

"That fire trick, how did you do that? I never seen an angel possess such abilities." He simply said. Alexandria turned her head slightly to ease in on the conversation. I guess she was as curious as he was. "Well, ever since the beginning of my existence, I've always been interested in fire, or the creation of it. I just picked up the abilities over the thousands of years. My fire abilities strengthen as my anger increases, so don't piss me off." I stated as I sipped another sip of wine. "I definitely can tell that you have a temper...I can see why my brother likes you." Alexandria said as she got up from her seat to get another drink. "That's not entirely true." He said confidently. I just looked at him, but before I could say anything, I noticed something else out the plane window.

"Get down!" I screamed as something flew into the plane causing all the outside air pressure to come in the plane. The plane instantly began to descend as Ruin, Alexandria, and myself started to fall towards the ground. I ejected my wings and flew toward my Alexandria until I was stopped by a winged being attacked me. Looking at its face assured me it was a demon, so I wasted no time tearing it apart. I could see Ruin and Alexandria ripping apart all the demons that came their way as they fell towards the ground. I hurried and grabbed Ruin as he grabbed Alexandria, saving them from a great fall.

"What were those?" Alexandria asked as she brushed off her clothes. "Demons." I said watching as our plane crashed in a field about a mile from us. The explosion was overwhelming to say the least. I looked around to see where we were at exactly...I got nothing. "Where are we?" I finally asked. Ruin looked around the vacant area before answering. "We are about 250 miles away from home. There's a small town up the road we could regroup at." He said pointing toward its location. I looked wearily towards it direction. "Let's go before more of them show." I said as I began to walk in toward the town. Ruin and Alexandria's faces were beyond calm, which I thought it was unusual. "We been through our share of battles Natalia. Don't worry about us." Ruin said as if he was reading my mind. "I can see it in your eyes." I simply said. "Our father must be killed. I am determined to hunt him down. I know he sent those beasts after us." Ruin simply said. I was surprised by his demeanor. This was a different vampire, this was a fighter. "Just when I thought I couldn't get more attracted to him." I said to myself.

(Lyla)

I tried my absolute hardest to not utter a word, but Joshua made sure that wasn't going to happen. The moment we pulled off, he began talking in his annoying and slight cocky manner. Restraining myself was my only issue at this point.

"Where are we now?" He asked for 20th time. "We are about to cross into America. Let me do all the talking, okay?" I insisted. He smiled as he pulled out a pack of Starburst from his pockets. "I wasn't planning on talking anyways. Just remember that I don't have a passport." I looked at him with a blank stare. "Me neither. Just hush for a second." I said as we pulled up to the gate. "Hello miss, passports?" The man at the gate asked. I smiled I looked at the man. "Just let us through the gate. It's quite an emergency." I simply said. The man's eyes got wide as he looked at us. "Of course, ma'am, safe travels." He said as he waved us to go through. I smiled and hit the gas, not bothering to look back.

"What the hell was that!?" Joshua said completely stunned. "It's an angel trick." I simply said not looking at him. "So, you have mind control over people? Is that why I decided to go with you on this road trip?" He asked as he placed another Starburst in his mouth. "No, it only works on weaker human minds. Trust me, if it worked on you, this would've been a quieter ride." I said smiling to myself. "Someone has jokes I see." He said as pulled his chair lower as if he was finally deciding to take a rest. "I have a question? Why did that son of a bitch brother of yours send you instead of coming himself? It would have been nice to see him." He asked. "Well, he is training somewhere for this fight. He will be with us soon. How do you two even know each other." I asked. "We used to work at a lumberyard years ago. He was one of the strongest people I ever known. We used to wrestle almost every day after work. He was also the only person I know that could drink me under the table. He found out what I was and never told anyone. We been friends ever since." He said. Adam's time on this planet must have been eventful. I couldn't even imagine my brother working in a lumberyard. "Did he ever tell you what he was?" I asked. "Nope, never. I should've known something was up with him though. I just never put two and two together. Even if I did believe he was something else besides human, an angel would have been my farthest guess." He said as he placed another piece of candy in his mouth. I smiled at him as he spoke about Adam, only making me miss my brother more. I can't wait until this whole ordeal was over.

I pulled in an empty gas station and parked the car. "I'll be right back." I said as I exited the truck and walked towards the front door. "Lyla?" An unfamiliar voice said behind my back. I turned to see a woman with dark red hair and menacing eyes. I took a closer look only to see that she wasn't a woman at all. "Who are you?" I demanded. "Hey, is there a problem ma'am?" The cashier asked as he stared at us. "No problem. Can you put 30 on pump 5 and exit the store." I said with my eyes still locked on this mysterious woman. The man placed the gas on the pump and ran out the store just as instructed. "Now, who are you!?" I repeated myself. She just smiled as she walked closer to me. "My name is Evelyn. I had the pleasure of running into your lovely sisters. I couldn't help myself to meet the baby of the group. I can't believe they chose to leave you all alone." She said as she examined me. "You underestimate me." I said as I punched her in her face causing her to fly into an aisle of juice and soda. Her clothes were soaked, and her face was furious. "Why you little..." She said as she kicked me out the window. "What the hell!" I could hear Joshua yell as he exited the truck and helped me up. "Demon!" I said pointing towards the store. Evelyn walked out slowly cracking her neck. "Finally, some action!" Joshua said as he began taking off his shirt and shoes. "Who is your little friend and what exactly is he doing?" She said looking puzzled. "Transforming." I said as I looked at Joshua. He smiled as he transformed into a huge wolf. "What the...?" Evelyn said as Joshua pounced her. I quickly ran behind him in an all-in attack. Joshua managed to clamp his jaws on her neck. Evelyn screamed in agony. Her wings began to sprout as she took to the sky with Joshua. "Oh no!" I said as I sprouted my wings and followed them in the sky. Joshua's grip began to weaken as Evelyn reached higher limits. She finally shook him off and Joshua's body began descending from the sky. I caught him effortlessly and placed him on the ground. I looked back in the sky only to see that the wounded Evelyn was nowhere to be found. "Damn." I said trying to find where she went. "I got her scent. She is long gone." I turned to see a shirtless Joshua standing looking up in the sky. "She said she ran into my sisters. We have to move." I said as I got back in the truck. Joshua pumped the gas and we drove away from the utterly damaged gas station.

Chapter 17
Fate

(Adrian)

      As I looked among the group, I couldn't help to notice my intense new power surging within me. Scarlett looked at me as if she could feel it herself. My hatred for my enemy was grand and I felt no one or nothing could stop me from the onslaught I was prepared to bring.

      "Baby?" Scarlett said distracting my current thoughts. I grabbed her waist and pulled her close to me. Her body was warm and vibrate, exactly how it always is. I wasn't excited about her going to Brazil, especially since I don't know this Zachariah personally, But I was willing to do anything to keep my fiancé safe.

      "It is time." Gabriel said referring to Melody and Scarlett's departure. Melody nodded and walked towards me.

      "It's going to be okay. I promise." She said looking at Scarlett, then to me. I nodded as I kissed Scarlett's forehead and released her from my arms. She looked up at me, eyes filled with water. It was a look I never seen before. It was a look that did' assure me if we would see each other again. "I will come for you. No matter what happens." I said passionately. She smiled and grabbed my face. "You better, because if you don't I will find you and kill you myself." I laughed as I looked her in the eyes. "I love you Scar." She looked at me effortlessly. "I love you Adrian, come back to me." She said as she kissed my lips. It was the deepest kiss I ever felt.

      "I'll see you soon." Scarlett said as she walked away towards Melody. Melody smiled at me as Scarlett stood by her side. I smiled back at her, which is unusual because I only smile around Scarlett. Victoria and Gabriel both gave their goodbyes as I stood there still staring intently at Scarlett. Melody spread her wings and for the first time I notice that they were not white like Gabriel's or black like the demons we fought, but it was more of a greyish color. Melody smiled at me one last time as her and Scarlett disappeared in the sky. I stood there, starring at the sky even after they were long gone.

"Gabriel?" I called to her. She stopped whatever she was doing and came to my question. "What is it Adrian?" She asked in such a concerned manner. "Why is Melody's wings a different color than everything I've seen so far? Will my wings be that color also?" I asked. "Well, You and Melody are called Nephilim's. Meaning you are the child of a demon and an angel. This means that you have a darkness within you as well as a lightness. They are at constant battle within your body. Melody was on the verge of death, so she made a sacrifice to regain her power and reach powers she never knew she had. She tapped into her dark energy, which cause her wings to turn black. Over time, she has learned to control her power, causing her wings to take on both colors." Gabriel explained. "Do I have this power too?" I asked. She looked at me with bold eyes. "Yes, and we are going to need you more than ever since Melody is not here." She said. I looked around at our team. "How strong was Melody?" I asked catching everyone's attention. "She is the strongest of us all." Gabriel said looking me in my eyes. I was speechless at the power my sister had. I had no idea that she possesses such abilities. I looked at my hands only to except that this power was mine as well. I just had to figure out how to use it.

"This demon, Demetri, is powerful, but he isn't the only one of the released beings. He will be the one we will go after first." Gabriel announced. "What about your sisters and the ones that Adam chose? Shouldn't we wait for them?" Victoria asked. "We have no time, he could be anywhere. We must strike now. Our powers combined will certainly over power him." I was beyond ready to kill the son of a bitch more than they were.

"How do we find him?" I asked. Gabriel looked at Victoria and Dawn. "Finding a full fledge demon isn't going to be easy." Victoria said as she looked at us. "Yeah, it won't be an easy task at all, but I'm sure with our combined magic, we could do it. but it will take a few hours. Can we use your home?" Dawn asked me. I nodded. "Do whatever you have to do. This is my number. I'll be right back." I said I walked around the house to the garage. I started up my mom's car and sped off without looking back. Gabriel didn't bother trying to stop me as if she knew where I was going.

I drove down the empty damaged streets with ease and stopped where my damaged car was. Looking at it beat up like this only made me hate this whole thing even more. I picked up the pistols that Gabriel blessed and checked them to make sure they weren't damaged. They weren't. "I'm going to need these." I said to myself as I began walking back until I heard something behind me. I immediately turned around and aimed my pistols directly in front of me only to be amazed at what I saw. My car was fully restored. I couldn't believe what I was seeing right now. I stepped closer to make sure this wasn't an illusion. It wasn't. It was my car. "Do you like it?" I turned to see a woman standing with long black curly hair down her back. She was wearing a red dress and smiling at me. She looked as if she knew me.

"Did you do this to my car?" I asked still pointing my guns at her. "Yes, do you like?" She asked without moving. "What are you, and how did you do that!" I asked. "I'm an Angel and I'm here to help you. We don't have a lot of time, so we must go Adrian." She said as she got in the passenger side of my newly rebuilt car. I hesitated briefly, but something about her made me trust her. I hopped in the driver's seat and started it up. "Where are we going?" I asked. "We are going to teach you how to use your powers." She simply said. I placed the car in gear and sped off to an unknown destination with an unknown being.

The ride was quiet. I didn't speak and neither did she, unless she was giving me directions. I followed them until we reached an abandon baseball field. It used to belong to an old high school that was demolished a few years ago. I hoped out the car and examined the area. "So, this is where we are going to do this?" I ask blankly. She began to walk deeper into the field, ignoring my question. "Hello?" I asked impatiently. She stopped walking and her wings ejected from her back. I looked in amazement as she took to the air in a spectacular way. She then charged after me with an almost invisible speed. I dodged her attack barely. "What the hell!?" I screamed as she began to attack me again. I dodged her second attack barely again, but this time she sliced my face with her wing. "I could feel the rage building inside of you. Release it!" she demanded. I began running towards her, prepared to knock her head off. She flew toward me and grabbed my neck, dragging me to the skies. "Here's your next lesson." She said as she dropped me hundreds of feet from the ground. "Your wings! Expand them!" She yelled. As I was falling to my death, all I could think of Scarlett. Dying wasn't on my agenda today. I could feel my wings eject right before I hit the ground. I flapped my new-found wings as hard as I could, causing a small dust storm between us. She smiled at me as she landed on the ground. I followed her, awaiting what she would say. I still haven't managed to ask who this woman was, but her teaching me about my abilities was helpful.

"Your power is limited...you are still holding back." She simply said as she examined me. "What do you mean? Why is everyone saying this shit to me? I just gain these abilities today!" I said impatiently. She just looked at me. "The timing is not the issue. Your sister mastered her power in a matter of hours...You are holding back? Why?" She asked. "I'm not holding back...and how do you know my sister?" I simply said annoyed. The mysterious woman walked around me, examining me. I stood still just looking at her. Who was she and what was her purpose for doing all of this? I couldn't help to not think it, but I didn't care that much to ask. "You have seen your future, and you still won't go of your potential? I find that...interesting. I see darkness in your heart, except for one thing. A girl?" She asked. I said nothing. "You are in love? Please don't tell me your love for this girl? I swear you and Melody with this love thing. In fact, it could be the one thing that could release your power?" She said thinking to herself. "Scarlett has nothing to do with this."

"She has everything to do with it. You were meant to be a monster. A powerful monster. Scarlett has steered you away from that life and I'm proud of it. Unlike your sister, you were born with the darkness. Your father and I tried to convert her, but we failed in our efforts; not because of her, but because I was following the wrong power. Looking at you now, I see something much more. I was wrong and I truly apologize for this burden I have given you two." She said. I took in every word she was saying. "What are you saying to me?" I asked as I clinched my fist. "Yes, what you thought when you first met me...I am Amora. Your mother. I know that Gabriel and Melody have found you first and have told you a great deal about me. All of it is true, but I have had a change of heart." I couldn't believe what I was hearing. Standing in front of me was a woman who I was told was evil, powerful, and surely dead. But here she was, standing in the flesh. He skin was so vibrate, she looked like an angel. I couldn't feel any evil from her though, which confused my freshly new senses.

"Why shouldn't I kill you right now?" I said as I paced myself. She smiled as she walked towards me. "Because you can't, and you need me." She said. I ejected my wings and began to walk away. "I don't care what you want. I need to get back…" I said as I started to walk away. "Don't you want to save her?" Her words stopped me in my tracks "What did you say?" I said turning around. Amora began walking towards me again. "I know what that witch showed you. The death of your fiancé, Scarlett. What she showed you would be the outcome if you don't embrace your power correct?" She said. I could feel my anger and frustration building. "I know I have done horrible things in this life, but I want to make things right. We can destroy the Darkness together. Help you save your fiancé. Unlock your potential so we could save this world. I woke up from certain death for a second chance. I just want to make things right." She said. I looked at my mother for a long time without saying a word. I didn't know if she was lying or telling the truth, but I did know I would do anything to save Scarlett. Whatever I needed to do to get this new power, I would do it.

(Natalia)

I knew my sisters needed me, but I was stuck in this tiny town called Brimmore trying to figure out our next option. We walked to a local bar and sat at the booths. Every eye was on us because not only were we all stunningly beautiful to the weak human eye, but we were outsiders. They knew we were not from these parts. Alexandria grabbed a napkin from her pocket and wiped the seat before she sat on it which caused even more attention.

"Let me get a drink. "Ruin said as he looked intently at the bartender. "You want anything?" He asked me. "Bourbon, no ice." I said to the bartender. Ruin smiled as he turned his head to his sister. She looked at him and turned back around. "I rather half blood." she said disappointingly. The bartender quickly left to fetch the drinks after her comment. "Alexandria!" I said under my breath. "What?! It's true." She said. Ruin shook his head and I just laughed at the whole altercation.

I took a sip of my drink and began thinking. "How are we going to get to America now? We are in the middle of nowhere." I said to myself. Ruin smiled and took a large sip of his drink. "Don't worry...I know how we will get there. I should've did this in the first place anyways." He said. I looked at him in confusion. "What are you talking about?" I asked. He finished his drink and stood up. "Bartender!" He called out to him. "I need you to go in the back and tell Ramos that Ruin is here." The bartender didn't say one word as he exited to the back. Alexandria and I both looked curiously. Less than a minute later, A man walks out with a head full of brown curly hair. He smiles at the first sight of Ruin. "Ruin! What has it been? 60, 70 years?" He asked. "74 my good friend." He replied. "What do I owe this visit?" He asked. "Well, this is my lovely sister Alexandria, and this is an angel named Natalia. We need your help." Ruin said. "He looked at Alexandria and then to me. "Oh my..." He said he placed on his glasses to examine me. "A real angel. I never seen one in person. You must really be in some shit. The end of days?" He asked. "It could be if we don't hurry." I say as he continues to examine me.
"Oh of course. Follow me." he said as he led us to the back of the bar. "Who is this guy?" I finally ask Ruin as Ramos led us to an

unknown destination. "Ramos is a witch who helped me fight Devorus back in the day. He is also what is called a gatekeeper." He said. "A gatekeeper? A gatekeeper of what?" I asked. "Well, some of the most powerful witches have the power to create gateways or portals to places all over the world or even other worlds. Due to the structure of the witch's code, there are only 99 gateways, and Ramos has one." I was blown away by his knowledge of it all. "Okay. So where are you guys headed?" Ramos said as he stood by a closed door. "Los Angeles." Ruin simply said. "Be careful." Ramos said as he opened the door. "Thank you, my good friend." He said as he hugged his friend. One by one we walked through the portal and to my surprise, once we walked through it, we were in Los Angeles in the middle of the empty street in front of a damaged hospital. "Ruin and Alexandria looked at the massive damage that has already took place. "This is bad." Alexandria said as she looked in awe. "Follow me, my sister will have all the answers." I said as I took flight. Alexandria and Ruin speed kept up with me easily until we ended up at a house I never been before. We walk toward the opening to where a door should've been only to be stopped by Gabriel.

"Oh, my sister! I have missed you." she said as she hugged me. I smiled as I held her back. I missed her just as much. "These are the vampires Adam told me to bring. This is Ruin and Alexandria. They are royalty, so treat them as such." I said jokingly. "It is a pleasure to meet you Gabriel, it is an honor." Ruin said with his usual charm. "Pleasure to meet you." Alexandria said as she took off her glove to shake her hand. "It is nice to meet you both. I appreciate you coming all the way here." Gabriel said. "It's no problem, we know if Adam needs us. it must be important." Ruin said as he looked around the house. "Where is Adam? Where is his mate. I was sure that we would meet her on this journey." Alexandria said as she began to inspect the house for him. "Adam is training somewhere that I do not know of." Gabriel said before I could answer. "Oh..." Alexandria said quite disappointed. "...Well, where is his mate? I would love to meet her." She asked once again. I noticed her absence as well. "Melody is with Zachariah..." She simply said. Now I was confused. "Why is Melody in Brazil? We need her now more than ever." I said. Gabriel just looked at me as she was trying to come up with words that were untrue. "Gabriel, can I talk to you outside?" I asked grabbing her arm. Ruin snickered as he sat down on the couch. "Have you forgotten we are vampires? There's not too much you could hide with these ears, so just tell us what's going on." He said. Gabriel bit her bottom lip as she looked at Ruin then to me. It was obvious she was hiding something. Lying was never her strong suite.

"But I promised Melody that I wouldn't say anything." Gabriel protested. "Gabriel!" I said surprisingly. She turned from facing me and faced the group shamefully. "Melody...She is pregnant. That's why she is in Brazil, to protect the baby." She said. "What?" I said stunned. Both Ruin and Alexandria's eyes widen as the listened to the shocking news. "Wait, what!?" Victoria said as she came out of the back room with Dawn unaware that we had new visitors.

"Are you serious?" I asked. Gabriel simply nodded. "It's been growing for a while, we were just to wrapped up in preparing for The Darkness, that none of us noticed." Gabriel said. "No freaking way! Oh my God! My baby sister is going to be a mother! Why didn't she tell me?" Victoria said as her and Dawn's attention went to our new visitors. "Who are you guys? More of Adam friends?" Victoria asked. "Yes, this is Ruin and Alexandria, Vampire royalty." Gabriel introduced them. Victoria smiled and introduced herself while Dawn just stared at Ruin as a piece of meat.

"She didn't want anyone to worry, and she didn't want Adam to know last. I think it's too late for that now. That's why she didn't say anything." Gabriel announced. The room was filled with joy and conversation, which I felt was good for our group. I looked around to acknowledge the sheer power in the room; Not counting Adam, Melody, Lyla, and whoever she was sent to get. I was excited for this fight, probably more than anyone else.

"Sorry to change the subject darlings, but this demon, tell me about him?" Ruin asked. Dawn made her way to the couch, right next to Ruin as if she was a horny schoolgirl. "Wow, you are so handsome. Like in a vampire-kind way." Dawn said as she touched Ruin's face in an amazement. "Let me guess, you are a witch with a vampire craving? Don't worry, I get it all the time." He said so cool. Dawn face seemed like it just melted at his voice. "So, about this demon? Who is he and how do we kill him?" He asked. I sat down to engage myself in this conversation. "Well, his name is Demetri. He is a powerful demon, one of the most powerful I've ever encountered. He has the power to open the gates of Hell and unleash demons upon this world." Gabriel said. "How is that possible? No demon could have that amount of power." "I said. "I don't know Natalia, demons were chasing Melody and I in the streets this morning." Gabriel said. "So, what's the plan?" Ruin asked as he folded his legs. "Well, Victoria and Dawn are creating a spell that will give us his location. Once we have a location, I say we bring the fight to him." Gabriel said as she looked at all of us. I smiled at the thought of the idea. "I love it!" I said as I stood up and paced across the room. "I love it to. So how many of us will it be? Or in other words, who else will be joining us in this fight?" Ruin asked. Gabriel smiled before she answered. "Well let's count; Me, Natalia, Victoria, Dawn, my other sister Lyla and whoever she is bringing with her, Adrian, your sister, yourself, and Adam. It would be 10 of us fighting sided by side." Gabriel said. "I like those odds. Who is Adrian? Is he here?" He asked looking around. "Adrian is Melody's brother which makes him a Nephilim as well. We are in his home right now. He stepped out briefly, but he should be returning soon." Gabriel said.

"Oh, and the spell is done Gabriel! We know where this demon you speak of is located.

Victoria announced. "Where?" I said as I felt the excitement build in my body. "He is in Vegas! Las Vegas! Why the hell would he be there?" Dawn said confused. "He's a demon that's been locked up for what seems like an eternity, Vegas is a perfect stopping ground for him since all demons feed off the sins of man." Gabriel said as she got up from her seat. "Well what's stopping us? I think we should move now. I know Devorus won't be too far behind." Ruin said as he stood up too. "Devorus?" Gabriel asked. "Our father who was recently released from The Darkness. We also had a run in as well." Alexandria said. "Well, okay, let's call Lyla and tell her where to meet us and let's end this demon." I said as I leaned against the wall. I began to say something else until I felt a powerful presence close by. I notice everybody felt the same thing as I because the room went silent. "What is that?" Gabriel said as she looked out the window. "It can't be?" Gabriel said as she exited the house. I followed right behind her only to see a sight I thought I would never see.

Standing in front of the house was a young man I never seen before and Amora. someone I thought was long dead. She stood there looking as vibrant as usually, smiling in a way I never seen before. "Adrian? Amora?" Gabriel said as she walked closer. "Hello Gabriel, it's nice to see you again."

Chapter 18
The Immortals

(Scarlett)

"Wait!" I said as Melody pulled me through the airport towards our flight. "What is it?" She said with her soft voice. "Something is wrong, I can feel it." Melody looked at me as if she could feel something as well. "What are you feeling?" She asked me. I stared blankly, developed in my thoughts. "Adrian...I feel like he is in trouble. I just think he is going to need us. We have to go back." I said still gazing at the distance. I could feel that his heart was conflicted. I could also feel his power, which is something I never could feel before.

Melody stood in front of me, interrupting my vacant stare. "I thought leaving would be the safest thing? Going back will only put you back in danger." She said. "I don't care about any of that. All I care about is saving all that I have left. Wouldn't you do the same for the ones you truly love? I know I don't have wings and super powers, but I can shoot anything, and I won't go down without a fight! I will fight in your place." I said. Melody smiled at me and grabbed my hand. "I would do anything for the ones I love." She simply said. I smiled back at her as we turned around towards the exit.

Once we got outside Melody stopped and looked at me. "This fight will not be easy Scarlett. I'm terribly sorry about Carmen, but there is a possibility that there will be more will be hurt or worse in this fight. We don't know what we truly are up against and that is the most frighten part. I don't know what is going to happen..." She said. I could feel her concern and I knew she meant every word. "I am a fighter. I will fight until the very end." I said. Melody smiled as she took my hand. Her wings ejected in front of the large group of people. I looked around to see hundreds of eyes all on us. "There's no point of trying to be conspicuous now. We have a world to save." He said as she lifted my off the ground. With one flap we were one with the sky.

(Lyla)

"So, was that the bitch that fucked up L.A.?" Joshua said as I floored the gas pedal. "I think, I'm not one hundred percent." I answered. Seeing Joshua transform and almost tear Evelyn apart was a sight to see. I'm starting to believe that he could be more powerful than I anticipated. "Does it hurt...when you turn?" I dared to ask. "Nope, I barely feel it." He simply said. I was intrigued by him and his werewolf abilities. "How did you become what you are? Is that whole bitten on a full moon thing true? All I know is the lore." I said laughing. He smiled before answering "Well, its genetic. I was born this way. The first full moon after my 13th birthday is the day I did my first transformation. Once I got older, I've learned to control it more. Now I can transform as many times as I want, when I want. Full moons just make me stronger." He said as he rolled down his window.

"Wow, that is really interesting. I know it must have been hard for you in your younger years." I said. It's been in our family for generations. My father prepared me for it, so when it came I was ready." I smiled and continued to drive like a mad woman. "We need to hurry up." I said to myself. I was beyond worried about my sisters and what was going on with them. "Can't you fly like super-fast or something? All I know is the lore." He smiled. "Yes, I could get to California in a matter of minutes." I said proudly. "I think we should ditch this car. I could run a lot faster than this truck. I could follow your scent." He said. I stopped the car instantly and turned to face him. "How fast can you run exactly?" I asked curiously. "Fast. Stop asking me one hundred questions!" He said. I almost forgot that he was a jerk. "Okay fine! Catch my scent and try to keep up!" I demanded. He smiled as he exited the car.

"Show me your speed." I said as I ejected my wings. He looked at me with that cocky smug look that I hated. "Just make sure you I got some clothes when we get there!" He said as he transformed into his beautiful form. I smirked as I took to the sky. I looked behind me briefly, only to see that he was keeping up.

Demetri (Las Vegas)

The wind was calm, not what I expected being that this was "the land of sin" and all. I stood on the roof looking over the beautiful city only thinking one thing...destroying it. I ran my hand through my jet-black hair and looked in disgust at the millions of people living their lives unaware of what was to happen to them. I hated mankind. Everything about them. I despised them. Ever since I was freed from The Darkness, I been dormant. Watching and learning the human species as if they were insects under my microscope. They are a weak species; full of sin, doubt, fear... A species that doesn't deserve all that they have been given.

Once I was awakened, my first mission was to find Adrian, which wasn't hard at all. His dark energy was dormant, but it was vibrate as well. He was filled with such rage, such power; I could not wait to meet him myself. A Nephilim walking among mankind was beyond my comprehension. I knew it would be a matter of time before his sister and Gabriel would find him. I also knew that turning him to their side would truly be a task.

"Father?" My thoughts were interrupted by the only being I cared about. "Yes Evelyn? What current information do you have for me?" I asked looking at her only to notice that her clothes were torn through. "What has happened?" I asked very much concerned. Evelyn looked down upon the people of Vegas. "Gabriel and her sisters. They have recruited 'other' entities to help them fight." She said without looking at me. I was confused. "Entities?" I asked. She then turns to me and showed me her arm. "A werewolf did this." She said as I examined the huge bite mark. "I need to recover. We need to unleash our plan among the world. I don't know how many more allies that they will have." She said looking back towards the people. "You are right my daughter, but we have allies too." I said as I heard a familiar friend desended from the sky.

"Devorus. It's good to see your old friend." I said as I turned around to greet the vampire king. "Ruin and Alexandria are here in the states. Thank you for the demons you sent to me. They brought down their plane. Stalled them." He said. I smiled. "That's excellent. We just need two more hours before the it can be open. We are right on time." I said as I stood there motionless. "To open The Inferno Chamber, correct?" Devorus asked. "Yes. The eternal flames will engulf all that enters while it's pressure will suck everything in this world inside it. All life will be consumed. Well, all life that is not powerful enough to withstand it." I said smiling to myself. "If the Inferno Chamber will consume the human beings, how do we stop Gabriel?" Evelyn asked. Devorus smiled at me as I smiled back. "I have a plan. Don't worry. Now let's go have some fun while we wait, shall we?" I said as I walk towards the ledge. "I agree..." Evelyn said as she walked to meet me. Devorus smiled as he follows. We all took a step off the ledge and landed on the Las Vegas busy street effortlessly. All the bystanders were in shock as we walked unharmed. I pulled out my gift, given to me by Lilith herself, Black Supreme. "Once it's gathers enough dark energy, it will create an entry to The Inferno Chamber, sucking everything inside of it." I stated. "It is the source of how I can unleash demons among this world my friend." I explained to Devorus. "I opened it once already when I had my run in with Gabriel and Melody." He smiled as he gazed upon it. "Gabriel and her sisters won't even stand a chance." I said. Devorus smile began to widen at my devious plan and it was caused for. "Where is Lilith?" He asked. Evelyn looked at me with wide eyes as Devorus uttered her name. "I haven't heard from her. I'm sure they are devising their own plan. I don't have the time to wait for them." I simply said. Devorus looked briefly before tuning his head. As if he knew I was lying through my teeth. Lilith was the one who led me to Adrian in the first place. She believes that he will be our greatest asset in the ultimate battle between good and evil.

I looked at my watch I stole from a man I killed earlier today. "I guess we could start earlier than expected. I grow bored of waiting." I said as I examined The Black Supreme. "Shall we?" Evelyn said as she moved all the pedestrians in the street with just a flick of her hand. Every human began flying towards where ever she flicked them. "I made some space." She simply said. I smiled as I threw The Black Supreme in the street. The streets began to shake creating cracks that made the city tremble. A large orb of black energy began to appear causing the skies to turn dark as if a thunder storm was brewing. "In about an hour, it will be ready." I laughed to myself. I could feel that we would be in a fight before everything was said and done. I hoped for it.

(Melody)

I felt something familiar...too familiar as I landed back to Scarlett's house. "Adrian!" Scarlett said as she ran into his surprised arms. "Amora?!" I said as prepared myself. She smiled at me as she raised her hands. "I come in peace my precious daughter. So much power. You have improved dramatically since our last meeting." She said. I balled up my fist. "How are you alive? And what are you doing with my brother?" I demanded. "You released my soul once you released The Darkness. Where did you think I would go? And as for your brother, I just wanted to help him unlock his power. We are going to need him to defeat Demetri." She said. "Wait, why would you help us? This is what you wanted to happen anyways. How stupid do you think we are?"

I said as I began to walk towards her. Adrian began walking towards me, stopping me. "What are you doing? WE cannot trust her. She tried to destroy me and everyone in my world just a few months ago. You know nothing about her!" I said to Adrian. His face was stern and emotionless.

"I feel there is truth in her words. I think we should give her a chance. Plus, I also feel that she wouldn't approach us if she wasn't on our side. I know you by yourself could kill her, look around you. There are plenty of us." He said looking towards the house. I noticed a few new people that Natalia must have brought with her. They looked beautiful, like something straight out of a 'Twilight' novel. The female gave me a very serious glance as if she was trying to figure me out. "That was going to be interesting conversation." I thought to myself.

I looked back at Adrian only to see his eyes were glued to me and his hand was glued to Scarlett's hand. I gave a glance to Amora as she stood there anxiously. "Come on, introduce me to the ones that look marble." I said as I walked towards the house. "Does that mean I'm okay?" Amora called from behind us. I didn't answer back, still contemplating if I should kill her again. "Do you believe her?" Gabriel said the moment we reached the doorway. "No, but Adrian does, and I guess I have to trust my brother's instincts." I said as the unfamiliar woman walked towards me.

"Melody!" Natalia said as she hugged me. "Natalia! I've missed you so much! Are these the recruits Adam sent you to find?"

I asked. "Yes, this is Ruin and Alexandria. They are vampire royalty from Paris. Who know Adam knew princes and princesses?" She said as she laughed. "Wow, vampires? This day just keeps coming with surprises. Hello, I am Melody. It's such a pleasure to meet you. Thank you for coming all this way." I said as I shock Ruin's hand. I stuck out my hand toward Alexandria with the full intention of her shaking it only to have it hanging. Alexandria just looked at my face and then to my stomach. "Nice to meet you." Alexandria said very fast as she walked away. "Umm okay?" I said in confusion. "I'm sorry about that. She has had a crush on Adam for years. To finally meet his mate in person was probably too much for her." Ruin said. "Oh, well I can understand that." I said as Adrian and Scarlett walked up behind me. "Oh, this is my brother Adrian and his fiancé Scarlett. This is actually their house we are in." I said as I introduced Ruin to them. I left before I could hear their conversation. "Victoria!" I called only to have her run into me. "What are you doing here? I thought you were going to Brazil with Scarlett? She asked. "Plans change, I feel like I'm needed here more. Any word of Demetri?" I asked. I could see worry spill all over her face. "Well I was just about to tell the group what is happening." She said. "What? What is happening?" Gabriel said as she appeared by my side. "Demetri, he has used a device that is opening a place called The Inferno Chamber. It's basically a level in Hell where the damned are burning for an eternity. It's a place that we must not let him open. There is great power around him." Dawn said as she entered the room. "Why would he want to open this place? What is his plan here?" Natalia asked. "What would be his intention?" Ruin said from the corner. "He is planning to suck the entire world into this chamber, trapping innocent souls...that is his objective." Amora said as she walked in the house. My fist was once clinched again. "Why would we believe you Amora?" Natalia asked as she stepped to her. "Because it's the only logical explanation. Why else would he open such a powerful portal? It's a page right out of Lilith's motives." She said as she sat down. I looked at Gabriel only to see that there may be truth in what she is saying. "It does make sense. Use the chamber to destroy all life on earth. But there is one flaw in his plan." Gabriel asked. "What could that be?" Amora asked. "If he opens The Inferno Chamber, he knows that it will not be able to suck us inside of it. We are way too powerful. This will not destroy us." Natalia said. Amora stood up out her seat. "Destroy you? Destroy you? Oh, darling, you still think it's about you. Destroying you is the last of his worries. Destroying this beautiful world God has made is the main objective. We are talking about a demon with unlimited power. The world has never encountered a threat with such malice." Amora said as she looked at us all.

"How much time do we have left before that portal opens?" I asked. Victoria looked at her watch. "In about an hour. We need to move." She said. Dawn and I have enough magic to teleport four of your guys to Las Vegas." Victoria announced.

"What have I missed?" Lyla said as she entered the house with a tall naked man. "Umm, Lyla? who is your friend and why is he naked?" I asked the obvious question. "This is Joshua. The one Adam told me to find. He is a werewolf, so when he transforms into a wolf he doesn't take his clothes with him." she said simply. "Hello!? Can I get a pair of fucking pants!" Joshua yelled in the door way. Adrian laughed, which was a rare sight indeed. "I got you." Adrian said as he went upstairs. "Well me and my sister would like to take that ride." Ruin said to Victoria. "Me too!" Scarlett said. Everybody that didn't know who she was just looked at her. "I know you love your mate, but coming out there is suicide mission. If that portal does open, you will be sucked in there. An eternal abyss. I don't think you understand what you are getting in to." Ruin said. Scarlett smiled at him. "Listen, I don't care what the fuck you are or what you can do, but I'm just as strong as any of you. I have had Adrian's back since we were kids and today is no different. Ride or die!" She said. The room went quiet. "Here you go." Adrian said as he threw a pair of pants at Joshua. "Thanks man, and I will like to take that last slot...I'm tired of running." Joshua said to Victoria. She nodded at him. Okay, everyone else we could fly there in the same speed that it would take to get them to get there. Let's go." I announced. We will meet up at the Mandaylay Bay hotel." Dawn said. I nodded as I left the house. I passed Amora and through her a mean glance. "I swear if you do anything, I won't hesitate to kill you again." I said. She just smiled. "I don't trust her Gabriel. She is up to something." I said. "She wouldn't dare try anything. There is way too many of us." She said as she took to the sky. I hesitated as I watched my sisters back together again. I glanced around only to awe at the power we had around us. Adam really did know a lot of powerful people. I hoped that he would return soon. I could feel the fight of our lives was just beginning.

Chapter 19
Battle in the City of Sin

(Victoria)

As we appeared in an alleyway right behind the luxurious hotel, I could hear screams and explosions, and earthquakes all around. Ruin and Alexandria seemed unphased by it all, instead they were looking for it source. "Do you smell it?" Ruin said. Alexandria closed her eyes and opened them toward the north. "Yes, Its father." She said. "Father?" I asked. "Yes, our father is from The Darkness and he is here working with your demon. We must stop him first. Will you be alright?" Ruin said. I nodded. "Of course! Go guys!" I lied. They nodded and disappeared. They were so fast I couldn't catch them with my eyes. I wasn't ready for this fight.

"What are you doing?" Dawn asked me from behind. "I was waiting on you guys of course." I lied once again. Standing with Dawn was the tall werewolf man and Scarlett. "Okay so what's the damn plan? I tired of getting stuck with girls today!" Joshua said as he began to walk away. "Wait!" Scarlett said. "The plan is me and you go out there and fuck some shit up, and Dawn and Victoria can cover us." she said raising her two pistols. He smiled at the idea. "I love that plan!" He said as he transformed into a huge wolf. "Oh my!" I said out loud. "Oh, my is right!" Dawn said right behind me. We turned the corner only to see the demon I've been tracking. He didn't seem to be excited or surprised to see us. "Finally, the heroes have arrived!" He said as he vanished and lady flew towards us. "Remember me bitch!" Scarlett said. "Oh Scarlett, no hard feelings, right? And I see you know this dirty wolf too. I can't believe I get the opportunity to kill both of you by myself." She said. "This time, there will be a different outcome. I'll kill you myself." She said as she began running towards her. I thought Melody was the bravest person I've ever met when we were in Africa. But looking at Scarlett, I had to take that back. She was about to go face to face with a full fledge demon. "We have to help her!" I yelled at Dawn. She nodded as she created a large bright beam towards Evelyn, blinding her. Scarlett took advantage and drop kicked her until a car and started pounding her with the butts of her gun. Joshua bit into her arm and tossed her into a nearby building. Scarlett didn't hesitate at all after she ran towards the rumble to finish her onslaught. Evelyn emerged angry and took to the sky.

"I will truly enjoy your death. I just feel sorry that your fiancé won't get a chance to see it." Evelyn said as she looked down upon us. Scarlett just smiled as she took her guns off safety and started shooting at her relentlessly. "Icedramense!" I scream a spell as I watched ice beams fly out my hands. "What the hell!" she said as she looked at me trying to freeze her. She flipped over a car towards me. "Victoria!" Dawn screamed at me signaling me to move, but I was much too slow. My body managed to dodge the car, but my arm wasn't. My arm was impaled under the car. I tried to stay awake, but the sheer pain I was feeling was far too great. I closed my eyes and I listened the voices and sounds of the world...

(Melody)

Las Vegas was in a state of panic. That's the first thing I noticed once I landed on the ground. I looked around to see Natalia, Lyla, Gabriel, Adrian, and Amora to my side. "I can sense Devorus is here. If I know Ruin, he is going straight after him. I need to go help them." Natalia said. "Of course, Natalia, be careful." Gabriel said. "Lyla, find Joshua, Scarlett, Dawn, and Victoria. I sense they could use your assistance." Gabriel also said. Lyla nodded as she flew towards them. "Shouldn't I go with her? Scarlett may need me." Adrian said. "No, we need you here." Amora simply said. Adrian didn't fight with her which was odd. I didn't understand what she told him or what hold she had on him, but I was vigilant to everything that was happening.

"Adrian, it's so nice to see you again. I see you brought big sister, mother and Gabriel with you." Demetri said as we approached him and his black portal. "This ends now." I said as I stand in front of the others. "What about the baby? You are willing to be so reckless and fight anyways?" He asked. "Don't worry about my child!" I said as I struck him so fast he didn't have time to block it. He flew into the closest building.

"Okay, Gabriel, how do we turn this portal off?" I asked. Gabriel and Amora examined it together. "He is using The Black Supreme. How? I thought it was destroyed? We have to destroy the stone to destroy the portal." Gabriel said. "How do we destroy the stone?" I ask. "Only a pure life of light can destroy the stone made of complete darkness. And by the looks of it, neither of you possess that." He said as he reappeared and knocked Gabriel into a car. Adrian braced himself. "Neither of you possess that, except you..." He said as he looked at my stomach. "Gabriel!" I screamed to make sure she was alright. "That baby that you are carrying, that is the light that can destroy the stone. You would have to jump in the portal as soon as it opens to save your world." He said. "He is right darling, it's the only way." Amora said as she came to my side. "What? I don't believe you nor do I trust you!" I said as I threw another punch at Demetri only to see him dodge it and aim for my stomach. I braced for the impact, praying the blow wouldn't kill my baby. but right before he could hit me, Adrian's boot flew across Demetri's face causing him to fly once again into a building. "I got you sis." He said as he helped me up. "This fight might be too dangerous for my nephew or niece. Let me take care of him. He did come after me first." He said. I nodded at him. "Not without me!" Gabriel said as flew out the rumble and assisted Adrian. "Good luck guys." I said as they flew away towards Demetri.

"He wasn't lying darling." Amora said as she came to my side once again. Her utter presence was pissing me off. "Why aren't you helping them?" I asked impatiently. "Because I'm helping you. Killing him won't stop this portal to open. You must make the sacrifice to save your world. Honestly, I didn't care what happened to this world before you killed me. Heaven for me was out the picture and I know could deal with Hell and its eternal torture, but God didn't send me to neither. He sent me to The Darkness. A world built in an eternal darkness. Eternal torture. Eternal prison. That brief amount of time I was in there felt like an eternity. There I realized that my actions were beyond wrong and unforgivable. I want to make things right with my children." She said. Her words sounded true. I believed her, but if what she said was true, I would have to sacrifice myself. Was this how it was supposed to be? I thought of Adam returning only to find that I am dead. He would never forgive himself. This may be the only way. No, this was the only way. I watched my brother and Gabriel fight Demetri in the skies. I could also see Lyla and Scarlett fighting Evelyn. I also looked at the hundreds of people hiding and running for their lives. I thought of the billions of the people on Earth who didn't deserve this outcome of life. I couldn't let their lives end. I just couldn't.

I placed my hands on my stomach and said a prayer as I stood in front the portal. I clinched my fist and prepared for an eternal torture, just as Amora said.

(Natalia)

Ruin and Alexandria were in full pursuit of Devorus. I came to the action just in time. "Natalia!" Ruin yelled as he signaled me to follow them. Devorus flew into a casino called 'The Flamingo' destroying its entrance entirely.

"Ruin, my son are you sure you want to do this?" He said as we entered the shattered building. "I'm positive." He simply responded as he braced himself. Alexandria gave me a look that told me to be ready. I certainly was. Devorus smiled as he grabbed two people running for their lives. "Have fun with these two. Me and your brother have unfinished business!" He said as he bit the flesh of the two people. "Coward!" Alexandria yelled. Devorus smiled as he flew into Ruin taking him high in the sky. "Let's go!" I said as I started following them only to be stopped by Alexandria. "We must handle them first. The vampire blood is in them. The blood of our father will turn them into monsters. They will feed on every living human if they are not stopped." She said as she looked at them transform. They were screaming in anguish and suddenly, they just fell to the ground. "I can't hurt innocent people." I said trying to be reasonable. Alexandria didn't take her eyes off them as they lay motionless on the ground. "The people they were are gone." She said. Suddenly the two stood up and looked up at us. One was a blond male and the other was red head girl. Both couldn't be no older than 25.

"I can smell your blood and it smells exquisite." The male said. "I don't want to hurt you two." I said as I started to walk backwards. "I don't either." The woman said as she began sprinting towards me. "Damn." I raised my arm and hit her body causing her to fly to a slot machine. The man started to run towards me until I kicked him in the chest causing him to fly to a buffet table. "Let's go." I said as I began to walk out the building. "That's all you got?" I heard the blond male say. I turned astonished. "Why is he still standing?" I asked. Alexandria looked at me appalled. "Did you think vampires could be killed by a kick to the chest? You must detach their heads from their bodies. Try not to get bit though. I don't know the outcome of a vampire who bites into an angel." She said as she ran towards the female. "Okay, nice chat." I said as I dashed after the male. His teeth were sharp as he flashed them to me. "You are so beautiful." He said to me as lounged after me. I kicked him away causing him to hit another slot machine. "Thanks." I said as I engulfed him with flames. His body was screaming as I pushed more flames on him until I saw nothing left. "I guess they can die from fire too." I said to myself as I walked to the exit. Alexandria met me holding the head of the woman. "Did you take care of that?" She said as she tossed the head to the ground. "Of course. Now let's go." Alexandria nodded as she looked up to the sky.

"I see them!" She said pointing at the top of a hotel. "Okay, lets finish this!" I said as I flew up to their location. Ruin and Devorus were blow for blow as I landed on the roof with them. Devorus smiled as he saw me. "The angel with fire. Why do you keep intervening? This is a family issue." He said as he kicked a tall building structure that was sitting on top of the building towards me. "Nobody wins when the family feuds." I said as I use my flames to melt it before it touched me.

Alexandria landed next to Ruin as the both got ready. I flew next to them and prepared myself. "One of us will not survive this." He simply said. "You are right!" I said as I took to the air and started shooting flames relentlessly. Ruin and Alexandria attacked him together at lighting speeds. Ruin grabbed one of his arms and Alexandria grabbed his other. "Now!" They scream at me. I fly down as fast as I could and with one strong swipe, I kick the head off the mighty Devorus. They let go of his lifeless body and watch as his head rolls to the edge of the building. Ruin walked over and picked up his father's head. Alexandria walked over as well. I could feel the emotion between them.

"It's over." Alexandria said as she rested her head on her brother. Ruin looked down at the chaos that was below us. "No sister, this is far from over. Look at what this beautiful city has become." He said as he turned to face me. "Thank you, Natalia, for everything. We couldn't have ended him without you." He said as he kissed me on the cheek. I could feel my body get all nervous again. I wanted to stay strictly on the mission. I wanted to hide my feelings from this man all together, because I knew love wasn't for me. I wasn't my brother. My attitude alone would be too much for any being. I knew this wasn't a fairy tale, but there wasn't a better time to do what I wanted to do since I first saw him again. "Just in case you die before I see you again." I said right before I kissed his lips, passionately. I felt my body, soul, and mind drift into a state of unconsciousness. I was at his will.

I pulled back only to notice his eyes were still closed. Alexandria smiled as she witnessed the entire thing "Just in case I die right?" Ruin said with his eyes still closed. "Right." I responded embarrassing. He smiled at me with the smile that I loved. "I'll try my hardest not too." He said. I smiled and turned away as if I was about to leave. "Where are you going?" He asked as he grabbed my arm. Before I could answer, He kissed my lips, and this time I felt an intensity I never felt before. It felt like my body was on fire.

He released my lips and I could feel my knees buckle. "Just in case you die before I see you again." He said. I smiled as I took to the sky. As hard as it was to get rid of the butterflies I was feeling, I had to make sure my sisters were okay. There were still threats that needed to be vanquished.

(Lyla)

"Victoria!" I screamed as I landed to her aid. "I'm using my magic to stop the bleeding, but we need to get her somewhere safe. Is there anything you can do?" Dawn asked me. I started examining her and quickly noticed that there would be no saving her arm. "No, my powers can only go so far. We need to get her out here." I said. "My magic is mediocre compared to Ms. Catherine's. I can take her to back to our school. I'm sure Ms. Catherine can help." She said as she picked her up. "Okay, hurry with her! She is my sister!" I cried. "Dawn looked at me with tears in her eyes. "She is my sister as well." She said. She uttered some words that I couldn't announce, and they vanished.

I looked at Scarlett and Joshua fight the malevolent Evelyn. I flew over there instantly with rage in my heart. "Evelyn!" I screamed. Scarlett and Joshua turned around to witness me. Evelyn smiled at me. "You have caused enough pain. It's time to finish this." I screamed. "You can try!" She said. The rain began to fall vigorously. "The portal is about to open! You are to late!" Evelyn screamed. "You are not going to be alive to see it." I scream as I charge after her. I crash into Evelyn as we crash into a building. I began punching her in to the floor. She catches one of my fist and headbutts me off her. She kicks me in the stomach which flies me out of the building into a parked car. Scarlett comes to my side, hopping off Joshua's back. "Are you okay?" Scarlett said as she helps me up. "Yes, thank you." I said as I get to my feet. Evelyn appears with a giant pipe.

"I cannot be killed!" Evelyn screamed. Joshua howled as we prepared for a fight that seemed unwinnable. "I'm going to bring her down to the ground; that way we can have a better chance." I said. "Okay, that's our plan. I'm Scarlett by the way." She said. "Lyla. Nice to meet you. Wish it were on better terms." I said. She laughed.

"Okay, here I go!" I said as I took to the sky towards Evelyn. She swings the large pipe only to miss completely. I tackle her body driving her the street. She kicks me off her and attempts to fly away, but Joshua quickly rips into her flesh with his massive teeth and large claws stopping her in her tracks. She screamed and hollered as she shook him off. Scarlett began shooting her down and

I could see Evelyn damages start adding up. "Foolish girl! I've had enough of you." She said as she held her by her throat. "Lyla! Help!" She screamed. "I will make sure your death will be seen by everyone, especially your soulmate!" She said as she flew higher in the air. Joshua turned back into a man as he watched in horror. "You got to save her!" He screamed. I flapped my wings and headed straight towards them fighting against the severe rain.

(Adrian)

Demetri was powerful, but Gabriel and I was holding him. I could feel the portal beginning to open. Demetri knocked Gabriel down into a car, which only left me and him. "You can't defeat me Adrian. I think you know this." He said. I didn't say anything. "I can feel the rage and confliction in your heart. Let me show you power you never thought existed." He said. "I will never become anything like you. I will kill you myself!" I said as I strike him causing him to fly in a billboard. I immediately fly right behind him pounding him with my fist. Blood was evident all over my hands.

"Unleash your rage!" He screamed. I blacked out as I punched him continually. "Scarlett." He said as I pounded him. "What did you just say?" I said stopping my fist. "She will die because you were afraid to unleash your power." He said. I just looked at him. I refused to believe what these angels and demons say. I control my own life. This was no longer my fight. I released Demetri and searched for Scarlett only to find her being chocked by Evelyn hundreds of feet in the air. "Scar?" I said in disbelieve. At that moment Evelyn threw Scarlett, dropping her as if she wasn't anything. "Scarlett!" I scream as I begin to fly towards her. I flew as fast as I could, hoping and praying that I could catch her. Evelyn threw Scarlett which such force that neither I or the other angel could catch her in time. I picked her lifeless body off the pavement and held her in my arms. I held her little hands and notice my mother's engagement ring. I forgot that 24 hours ago we were regular people with plans of the future. Plans to get married, have kids, start a family. I looked at my best friend, my fiancé, my soul mate. Dead in my arms. I placed my head in her lap.

"I'm so sorry..." The winged angel said as she dropped by me. I could see the tears running down her face. I didn't say anything. I placed Scarlett's body gently down and with all my speed I flew towards Evelyn running my arm ran right through her body. "Finally, you have embraced it." Evelyn said as I can see her eyes close. I flung her lifeless body off my arm and came back to Scarlett. "This is no longer my fight." I said as I picked up the love of my life. I began walking toward the portal.

Chapter 20
Return of The Archangel

(Melody)

I could see the portal begin to open as it started sucking up life. "Go on my dear. Save your world!" Demetri said as he landed next to me. Amora attempted to attack him but was swatted away effortlessly. "You are merely a shadow of your former self." He said as he turned his focus on me. "You are a monster!" I screamed. He just laughed at my anger. "Forgive me." I said as I thought about my child and everyone I would be leaving behind.

"Wait!" I heard a young woman call from behind me. She was young and simply beautiful. I looked at her without saying anything, only because she had Adam's gorgeous eyes. "What are you doing?" Demetri said as I stop to stare at this mysterious woman. She smiled at me before she vanished just as quickly as she came.

"...I'm coming for you." The voice that I loved entered my thoughts. The voice that I missed. Could It be? My hesitation was rewarded.

(Adam)

I felt intense power as I looked down among the world. "Are you sure you don't want us to assist you? We don't know how this will all end." Roy said as he handed me a sword. "No, this is my mess. I will clean it up. Thank you for everything friend." I said as we shook hands. "Ok, I understand. Good luck Adam. I'll see you soon brother."

I could feel the world shake as I flew from the heavens down to Earth. I flew straight to the portal and stopped to examine it. "Could it be?" Demetri said in shock. I didn't even acknowledge him. I flew into the portal and reached for Melody. "Take my hand!" I demanded. She found my hand and grabbed it. Effortlessly I pulled her from the portal and grabbed the stone. I crushed it in my hands, causing the portal to disappear.

"Sorry I was late." I said as I looked at Melody's surprised face. She couldn't say anything, she just stared at my face in bliss. "Its…It's really you?" She said. I nodded. "Yes, my love, it is." He said as he started to look at my stomach. "It's so good to finally meet you as well." I said as he kissed my belly.

"That's... That's impossible! No being could come and go in that portal. No one is that powerful!" Demetri said reminding me that he was still present. I turned toward him, and I grabbed him by his neck. "You have caused my friends and family to much grief!" I said as I slammed him on the ground. I placed my boot on his back. "I hate demons!" I ripped both of his wings off his back. He screamed in utter pain. I then placed my boot on his neck and pressed down until his body life was no more. He engulfed in flames as he disappeared.

Melody ran into my arms as if she would never leave. "Adam!" Gabriel said as she ran towards us. "It's good to see you too Gabriel." I said as I hugged her. "I see you have become an arch angel?" She said. "Yeah I noticed the four wings." Melody said after her. "I needed to get to the strongest I could possibly be. It was the only way." I said as I looked around. "Where are the others?" I asked. Melody began looking around too only to fall to her knees. "Adrian…he is in so much pain. Victoria too. Where is she?" Melody said. "She is with Dawn, she is in critical condition and Scarlett…" Lyla said crying as she landed near us with Joshua. Natalia, Ruin, and Alexandria came soon after. "Where is Adrian?" Melody asked. "He is coming." I said as I saw him walking carrying Scarlett's body. Melody fell to her knees sobbing. Everyone was silent as he walked towards us. I could see his eyes were filled with sorrow. He stopped in front of us and just looked at me. "The love of my life is dead. I blame you. I blame you all. I am no longer apart of this war, so let me be. If anyone dares to contact me or find me, I will kill them." He said. He spread his pitch-black wings and disappeared in the sky. Everyone just remained silent. Adrian's grief was far too strong to be ignored.

***

"Where's the vodka!? I know you have it!" Joshua said as he went through my cabinets. "Look in the one in the left." I said as I sat on my love seat. Melody cried herself to sleep on my lap. I looked out the window thinking about Adrian and Scarlett. "You can't punish yourself Adam. It was nothing you could do old friend." Ruin said as he sat next to me. "No matter what, I will feel responsible if anything happened to any of you. I dragged you out of your lives to help something I started." I said. Ruin smiled. "You know Alexandria and I would always be here for you." He said. I then glanced at Alexandria as she spoke to Natalia. "I know brother." I responded smiling. "I got a question for you though?" He asked. I looked at him. "Yes, what is it?" He looked at Melody. "All of this, how do you expect this to end?" He asked. "With all of us together." I said. Ruin smiled. "Well, you don't mind if we crash here do you, until we find a place? We figured we should stay in states until all of this is over." He said. "I gave him a funny look as he asked his question. "You sure it has nothing to do with Natalia? You haven't stopped looking at her since we got here." I said as I looked at him, waiting to hear whatever answer he was going to give. He took a huge sip of his glass and stood up. "I don't know what you are talking about." He said as he walked away. I laughed at him as I turned my focus back to Melody, who was just starting to get up.

"Is everyone still here?" Melody asked as she rubbed her eyes. "Yes, my love, how are you feeling?" I asked looking at her stomach. "Sad, but the baby is great. How did you know? I have a thousand questions." She said as she sat up on the couch. "I could still read your mind, you just couldn't read mine from my location." I said. Melody's eyes grew big as if something just came to her. "I saw someone, just before you arrived. A young woman came to the field and stopped me from going further in to the portal. She came out of nowhere baby and just vanished as quickly as she came." She said. I was blown away. "Who could this woman be?" I asked in confusion. Melody sat up against me as she kissed me the side of my face. "Maybe she's our guardian angel, striking once again." She said. I smiled at the thought. "She just might be." I simply said as I continued to ponder about our mystery woman.

"I just wish we could have saved him." I said sadly. "I wish I could be there for him right now. This is just all so bad. Where is my Victoria? I need to go to her." She said as she got up. "I just got off the phone with Catherine before you woke. They are doing some magical procedure on her at this moment. She will be just fine. We can go see her in a few days." she sighed and sat back down. "What are we going to do? Everything is so bad. Plus, I'm pregnant! I already know that this is not going to be a typical pregnancy. How do you feel about this? I just have a lot to say since you were gone for three months. I think I have a right to be upset. How could you leave your pregnant girlfriend alone for three months!" She rambled on. I couldn't even look her in her eyes as she spoke. I deserved to be in the hot seat. "I am sorry my love, I never thought it was possible, but I felt it the moment you feel to the ground holding your stomach. I wanted to come to you, but I had to know I was strong enough to protect you and our baby. Your fighting days are over by the way." I said as I placed my head on her stomach. "I am so excited about our future and our baby. I know everything will work out for all of us. I love you." I said. She smiled at me and placed her hand on my cheek. "You must've read my mind." She said. I gently kissed her lips as if it were my first time kissing them. They were just as soft as I remember them. "Nope, I just know what to say." I said laughing.

"Hey, nobody wants to see that!" Joshua said as he sat down next to us. "I don't think we properly met? You are the wolf I heard so much about. I'm Melody. Thank you for coming out and helping us." Melody said with such charm. "Well, I really came to see your asshole of a boyfriend, but you gave me a better welcome than your annoying sister." I laughed as he talked about Lyla only knowing it was a matter of time before she would respond. "Excuse me, you arrogant jerk!" Lyla screamed from the hallway. "How dare you call me annoying! You are the worst! Adam, why did you even send me to get him?" She yelled as she came storming towards us. "I thought you two would hit it off." I said smirking. "I saved her life twice since I met her, so I guess it worked out in her favor. I'm going to go on vacation. This shit was a little over the top for me. Adam, thanks for the invitation though." He said as he walked away. "Wait, you are leaving?" Adam asked as he stopped him. "I have things to do. This shit was crazy. Look around the room. You have plenty of help." He said as he headed towards the door again. "Alright old friend. Thank you for everything." Adam said as he stuck out his hand. Joshua looked at his hand then brought his eyes back too Adam "It was nice to see you. When you are done saving the world, come have a drink with me." Joshua said as he shook his hand. Adam nodded as Joshua threw Lyla one more glance before exiting. "I really don't like him." Lyla said as she rolled her eyes. "Aww, Lyla you are just so adorable." Melody said as she hugged my sister. Lyla smiled "I've missed you so much Melody. I'm so excited to meet the newest edition of our family. When are you supposed to be due?" Melody instantly looked at me. "I really don't know, but what I do know is that he is growing fast." She said. I looked at her with wide eyes. "He?" I asked. "I have a feeling." She said just as fast as I did. "We would need to find out more information. I am very much concerned." Gabriel said as she walked towards us.

(Melody)

I noticed Amora in the corner looking out the window. "I'll be right back you guys." Melody said as she kissed Adam. He smiled at me as I walked toward Amora.

"Amora..." I said as I walked in her view. She looked at me with eyes of joy and worry. "My precious daughter, you should sit. You been fighting and saving the world. I know it must be stress on the baby." She simply said. "I know. Adam said that I am done with the fighting. What are you doing here? Nothing has changed between us. I cannot stand the sight of you." I responded. There was a brief quiet moment before any of us spoke again. "Trying to make things right. I tried to help him Melody. I failed you and I failed him." She said. I could feel Adam's eyes luring at me. Maybe I could have a change of heart. "We have nothing but time. I just want you to know that you have done some awful things, But Adam still sees good in you. I know he does. And if he sees it, then I will try. I will try to forgive you Amora because I will soon be a mother and I couldn't live with my children hating me, but I promise, if this is all a trick of some sort, I will not hesitate to finish you myself." I said. Amora smiled at me. "Thank you. That means so much to me. I will be here for you, Adam, and the baby." She said.

"I always knew you would come back to your senses." Adam said as we approached us. "Well you knew me best." She said quietly. "So... what's next? Lilith is still out there, and we have no way of finding her." Melody said. "Lilith must be working on something...something massive. I suggest we prepare myself..." Amora said as she continued to look out the window.

***

Epilogue
The King of The Darkness

(Adrian)

I stood there motionlessly at my fiancé's funeral, thinking about the last talk we ever had. I remember it being as intimate, and as personal as any of our many conversations. I knew my happiness went down in the ground as so my love. All my feelings were gone, and all my emotions were numb. No one tried to reach me nor find me which was smart on their behalf. My trust in God and his angels was non-existent. I wanted to spend the rest of my days alone in the mountains and that's where I planned on going after the funeral. I've cried and lost more than any normal man.

I stood at Scarlett's grave for hours after the funeral. I didn't say anything, I just stood there. "I'm sorry for you lost." An unfamiliar voice rang from behind me. I didn't turn around or say anything. "I know this has caused you much grief Adrian, but I can help you." She said. "I can't be helped. Now please leave me alone." I said maintaining my anger. "I can bring her back Adrian." She said. I turned around to face whoever this was. "Who are you?" I asked. "My name is Lilith. I have powers that are not of this world." She said. I looked at her as if I wanted to drive my fist through her fragile body, but I didn't. My soul was desperate. And if she was lying I would kill her anyways. "Okay you have my attention." I said. "I'm building an immortal army and I want you to be its leader." She simply said. "Why me?" I asked. She looked at me in surprise. "Because your power is impressive, remarkable. I saw you in Vegas. I saw you rip a class 3 demon in half. I see you potential, and with some training, you could be the most powerful being in existence." She said. This woman knew who I was, what I was. "So, what do you say? Are you in or are you out?" She said as she stuck out her hand. The wind started to pick up. "Are you going to bring back Scarlett? How?" I asked. She nodded. "Once you agree to lead my army she will back to you." I looked up at the sky and shook her hand. She smiled. "You will be my king. The king of The Darkness. You will rule over this world. I will be in touch." She said right before she vanished. "Hey! What about our deal!?" I screamed.

"Adrian? What are we doing out here?" I heard the voice that I thought I would never hear again from behind me. I could feel a tear run down my face. I turned around and saw the most beautiful being in my world. My soulmate. "Adrian? Why are you looking at me like that?" I wrapped my arms around her and burrowed my head in her shoulder and sobbed. Scarlett held me just as tight unaware of what dark future awaited…

PHASE III:

The

Immortal

War

Chapters

Prologue

I stared in the distance, looking blankly at the nothingness in front of me. The sky was as black as my heart and as cold as my skin as I noticed it above me. I stood there alone, contemplating all my actions and decisions that led me to this point in my existence and I could not do anything but smile.

This world belonged to mankind, and it's been like this since God created them; but my intentions were to change that completely. When I was awoken from The Darkness, my first goal was to destroy this world and its entirely. I had no intentions of purifying anything. My mind quickly changed after I witnessed a being who shadowed my power, Melody. The prodigy child refused her destiny and stood toe to toe with me and survived. I have never seen a power so strong, until now.

Adrian was filled with hate and rage; these were the things that made him powerful. These were the things that attracted me to him. After the Darkness was released, I went into hiding. Not because I feared whoever intended to stop me, but because I wanted to watch and observe the world through my eyes. I witnessed Demetri's attack in Los Angeles as well as Devorus's acts in Paris and I wasn't impressed. They both failed in their missions, which I knew they would, but they succeeded in one; Exposing the power of

Adam and his foolish friends. I saw the power that they possessed, and it was magnificent. I decided to create a team of my own.

Morgana, an ancient being that was created to be the protector of earth. After realizing her true powers, she started abusing it and was banished into The Darkness. Her powers are unlimited, and the world is the source of her power. Ever since she was casted into The Darkness, she has become my greatest ally. She has created an army for me of monstrous beings that cannot die. I needed someone to lead this army across the world, destroying everything in their path...

"They are in position. What shall we do?" Adrian asked as he entered my chambers. "I was just thinking about you." I said as I turned to face him. In the time since he has been my protege, his growth and appearance has changed. His black curly hair has begun to flow down his neck to his back. His physical appearance seemed more in shape. His demeanor was that of a soldier, a leader; one who would stop at nothing until mission was complete. His eyes were black with focus; he was ready.

"I think you are ready." I simply said as I placed my hand on his check. "What do you think Morgana? Is he ready?" I said as Morgana entered my chambers. Her long black hair followed her shadow as she walked.

"Absolutely. No one else could led this army. You were created for this." She said as she took a seat and observed. "What do you think Scarlett?" I said. Adrian's face remained emotionless until I spoke her name. Scarlett walked out of her chambers. "He won't do it! Adrian this is not you! Please wake the hell up!" She screamed as the shackles on her arms and feet rattled. "I'm annoyed with her already." Morgana said as she turned her sights elsewhere. "Why must you continue to fight me?" I asked as I walked closer to Scarlett. "Because you are a monster! I don't know what your hold is on Adrian, but once he breaks out of this trance he will kill you!" She screamed. I stood in front of her and smiled. "Adrian will do whatever I say because if he doesn't I will kill you and kill him and destroy all life anyway." I said as I walked away. Adrian's face was filled with rage. "You are pathetic!" She screamed as she spat on my feet. "How dare you..." I said as I launched towards her and grabbed her neck. I felt a sharp pain go through my abdomen. I turned to see Adrian's sword inside my body. I quickly released Scarlett and turned my sights towards Adrian. "My child, your anger is your greatest ally, and yet, your greatest enemy." I said as I pushed him against the wall. He didn't fight back, nor did he say anything. His eyes were focused on his beloved. I pulled his weapon out of me and sliced it across his handsome face, leaving a scar that would for sure be permanent. "Now you will live with a scar that will forever show your disloyalty. Morgana created a mask to cover his face out of nothing and took them both out of my sight. Morgana smiled as she took Adrian away. Scarlett was dragged back in her chambers which left me by my lonesome once again.

"You asked me to bring the girl back in hopes of controlling him? This will never work Lilith." A voice sand from behind me. "Yes. His soul is weak. He will do whatever it takes for her survival. Love, what a foolish emotion. This world will soon fall to me soon. Are you jealous?" I said not turning to his voice. "Quite frankly, I'm just a little sad that you didn't ask for my help. How could you attempt to destroy the world without me?" He said as walked closer behind me. "I know you have dominion over this world, Lucifer, but I feel that you will enjoy what happens next. Plus, you helped enough." I said as I smiled. He walked to the side of me and folded his arms. "You will fail, Lilith. I will come to you three times in total, this of course being the first, And I will extend my hand to assist you. You will accept me on my third and last visit." He said smiling. "I'm not one of these weak-minded humans. I will not fall for your tricks Lucifer. It is good to see you though." I said. He smiled at me as he kissed my check. "It's always good to see you Lilith." He said as he disappeared just as fast as he came. I folded my arms as I thought about his words. "We will see..." I said to myself.

Chapter 22
Full House

(Melody)

It has been six months since our fight in Las Vegas and quite actually, it's been a quiet six months. Adam, the love of my life has returned and saved my life at the brink of death, which is something he has become very good at. Having him back has brought more love and happiness in my world. Gabriel and Lyla have been doing worldwide searches on the whereabouts of Lilith and the unknown fourth and final being that was released from The Darkness, only to come to dead ends. Where ever they were, they didn't want to be found. I could only imagine what Lilith's plan was. I could still remember the first time I met her. She was so alluring, her blank face read that she didn't care about anything but her own agenda.

I looked down at my growing belly only to be joined by Adam. He hasn't left my side since his dramatic return. "What are you doing up?" He said as I attempted to walk to the kitchen. "I'm just going to fix me and the baby a bowl of cereal." I said as I looked into his mesmerizing eyes. He gave me a look. "Cereal? I don't remember buying cereal this week." He said looking around. I smiled as I grabbed the box.

"Good morning Adam." Alexandria said as she exited the guest bedroom and winked at me. I smiled back at her. "Oh, I see..." He said as he smiled at both of us. Alexandria and I have built an 'interesting' relationship in the past few months. I never thought I would be best friends with a vampire princess, but I'm not one to object such a sweet soul. Her and Ruin got a condo in Adam's same building, but Alexandria leaves on the count of Natalia and Ruin 'late night' rendezvous.

"Another long night?" I asked as Alexandria sat down next to me. She gave a blank look of distraught. "You have no idea. I love my brother to death...but to hear him have sex for hours on end is enough for even me. Sorry for barging in on you two every night."

She said as she placed her head on the kitchen counter. Adam looked at me as he laughed to himself. "I still can't believe that Natalia and Ruin..." I said to him through my mind. "I did. I knew they would hit it off, I just didn't know they already met prior." He answered. Alexandria looked at us suspiciously. "I hate when you guys do that." She said as she poured herself some coffee. "Do what?" I said smiling. "When you two read each other's mind. I find it very rude." She said. She could turn to her prissy queen ways in a heartbeat. "I'm sorry Alexandria, you are welcome here anytime." Adam said. "Yeah, yeah..." She said as she waved him off playfully. Alexandria turned her sights on my belly.

"How's the little one?" She said as placed her hand on my stomach. "He is doing just fine. All he does is eat and sleep all day. He must be mine." I said laughing. "I'm telling you, it's going to be a girl." Adam said in the background. "I'm telling you that you are wrong." I answered back. I was one hundred percent sure it was a boy. Adam and I decided not to go to the hospital because I didn't think it would be a great idea, on the count that we don't know how this pregnancy will turn out. Never has a Nephilim and an Angel made a baby before, so Adam and I thought It may be a little too unpredictable if we did decide to go. I glanced at Alexandria only to witness a sadness in her that I have seen many times before.

Alexandria laughed at us as we argued over the sex of our baby, but I could tell the topic was a little upsetting to her. In our time together, I've learned several interesting facts about Alexandria and her vampire traits. One thing that I learned is that vampires can't conceive a child. Alexandria would spend her entire lifetime (which is a long time since she doesn't age) childless. It breaks my heart every time that I think about it because I know it is something she longs for. Another thing that is heartbreaking is the fact that she has been in love with Adam for over 50 years. Ruin told me that a few months ago. Adam, of course, is clueless to all of it, but it is evident on Alexandria's face. I can still remember the first time we met and how she just stared at me. I couldn't put two and two together at first but even now it's obvious. She would look at him for a half a second and then put her sights on something else. Vampires are incredibly fast, but I am faster. She is such a beautiful girl, I'm sure she will find a love so great one day.

"I smell your mother coming up the elevator Melody. I will take this time to excuse myself." Alexandria said as she stood up and walk towards the door. "Wait. You don't have to leave." I said stopping her. She smiled at me as she looked into my eyes. "It's okay. I have to feed anyways. I can only live off human food for so long." She said. I instantly started thinking about how she was going to feed, but I wouldn't dare to ask. "I see that face. I'm going to raid a blood bank. I wouldn't dare kill any of your Americans." She said as she smiled. "Okay Alexandria see you later?" I asked. She smiled at me once again until she turned her focus towards the door. "Who is this?" She asked right before a knock at the door. I look through the peep hole and smile the moment I see who it is. "Melody, I guess you are official all moved in!" Jason House said as he entered the condo. "Yeah, I am. I'm your new neighbor!" I said as we embraced each other. "How is my niece...Hello...." He started but was quickly sidetracked when he saw Alexandria. She looked at him briefly before touching his face. Adam and I looked in awe. "You have a nice-looking face." She said as she examined Jason. Jason just starred and didn't say anything. I don't think he could say anything. Her beauty was just as intimidating as Adam's angelic sisters. "Okay Melody, I will see you soon. Goodbye Adam." Alexandria said as she walked out the door. "Okay, be safe." I said which didn't make sense since she was indestructible anyways. Adam waved and just like that she was gone. Jason was still speechless.

"Adam, we need to talk." Jason said as he walked towards the kitchen. Adam immediately took out one glass and poured him some vodka. "Why didn't you say anything? I think she likes you." Adam said laughing at him. "Why do you have so many beautiful friends and family? I swear, every time I come here nowadays, there is a beautiful woman here." Jason said as he took a huge swig of his drink. "Um, what about me!?" I said playfully. He looked at me and waved his hand. "You don't count." He said causing us all to laugh. "Who was that enchanting woman I just met?" Jason asked. Adam and I both looked at each other. Jason has been my friend and music teacher for years, but he knows nothing about what I am, what Adam is, or what any of my friends and family are. He knows nothing of angels, demons, vampires, or werewolves and I wanted to keep it like that. I didn't want to drag my human friends in to all this madness.

"Her name is Alexandria. She is visiting from Paris to help us with the baby." Adam said as he sat down next to me. I quickly laid my head on his shoulder. "Wow, when will she be back?" He asked. Adam smiled as we looked at Jason. "Later tonight probably." I said. Jason flopped down on my love seat. "Okay okay, I'm back to normal. Oh, can someone please call Nathan. He has been a mess since Victoria left again to New Orleans." He said. I immediately felt a sudden sorrow in my heart for Nathan as Jason spoke.

Victoria and Matthew have been married for quite some time now, but after I met Adam and both our worlds went into mayhem, she hasn't spent much time with him. She has been too busy mastering her newly witch abilities and saving the world, which Matthew knows nothing about. In Vegas, she lost her arm in a fight with a demon and almost lost her life. Thanks to Dawn, she managed to get her back to New Orleans just in time to be healed by Miss Catherine, The most powerful witch in existence. Victoria now has these magical white bands surrounding her missing arm, and through magic, her arm exists. The bands must never be removed, because they give her arm life. I feel horrible about what happened to Victoria, I feel horrible about what happened in Vegas. There is not a day that goes by that I don't think about Adrian, Carmen, and Scarlett. I single handedly blame myself.

"She is doing fine. New Orleans has the best arm doctors in the world. She will be home soon." I lied. We told Jason and Matthew that she broke her arm and we are trying to keep her secret safe. "Okay, well I'll past the message. He just misses his wife." He said as Adam looked at me with eyes of worry. "We will have to tell him. Victoria cannot hide this secret forever." Adam said in my mind. I simply nodded at him without responding. "Well I just wanted to drop by and send you that message and check on the baby." Jason said as he stood up. "Melody! It's your mother." My mom said as she entered through the front door. "Mrs. Eve, even you have a key?" Jason said as he was the first to greet my mother. "Of course, honey. My baby girl is pregnant, and I need to reach her at all times." She said as she hugged and kissed Jason on the cheek. "Hey mom." I said as I hugged her next. "Mrs. Eve, it's always a pleasure." Adam said as he took her bag. "My dear Adam." She said as she kissed his check and turned her sights on me. "Now Melody, you know you should be resting. Adam, I thought I told you to make sure she doesn't get up after all the running around she's been doing in the last few days?" She said. "You know your daughter. She is too driven." He said as he smiled. My mom sighed as she took a seat. "Well I will see you guys later." Jason said as he exited. Everybody said their goodbyes and then there were three.

"Have you spoken to your sister?" My mom asked. "Not for a few days, she is back in New Orleans." I responded. "Okay, any additional information on this Lilith and her whereabouts?" She asked looking at Adam. "No mama, Gabriel and Lyla have been searching for anything since Vegas. We have yet to find anything." Adam responded. "This is bad darlings." My mom said. Once she said that I had a very bad feeling grow within my head. Adam immediately came to my side. "What is it?" He said but quickly closed his eyes and felt the same thing. "Turn on the news ma." I asked as I stood up and went to the bedroom to change. My mom turned on the news without hesitation. "Mom get away from the doors and the windows." I said as Adam laced his boots. "Oh my God!" My mom said as she watched the news. I glanced at the television only to see our building. I turned up the volume to see what the reporter was saying:

...The SWAT and the Chicago Police are surrounding the building where suspect and supposed terrorist "Melody Eve" resides. She was present in the Los Angeles and Las Vegas terrorist attack which caused hundreds of lives and even more injured. We are live right now and hopefully we will have her captured with a matter of minutes. We will keep you posted with details...

I looked at the news in awe, amazed that I was being hunted by the government. Adam grabbed my hand. "I don't want to hurt anyone, but I will to get you and your mother out of here." He said as he looked at us. "Let's just leave now, they can't over power us." I said as I headed toward the window. My mom grabbed my arm. "They might not be able to hurt you, but that baby?" She said as she looked at my belly. "They just breached the lobby." Adam said. "We might have to fight our way through this. That helicopter has powerful weapons on it. I don't want to risk your mother's life." Adam said as my mom stood behind us. "That is our plan...Mom, stay behind us at all times." I said. She nodded. "They are on our floor, brace ourselves." Adam said as he stood behind the door. I stood in front of it, ready for whatever.

A large bang knocked over the door as the first SWAT officer entered the house only to be knocked across the house by Adam. I threw the coffee table at the next one that entered and that's when they started shooting. Adam's wings expanded creating a shield from the spraying bullets. The helicopter began shooting through our home, destroying all of Adam's furniture. I pushed my mom out the way and rolled with her. Adam continued to fight all the SWAT officers in the hallway. "Cease fire!" I heard a voice in the hall way scream. The gun fire stopped suddenly. "Come on mom." I said as I picked her up and assisted Adam in the hallway.

"I know who you are Mr. Tyler. You currently work for real estate or did before you stopped showing up months ago. It's funny how many jobs I have for you over the past 101 years." The SWAT man said. He looked as if he was in charge. I got a different energy from him. "Well, it seems as if you did your research." Adam simply said. "Your biology is none of this world. That much is evident, but we are not after you Mr. Tyler." He said as he looked right at me. "My name is Captain Ralph Black and I need you to put your hands where I can see them." He instructed me. "You don't understand. We are the good guys." I said. "You and your winged friends destroyed half of Las Vegas. I don't know what you people are, but we took many precautions to stop you here and now." He said as two policemen walked from behind him holding Jason. "Jason!" I yelled as they held guns to his head. "Now surrender yourself now or we will shoot him." Captain Black yelled. The floor began to shake causing the SWAT team to begin to fall. "What the hell!" Captain Black said. Suddenly, Natalia comes flying through the floor, knocking Captain Black to the floor. "Shoot him!" He screams as he falls to the floor. I then notice Ruin and Alexandria climb up the hole that Natalia created. Ruin immediately starts fighting the SWAT teams as Alexandria grabs Jason. "You thought we were going to miss this!" Natalia said as she swiped a SWAT officer away. "Thank you. I must get Mrs. Eve out of here. Alexandria has Jason, right?" Adam asked. "Yes, we all need to get out of here. Do you have a place under the radar?" I asked them both. Natalia smiled. "Ruin knows a witch who could probably help us. but we have to get out of this crossfire." Natalia said as she continued to fight. "Okay, let me get us some space." I said as I expanded my wings and with one flap all the remaining SWAT officers went flying towards the opposite side of the hall. "Let's go!" Adam yelled as we ran away from the men trying to kill us. Adam, Natalia, Ruin, Alexandria, my mom, Jason and myself ran into the nearby elevator and pressed the roof.

"Ruin, how close is the closes gatekeeper from here? We need to get out of the city." Natalia asked. I didn't know what they were talking about, but I didn't care as long as we got out of here. "I'm not sure, I'm not familiar with the states." He said. "Have you guys forgotten that I am a witch? I might be old, but I still have some tricks." My mom said. "So where do we have to go?" I asked. "Nowhere. Hold hands everyone." She said as she pulled out this black rabbit's foot. Everybody followed directions and held hands. "Leftium!" She said and the next thing I know we were in a grass field in front of a massive mansion.

"It worked!" I said as I looked around the unfamiliar place. "Where are we?" Natalia asked as she looked around. Ruin and Alexandria smiled as they stared at the mansion. "We are in New Orleans. Right in front of Madame Catherine's school." Ruin said as she began walking towards the entrance. "I figured this would be the safest place to go." My mom said. I nodded as I looked at Jason passed out on the grass. "Adam!" I screamed as I came to Jason's side. "I think the magic was a little too powerful for a normal human. He needs his rest." My mom said as Adam picked him up.

We reached the front door only to be welcomed by Miss Catherine herself. "My dear sister! You all are right on time. I have news..." She said smiling. Victoria came right behind Catherine and I could feel her power. Her new power. I hoped Miss Catherine had some good news.

(Captain Black)

       "What do you mean they are gone?!" I screamed furiously as I stood in the lobby with my proficient SWAT team. "They disappeared in the elevator sir. It's like they disappeared into thin air." One of my soldiers said to me. I was beyond mad, but well prepared as I stepped outside and took off my hat. "What exactly are we dealing with Ralph? These people are flying through floors and disappearing in elevators. What the hell?" My first Sergeant in line, Sgt. Jones, said as he approached me. "I don't know, but I will get them." I simply said as I walked away. I sat in my car and waited for Shawn. I took of my gear and turned off my radio.

       "How did it go?" Shawn said as he entered the car. I turned on my tracking device. "Melody isn't the only angel, Adam and some other woman had wings as well. They had other accomplices as well, but I still managed to place the tracker in their friend Jason's pocket. You were right about them saving him." I said as I waited for the device to stop loading. "Whatever they are planning we will be able to hear everything and know their every location." He said. I looked at the device and what it read confused me. "They are in New Orleans? How could they get there so fast?" I asked. Shawn looked at the device. "We still don't know the limitations of an angel's power or they could have a witch with them. We just won't know for sure, but we need to get out of here." He said. I began thinking about that tragic day that made me so relentless to capture this Melody Eve and every other entity that was there in Los Angeles. How could I forget...

Chapter 23
The Story of Captain Ralph Black

(Captain Black)

6 Months Earlier...

"Good morning daddy." I heard my son say as I laid in my bed, exhausted from a long night of work. "Hey little man, what you are doing up so early?" I asked. His little hands grabbed my face and smiled. "Can you play with me?" He asked, which is something that he would ask at least a hundred times in a day. "Of course, little man, just let me get up." I said as I rolled over to my stomach. I felt his little feet climb on my back. "Daddy! You always say that!" He said as he stood up on my back.

My son, Nathan, is my everything. He is only five, but he has such much joy and happiness in his life that he is the reason I decided to smile these last five years. His mom and I separated when he was only one, so our relationship is strained. I get to have Nathan every other weekend and a few days in the week. My job is stressful and takes up most of my days and nights, but on this day, I was off just to spend time with my mini-me. I had a lot planned today, so I knew he would not let me sleep late.

"Okay, what do you want for breakfast?" I ask as I sit up in the bed and rub my tiresome eyes. "Pizza!" He screamed at the top of his lungs. "Okay, okay. Pizza it is!" I laugh as I get up and throw Nathan on my shoulders. The sun is shining bright on this nice Los Angeles day. The weather was great, and we were in a great mood. "Okay, go watch your shows while I order this pizza, okay little man?" I said as I picked up my phone. He smiled and ran in front of the television. "Shit." I said as I looked at the missed call from Nathan's mother. I knew she was going to give me a tough time about something. I dialed her number back and prepared for the worst...

"Hello?"

"Yes, Trish, how can I help you this morning?"

"Well, it's nice for you to finally wake up. Where is my baby?"

"He is fine, watching T.V. We are about to go get some food. Is that everything?"

"What kind of food?"

"Pancakes."

"Oh, okay, because I know how you are. You would give him any unhealthy thing, if he asks for it. Then he comes home thinking he can eat pizza and Ruffles all day. You confuse him when you do that."

"Okay, are you done? We have things we have to do today."

"No need to be rude. I'm just making sure you are doing your job as a dad..."

"I don't need you to 'make sure' anything! I have everything under control. Now are you done?"

"Do not tell him about getting shot the other day. I think Nathan over heard my conversation with you LT. Of course, they called me since you have no other emergency contact."

"Why would I tell him about that? And I've been meaning to change that."

"You have been saying that for years...Are you okay though?"

"Yeah, it was just a shoulder wound. Nothing big."

"Well, you need to be more careful out there. I've seen you in action. You are far to reckless. Think about Nathan next time you want to run into a warzone."

"I think about Nathan every day! You know what I'm done talking to you about this. Are you done Trish?"

"Yes Ralph, I'm finished. Let me say hello to my baby before I leave,"

"Really Trish, you just saw him seven hours ago. Let us have our man time."

"That's what you call it? Okay, I'll leave you be. Tell him I love him then?"

"Absolutely."

"Okay then, I'll talk to you later today."

"Okay Trish, talk to you later."

"Okay bye."

"bye."

I ended the call and ran my hands through my hair. "I don't like her." I lied to myself. Trish and I go back since high school. I've known her for about 15 years and our relationship is still evident. She is highly annoying, but I know she comes from a good place. She claims that I'm too stubborn and put my job over my family. That's why our relationship came to an end. Of course, it was my fault. My job does take most of my life and she hated it. The thing is that I love what I do. Special forces, detective, SWAT, it doesn't matter how dangerous the mission was, I wanted it. I did eight years in the Marines as special forces until the government bought out the rest of my contract to assist C.I.A. and the F.B.I. As you can imagine, that left little to none time for family time.

"You ready for pizza!" I asked Nathan as he was fully involved in his cartoon. "Pizza!" He screamed as he began jumping all over the couch. "Okay, come here let me get you dressed." I said as I searched for his clothing bag. "No daddy, I can get dressed by my own self." He said as he started going through his bag picking out clothes. "Okay little man, go ahead. Tell me when you are done." I said as I ran upstairs to put on my clothes.

I looked in my top drawer and pulled out my pistol and quickly put it back. "I'm with my son, I won't need it." I said as I ran back downstairs. My pistol is so a part of me that it's always hard to part with it. "Are you ready little man?" I said as he ran into my arms. "Yup!" He responded. I unlocked the car and watched Nathan run to the passenger seat. I looked at the sun as it blazed upon us. I just knew it was going to be a good day. "You ready!?" I asked as I started up the car. "Yes! Can I drive this time?" He asked. "Well, you still got about ten years left before you could get behind the wheel." I said laughing. "I can still drive my bike, right?" He asked. "Of course, little man." I said as I pulled out of the driveway.

We pulled up to this small pizza spot that's been my favorite since I was a kid. It's 24 hours, so I knew it would be open this afternoon. "Ralph! I see you brought little Ralph today!" The store owner, Mr. Cabzo, said as we walked in. "Yeah, I got little man with me today." I said as I picked him up. "Say hello to Mr. C." I said as Nathan smiled. "Hello Mr. C." Nathan said joyfully. "Hello little Ralph, looking just like your mother every day." He said. "Unfortunately." I said as I placed Nathan on his feet. "Find us some seats little man." I said as Nathan went on the hunt. "How is that going?" Mr. Cabzo asked. "It's going, she just called me this morning, giving me a large rant about being a good dad." I said shaking my head. "I believe it, she is firecracker, even back when she was a teen. I'm sure you know that more than anyone." He said. "If only you knew." I went to sit down next to Nathan at the table he decided, and of course he chose the one by the window; the one he always chooses. "The usual?" Mr. Caboz asked. I nodded and turned my focus to Nathan. "So how is home?" I asked. "Home is good. I'm learning a lot of stuff at school too." He said with much excitement. Mr. Caboz drops off the pizza filled with pepperoni and sausages, Nathan 's favorite. "What is something that you learned?" I asked as I place two slices on his plate. "That elephants are the biggest animals!" He said with a mouth filled with food. "Oh really? I didn't know." I said as I took a huge bite.

Right before I could say anything else. Two cop cars sped right pass us with their sirens extremely loud. I glanced out the window trying to see where they were stopping at. "Oh, it's just the hospital." I said as I continued to eat my food. Moments later, three more police cars and a SWAT van pulled up in front of the hospital. "What the hell is going on?" I said as I looked out the window. "Daddy?" My son said gaining my attention again. "Yes son?" I asked. Just as I said that, two people jumped out the window of the hospital, but started flying. "What the hell!?" I said as I stood up from my seat. I could hear Nathan saying something, but I was so focused on what I was seeing, I couldn't make out any of his words.

As I watched them fly around, a huge earthquake started up causing everything and everyone to fall amongst themselves. "Come on Nathan!" I said as picked him and ran to the car. "Daddy! Daddy!" I could hear Nathan scream as I placed him in his seat. I ran to the driver's side and started the car up. "Hang on son!" I said as I pulled off. Flying winged creatures started to appear from   the cracks the earthquake created. "This is not happening! It's impossible!" I said as I drove through the rumble and winged creatures. Flying in the roadway was this woman. I will never forget her eyes. There was another woman flying with her, but I didn't get a good look at her face. The woman I could see was fighting off these things. A car flew past me with a woman and man shooting these things out the windows. I looked behind me only to notice hundreds of the winged things right behind me. I pressed my foot down on the gas petal trying to escape whatever that was happening.

Suddenly, A man was standing in the middle of the road. Nathan was screaming at the top of his lungs as he looked out his window. "It's okay baby, daddy is going to get you out of here." I said to him and myself. The car attempted to hit the man standing in the road, only to get knocked away like a fly in the air. "Oh my God!" I said as I tried dodge the car he knocked away. I hit the break to hard and we started drifting. I saw that we were going to take a hard hit. I leaned over and make sure Nathan was bulked in. "I love...." Pain came first, then darkness...

I woke up in a hospital unable to move. "Nathan!" I screamed hopping he would hear me. I knew he would hear me. A doctor and my boss, Commander Davis, came from the hallway. "Where is my son!?" I screamed as I struggled to sit up on my bed. "Mr. Black, my name is Dr. Lee, you have suffered many injuries. You are lucky to be alive." The doctor said. "Where is my son?" I repeated. Commander Davis and the Dr. Lee looked at each other before answering. "I know this may be hard to hear right now, but your son did not survive the car accident. We tried to revive him, but to no prevail. I am very sorry for your lost." He said as he left the room. I heard what he said, but I didn't believe him. How could I believe him? "Where is my son?" I repeated. "I'm so sorry Ralph. Take as much time as you need." The Commander said as he left the room. I sat in that bed with no emotion, except one, sorrow. My son was dead, and that was something I would have to deal with for the rest of my life.

I stood at my son's funeral with sadness in my heart and anger in my soul. Trish hasn't spoken to me since that tragic day, but I can tell she hates my very soul and wishes I died instead of our son. The tears fell from my eyes as I fell to my knees. I grabbed a handful of dirt and dropped it on my son's coffin. "You don't deserve to be here!" I heard Trish yell as the pastor was saying his final words. I didn't say anything because maybe she was right. "You killed my baby you son of a bitch! You killed my child you ignorant son of a bitch! I hate you for living! I hate you for breathing!" She said as she ran to me and began punching and slapping me until people began pulling her off me. I didn't fight back or even respond. I just got up and walked away from the burial site. I felt her pain because we shared it. I felt responsible for my child's death and she was right, I didn't belong there. I hoped in my car and drove home.

I loaded my pistol with a full clip as I looked in the mirror. I held Nathan's shoe in my other hand as I thought about him. I place my phone, a picture of my son, and my badge on the table in front of me and pressed my gun on my head. I hesitated briefly before putting my finger in on the trigger. "God please forgive me." I said as I prepare to pull the trigger and end my pathetic life. Just as I close my eyes, my phone begins to ring. "I thought I turned you off dammit!" I yell as I place slam my gun down and answer the phone:

"Yeah, what do want?"
"Ralph, we found a breakthrough on the Los Angeles and Las Vegas terrorist attacks."
"What breakthrough? Did you find out what the hell those things were? What breakthrough did you find out!"
"No Ralph, but we found out who that woman was you spoke about. We linked her to both attacks. Her name is Melody Marie Eve, college graduate, no prior record. She seemed normal until December after she was involved in a car accident. After that incident, she stopped showing up for work."
"Melody is her name, huh? Okay, what else do you have for me? Is that all?"
"No, I have more. Her parents are unknown which I find also strange. She was adopted, but there are no records of who her biological parent are. Her step sister, Victoria Meagan Eve, has also disappeared from her job as well. But that's not the best part..."
"Okay, spit it out!"
A man by the name Adam Tyler saved Melody in that car accident. We pulled up Adam Tyler's files and came across that he has no birth certificate, no social security, no nothing. It's like the guy came out of thin dust. We also have several records from him tracing all the way back to 1909! We checked all the files over and over and it's

still the same. You would think that he is an old gesture, right? Nope, he looks younger than us."

"How is that possible? What are we really dealing with? People with large wings who don't age? It sounds like something from a comic book. How do we stop them?

"Well boss, I don't know what we are dealing with, but I think I might have found someone who might."

"Who are you talking about?"

"Two years ago, we arrested this crazy guy who said that he was monster hunter or something like that. Young guy, about in his late 20's, His name was Shawn McQueen, goes by the name, 'The Hunter.'

"Yeah, how could I forget. He was wacked out of his mind. I know you don't think he would actually know something that could help us?"

"Well, he did take down our whole team by himself, which means he was skilled at what he did. And check this out, he was in Las Vegas during the attacks. He is the best lead we have. It won't hurt to check him out."

"How can we find him?"

"That's actually the easy part. He is here right now. And he only wants to speak with you."

"What? Why is he there? Why does he want to speak with me?"

"He said that you are ready to listen now."

"I'm on the way now."

       I hung up the phone and sat there briefly. "Maybe another day." I said as I look at my gun and place it on my holster. I put on my jacket, place my badge and the picture of my son in my pocket and walked out the door. These things are the reason my son is dead, vengeance was all I wanted.

       The police station was stunned to see me as I walked in. I haven't been here in weeks. "Right over here Captain Black. He has been waiting for you." One of the police officers said as he pointed to Shawn 'The Hunter' McQueen. He looked at me with a look I knew all too well, sorrow.

       "You are very brave to come here today. I could lock you up right now with all the cases I have piled against you Mr. McQueen." He looked me right in my eyes. "Yeah, you could, but you won't." He said. "And why is that?" I responded. "We need to talk, but not here." He said as he started walking out the building. "Hey, where do you think you are going?" I yelled. He stopped but didn't turn around. "It's the end of the world Ralph. I have no time to sit around and lollygag with you while people are dying. I came here because I thought you were ready to listen, since what has happened to you, but if not..." He stopped talking and just continued walking. I thought about what he said, and it was just something about him that caused me to trust him. "Okay. Hold up." I said as I followed him out the building.

"Get in." He said as he hopped in his battle ready S.V.U. "Wow, is all this equipment licensed?" I asked as I looked at all the computers and weapons in his truck. "I'll answer all your questions once we get to our destination." He said as he continued to drive.

We pulled up to what looks like an abandoned house on the outskirts of the city. I didn't ask any questions as we walked up the steps to the house. He stopped at the entrance of the house and stood in front of me.

"Ralph, there is no coincidence that me and you are standing in front of each other again. Do you believe in fate?" He asked me. "No. I believe that we are in charge of our own lives." I said. "Okay, well do you believe in God?" He asked. "I did, until he took my son from me. Now, I believe in myself." I said. He looked at me, but not in a judgmental way, but in an understanding way. "I'm sorry what happened. I saw it on the news. I figured now you would be more open to listen to me." He said. "Listen to what? That you hunt monsters that hide under people's bed? Come on now." I said as I began to walk down the stairs. "You saw them come from underground. Winged creatures who ultimately got you injured and your son killed. What do you think they were huh? Huge bats or maybe they were just in your head?" He yelled at me. "Don't bring up my fucking son again or I will kill you, do you understand!" I screamed back as I pulled out my gun. "What you saw out there, they are called demons. They come only in two forms; Their demonic form, which is the way you saw them. The other way is their human form. in that particular form, they look human. The stronger ones create skins to blend in with us." He said. "What the hell are you talking about? You are crazy!" I said as I took in his words. "Am I? You think I enjoy knowing this? You think I enjoy killing demons for a career? These 'monsters' that you find so crazy, are the same ones who murdered my entire family. You think you are the only one who has lost someone?" He said as he looked away from me. His words were truly haunting. I had no idea.

"I believe you." I said. He looked at me and pulled out his keys. "It's about time." He said as he twisted his keys in the door. I awed as I walked in the house. There were maps, guns, stakes, swords, all types of stuff. "This is our main headquarters. As you can see, there are more monsters than demons in this world." He said as I looked at everything. "What else is out there? Aliens?" I asked in confusion. He smiled before he answered. "I'm afraid there is no such things as Aliens, but vampires, werewolves, ghost, shapeshifters, witches, ancient beast, etc. These things exist for sure. The world you know of is so small. We share this earth with hundreds of species that you only seen in horror movies and nursery rhymes. We are definitely not alone in this world Captain." He said as he handed me a large notebook, "What is this?" I asked as I investigated the book. "That is our record book of everything that we came across." I looked at all the different creatures and just couldn't believe what I was seeing. "I brought you here because we need your help." He said as he sat down. "I know how to hunt people, not monsters." I said as I continued to go through the book. "It's the same thing, just with different methods. The demon that is responsible for killing your son, his name was Demetri, but there will be more. Stronger ones, I feel something bad is coming." He said. I closed the book. "Like what exactly. The end of the world? The Revelations?" I asked. "That's what I thought originally, but the signs didn't add up. For the Revelations to begin, there must be an Antichrist present, along with the four horsemen, and of course Lucifer. None of these entities are present on earth, or at least in a physical form." A young woman said as she came from the stairs carrying a huge book. "Oh, this Lynn, she was touched by an angel when she was young, which gave her interesting powers." He said explaining her. Her tangled hair covered her face. "Powers like what?" I said curiously. "Well, I have really good insight on what is going on. I see ghost, and I can detect the precise location of any being. No matter how powerful or non-human they may be." She said proudly. "This could come in handy. I need to find a woman named Melody Marie Eve. I think she is one of those demon things in a human body like you explained." I said. "Maybe, but I'm not one hundred percent sure. That's what we are trying to find out." Lynn said as she sat next to us." How do you know who she is? What is she? If we are going to work together, I need to know everything." I demanded. "Hey, remember, we are on the same side." He said as he looked at me. "Okay, I just want to know what we are up against." Lynn looked at Shawn then back to me. "What is happening now may not be The Revelations, but it could be just as bad. It has been said that there was a place where God put his most dangerous and most evil creations. It's a world called The Darkness. It was thought to be only a myth, but a few months ago, The Darkness, was opened and it released several powerful beings that are responsible for the events that took place in L.A. and Vegas. Melody just recently came into my radar these past couple months, right before The Darkness was released. I'm not sure what her intentions are or if she even opened it, but it is quite suspicious." She said. "This is madness. Okay, so this Melody opened this mysterious world and unleashed all this crazy stuff on us. How do I find her and how do I kill her? How can we close this Darkness thing too?" I asked. Lynn looked at the book then back to us. "Well closing The Darkness isn't an issue since It closed just as fast as it opened. Our problem is that we must destroy the beings that came out. And as for Melody, I know how to find her, but killing her is a whole other problem. We have never faced anything like her before." She said. Shawn flipped through the book and stopped at one page. "We believe she is an angel. It's the only thing that makes sense and unfortunately, there is nothing in creation that can kill an angel, well, nothing we can get our hands on." He said. I was amazed. "An angel? I thought they were meant to protect us from these demon things. Why are they trying to kill us?" I asked. "Lucifer was an angel too. We won't know anything until we confront her. I just think it's a suicide mission to challenge her now." Lynn said as she stood up. "If we can't kill her, what do you need from me?" I asked. "Help us find a way to kill her and the other beings that was released. You have the skills and the resources. I don't know how much time we have left." He said. I looked at them and pulled out my phone. "Okay, teach me everything you know. I need to know how to kill whatever stands in my way. I want to learn how to be a hunter. Then we will find a way to kill Melody and I will get a team together to take her out." I said. Lynn smiled at me as she threw me a few books. "Get to reading." She said.

(Amora)

I stood at Scarlett's grave for hours, in awe that her body wasn't present in her coffin. I placed my hand on the ground and closed my eyes to see if I could find her location. I felt nothing. The wind blew through my hair as I stood up and looked in the sky. I've been searching for my son since he took to the sky and abandoned us all with his deceased fiancé. I was concerned about his location and state of mind, but now I was more concerned about Scarlett's body. I underestimated how powerful love could be.

I dropped a white rose and I took to the sky. I knew I must inform Adam and Melody that Scarlett's body was missing, for maybe they would have a better explanation than me. I wondered why anyone hasn't come to her grave site. Why was I the first and probably the only? I had many unanswered questions and concerns, and I was bent on answers.

I flew to Adam's condo only to notice that it was being raided by the police and other men with weapon. I could feel that they weren't there, but the arrogance of mankind thinking they could vanquish us with their pathetic weapons. I gazed upon them in utter confusion. "What are they doing?" I said to myself as I folded my arms. A helicopter soon turned his sights on me as I remained airborne. "Are you serious?" I said to the flying machine as it started pointing its guns towards me. Without hesitation, it started firing at me which only made me upset. "I'm not your enemy!" I screamed as I dodged the pathetic attempt to injure me. They remain shooting at me until I patience reached its limit. "Okay, fine." I said as I flew right through the chopper causing it to explode. "I'm not my daughter nor Adam." I said to myself. "I need to find Adam." I said as I flew out of sight.

Chapter 24
The Death of an Angel

(Gabriel) London

"I don't feel anything here either." Lyla said as we stood on the roof of a beautiful building. Our search for Lilith and the other entity was beyond even my power. "I don't either Lyla." I said as I continued to look down amongst the people. "What is wrong sister? Are you flustered by our search?" She said. She was one of the sweetest souls I knew. "No, Lyla, Its nothing." I simply said. Lyla walked towards me and grabbed my hand. "What is it?" She asked me. I continued to look down, not fully prepared to look at Lyla's investigating eyes.

"I just don't know.... If we can win this fight." I said finally. Lyla managed to stand in front of me. "Why are you having doubts? We have a wonderful team, plus we have Adam." Lyla said. This was true. We did have a powerful team filled with all types of allies, but I just wasn't sure about our chances of actually defeating Lilith. Her power was limitless and unknown to us. We had no idea of what she was capable of.

"I know, but this whole thing. Will there ever be an end? Lilith has powers we can't even fathom, how can we stand against that?" I said. Lyla just stared at me in disbelief. "Gabriel, I can't believe what you are saying. You are our fearless leader. We will win! You have to believe." Lyla said as she hugged me. "I'm sorry Lyla, I been on Earth so long that I'm starting to take more and more of their emotions." I said. Lyla laughed as we both looked amongst the horizon. I seriously had a bad feeling and I don't know where it came from, but it was there lingering within my heart.

The wind started to pick up and dark clouds started to appear. "Do you feel that?" Lyla said as she looked at the sky's sudden change. I looked up as well, bracing myself for whatever it could be. "This is not a storm. Something is coming!" I said. The rain began to pour just as the thunder started to roar. "Look!" Lyla said as she pointed in the sky. I followed her finger to see a big dark hole open in the sky. "What is that?" Lyla said as we starred at it. "The Darkness? They learned how to come in and out of it. That's why we couldn't find them here, because they weren't on this world." I said thinking out loud.

Coming out of the huge hole was a being I never thought I would ever see again. "Morgana." I said as I took a step back. "Morgana? Who is that?" Lyla asked. "I knew this fight would happen one day. Stay back Lyla let me handle this." I demanded. "No, I won't let you fight by yourself." She said. "Lyla! Do as I say!" I yelled. Lyla didn't say anything. She just took several steps back.

Morgana landed on the building and didn't say a word. She just stared at me in anger of course. Thousands of years ago, I was sent to earth to destroy the powerful Morgana, for she was created to take care of the earth, but instead she used her power for her own benefits. I casted her and entrapped her in the earth's core, killing her. I guess it made since to place her in The Darkness, rather than Hell. Her power was quite magnificent. She could use the earth's power to her will. Control of all the natural elements.

"You don't look to happy to see me." Morgana said as she smiled at me. Her beauty hasn't changed a bit. She was mesmerizing. "Why would I be happy to see you?" I responded. She looked at me then to Lyla. "You should've brought more back up with you." She said as she looked back at me. "She is not my back up. I will handle this on my own." I said as I ejected my wings. "You know, I was told to wait, but I couldn't wait to redo our last encounter. I will enjoy every moment of this." She said. "I stopped you before, this time will be no different." Gabriel responded. Morgana placed her hand on her face. "Well, since you are about to die anyways, I don't think it would hurt to tell you...and plus I don't really care. I'm not fond with keeping secrets. I want to give you and your band of rejects a fighting chance." She said with a menacing laugh. "Whatever you have planned we will prevail!" Lyla screamed from behind me. Morgana continued to laugh. "Really? Well, I have created an army that will destroy everything on the face of the earth. I used my abilities while I was in The Darkness and created beings that I'm sure are unkillable. I'm naming them 'The Immortal Army.'

Oh, and that's not the best part, the army is being led by one of yours. The broken Adrian. His heart has become truly dark, which will work well for us. This is the final frontier for earth. This is how it will end. In six days, everything you cherish, everything you love, it will die. We will destroy everything!" She said with such rage that I had no choice but to believe her. "You are a monster! What have you done to Adrian?" I screamed at her, thinking about Adrian and all the pain he must be going through. "We've done nothing to the boy but make him live out his destiny. All he needed was a little push." She said as she began laughing. "What have you done?" I repeated myself. "We used the only thing that he cared about. Lilith found a way to bring Scarlett back from the dead. Adrian has no choice, but to obey his master. He does quite a fantastic job at it, but you shouldn't worry about him. You should be more worried about yourself." I braced myself as my wings began to flap. "This ends now!" I scream as I take to the sky hoping Morgana will follow. "Go! Warn the others!" I yell at Lyla. She hesitates before she moves. "I cannot leave you!" She screams back as her wings began to flap. "Leave now! That's an order!" I demand. Morgana smiles at our conversation. "You think I will let her escape? Both of your graves will be right here on this roof!" She said as large thunderbolts began descending from the sky towards Lyla and myself. I dodged them and dived into Morgana, crashing into a nearby building. Lyla came right behind me, punching Morgana further from us.

"I told you to go! Adam needs to know what they are planning! If we both die in this battle, everything is lost!" I said as I got to my feet. "No one is dying today Gabriel. Together we are stronger!" She said. "No, this is my fight Lyla. I need to do this on my own." I said as I stared at her. She nodded as she hugged me tight. "I love you, Gabriel. And sorry for the hug. blame Melody." She said as she released me. "I love you too Lyla and it's okay. I like it." I said as I smiled, but I knew that it was a chance I wouldn't make it out of this fight alive. If Lyla shared the information we learned from Morgana, then maybe we would have a fighting chance.

A large thunderbolt shocked Lyla, causing her to fly off the building structure. "Lyla!" I said as I attempted to go after her, only to be grabbed by the back of my hair. "Where do you think you are going?" Morgana said as she threw me through a couple walls of buildings close by. All I could hear is people screaming. "I'm going to take my time with this." She said as she kicked me out the window. I managed to catch my fall as I flapped my wings. I could see police cars and police men coming towards me as I landed on the ground. "Freeze! Get on the ground or we will shoot!" I heard them say. "It isn't safe. Please evacuate this place!" I yell at them. Morgana lands in front of me, smiling at the police men. "You too, lady, Get down now!" They yell at her. I could see that they were more scared than anything. "Get down? How cute." She said as she raised her hands. A huge earthquake began, creating large cracks in the ground. "Stop!" I said as I dived towards her again, knocking her into a police car. The cracks in the ground were getting bigger by the moment. I grabbed as many people as I could, saving them from falling in. "You can't save them all!" Morgana said as she picked up a bus and launched it towards me. "Oh no." I said as I caught it and slammed against a building. Two helicopters began shooting Morgana vigorously. "Fools!" She said as large thunderbolts hit both, causing them to explode in a ball of a fire.

I looked in horror at all the death and destruction that was around me which only fueled my hatred for her. I flew towards her only to be knocked into another building. "You have gotten weaker. You time on earth has really hindered you." She said as picked me up by my hair. I struggled to release myself only to be thrown into a truck. As I fell to the ground, I noticed the man that was driving the truck. He looked as if he was stuck inside. I raised my hand to attempt to help him only for Morgana to destroy the truck with a bolt a lightning. The explosion caused me to fly into the street. I managed to get to my feet, only to realize this was a fight I couldn't win. I looked around only to see the mayhem Morgana has caused. The rain was still pouring, but it wasn't enough to put out the many fires around the city.

"You are pathetic Gabriel. I was really hopping for more of a fight. If this is the best that you have, then your little team won't stand a chance." She said as she lands a few feet away from me. "You are wrong. We will defeat you." I simply said as I thought of one final move. She just laughed at me, unphased by my words. "Laugh at this!" I said as I flew as fast as I could, grabbing her in the process. "What is this!" She screamed as she tried to get loose. I used every bit of my energy to hold her. I flew into the clouds and placed my arms around her stomach and dove back down into the ocean with a speed I never reached before. I continued to descend even after we hit the ocean floor, attempting to reach the earth's core. I knew once I reached the earth's core, my body wouldn't survive the impact; but I was hoping that I could destroy Morgana in the process. It was a sacrifice that I was willing to take to protect my family. I began to think about my time on Earth and all the great moments I got a chance to have. I thought about my family and my new extended family. I thought about never getting the chance to meet the Adam and Melody's miracle child. This was for them and the rest of the world.

I could feel us getting closer to the core. I used every ounce of my power as he drove through miles of the earth's mantle. "This is it." I told myself as I reached my goal. In a blink of an eye, all my feelings, all my pain, everything was gone. It was done. I was done.

(Joshua) London

"Another one." I said to the bartender. He nodded and poured me a glass of some unknown London drink I been sipping. I didn't give a rat's ass what I was drinking if it would get me fucked up. I was still pissed about everything that happened back in the states. That bastard Adam and his fucked-up version of the super kids expect me to fight a war that I didn't start. People died and that wasn't cool, but I think the thing that bothers me the most is that guy and his dead girlfriend. The way he carried her body towards us still is an image in my mind that I want to forget.

After all of that. I managed to finally get my passport and go to the one place where I knew I could get wasted and fuck escorts all I want, Amsterdam. I ended up in London just because the trip wasn't far, and someone told me they had good bars. I checked my phone only to see three missed calls from Adam. I'm sure something must of went down, but I didn't feel like being bothered with saving the world on my vacation.

"Another one but stop giving me that fucking ice!" I demanded. The bartender looked at my angrily. "Hey, watch your mouth American!" He said. I finished my drink and smashed his head against the counter, knocking the bartender out. "I'm not from America, jackass!" I said as I threw a ten-dollar tip at him. Just as I did that, it began to rain out of nowhere. "What the hell?" I said as I heard people scream from outside.

"You have to be shitting me!" A giant black hole sat in the sky. I went back in the bar and grabbed a bottle of vodka and walked back outside in the rain. "This isn't going to be good." I said as I took a large gulp of the bottle and pulled out my phone. I called Adam only to find out that whatever the black hole thing in the sky was, it destroyed all service for phones. "Fuck!" I transformed in a wolf and ran towards the hole. I didn't know why I cared, but a part of me did.

I stood in front of the hole, examining it. "This shit is crazy." I thought to myself. I looked up only to smell someone very familiar "Lyla." Just as I said that, her body flew out of a building. I couldn't tell if she was alive of not. I used my claws and climbed up the building catching her body before hitting the ground. She was hurt and unconscious. I placed her on my back and began running.

When I noticed I was out of the city, I stopped running and placed Lyla on a tree. I transformed back to my human form. "What the fuck is going on?!" I screamed to myself. I looked around for some clothes until I noticed a JCPenney's on the corner. "I'll be right back." I said to a knocked-out Lyla as I walked towards the store. "Nobody mind me, I'm just here to get some clothes." I said as I walked in the crowded store naked. "Sir, I'm calling the police." The cashier said as I walked past her. I ignored her as I found a shirt, pants and some shoes. "I miss my bottle." I said as I got dressed in the middle of the store.

"Wake up!" I said as I slapped Lyla in the face attempting to wake her. Her eyes slowly opened as if she had been sleeping for years. She looked at me in surprise. "Joshua?" Sheaid as she continued to look at me. "Yes, Unfortunately." I thought Lyla was one of the most annoying people I have ever met, but it was nice to see her face again. "Where are we? Gabriel! We need to go help her!" She said as she attempted to fly, but quickly fell right in my arms. "Look at you! You can't fight. You got your ass handed too. What in the hell happened?" I asked. She leaned on the tree and looked up at the sky. "We were attacked. I was shocked by lightning and that's the last thing I remember." She said as she continued to look at the sky. "Oh my God, look! Its Gabriel!" She said pointing at the sky. Coming down like a comet in the sky was Gabriel and some other woman. I never seen anything move that fast. They crashed in the water, causing waves to rise at unbelievable heights. "We need to go." I said as I saw the waves start to crash on to the land. I picked up Lyla and began running back into the store. "What is she doing?" Lyla asked as we ran to the roof. The water crashed against the building causing us to fall over each other.

We stood on the roof as we watched the city go under water. We both waited for Gabriel to arise from the ocean, but she never appeared. "She will come up Lyla." I said as I looked at her. Lyla didn't even look my way. Her eyes were focused on the ocean. "No, she won't." She said as she fell to her knees and sobbed. I didn't know angels could sob, but Lyla's tears ran down her face like a river of sorrow. I held her in my arms, finally realizing that this fight was bigger than me. This fight was bigger than all of us and watching everyone fight and lose their lives in the process was something I couldn't allow to happen anymore. I was prepared to join this fight and join it permanently. I didn't want to see any more pain.

Miss Catherine's mansion was beyond massive. All the stories I've heard about it were under told. I glanced at all the beautiful murals and artifacts that were on display throughout her home.

"Welcome family and friends. This is our school of witchcraft. You will be safe here." Miss Catherine said as we followed her through the house. "It is a pleasure to finally meet you." I said as I extended my hand to her. She smiled as she shook my hand. "The pleasure is all mine. It's not every day an angel comes to visit this part of town." She said as she turned back around. "Follow me. I have something to show you all." She said.

"Victoria! What has happened to your arm?" Mrs. Eve said to her daughter. Victoria looked at Melody then to her mom. "It's a long story, but I am okay." She responded. My mom examined it and placed her hand on her heart. "Oh, my goodness! Your arm is completely gone!" Mrs. Eve said as she looked closer at it. I looked at Melody only to see the hurt in her eyes as well. I know she still blames herself, and it kills me.

"A demon threw a car at me and I lost an arm in the process. My friend Dawn and Miss Catherine saved my life and gave me a magical arm if these bandages stay on me. I have gotten a lot stronger since then, and I guarantee that nothing like that will ever happen to me again." Victoria said as she looked into all our eyes. I could feel her newly power and it was quite impressive. Mrs. Eve was devastated by Victoria's arm, but she didn't say anything. She just kissed her cheek and continued to follow Miss Catherine.

"This is my panic room. No type of magic or anything can find you while you are here. We have found a breakthrough in your search for Lilith." Miss Catherine said as she looked at us. "What have you found?" I asked. "You won't find Lilith, because she is not on this world. We believe that she is dwelling in The Darkness." Dawn said as she appeared in the room. "Hey guys. Long time no see." Dawn said as she walked passed us and stood next to Miss Catherine and Victoria. I could tell her power has improved as well.

"Lilith is living in The Darkness? How is that possible? The Darkness closed as fast as it opened." Melody said confusingly. "We believe that Lilith has somehow found a way to travel between The Darkness and our world and that she has been hiding in The Darkness because she is planning something." Miss Catherine said. "It makes sense. If Lilith was planning something and wanted to do it undetected, The Darkness would be a place that she could do it." I said. "Okay. So how do we get to The Darkness?" Ruin asked as he took a step forward. "I don't know, and even if we did, we don't know what's in there. Its way to risky." Dawn said. She was right as well. Going through The Darkness was extremely dangerous because we don't know what was waiting on the other side, but waiting for Lilith to attack us wasn't a better idea.

"What's going on?" Jason said as he awoke. I looked at him and I could tell he was confused. I looked at Melody only to see her in an awkward position. Through everything, her beauty was always mesmerizing. I couldn't wait until all this was over, so we could just 'be' together. I haven't even gotten the chance to enjoy our pregnancy since I returned, because of all the things that has been happening to us and our family.

"Jason, let me explain..." Melody said as she walked closer to him. "No, let me explain. I was kidnaped by a federal agent and used for bait to lure you Melody because apparently, you are a demon who is bent on destroying the world. What the hell!" He said. I couldn't say anything because I didn't want to be the one to tell him the truth about this world. "Jason, whatever they told you, it's not true. You know me." Melody said putting her hands up. "I did know you Mel, but I saw a woman fly through a floor. I saw wings on Adam's back. Matthew has been worried sick about you, Victoria, and here you are. I saw some impossible things that need explaining! So, stop lying to me!" He demanded. The room was quiet, but I knew someone would finally tell him the truth. "Melody is a Nephilim, which means her mother was an angel and her father was a demon. So, whoever told you that information was half right. Adam and his sisters are angels. Victoria and Mrs. Eve are witches and my brother, and I are vampires. There are many forces that are trying to kill us and I'm sorry you had to find out like this, but we have no time to waste on human feelings, no offense." Alexandria said as she went off in a rant. Jason was stunned, but he didn't say anything. He just sat down and looked at us all. "Okay. Okay. Sorry about that." He said. Melody went and sat next to him. "So, what's the plan?" Melody said as she looked amongst us.

"Well first we need too..." My thoughts were interrupted by a severe pain in my heart which caused me to fall on my knees. "Adam!" Natalia and Melody came to my side instantly. Natalia stood up and left the room. "Hey, what's going on?" Ruin said as he followed her out the room. "It's Gabriel. She's gone." I simply said as I stood up in disbelief. "What do you mean, gone?" Melody repeated. I couldn't have managed to say anything else. "Adam!" Melody called my name, but I still couldn't reply.

"Hey guys! You all need to come see this." Ruin called from the other room. Without a word, everybody stood in front of the television watching in awe at what we were seeing. The news reporters words were devastating:

Reporter: At about 3:00 this afternoon, destruction and devastation were the
only words being used in London, England as it became the third city
to be attacked by this unknown force. As you can see here, a large
black hole appeared within the sky releasing one woman who caused rampage
amongst the city killing thousands of people. Apparently, the unknown woman
was fighting one of the many winged people we have been seeing within the
last 6 months. The Prime Minster is preparing to go to war with whatever
these beings are. We have footage of the devastating battle that left most
of London under water...

As we watched the footage I could see Gabriel fighting for her life. "Who is this woman?" Alexandria said as she pointed. "Her name is Morgana. Humans know of her as mother nature. Gabriel defeated her before the first human was even created. She must be the fourth being released from The Darkness." I said looking at the television.

Reporter: As you can see, both mysterious women crashed down back to the oceans causing huge waves which flooded three-fourths
of London. The two women have yet to resurface and the dark hole in the sky
has yet to disappear. We sit and wait until further information about this disaster.

"Gabriel." I said as I looked at the television. "It can't be! It just can't!" Melody cried. "Melody calm down." Alexandria said as she tried to confront her. "No, I can't calm down. Gabriel was my sister too and she has done so much for me and accepted me when I didn't accept myself. She has always risked her life for me and when she needed me the most I wasn't there." She said as tears ran down her eyes. "Melody." I said but her tears blinded her from me. "First my beloved Scarlett, now Gabriel. All these deaths are because of me. I released The Darkness and every life that perished since then is because of me." Melody cried as she started clinching her stomach. "Melody!" I yell but to no prevail. She closes her eyes and falls towards the ground. I catch her effortlessly and hold her in my arms. "The amount of stress she is experiencing is affecting the baby." I said as I look at her body. "Oh my God! What do we do? We can't take her to the hospital." Mrs. Eve said as she came to our side. "Melody!" Victoria screamed. "I will take her. We have medicine and certified witches who can take care of her." Miss Catherine said as four witches came and took my love away. I watched until she was out of my sight.

"She will be alright Adam. I know it." Alexandria said as she gave me a hug. I couldn't say anything. I just stared blankly. "Adam, we need to find Lyla!" Natalia said as stood in front of me, snapping me out of my trance. I almost forgot that Lyla was with Gabriel. Gabriel must have fought hard enough so Lyla could escape. She was truly a leader.

"Gabriel sacrificed her life for all of us, we must keep fighting. We cannot let her death go in vain. I refuse to let any more of us die before ending Lilith. Natalia, Victoria, and I will go to London to find Lyla. I will travel in The Darkness alone to find out more information, so we know exactly what we are up against." I said as I looked at everyone. Victoria stood up and confronted me. "I like your plan, but I feel that you should stay here, with Melody. She needs you more than we do. Natalia and I can find Lyla and travel to The Darkness and find out whatever we need. While we are gone, you guys should prepare yourself. It's time to end all of this." Victoria said. "I think that's a great idea." Miss Catherine said as she looked at me. I nodded in agreement as they spoke. "Bring back Lyla." I said seriously. "We will." Natalia said as she wiped away dry tears. Victoria held out her hand for Natalia to hold. Ruin gave Natalia look and she threw a weak smile at him. "Okay, here we go." Victoria said as the disappeared.

"What do you need from me Adam. I just want help." Ruin said as he walked up towards me. "Actually, I do need something." I said as I walked towards Jason and dung in his pocket. "Hey, umm, what's happening." Jason said confused. I smashed it before I pulled it out. "What is this? I heard it while I was carrying him." I said as I showed him the device. Ruin looked at it briefly. "It's a tracking device with a voice recorder." He said as he looked back at me. "This doesn't look government issued, but handmade instead." He continued. "What does that mean?" I asked. "I've seen this model once or twice in my lifetime. You are right, it's not government issued. By the looks of it, it seems like a hunter made it." I sighed as I shook my head. "A hunter?" I asked confused. Ruin smiled at me. "People whose job is to kill the monsters like me. I don't think they truly know what you are yet, but they traced us. If I was a betting man, I would bet they are on their way here now. The only thing I don't understand is how is the government and hunters working together?" He asked. "Well, after the attacks in these major cities, they probably had no choice." I thought out loud. Ruin sat down next to Alexandria. "Do you still got a scent on that agent who we fought?" I asked. Ruin smiled. "Of course, should I pay him a visit?" He asked. "Before he pays us one." I said. Ruin smiled as he and Alexandria got up and exited the house. I looked at the smashed device once more before I dropped it on the floor and went the bed side of Melody.

Chapter 25
Loss, Rebuild, Prepare

(Captain Black)

I was looking at a picture of my son as the helicopter landed in downtown New Orleans. Shawn and I were on a full pursuit to find and obtain Melody. I already called the whole New Orleans police force and put them on full alert. "We can't attack them like we did before, for obvious reasons. We need a more solid plan." Shawn said as he loaded his gun. "We do. These people are out of our lead. What has Lynn found?" I said as we exit the helicopter. "Nothing yet, but I'm sure we will get a breakthrough." He said. I nodded as I looked up to see Commander Davis walking towards me. "Just follow my lead." I tell Shawn as Commander Davis stops right in front of me.

"Ralph! What the hell! You are in some shit! You took my squad team to raid a Chicago condo in hopes of what? No warrant, thousands of dollars in damages! And now you are here! Why!?" He screamed at me. "Sir, we found the terrorist who is responsible for the L.A. and Las Vegas attacks. I took all precautions to obtain her, but we failed. I placed a tracker on them, which has led us here. This is my new partner, Shawn McQueen, he has knowledge of the beings we are dealing with." I said. "So, what are dealing with Ralph? These things are destroying entire cities! What information do you have and why haven't you informed me about anything? I could have you locked up for this shit!" He said. "You could, but you know, and I know that you won't. We are looking at the end of the world sir. The end of the fucking world! I'm going to do whatever it takes to make sure it doesn't end while I'm on here." I screamed. I could feel my face turning red with rage. "I know that you feel obligated because of what happened to your son, and I'm sorry for that..." He started but I interrupted him. "Don't bring up my son! These sons of bitches got him killed! You have no idea what I feel! I will find and stop them from killing anyone else." I said as I continued to walk. "I also need a unit of your best within the hour. We have their location and I don't plan on failing twice in one day."

Commander Davis stood there motionless. My anger was evident, and he wouldn't dare to challenge it, not today at least.

"So, what's the plan? We still don't know what we are up against. They dismembered my last team like they were children." I said as we entered an empty room used for meetings. Shawn paced around the table as he thought to himself. "I was thinking the same thing. I thought Lynn would have found something by now. I don't think we are just dealing with angels." He said as he sat down.

"You're not." An unfamiliar voice said in the corner of the room. I immediately pulled out my gun and pointed at the unknown man. He didn't even flinch. "If I wanted to kill you, trust me, you would be dead." He said as he folded his arms. "Who are you and how did you get in here?" I asked. Shawn stood up and stared blankly at him. "Ruin. His name is Ruin. He is a prince. A vampire prince. I thought your existence was simply lore, but here you stand. What could you possibly be doing here?" Shawn asked without hesitation. I continued to look at him truly amazed at what I was staring at and the sheer knowledge Shawn had on these creatures. I was more than happy he was fighting on my team.

"I came to return this..." He said as he threw the tracking device on the table. "...also, I came to find out why are you following us? Believe it or not we are trying save you and the rest of your race." Ruin said as he smiled at us. "Save us? You are your little flying friends destroyed two of our beloved cities and your hands are covered in the blood of hundreds of the innocent people!" I screamed at him. He looked at us in confusion, is if he wasn't aware of what I was saying. "There is a war upon us and despite what you know about us, we are on the same side. My winged friends you saw are angels, and they are fighting for us the most. How dare you send your troops to fight us?" An unfamiliar woman said as she appeared from the shadows. "Who the hell are you!" I said as she startled me. "My name is Alexandria, sister of Ruin and princess to the throne. Now who are you and your hunter?" She demanded. Her beauty was intimidating, but her voice was firm. Ruin stood behind her as she took the floor.

"My name is Captain Ralph Black and this is my partner Shawn McQueen. Ever since the first attacks we have been following Melody Marie Eve and Adam Tyler in these events, but now you say that they are the good guys. So, now I ask you, who and what are we fighting, and what can we do. I want to save this world from whatever forces that are trying to destroy it." I said.

Alexandria looked at her brother for a moment before turning her eyes back on us. "Her name is Lilith. She is the first woman to ever be created, before Eve. After her creation, she abandoned the Garden of Eden and as punishment, God himself created a prison for her called "The Darkness." In this prison are God's most dangerous creations. Creations that only live for destruction and death. There were four powerful beings who took up most of "The Darkness." Devorus, a powerful vampire king, the absolute original; Demetri, A demon king; Morgana, the goddess of the earth; and of course, Lilith. Devorus and Demetri were defeated in your Las Vegas. Lilith and Morgana are what is left." She said looking at us intently as she spoke. I listened to her every word, only to be speechless by the true horrors that await.

"Wait, are you telling me that Lilith is responsible for all of this? How did she even get free from her cage?" Shawn said as he looked at Alexandria. "It was an accident, and it is no longer of importance. What is important is stopping her before more lives are taken." Ruin said as took a seat. "And how do you suggest we do that?" I asked. "Well, first off, you and your soldiers can stop trying to attack us. It won't work, and it will only piss me off. We are working on a plan as we speak. What have you guys come up with? I'm sure your hunter has some information?" Ruin asked us.

"Well, we don't have much. I have someone on a mission now, but until we hear anything back, we are in the darkness. What are you guys going to do about the giant hole in the London sky?" Shawn asked. "We have a few of ours there now. We think it's an open portal to "The Darkness." Closing it before anything else comes out is our main concern." Ruin answered as he started walking toward the exit.

"Hey, where are you going? We could use your help." I said trying to stop them. "Sure, you could, but you are of no use to us. We need warriors who are willing to put their lives on the line. I don't think you two are ready for this scale of war." He said as he walked out. Angrily I followed.

"Hey! You don't know what I have lost to get to this point. I am ready and just as qualified as you to fight. We are coming with you!" I demanded. Just as I said that my phone rang. "It's Lynn." I answered it hoping to hear some good news.

"You are going to need our help now. We found a weapon that could kill this Lilith." I simply said. Ruin smiled as he turned to exit the building. "Follow me." He said in his haunting voice.

(Natalia)

The waters were residing as Victoria and I walked through the wet, damaged streets on London. All I heard were police sirens and chaos, but not even that could take away the rage I was feeling. The loss of my sister was more than devastating. It was life changing. It showed my true mortality on this world. She was gone, and there would be no way to bring her back.

"I can feel her, Natalia. She is close, but she is not alone." Victoria said. "I can feel her too, right up there." I said as I expanded my wings and flew to the roof of a building that has been abandon right before the water hit. "Lyla!" I said as I ran to her. She was hurt but she was standing. She was not the angel I grew up with. I was looking at a much more powerful sister.

"She is gone." Lyla cried to me. I held back tears as I held her in my arms. "It's okay Lyla. She sacrificed herself to save us all. We will finish this." I said as I looked up to see Joshua, which was surprising to me. "What are you doing here?" I said as I stared at him. "I was in the neighborhood. Your sister needed help, I helped." He said as he looked at my damaged sister. "He saved me, Natalia. So, he is not as worthless as you originally thought." Lyla said as she smiled. "Worthless!" He screamed. "When did you say that!? We hardly ever spoke." He yelled. I smiled to myself before answering. "I said it when you decided to walk away from all of this. It seems like fate has brought you back with us." I said as I lifted Lyla up. He didn't say anything, he just turned his back and looked at the water. "Come Lyla, let me heal you." Victoria said as she places her hand on her. We watched as all her bruises disappeared and her strength regained.

"I feel great!" Lyla said as she spread her wings. I smiled as I watched her fly around and land back on the roof. "I'm glad you are back, sister." I said. "Umm guys..." Joshua said as he stares up blankly at the sky. I look to see where his eyes lay only to witness the impossible. "How could this be?" Emerging slowly from the water was the very much alive Morgana. She was banged up and injured for sure, but she was alive. "How could she survive an attack like that?" Lyla said as her fist began to ball up. I looked in awe as I saw her fly back into the giant dark hole that stood above the city.

"Who is she?" Joshua said as he looked in awe as well. "Morgana, mother of the earth. How is she alive?" I said as I watched her disappear into darkness.

"We must follow her. End her now!" Lyla said as she began to fly towards the hole. I quickly grabbed her. "No! We have no idea what awaits in there. And I refuse to lose anymore life." I said. "Well, I think that you should go Natalia. Not to fight, but to investigate. See what we are truly up against and then get out of there. We could prepare better if we knew what exactly we were fighting. That's what Adam would do." Victoria said as she looked at me. "She is right. That information could give us a slight advantage." Joshua chimed in. I looked at the hole and back at my sister, Joshua, and Victoria. "Okay. I will go." I said as I looked back at the hole. Lyla walked in front of me looking me right in my eyes. "Please, Natalia, be careful and come back to us." Lyla said. I hugged her for what felt like an eternity before letting her go. "Take care of my sister, wolf. She seems very fond of you." I said to Joshua without turning around. "Yeah, sure. Just don't die." He said smiling. I threw a smile at him and I was off. With one powerful flap of my wings I was staring face to face with the giant hole. I examined briefly before flying directly into it unphased by the what awaits. I was motivated by vengeance, not fear.

I looked at the desolate grey desert of rock and mountain as I descended to the ground. The clouds were grey and filled with lightning and thunder with no sight of rain. This was "The Darkness" indeed, but I wasn't afraid. I saw no other being as I roamed across the empty valley of nothingness, until I saw something that didn't fit the area. Sitting high on a very large mountain was what seemed like a castle or a fortress. I flew closer, but close enough that I couldn't be seen by anyone. I stood on the balcony, outside of a large window. I looked in not only to see a battered Morgana, but Lilith as well. I managed to keep my rage in order as I listened to their conversation...

Morgana: She was a lot stronger than I anticipated, but she is no more.
Lilith: I knew you couldn't wait to kill Gabriel. I wondered what took you this long.

Morgana: I waited to stick to the plan, but I figured one less angel would give us even better odds.

Lilith: There are no odds, only victory. I have foreseen it. How is my army doing?

Morgana: They are on schedule. In four days, every soldier shall be complete.

Lilith: Where is my Adrian?

Morgana snapped her fingers and two of her monsters came out of a dungeon carrying a very different looking Adrian. His long hair covered much of his face, but it didn't cover a huge scar across his face. His power was almost frightening, and his heart was black, but I could still since light within him. He was carrying a large helmet that kind of resembled a Spartan's. "What was he doing here?" I asked myself as I continued to listen.

Lilith: How is my powerful leader?

Adrian didn't say anything. He didn't even look up at her.

Lilith: Adrian?

Adrian: Scarlett. I want to see her.

Lilith smiled as she walked to a caged door and opened it. To my disbelief, Scarlett came running out with large shackles on her ankles. I couldn't believe what I was seeing. Scarlett was alive, but it looks like she was a prisoner. Adrian ran to her and I watched them hug each other deeply. Something wicked was happening here and it hurt me to know I couldn't do anything to save them. I would surely get over powered. With an aching heart I flew back to the hole and flew inside of it. I stood there, trying to piece together everything that I saw.

"What happened?" Lyla asked as I landed next to her. "Victoria, get us back to Miss Catherine's. We have to prepare." I said with the image of Adrian still in my head.

(Adrian)

Scarlett's embrace was beyond soothing to my body. I didn't want to let her go, but I knew Lilith would only hurt her if I refused.

"I missed you. Are you okay?" She whispered in my ear. "Yes, I'm fine. It will all be over soon, I promise." I said as they took her away just as fast as she came to me.

"Wait." Lilith said to the monster who began to carry her away. I looked at Lilith to observe what she was doing. "Unshackle her." Lilith demanded. Morgana watched in curiosity. I could tell she was unaware of her motives as well.

The monster followed orders and Scarlett was free. She looked at me then to Lilith, prepared for what type of torture she would have for her. Lilith walked to her and smiled. "Rest yourself. I'm not going to hurt you." She said as she snapped her fingers. Suddenly, Scarlett's cuts and scars vanished, even her dirty gown was transformed into a beautiful clean white dress. She was beautiful. She was always beautiful.

"I think I went about this all wrong. Would you follow me?" Lilith said as she began walking down a long hallway. I held Scarlett's hand as we followed her to huge room that I never seen before. "You have showed me your loyalty, Adrian. You are my powerful leader of the world's most powerful army. I think you finally deserve this." She said as she placed her hand on my shoulder. My outfit quickly transformed into an outfit of a warrior. It was surrounded by black armor that was clear as glass, but as hard as diamond. "Here, take this as well. You have earned it." She said as she held her hand up to the sky and out of thin air, a large sword appeared in her hand. The sword was longer than her entire body and the blade itself looked as if it were at 12 inches thick. It was an amazing weapon.

"This is The Sword of Death. Only one other being has wield this specific weapon, and his name is Death. He created the sword with the souls of his victims. He gave it to me as a gift. It's the ultimate weapon for a soldier of your power." She said as she gave it to me. I looked at it before driving it into the floor. "Thank you." I simply said. Lilith smiled at me as she started to leave the room. "This is your new quarters, both of you. You are stronger together and I need you to be at your strongest." She said as exited the room. I watched as the door closed behind her and was still in awe at what just happened.

"Adam! Why didn't you strike her down when you had a chance? We have to get out of here." Scarlett said as held my face. "I couldn't. It was a risk I wasn't willing to take. Your life will never be a liability. Never again." I said as I looked her in her eyes. I missed her so much, words couldn't even explain what I was feeling.

"Why would she do this? She knows that escape is all we want. Why would she make this so simple?" Scarlett asked. I looked out the large window before answering. "Because she will kill you if we tried. She knows that I know that. Plus, I know we will rage war against the world in a matter of four days. I guess this is like my last supper." I said sadly. Scarlett came behind me and held me. "Are you really going to go through with it?" He asked as she rested her head on my back. "What do you mean?" I responded confused. She then walked in front of me and looked at me intently. "Are you really going to kill innocent people in Lilith's name. This is not your war Adrian," she announced. I took a deep breath before answering. "I would do anything to protect you Scarlett. I must fight because if I don't, you die. I don't care about this world or anything. You are the most important thing that I care about in existence. The world can burn if you are alive. I love you Scarlett." I said as I turned to her. She didn't say anything, she just looked at me with those gorgeous eyes. "Come to me." She said as she sat on the bed. I could feel that she needed me because I needed her. I walked towards her slowly, taking off each piece of my armor as I got closer to her. The armor made loud thumps as each on hit the floor. By the time I reached Scarlett, I was completely in the nude. Scarlett marveled at me as she crawled towards me on knees.

"Adrian." She said with a voice so beautiful, it only filled my passion for her more. I placed my hand on her neck as I laid her body on the bed. Her skin was just as soft as I remembered. She stared at me as she lifted her dress and pulled off her stockings. My lips made their way to hers, and it was as an explosion erupted within my heart; A heart that has been cold and unbothered for quite some time now. I lifted her off the bed as we kissed, tearing every inch of her clothes off her body until she was fully amongst the nude as well; a sight I haven't seen in what feels like forever.

She ran her hand through my newly long curly hair as I place her on the wall. I look at her before I placed myself inside of her. "Oh, Adrian! I missed you." She said as I continued to go deeper inside of her. I held her effortlessly as I continued to thrust myself inside of her. "Adrian!" She screamed, but I said nothing. Being inside of her was a paradise of its own and words were useless in this type of engagement.

I place her back in the bed as I turned her around. I grabbed her beautiful hair and placed myself inside her again, only this time, I gave her every inch of me. She placed her head in a pillow next to her as she took every stroke. I could feel the bed about to collapse under us, so I spreaded out my dark wings and lifted us in the air. Scarlett looked back at me and turned her body towards me, knowing I would never drop her. "I love you Scarlett." I finally said as we looked each other in the eyes. "I know you do." She said as I carried her in my arms as we glided in the air.

I slowly descended into our bed and we laid in each other's arms. Scarlett turned her head towards mine and just stared at me. "What is it?" I asked afraid of what the answer might be. She looked at me then down to my chest. She looked at all the scars on my body from all the training I have endured. "What have they done to you? How did we get here Adrian?" She asked the question I never wanted her to ask.

Scarlett doesn't remember dying. In her mind, she was fighting in Vegas, got knocked out, and ending up at the graveyard with me. Soon after that, Lilith and her demons grabbed and took her away and that's how we ended up here in the first place. I felt the truth would be too much to bare so I decided to keep it away from her.

"I don't know Scarlett. We were sucked into this war because of my sister and her foolish friends. And now we stand as prisoners, forced to fight against the ones trying to save it." "We can't do this Adrian. We just can't." She said. I looked up at the ceiling with a blank stare. "I told you Scarlett, I don't have a choice. It's either you or them. I chose you every time." I simply said. Scarlett was quiet with her thoughts. I knew she was thinking of a solution, something she has been doing for me since I've known her.

"Adrian?" She simply said. "Yes?" I replied. "You said earlier that '*Your life will never be a liability. Never again.*' When has my life been a liability? You have been saving me my whole life." She said. Images of her dying in my arms came flashing back to my head. I tried hard to push them back deeper in my head.

"I should have been there when Evelyn kicked down your door and sent you to the hospital. I should've been there when...when you almost died in Vegas. I have fucked up with you for the last time and I refuse to lose you, Scarlett." I said to her, but as I looked in her eyes I could tell that she could see right through me.

"You could never lie to me Adrian, so why are you lying to me now? She said as she exited the bed with the sheet wrapping her body. "What are you talking about?" I said surprised that she still knew me so well. "I know there is something you are not telling me. I can feel it. I also know there is something different with my body as well. Something is off. Every time I dream, I go to this beautiful place that I cannot put in words. I see my parents. Adrian, I also see Aurora; Just as beautiful as I remembered. Why am I having these dreams? Why does it feel there is something in my body that doesn't belong? Why are we here Adrian!" She demanded. I looked at her in complete shock, unaware of all these things. "My mother. You've seen my mother?" I asked as I walked closer to her. "Yes, Adrian. She even spoke to me. She said, '*Protect him, for this is the time when he will need you the most.*' Her eyes were filled with a worry I have never seen. What is going on Adrian? Talk to me?" She asked. I said nothing, for the truth would hurt, but a lie would hurt her far more.

She went in her gown and pulled out something I haven't seen in such a long time. "Is that my mother's ring? I didn't know you still had it." I said as I grabbed her hands. "I kept in my pocket. I couldn't risk anything happening to it. But my point is that when you proposed to me, it was an agreement that I was going to be your wife. I may not have the title right now, but I think our lives together are so much more. We been through everything together, don't you think you owe me the truth...?" She asked me. I could see a tear began to fall from her eye. I wiped the falling tear before it fell of her face.

"Scarlett. The truth...the truth would kill you." I said as I consoled her in my arms. "I feel like I already been dead, and this is my Hell." She said as she looked up at me. "We are dead, aren't we? We were sent to this place together to live in an eternity that we cannot escape." She said as she dungs her head in my chest. I took a deep breath before uttering a word. I knew the outcome would not be good.

"No. This is not Hell. And no, you are not dreaming. You are here because of me. Scarlett, you died in Vegas. Evelyn killed you like she said she would. I carried you in my arms, cursed everyone that was there and flew you home. I buried you myself and grieved for you for seven days not leaving the cemetery. I buried you right next to my mother. We don't have any family, so it was just us at your site. After the seventh day, Lilith approached me and offered me a deal. She said she could bring you back if I lead her army. I didn't give a damn what she wanted me to do, if you came back to me. You did and that's all I cared about. Having you was all I cared about. I couldn't come to tell you the truth because I knew you would look at me like this."

It was quiet in the room. I finally managed to look at her only to see her hand on her mouth and her eyes were watery. "Scar?" I said as I reach my hand towards her. She looks up at me and slaps me across the face. "How could you do this? How could you? I died? How?" She said as she fell against the wall. I looked at her as I could feel the sorrow in her heart. "I'm sorry Scar." I said as I got on my knees. "I'm sorry for slapping you. That was for lying to me. So, now that I know the truth, we must find a way to free ourselves from this place. I appreciate you putting my life first, but the world shouldn't have to parish because of me. Find a way Adrian, because I can't let you fight." She said. Right when she said that, I got an idea. "I will find a way Scar...But for now, I need you sharp and on my side. What are you willing to do?" I asked her as I started putting on my armor. "Anything. If it comes down to us fighting the world then that's what we have to do." She said as she grabbed my arm. "But I don't want to fight the world. I want to fight Lilith. Melody, your sister, has saved my life and yours. That is who we need to get in contact with. Maybe she can help us baby." she said as she looked at me. I thought of something very similar in my mind.

"Okay Scar, I will pay her a visit." I said as I placed my last gear on and grabbed my giant sword. "You are taking this being dead and coming back alive thing very well." I said as I looked her. "Stranger things have happened. I just can't believe that you brought me back." She said as she embraced me. "Really? You don't believe it?" I asked. "She smiled at me before answering. "Well..." She said as she gave me one more kiss. "I'll return soon." I said as I left our room quarters and walked towards Lilith's den.

"My fearless Adrian. Do you like your new living arrangements?" Lilith said as I walked in her presence. She was alone starring out the window as usual. "Yes. I am grateful. Thank you." I said as I stood before her. Her smile was inviting yet sinister. I wanted to strike her down, but I thought about Scarlett and our plans. I had to play as cool as possible.

"I wanted to ask for permission to Earth. I want to approach Melody and test her true strength, for I think she is the strongest amongst them. I want to test it out on my own." I said as I starred at her without budging. Her smile grew as she walked towards me. "I knew you would live up to your demonic reputation. Melody was my first choice between you two, and not because she was stronger than you, but I got more joy from turning good into evil versus evil into eviler. That was a mistake, my only mistake. Finding you has been my best decision. Go along and find her. Kill her if you can. The least of them the better." She said as she placed her hand on my face. "Make me proud my child...and I'll give you more than your heart could possibly desire." She said as she turned back towards the window. "Of course, Lilith. I won't disappoint you." I said as I placed my helmet on. I expanded my wings and flew out of the window and headed toward the open portal without looking back.

(Melody)

I awoke from my sleep and immediately placed my hands on my stomach. To my surprise, I felt a little heartbeat that has become so dear to me within these last few months. I looked in shock as I continued to rub my belly, bursting in tears that my child hasn't left me yet. "Adam!" I screamed only to watch him instantly appear right next to my side. He was always faster than my own thoughts. He appeared so fast, I forgot briefly on what I was even calling him for. "The baby, our baby. I can still hear him. He's okay." I said happily as I placed his hand on my stomach. His smile was priceless. "You still think it's going to be a boy, huh?" He asked looking at me with those eyes that would usually make my body tingle, but at this moment, I gave him a look I knew he couldn't resist. "Yes. Don't you think it's too many women around here anyways? A boy could definitely liven this place up." I laugh only to be kissed repeatedly all over my face. I was loving the all of this. I feel ever since Lilith and The Darkness happened, Adam and I haven't been as affectionate as we want to be. Everything is about saving the world nowadays. Miss Catherine walked in while interrupting our intimate session. Adam and I laugh as we fix our composure.

"Looks like you are feeling better." She said as she stood next to me. "Yes, thank you for everything. The baby is fine." Adam said as he held my hands. I could feel that he was happier about it than I. "May I have a look see?" Miss Catherine said. "Of course, please." I responded as she placed her hands on my stomach and closed her eyes. "Remarkable." She said. "What! What is it?" I demanded. "The spirit energy within this child is incredible. "I have never seen anything like it." She said as she looked in amazement at my stomach. I looked at Adam in confusion. "Spirit energy?" I whispered to Adam only to see a bright smile. "It's the energy you have within yourself. I just recently found this definition out today as well." He said as kissed my forehead. "This child will possess many gifts. Many powers and abilities." She said. She let go of my stomach and looked at me with concerning eyes. "Your child would be unlike anything this world has never seen before." She continued as she smiled at Adam and I. "Thank you Miss Catherine." I placed my hands back on my stomach. "Do you need anything dear?" She asked as she started to leave the room. "No, thank you." I answered with a smile. With one final glance she left the room. I continued to look down at my stomach only to remind myself of what got me here on this bed in the first place.

"Gabriel." I simply said rushing in the waves of sadness and lost. I didn't know what to think anymore or what do. I stood up in my bed as Adam held out his hand to help me. I could see the sorrow in his eyes just from me saying her name. I refused to believe that she was gone. "Gabriel, has she surfaced yet?" I asked hoping to get an answer I would accept. "No... She hasn't. I don't feel her anymore ever since she went in the ocean." He said in my mind. I could feel my tears beginning to fall down my face once again. "Dawn and my mother just happened to walk in just as my tears began getting the best of me. I hated crying in front of them, but I couldn't control it. My mother walked up to me and held me like a loving mother should. "My Melody, it will be okay." She said as she consoled me. "No... it won't." I answered as I got up and placed my face in Adam's chest, the one place I knew I would be safe and able to hide my tears. My mother frowned as she looked upon me. "Come on Ms. Eve, let's give them a little privacy." Dawn said as she grabbed my mother's arm and together they exited the room.

"What are we going to do, Adam? Without Gabriel..." I couldn't finish my words. Adam placed his hand on my wet check before he spoke. His eyes lined up with mine so perfectly. "We are going to fight. Fight for Gabriel. Fight for our family and all our friends. And we are going to fight for our baby. We will not let Lilith, or anyone take this world from us. We will save it." He said as he kissed me passionately on my lips. I grabbed his body close to mine, not prepared of letting him go any time soon, until we both heard another presence come close to the door.

"Sorry to interrupt, but your sisters has returned." Dawn said as she smiled at us. "Great!" I respond as Adam and I follow Dawn to the living room. "Mel! Are you alright!" Victoria said as she ran in my arms. "Yes sis, I am fine." She looks at my stomach, but before she can say anything, I interrupt her. "Everything is fine, the baby is okay." I said as I looked at her worrisome eyes. She nodded and stood next to me and Adam. "Lyla are you okay?" I asked as I walked to her side. "Yes, thanks to you guys. Joshua saved my life. Can you believe that?" She said shaking her head. Adam walked towards Joshua and smiled. "So, you decided to stay and join the fight after all?" He asked him. "Well, I got tired of saving you guys everywhere I go...plus, I have a score to settle with the chick who destroyed London. I'm here to the end this brother." He said as he stuck out his hand. Adam smiled as he shook it. I was happy to Joshua was back with us. I knew now more than ever, that we needed as much help as we could get. "Is everyone here?" Natalia said as she stood amongst us all. I could feel Ruin, Alexandria at the front door with two other figures, which I thought was great timing. "Yes, everyone is here. This is Ralph Black, a C.I.A. agent who shot at us this morning and this is his partner Shawn McQueen, a hunter. I think they could help us, so I decided to bring them with me." Ruin said as he entered the room. All eyes turned on his two guests. Ralph looked at everyone, but his eyes narrowed down on me. "All this time, I thought you were responsible for killing my son. I ordered a team of specialized soldiers to take you down and you proved that we were no match for you. I wanted to apologize for everything I put you and your family through." Ralph said as he looked directly at me. I began walking towards him. "I could look in your eyes and see that you been through pain. I am so sorry for that." I said as I stood in front of him. Ralph nodded as we both came to an understanding.

"Thank you, Ralph and Shawn, for being here. We appreciate it deeply." Adam said as he smiled at both of our newcomers. They nodded as the moved closer to our family. "Now that everyone one is here, Natalia, what have you found out?" Adam asked. Natalia walked in the middle of all of us before she spoke. "I entered the portal that opened in London only to find that it will lead to Lilith. She has a massive castle structure that I think she has been residing in since her freedom. Morgana, if you don't know, has survived my sister's attack and has returned to Lilith's lair as well." She began. I could feel my anger begin to build. I noticed everyone's anger as I looked across the room.

"But that is the least of our problems. Lilith is building an army. An army that will certainly invade this world in four days. These beings are of Morgana's creations of course, so we must prepare ourselves." She continued. "An army?" I asked. Natalia closed her eyes as if her next words would hurt. "Yes, an army...that is being led by your brother, Adrian." She said as she looked at me. I could feel the shock in everyone's eyes as the name of my brother rang throughout the mansion. "How? This cannot be? Why would he do this?" I said to myself. "It is true. Morgana told me herself." Lyla said. "He is not the same Adrian you remember. His heart has been manipulated by Lilith; But when I felt him, I still felt light within him." Natalia said as she placed her hand on my shoulder. "Scarlett. Losing Scarlett must have turned him completely. I saw in his eyes that he would never forgive us, but I never thought he would do this. Lilith must have a hold on him." I said as I paced around. "She does...While Lilith and Adrian were talking, Lilith brought out Scarlett. She was in chains as if she was a prisoner." She said. "How is that possible?" Victoria asked in confusion. "Somehow, Lilith brought her back into the living and is using Adrian to do her will. If he refuses, she will kill her. That is what I believe." Natalia said. "What kind of power must you have to bring someone back from the dead?" I asked. "A power that she does not possess. Someone else has done this. We have to save them." Adam said. "But how? They have an entire army. How can we expect to defeat them without...? losing anyone." Lyla said. Adam paced around for what seemed like an eternity. I heard his thoughts ramble from one to another. I thought about Adrian and Scarlett. The amount of pain that they have been through. We had to help them. I had to save them.

"I have an idea, but it will take a lot of magic and at least 24 hours of time." Victoria said as she stepped forward. "What idea?" Dawn asked as she walked towards her. "The Soul spell. We could do the soul spell." She said looking at Dawn and Miss Catherine. "No, my child, that spell is to complex, even for me. That would take weeks, maybe even months to complete." Miss Catherine announced. "Miss Catherine, my power has increased dramatically within my time being here. Dawn's power has increased too. Together, we can do it, but on a smaller scale." Victoria argued. "Is anyone going to tell the rest of the group what this soul spell is?" Ruin said as he looked at my sister and Dawn. He placed his leg on his on the coffee table as if he was ready to listen to everything that would be said. Ruin was quite amusing to me.

"Oh, I'm sorry. There is this very powerful spell called the soul spell. If done correctly, righteous souls from the dead would return to earth to help us fight Lilith's army. It takes a lot of time and power, but I think with mine, Dawn, Miss Catherine's, and all the other witches in the coven, we can pull it off." Victoria explained. "What are the side effects? I know there must be some type of danger to this?" Lyla asked. Victoria looked at us all then back to Miss Catherine. "Well, if the spell is done correctly, the righteous souls do return. But if done poorly or incorrectly, the evil souls would rise instead. So, we must do everything perfect." Miss Catherine said. "We can do it Miss Catherine." Dawn said holding Victoria's arm. I smiled at them, because I too, believed that they could do it. I always believed my sister could do anything. "Okay, we believe in you. What do you need?" Adam said as he grabbed my hand. Miss Catherine smiled at him before answering. "Nothing my dear, just your patience. Now come on girls, this will in fact be your greatest task and ultimate test." She said as she walked towards the hallway. "Good luck everyone." Dawn said as she followed Miss Catherine. Victoria walked towards me and gave me a hug. "Wish me luck Mel's, I'm going to need it." She said as she released me. "I believe in you sis." I said as I watched her disappear in the hall way,

"Well, that's a solid plan, but we need a plan b." Shawn the Hunter said. Which were his first words he uttered since he been here. I took my time to really examine him since I haven't had the chance yet. "So, you are a hunter correct? What exactly do you kill?" I asked. He looked at me in surprise. I figured that he thought no one was going to talk to him. "Um, I hunt demons, ghost, ghouls, whatever supernatural being that hurt people. That is my job." He simply said. I was intrigued. "And how long have you been doing this type of work? How did you get involved, if you don't mind me asking?" I asked. I saw everyone eyes quickly shift towards our mysterious stranger.

"I have been doing this since my family was murdered by a demon years ago. I spent years training and preparing myself for this." He said as he grabbed his pendant around his neck. I looked closely at what he was holding, and it was a picture of a woman and two children. I assumed it was his family. "I am so sorry." I said as I felt his sorrow as well. "Thank you." He simply responded. "Welcome to the team." Adam said as he shook his hand. Both Shawn and Ralph have lost a lot and I could feel their sorrows. It broke my heart. Adam placed his arm around me, for he too, felt my pain for them.

"Shawn is right though, I think we do need a plan b. We need all the help we could get." Alexandria said. "We are in New Orleans. This was the city where the first of our kind settled in America. I'm sure we can find a coven here." Ruin said. "Great! That would be incredible." Adam said. Ruin nodded as he stood up. "What about you? Don't you have wolf friends or something?" Lyla said as she looked at Joshua. "I have a few of my good friends, but nothing that could fight a war." He simply said. "Lead the pack, Joshua. I know you used to be the leader in that territory, until you gave it up to go on your own ventures. Lead the pack again. They will follow you." Adam said. "How in the hell do you know that?" He responded surprised. "Because I know you, my old friend." Adam said as he smiled at him. "It's not that simple, I would have to fight the current leader, then convince the other wolves to fight in a war that could get them killed. How do you suppose I do that?" He asked. "I'm sure you will figure something out." Adam simply said as he panted him on the back. "Shit." He said as he walked away from the group. "I will go with you...on a count that you did save my life. It's the least I could do." Lyla said as she smiled at him. "I think Lyla likes our wolf friend..." I said within Adam's mind, "That would be truly interesting." He answered back

Joshua threw a smile back at Lyla and looked at Adam. "After I do this, I want a half gallon, not a fifth, a half-gallon of any liquor that I want. You got me?" He said. Adam and I both laughed at as nodded. "Yes, we promise." I said smiling. Joshua grinned as he walked away and leaned against the wall.

"Should I get the military involved? I feel the world should know and prepare themselves. It could save more lives." Ralph said as he brainstormed ideas. "Yes, but that could also get more lives killed. The military are just people. We are fighting unknown threats with unknown powers." I said. "With all due respect Melody, we are soldiers and if there is threat that is opposing our country, we will fight. This is a threat that is opposing our world. We could get the armies of the world to fight with us." He said. I looked at Adam, knowing what he was saying was right. "If I knew my world were being attacked, and I had an opportunity to fight, I would. What can you do?" Adam asked. "I would need to go to the white house as soon as possible." He replied. "Okay, whatever it takes." Adam said. "Wait, before anybody leaves, I have something for you, Adam." Shawn said as he walked towards him. "My partner, Lynn, has found a weapon. A legendary and ancient weapon. A sword that crafted by ancient beings and an angel named Michael. It is rumored that this blade could kill anything." Shawn said showing him a picture on his phone. The blade was long and sharp. It was complete white with many unique designs on it. Adam and Natalia looked at it in amazement.

"The Blade of Michael. How did you find this? Where did you find this?" Adam asked is disbelief. "Lynn has a unique gift. She has the ability to feel spirits and locate them. The sword happens to be a spirt within itself. She felt the energy it was releasing, and she tracked it down. The sword is in Tokyo, Japan. I tell you this because I have killed hundreds of monsters, but Lilith is far too powerful for us to fight. I want you to use the sword to kill her once and for all. You could get closer to her better than me or Ralph." Shawn admitted. Adam continued to look at the phone, still in utter shock. I figured this weapon was the real deal the way he looked at it. "With this weapon, I could end all of this. We must retrieve it." He said as he looked at Shawn then back to me. "Yes, go Adam. If this weapon has that much power, we would be foolish not to. I will stay here and help in any way I can." I said knowing I would do anything to fight. Every fiber in my body wanted to go with Adam, but I couldn't risk injuring our child.

"No, Melody, I need you to come with me." I turned around to see Amora, standing right beside me. All the eyes immediately turned to her. "Amora, nice of you to drop by. What could you possibly want?" Adam said as he looked at her. "I had too, Scarlett's body is not in her grave and Adrian is nowhere to be found." She said. "Yes, we are aware. Lilith brought back Scarlett from the dead and she is using Adrian to fight for her army she is creating." I said as I looked at her. She looked in awe as I said these words. "I told Adrian that this would happen…If she couldn't have you, she would take him. Where are they? I must go to them now." She demanded. "No, you mustn't. We have a plan. As powerful as you are Amora, they will kill you. We already lost too much, not that I care about you. I just don't want to see anymore lost." Lyla said as she got up and left the room. Amora looked around the room until she noticed someone missing. "Where is Gabriel?" She asked. No one said a word, not even Adam. Amora held her head down briefly before turning and looking at Adam and me. "I... I am very sorry for you lost." She said. The room remained quiet for a while before anyone spoke again. "Thank you." Adam said. Amora looked out the window then back to me. "How is the little one doing?" She said to me. Everyone else also looked at me. "He is fine" I responded quickly. She gave me a weird look before she continued. "Okay well, I need you to come with me. I have to show you something." She asked. I looked at Adam only to see his eyes glisten off the reflection on the light in the house. "Go, my love, your powers are great. If you get into any trouble, I will be there." He said in my head. "I love you." I responded with a smile. "Okay Amora, let's go." I said as I headed towards the door.

      "Everyone has their missions. Let's get to it. We only have four days to save this world. I believe in every one of you." Adam said as he looked at every being in the room. I glanced at them too. Everyone was beautiful and powerful in their own way and for the first time after losing my sister Gabriel, I felt something that nothing could take away from me now. I felt hope.

Chapter 26
Lilith

(Lilith)

       I gazed upon my magnificent army as I stood from my balcony. Morgana smiled as she stood by my side. I owed her a lot, and I planned on giving everything her heart desired after this war was over.

       "I want to see them." I said as I continued to look in amazement at the soldiers down below. "Absolutely. Follow me." She said as she turned around. I took one more final gaze before following her to the ground below.

       "My babies. Bow down to your leader and queen, Queen Lilith!" She announced as we stepped on the dark sand. Every soldier immediately got at attention, standing completely still. I marveled at their unique features and superb discipline. "What are they made of?" I asked as we walked between them. "Minerals, dirt, rocks, any type of substance that can be found in this desolate place. They are strong and obedient. They will follow Adrian into war without an ounce of fear." Morgana said as she smiled at her creations. "With this army, defeat is impossible. My children cannot die as long as I have my amulet." She pulled out a gold amulet from around her neck. I examined it for the first time, unaware that she has been wearing this amulet since I known her. "What exactly does this amulet do? What is its power?" I asked curiously. Morgana placed the amulet in my hand, so I could further inspect it more. "I infused The Dark Supreme with my own power." She said as she took the amulet and placed it back around her neck. "Without it, I am powerless." She continued. I glanced at the army she has created and then I looked at Morgana. "What happens if you are defeated, or your amulet is destroyed in the fight? What will happen to this army?" I asked. Morgana smiled as she looked at me. "Nothing is going to happen. I killed the angel Gabriel effortlessly. No angel or any entity can kill the mother of the earth! I will destroy them, all of them." I looked at her briefly began I said anything. Her power was impressive, and she did destroy Gabriel, one of our strongest enemies. I figured she probably would overpower them. "I believe you. I was just worried, because if I felt you weren't strong enough, I would have killed you and took the amulet for myself. Nothing personal, I just can't let anything happen to my army." I said with a light smile. Morgana looked uneasy as she smiled too. "Yes, I will not disappoint you." She said as she got on one knee. "I know you won't. Finish arranging my army. I'll be in my chambers." I said as I waved my hands and disappeared within my castle.

As I walked up the stairs to my chambers, all I could think about was my hatred for the world and all mankind. The destruction of this world was all I could thought about. It was all I cared about.

"It seems you are really going to go through with this? A familiar voice echoed in my ear. I stopped myself immediately. "So, you are going to continue to bother me Lucifer?" I said as I turned around to see him smiling and leaning on the stair case. "Bother? Oh, no…I would never want to do that. I was just checking up on you and your progress. Where is Adrian? I would like to meet him." He said. "No. I cannot allow that." I said as I continued to walk up the stairs. He appeared in front me, blocking me in the process. "I don't think I'm asking." He said as he stood in front of me. I took another step closer to him so that I was able to be directly in his face. "You may have helped me throughout my existence and your power may be frightening to others, but not me. I am aware of your tricks and schemes and I will not fall for it. You know my power and you know what I can do, so stop with all the games. I love you Lucifer. My heart will always belong to you, but this is my battle. This is my war, and I could not imagine not wanting anything more than the destruction of every living being your father has created. I don't need your help!" I said as I looked him in the eyes. "So, you believe you are stronger than I?" He asked so calmly. "I believe you can't defeat me and, in a few days, you won't even be able to defeat my king. Adrian. I have huge plans for him after this war is over." I simply said as I brushed by him. His smile has yet to disappear.

"And you really believe this? All of this pondering over your own vendettas and your absolute quest for power has engulfed your mind." He simply said. I turned around in anger. "What are you saying? That my power does not marvel yours? You are nothing more but the original devil. The original evil. I am the improved form of you. I will succeed where you have failed repeatedly." I said as I continued to walk up the stairs. He began laughing out loud, only fueling my anger.

"You will be the cause of your own demise, unless you let me help you. What you are trying to do, you will fail. I love you Lilith, and losing you will hurt, but I will not save you from this." He simply said. "I won't need it." It was silent for a concise moment until I felt his hand on my neck. He pressed my body against the walls as he glared at me. "Remember who you are and what you have come from. Most importantly, remember all that I have done for you." He said as he smiled at me one more time before vanishing.

I held my neck, still stunned at the fact that Lucifer grabbed me. "I will kill him also." I said to myself as I sat on my thorn. I glanced at my book as I thought about the words he said. I closed my eyes in anger and remembered a grimmer time within my existence. A time that where I needed Lucifer to survive…

Lilith (Nerite, city 18 miles away from Babylon, Around 700 B.C.)

I managed to open my eyes only to the realize that I wasn't in The Darkness anymore. "I'm free?" I asked myself as I tried to stand up to my feet. I was alone and naked, standing behind the home of someone who loved pottery. I looked and gazed at man's creations in complete awe and disbelief; for I have never seen the creations of man. I have been locked away in my own dark paradise since fleeing from The Garden of Eden. I don't know why I was here, but it didn't stop me from observing. My body was weak, as if I just crash landed against the rocky terrain. I stumbled as I tried to walk, knocking over several pot sculptures in the process. I watched as the crashed on the ground.

"Hey! What are you doing back here!" A young man said as he came running to my aid. "Miss, are you okay?" He asked. "Adam?" I said as I tried to focus in on his face. "No, ma'am, my name is Josiah. I am just a potter, but it seems like you just broke two weeks of work." He said as he helped me up. "I'm sorry, I am not from this land." I responded. "Oh, well where are you from? Did you travel far?" He asked as he handed me water and bread. I looked at him, wondering why he was being so generous to me. "I came from a much darker place." I said as I began drinking the water as fast as he gave it to me. I never had the satisfaction of drinking water or eating bread, so I was amazed at what was happening to my body as I consumed it. "You don't have to rush, there is plenty." He said as he handed me another piece of bread.

"Where am I? What place is this?" I asked with a mouth full of food. "Well, this is my home, but if you want to be specific, we are in the city of Nerite. Are you looking for someone?" He asked as I began hearing hundreds of voices and noises. "I must leave." I said as I managed to get to my feet. "Wait, where will you go?" I ignored him as I walked passed his farm toward the busy streets of Nerite. "Wait! Take this?" Josiah said from behind me. In his hand he was holding a white robe and some sandals. "Put this on. People here wear clothes. Especially the women These garments belonged to my wife." He said as he handed me the items. I looked at them carefully before placing them on my body. "Your wife? She is no longer here?" I asked. He looked at the garments then to me before answering. "She was killed in a fire." He responded. I felt his pain in his voice, troubling "This world? It is ran by man?" I asked as I looked among the townspeople. "Well, we have a king who rules over this land, if that is what you mean." He said. "What about the women? What power do we have?" I asked studying his words. "None. Women here have no power in the courts or anything. Their main purpose is to have children with their husbands and take care of the household." He simply said. I was infuriated. "No power!? This is exactly what I feared. This is exactly what I knew would happen." I said as I continued to gaze into the Babylon streets. "What's wrong…Um, I never asked for your name?" He asked me. I finally manage to turn my sight to Josiah after spending time in my own thoughts. "My name is Lilith. I appreciate your hospitality and everything you have done for me. I will spare your soul because of it." I said as I kissed him. It was a passionate kiss. The first kiss I ever done. I pulled back to acknowledge his face. His eyes were still closed, which made me smile. "I will come back to thank you completely." I said as I started walking away only to stop myself again. "I have one more favor. Who are the beings that your kind fear? Where can I find them?" I asked. He looked at me in confusion. "I don't understand." He said. "I know there are beings in this world that man fear. Point me in their direction, I need to speak to them."

I said firmly. "Alright, wait here." He said as he departed into his home. I waited anxiously just looking among the people. I saw the lust within every man's eyes who walked past me. It only fueled my venture more. "Hey, what do you think you are doing?" I heard a voice say from behind me. I turned only to see an obese man and two others standing behind him. I could tell that all three men yearned to taste my skin with their lips and tongues. I was disgusted and angered by their ignorant approach. The sin in this world was overwhelming for me. I looked at them and only saw hatred, quickly reminding me that I, no matter how un human I have become, still was one of them. I had to change that.

"You are too beautiful to be out on the streets all by yourself. Let us take you to a safer place. A place where you can be more comfortable." The fat man said as he grabbed my arm. "Do not touch me." I said as I swiftly swiped his arm off mine, slicing it off. The man screamed in agony as a river of blood came out of his arm. I smiled as his pain as I finished him off as I placed my foot on his neck snapping it instantly. The two other men ran towards me, but I quickly grabbed their necks, snapping them as well. Everyone who witnessed it was in mere shock at the scene. An older man came amongst the deceased bodies and placed a knee, reviewing what just happened in his mind. I knew there was something different about him because of his holiness that surrounded him. Before I could examine him further, Josiah came to me with a map. "Oh, my Lord in Heaven. What has happened?" He said at his first glimpse at the bodies. "These men were trying to hurt me, I killed them for their ignorance." I simply said as I grabbed the map. Josiah looked at me in awe. "You must be an angel. God has returned!" He rejoiced. I looked at the dead bodies then back to Josiah. "I am no angel. I am something much more powerful. I shall return to you after my quest is done." I said as I stepped over the deceased bodies and began my journey. Josiah waved a me as I quickly disappeared into the crowd. I was looking forward to seeing him again. He was in fact the first human that I didn't want to kill.

After walking for some while, I noticed that the old man from earlier was following me for some unknown reason. As I reached a hill, I turned around a finally confronted him. "You have seen what I can do, so why would you be so foolish in provoking me?" I asked as I began walking closer to him before stopping a few feet away. "No, no, I do not want to provoke you. I was sent to deliver you a message." He said calmly. "Tell who ever sent you that I'm not interested." I said as I started turning back around. "The message is from your Father. He has words for you, Lilith." I stopped in my tracks. "What did you just say?" I said unaware of how this old man knows my name. "Your father says that you are here to prove yourself to him. He is giving you another chance of life here, on earth." He said. "Prove myself? Who are you?" I demanded. "He says that he sees immense potential in you. Enough potential to change this world in its entirety. You have the gift; your heart is just not in the right place." He continued. "Who are you!?" I yelled. The old man smiled. "I'm just a messenger, living out my God's word." He said. "Why didn't 'your God' come down and tell me this himself?" I asked. "You know better than to question him more than anybody." He replied. I could feel my anger begin to boil within me. "What you are planning to do, it will not get you into his Kingdom. It will only damn your soul. God brought you back to give you another chance. He loves you more than you could ever know. Do not do what you are planning." The old man begged. "Now, now…why would you want to stop her. She has her own mind and free will. This world is sinful, these people need to be punished." Another voice came from behind me. "What are you doing here, Lucifer?" The old man said as he stood his ground. "I heard all the commotion." He simply said as he walked from behind me. "You do not belong here." The old man said as Lucifer continued to walk in between us. "Hello, sweetheart, is this man giving you trouble; talking about a father who has left you?" Lucifer said to me. I said nothing. Lucifer's presence was intimidating, too intimidating to just speak through anger. "No, I was just leaving." I said as I turned around only to be stopped by Lucifer. "Wait, I thought you were trying to get to the Black Sea? Your map is incorrect and outdated. I could show you myself if you like?" Lucifer asked charmingly. "No, you mustn't go with the devil. He will only lead you to an eternal hell. Please listen, as God has sent me to save your soul." The old man begged once again. "God doesn't care about us. Look at his creations. Filled with sin and evil. I will cleanse them from this world and create an army to destroy this world and create a new. God is no longer someone I care about or answer too." I said as I turned back around towards my destination. "Now, Lucifer…I would love for you to show me the way." I said as he smiled at me. "God will not take mercy on your soul." The old man said as we began to walk away. "No, but I will." Lucifer said as he snapped his fingers. The old man suddenly went into flames as we walked away, screaming an awful scream. Lucifer didn't even look back to witness the old man, he was too focus on getting me where I wanted to be.

Lucifer an I walked for miles before either of us uttered a word. I found him to be quite enchanting to say the least. "What made you leave the Garden of Eden? I always been curious of your story." He finally said. "The idea of being created to be a man's partner was unbarring. I didn't think it was fair if we were made equally. I refused to abide by our father's rules, so I left. Being human also made me weak…that is something I could never stand for." I simply responded. "That shows strength. How could you be punished for thinking on your own? I agree with your decision completely, but what are you going to do about it?" He asked. "I am going to destroy everything He has created and start a new world. A world where there are no rules or no masters. I will show God that I can do a much better job than him." I answered. Lucifer smiled at me, but he didn't respond. I felt an appreciation from Lucifer, which is something I have never felt. "I chose to follow you because in my eyes, I looked at you as a God. You were banished from Heaven because you couldn't bear to bow down to mankind. I thought that was the most inspiring thing to happen in existence. Man is weak, filled with malice and sin, you were perfect. I didn't understand it, but I have been longing to meet you, so I could tell you this in person." I confessed. Lucifer smiled once again but didn't respond. "What is it?" I finally asked. He looked ahead and pointed. I followed his eyes to see a beautiful twilight in the sky. "My father was wrong to banish me, but he has paid the price everyday as he gazes upon his most precious possessions as they destroy themselves. All my brothers and sisters who opposed me are now my enemies. I am alone. Well, I was alone, until I found you. Another being who opposed your father's flawed plans. My time on this earth is limited, therefore you must be the one to fulfill what needs to be done." He said as he continued to look at the sky. "Where will you go?" I asked worried. "Years from now, my dominion over the world will solely be because of humanity's constant urge to sin. I will only be able to live through sinners, which hurts my feelings because I would have loved to see the world burn with my own eyes." He confessed. "You will be here to witness everything. I will make sure of it." I responded. He stopped and pointed to a large body of water. "This is the black sea." He simply said.

       I walked towards the body of water and looked in. "Why have we come here?" Lucifer asked as he approached my side. "Josiah, he said there were beings here than man feared." I responded as I continued to look in the dark sea. "And you believed him? Man are flawed remember. Why would you put your trust in one man?" He asked. "I trust him. I felt his attentions were good." I simply responded. He looked at me oddly before he began walking in the water. "Wait, what are you doing?" I asked as he stepped closer and closer in to the water. "You must be looking for Agatha, the siren?" He asked. I wasn't sure what I was looking for, but I knew there was power in this body of water. "I am looking for power." I replied as I followed him in the water.

Lucifer placed his hands in the water and called out her name. "Agatha, rise for me beautiful." He simply said. We waited until I heard voices from under the water become clear. "Lucifer. Such a wonderful surprise." A beautiful woman appeared from the sea. Her hair was pitch black, but her eyes were a beautiful shade of green. I noticed when she spoke, her mouth did not move. "Agatha, my darling, it's been so long." He said as he kissed her hand. She smiled as she blushed. "Agatha, I want you to meet Lilith." He said as he held her hand guiding her to me. "Could it be? Are you thee Lilith. The one who fled The Garden?" She asked as she observed me. "Yes, she is here on earth and she seeks your assistance." Agatha continued to look at me before she could say anything. "You are…mesmerizing. How did you get to here?" She asked me. I looked at Lucifer before responding. "We walked to you. A man said you are beings that they fear. I wanted to see for myself." I responded. Agatha laughed a boisterous laugh showing her many sharp teeth. "I love her!" Agatha said to a pleased Lucifer. "Men fear us because we eat man. We are the goddesses of the sea and the monsters of the land." She said as she dived under water, showing her large fish like tail which existed over her legs. "We will follow you, because of your history and because you have brought Lucifer to us once again. But we want to be able to destroy everything that we touch. We have been waiting for this moment for thousands of years and we will not disappoint." She said. I smiled with gratitude, as Lucifer smiled at me. "Shall we?" He said as he began to leave the water. Agatha followed right behind him. As she got closer to land, I could see her fish-like fin transform into a long snake body. Her tail was long and elegant; she was a sight to see. She held a large sword and shield and her hair was long enough to cover her breast. She slithered in front of the water and banged her shield and sword together. "Sirens! Your leader calls you to battle. Show yourselves and prepare to kill all of our enemies!" She yelled. Suddenly, hundreds of sirens appeared from the water, all ready for battle. I was amazed at the number of warriors we had. Lucifer smiled as they came out from underneath the water. "Being here on earth has weakened your abilities, close your eyes." Lucifer said as he placed his hand on my chest. I felt a surge of energy go through my body as he touched me, awaking powers that I forgot I had. "Thank you." I said as wings appeared on my back. "Are you ready?" He asked me. "I have never been more." I replied as we began to march through the night.

We took the city of Nerite within the night. Houses were burned, and temples were destroyed. Men, women, and even the children were killed without an ounce of compassion. The sirens had no remorse as the fed on the people of the city. "Lilith! What has happened!?" Josiah screamed as he came running out of his home. "Go far away from this place!" I screamed. He didn't move, he just looked in horror at all the destruction. A siren made its way behind him as we were talking. "No! Do not harm this one!" I yell at her. She nods and slithers away. "You must leave this place! Go now!" I screamed at him. "No, Lilith, you must stop this. You don't have to do this." He screamed. "I have to do this. This world is tainted. It is for the best. You will understand one day." I said. "No, he won't understand because his little mind can't comprehend it. Man deserves to be destroyed. All of them!" Lucifer said as he appeared behind me. With one swift move, He decapitated Josiah and held his head toward me. "Don't let man, become your weakness." He said as threw his head to my feet. For the first time in my life I felt sorrow.

"Lilith! This stops now!" A man's voice rang from behind me, but the loss of Josiah had me unfocused. I turned around to see two angels standing before me. "Adam and Gabriel. What a pleasure." Lucifer said as he approached them. "You know you cannot defeat us." Gabriel said as she took out her sword. "We must retreat. WE are no match for an angel let along two." Agatha said as she came to my side. I looked up only to see hate in my eyes. Without warning, I flew towards them only to get cut down by Adams blade. "Now, you will return to the place you came." He said as he plowed his sword inside my chest. I could feel everything become black and then it became nothing.

I was in The Darkness once again, but this time I was chained into my own dungeon. This wasn't the same place I created for myself, but it was. For what felt like an eternity, I sat chained up, harvesting my power, learning new abilities that I would never use.

"Lilith." Someone was calling me, but it was so faint and far away that I didn't think it was real. "I want to help you get free." I heard the voice again, but this time it was a lot more clear and familiar. "Lucifer?" I called out. "There is a way for you to be released..." He said. "Share with me." I said angry. "There is a stone called "The Black Supreme." This powerful object has the ability to free you and even open The Darkness and its entirety." I looked in amazement as he spoke. "How can I obtain this stone?" I asked. "You can't. It resides hidden on Earth, but I know where it is and I know the perfect being to retrieve it." He said. "Her name is Amora. She is a fallen angel who I have been manipulating for quite some time now. She will be the one to find the stone and release you."

I was speechless. Lucifer has always helped me and guided me. M appreciation for him was massive. "Is there anything else that is needed for all of this to work?" I asked. "There is one more thing…Once the stone ritual is complete, it will need a drop of blood from a Nephilim. That drop of blood must fall into the Lake of Death, which is located in a hidden cave." He said. My excitement dropped dramatically. A Nephilim? How is that even possible? Nephilim's haven't walked the earth for millions of years. No angel and demon could produce anything of that nature anymore." I responded. "Melody and Adrian. Amora's children with one of my most powerful demons. These two already walk the Earth. Everything is going according to plan, just be patient." His words were beautiful to my ears. I was in love with the devil. He was the only one trying to free me, so I would forever be in his debt.

"Once you are free, do not set out to destroy life alone. Wait for me, and we can do it together." He said. I agreed to the terms, but in my head, I knew what I had to do. What I was created to do. I would destroy all life once I was free and I sat a waited patiently until my prison was open…

Chapter 27
Before the Storm Came Rain

(Adam)

I thought about my beloved Melody as I flew to meet up with Lynn to fully undergo the information she had about Michael's Blade. I never thought that blade could be found after all these years, but I was happy that it was. The legend is that it was created to kill Lucifer in the ultimate battle between him and the army of Heaven. For it to be found now is a worrisome thought.

I flew to the location Shawn told me to go which led me to a house that was surrounded by trees and dirt. It was very isolated, which I figured it needed to be. Before I knocked on the door, a young woman opened it with eyes of sheer excitement. "You must be Adam?" The woman said as I looked at her. "You must be Lynn." She smiled as she moved her body to let me in. Her energy was quite amusing.

"Before we start, I just have to say; I never encountered a real angel. Like, I am blown away that you guys exist. I'm so used to chasing monsters and all types of other things, I just never thought I would meet a real angel. I have so many questions for you..." She said as she moved all over the place, fixing their home. "I am truly humbled." I simply said as she just stared at me. "Where are your wings? Like, do they just pop out when they want?" She asked. "Yes, I can eject them at any time." I said as I examined their home. It was filled with demon traps, artifacts, weapons of all sorts. I was really in the home of a hunter. Lynn continued to stare at me as I looked amongst their things. "How did you find Michael's Blade? That is a very hard find, even with my abilities. How did you find it so swiftly?" I asked curiously. "Well, ever since I can remember, I have been connected to the spirit world. Finding people, demons, monsters, artifacts, ghost, whatever, has been my thing. I came across your sword while I was looking for a weapon that could help us. This sword gave off an enormous amount of spirit energy. It made it easy to find." She simply said as she started her computer.

"Spirit energy?" I asked. "Yes, spirit energy. It's the amount of power your spirit has. I have the ability to see it with my own eyes." She said smiling. "Fascinating? How does it look?" I asked. She looked at me in confusion. "I thought since you were an angel, you could see them as well?" She said. "We don't have all the powers. Our father gave humans powers we could never imagine." I said. She smiled as she continued to type. "I doubt that, but I see them in colors. Bright colors. That's how I knew you arrived. Your energy was shining through the front door. It is one of the most powerful energies I ever felt." She said. "Have you ever seen someone stronger?" I asked. She smiled at me once again. "Yes, Melody's energy is actually quite frightening. I can sense she has balanced the demon inside of her. She is truly remarkable." She said as she got up from her computer. "Hey is your sword. It's in Tokyo, Japan. It was found years ago but has been kept hidden by a demonic spell over it. Somehow the spell was broken, and the sword has been moved to Tokyo. Whoever stole the sword, I can imagine is in some deep trouble. I can assume the demon who had the sword is looking for it, so if I were you, I would retrieve it has fast as you can." She said. "Demons had the sword all alone. No wonder we never found it." I said as I began to leave. "Do you need some back up? I may not know how to fight, but I have some tricks under my sleeve." She said as she followed me to the door. "No, it may be too dangerous for you." I said as I exited the house. "Thank you for all your help and welcome to our team. I know Melody will love you." Lynn smiled as she folded her arms. "No problem…" She said as she continued to stare at me. "Oh, I know what you want to see." I said as ejected my wings. "Wow!" She said right before I flew off into the clear blue sky.

I dropped down on the top of a skyscraper as I felt the swords location. "Okay, here we go." I said to myself as I dropped down to the entrance of the massive structure. "Excuse me sir, can I help you?" A man said as he approached me. He was wearing a uniform which made me assume he was the door man. "No but thank you." I said as I walked to the elevator. I could feel every eye on me as I walked passed all the people in the lobby. "Something is not right here." I said to myself as I pressed the elevator button that led me to the 57th floor.

I quickly exit and walked to room 5709. I could feel the sword was here, but I could also feel another presence in the room. I knocked on the door and awaited whoever was responsible for stealing it. "What do you want?" I female voice called through the door. "My name is Adam. I came a long way to talk to you. May I come in?" I asked. After a brief silence, she opens the door. A blond woman with blue eyes and an uncertain look opens the door. She instantly throws water in my face and pulls out a gun. "What was that for?" I asked as I wipe my face. She looks at me briefly before putting her gun down. "You not a demon?" She asked as she examined me. "No, I'm not. Wait, what do you know about demons?" I asked. She walks to her coffee table to place her gun down. "I already said to much. What do you want, Adam?" She said as she lights a cigarette. "My name is Adam and I know you came across a sword." I began. She looked at me in suspicious. "How would you know that? Are you a collector? Tell who ever your informant is that it's not for sell." She continued. "No, I'm not a collector. I came because I need the sword." I said. She laughed as she took another puff of her cigarette. "Who do you think you are? You people kill me. Do you even know what this sword is?" She asked. "The Blade of Michael." I answered. She put her cigarette down and picked up her gun. "Who are you?" She said as she began walking closer. "I'm an angel who needs that sword to kill a very powerful entity." I said. "Angel? Angels don't exist. Are you some kind of hunter? Listen, I need this sword, so I can kill all the demons that was released when the The Darkness opened." She said. "Wait are you a hunter?" I asked. "Cara Nightmare, you heard of me?" She asked. "No, I'm afraid not." I responded. "Oh…" She simply said disappointedly. "Listen Cara, you are in danger. That sword that you stole, the demon will find it. I need it for a much bigger purpose." I said. "I bet, but I can't let you have it. I need it to kill Lilith." She said. "How do you know about Lilith?" I asked. She looked at me before answering. "Every hunter knows about Lilith and that she resides in The Darkness. The Darkness was open, so I can assume she was the first one who jumped out. I done the research." She said. This woman knew a lot to my surprise. "I am sorry to tell you this, but you are no match for Lilith. She would kill you before you could even get close." I said. "Really? And you think you can get closer? Just because you are a man? Listen dude, I can handle myself, so I don't need your help. Now get out before I have to kick your ass. All over this hotel room" She said as she pulled another beautiful sword from her bed. It looked as if it belonged to a samurai or someone who studied the Japanese arts. "That's an amazing weapon." I said as I marveled it. "It was made especially for me and I feel I am about to feed it some more blood." She said as she got in position to strike. "I don't have time for this…" My thoughts were interrupted as I felt demons coming towards her room. "We are too late." I said as I turn my attention to the door. "Okay, I've had enough of you." She said as she started to strike me with her blade. Effortlessly I blocked it with the tip of my finger without even looking at her. "Impossible." She said in amazement. "Brace yourself." I said as the front door blew open.

"Cara Nightmare. I knew you would be the only one able to steal my precious sword from me." A demon walked in with three other men behind him. "Who are you?" I asked as I stood in front of Cara. "His name is Claudio. I been trying to kill this son of a bitch for years now." She said as she raised her blade at him. "Oh, you have a friend? How adorable. Fetch me the sword and kill them. I have things to do." He said as he stood back and let the other three men in. "These are people! How is he controlling them?" I asked. "It's his thing. He can control the minds of the weak." Cara said. I knock all three men out in a single blow. Claudio looks in amazement. "What are you?" He asked. I ejected my wings and grab him by the throat. "Oh my God!" Cara said in the background. "I hate your kind." I simply said as I looked at a shocked Cara. "Go ahead, finish him. I know you will have more satisfaction in it." I said as I smiled. Cara smiled as she approached Claudio with her blade. "Wait! Cara!" He screamed. "Go back to hell!" She said as she sliced off his head. I dropped his body as it dissipated into nothing.

"So, you are an angel after all." She said as she examined my wings. "Yes. That's why I need the sword. I can kill Lilith with it, I promise." I said. "So, I can assume that you have something to do with all the attacks I been seeing on the news?" She asked. "Unfortunately." I said sadly. "I don't appreciate you bringing this war to our world. Innocent people are dying by the hands of these demons." She said as she wiped the blood off her sword. "My friends and I will end it." I said. "You better, because every day you waste, hundreds of people are dying." She said as she walked towards the back of her house. I followed.

"Here she is, The sword of Michael. I'm only giving this to you because I believe you. Kill Lilith, close the The Darkness, save the world." She said as she handed me the well-crafted weapon. "Thank you, Cara. You are so skilled and well-educated in what you do. I would love for you to join our fight. There is an army coming and we could use your strength." I said. She relit her cigarette as she started packing a bag. "I appreciate the offer, but I have other lives to save. You continue to fight the big fight, while I fight the little ones. The Darkness not only unleashed Lilith, but it unleashed hundreds of less powerful demons. My job is here, but like I said, I appreciate it." She simply said. "Where are you going?" I asked as she walked passed me. "London. There is a huge hole in the sky, sounds like my type of work." She said as she grabbed her sword. "It was nice to meet you Adam the angel. I'm pretty sure we will meet again." She said. "I have that same feeling." She smiled as she walked right out the door. I looked at the sword and felt its power. I walked over the unconscious men and closed the door behind me.

I left the building only to see Adrian standing in the middle of the street with a large sword. Cars were beeping at him, but he remained still. His face showed no emotion, but his eyes were glued on me. "One of your friends, I guess?" Cara said as she stood by the entrance. "Yes. I'll take care of this." I said as I approached him.

"Adam, it's nice to finally meet you. I would like to have a talk." He simply said. "Of course." I said as my wings ejected. He smiled as his pitch-black wings ejected as well. We flew to an empty alley where we would be uninterrupted. "I've heard so much about you, I wanted to meet you personally." He said as he drove his massive sword into the ground. "Yes, so have I. I want you to know that I am very sorry about what has happened. Let me help you, Adrian. It's not too late." I said. "It is too late for me. I made a deal to bring Scarlett back to life, after you and your friends got her killed. There is no way of getting out of it with Scarlett surviving. She doesn't understand." He said with sadness in his eyes. "There has to be a way Adrian. I can find it." I said. "No, you can't. But I'm not here for that. I'm here to tell you personally not to oppose me once this starts. I have chosen my path and now I must walk it. I don't care about this world, your friends, or even you for that matter; but I do care about Melody. My whole life it's been Scarlett and me. Now, I have a sister that I know cares about me, and I know she cares about you. Killing you in battle would destroy her and I don't want to do that, but I will if you make the wrong decision." He said. "I cannot allow you to destroy this world Adrian. We can kill Lilith right now, together." I answered. "I'm sorry, but I cannot chance Scarlett's life. What limits would you go to save Melody?" He asked me. "I would do anything." I responded. "Well, you understand. I will come and destroy this world and Lilith will make a new one where Scarlett and I will live forever. I came to beg you not to fight. You cannot win, and your death would only be for nothing. I won't hold back anything for the sake of my love." He said. "Well, neither will I. I am fighting for my love as well. I am fighting for all my friends and family. I am fighting for every human, animal, species, I am fighting for this planet. This blackness in your heart has consumed you. You must let it go Adrian. You are not this person." I said. "You know nothing about me. This blackness has always been inside of me. I'm just accepting it. I'm accepting my fate and I hope you accept yours." He said as he flapped his wings and disappeared in the sky. I remained there for several moments, thinking about Adrian and how lost he has become. I feared the day that we would fight, but I knew that the day would come. I could feel the sadness overtake my heart as I flew to the clouds.

(Ruin)

      As Alexandria, Natalia and I walked the New Orleans streets, I couldn't help to wonder how these people could possibly be celebrating and partying as if nothing was going on. Were these people that blind to the fact that their world could end in a matter of days. The smell of alcohol was way more present than the smell of blood in this place. I looked over towards my sister, and I could tell her thoughts were much different than mine.

      "What are you smiling about?" I said to her as we walked the infamous Bourbon Street. "I find it quite amusing that nothing has changed after all these years. I find it quite fascinating." She said. "What are you guys talking about?" Natalia asked me as she moved closer to me. Her scent was remarkable. "The city of New Orleans has always been like this. A constant party. My sister and I used to live here years ago. Nothing has changed." I said. Natalia looked amongst the crowd then back to us. "Are you guys sure there are vampires that still exist here. I've been on earth for quite some time and I have never ran into one, well besides you guys." She said. As she spoke, I stopped in my tracks as I came across a bar hidden from the rest. "You just didn't know where to look." I said as I pointed to a vampire symbol on the front door of the bar. "What is this?" Natalia asked. "It's the mark of the Eastern Vampire. They must have settled here." Alexandria said as she walked to the door. I smiled as I followed her inside of the building.

      As we walked in, I noticed humans occupying the place. Loud music and dancing was all I could hear. "I don't sense any vampires here." Natalia said as she looked around. I walked to the bar and took a sit. "What are you doing?" Natalia said as she sat right next to me. "Be patient." I simply responded. Alexandria smiled as she pulled up a sit next to me as well. "What are you having?" The bartender said as he placed three shot cups in front of us. "Don't worry I'll take care of them." A pale man wearing a very expensive suit appeared behind the bar smiling at us. "It's not everyday royalty comes in my bar." He continued. The bartender scurried away as if he were afraid. "Ruin. Alexandria. Welcome back to New Orleans. You have been dearly missed. My name is Vlad. I am the leader of the southern Vampire clan." He simply said as he poured three glasses of blood and one vodka. "It is a pleasure to meet you. We thought this would be a lot harder." Alexandria said as she took a large gulp of her blood. "Why? You are in the biggest mecca for vampires. Our numbers have been increasing within the last 50 years and we are thriving. Brother and sister, we know about the return of Devorus. What is happening? It must be big if I'm seeing you two." He said as he poured us another shot. Natalia's face said it all. "Something is happening, but can we discuss this elsewhere?" I asked. Vlad smiled before answering. "Sure, but first, who are these beautiful women with you? I know she isn't a vampire or human to be exact." He asked. Before Natalia could speak, I answered for her. "You wouldn't believe me if I told you." I simply said. Vlad examined her further before responding. "You are quite an exquisite piece of work. I can see why Ruin has his eyes on you." I could see Natalia's face begin to build in anger. I was slightly annoyed. "Shall we? We have lost a sister. We have no time to waste." I said as I stood up. Vlad's eyes turned on me. "Of course. Follow me."

We followed him outside into the crowds of people. "I do apologize for earlier. I know how hard it is to lose someone you love." He said as he walked. "Thank you." Natalia responded. I could feel her rage within her heart. I know she would stop at nothing to get her revenge. I would follow her in to that battle. "Have you fed since you been in the city?" Vlad asked. I looked at Alexandria before answering. "We haven't had the time. Things have been hectic since our arrival." I said. "I understand, don't worry, we will take care of that." He said as he turned into an alley. There was a dark cave that stood before us, which was unusual since it was still in the city limits. "Follow me." He said as he went in to the darkness. Once in the cave, we went through a huge door with all five of the vampire markings of the world. "Here we are." He said as he opened the door. Once we walked in, there were hundreds of vampires drinking, fighting, it was their own sanctuary. "This is where all the vampires from all over the world come to enjoy themselves. Here you will be safe and undetected." He said as I continued to look around. "Ruin! Look!" Alexandria said as she pointed to a large mural of her and myself on the wall. "Yes, you are queens and kings here." Vlad said as he smiled. "Wow, you two are really royalty. I thought it was all a façade the entire time." Natalia said as she grabbed my arm. "My brothers and sisters! I bring you your king and queen of our thriving world!" Vlad yelled gaining all the attention of every vampire in the building. "He has something to say to all of us, so open your ears!" He continued. Every vampire turned to face us, and for the first time, I felt like a true king.

"My brothers and sisters! I have come a mighty long way and I am overwhelmed at the numbers I see today. You are in fact thriving…" I said causing them to cheer amongst themselves. "I have come to tell you that something is coming. An army who is being led by Lilith. Most of you know of her through stories and legend, but I come to tell you right now that she is real and more terrifying than her myth. She is coming with an army to destroy all life on earth. Now, you may ask, what does her hatred for mankind has to do with us? Well, I'll tell you. To her, we are nothing. She would wipe our kind out completely. Even with me and sister's strength combined, we would be no match. I come here to ask you to fight with me. I have called the help of werewolves, witches, and even angels to assist me with this battle…" I said looking at Natalia. She immediately spread her wings, showing her fierce power.

"My name is Natalia and I am an angel, here to fight amongst you. We have lost much in this battle, but with your help, we can overcome and save your world." She said as her wings disappeared. "I, your humble king, will not force you to fight. But if you choose not to, the fate of the world and your existence will not be promised." I said. "We will join you in battle with our lives." Vlad said as all the other vampires cheered in agreeance. I smiled at the reception we got. "Good job King." Alexandria said as nudged my shoulder. Natalia smiled at me as I looked back amongst the vampires.

"Don't be fools!" One vampire yelled causing all the others to silence themselves. I looked over to see a very familiar face. A face I thought I would never see again. "Don't be fools. Why would you risk your life for an unfit king?" He said as he stood up. "Evan?" I said with much surprise. "It couldn't be." Alexandria said. "Who is he?" Natalia said. "Oh, of course the angel doesn't know who I am. I am the rightful heir to the throne. The first son of Devorus!" He said as he began walking towards us. "Is this true?" Natalia asked. "Yes, Evan was the first child of Devorus, but his blood wasn't pure, so he could never be king. I'm actually surprised to see him here." I said without looking at her. "Unpure blood? What does that mean exactly?" Natalia asked. "My father courted a human girl before we were conceived. The woman died during birth, but the baby lived. He is a vampire, with human blood running through his veins." Alexandria explained.

"It's been a while brother. The rules have changed! I watched you kill my father, and I never forgave you for that. He was resurrected, and before I could see him again, you murder him twice with the help of your angel. Well, now I want to be king, so I could rule as he did. I challenge you brother, right here in front of all your followers. Then we may see who is fit to truly be king." He said as he stood right in front of me. "What are you doing!" A vampire said as he tried to stop him. Evan quickly drove his sword in his chest killing him instantly. The vampires began to roar as they all tried to approach him. "Wait. I'll take care of him once and for all." I said as I walked toward him. "Wait, what are you doing?" Natalia said as she grabbed my arm. "Don't worry, this will be over quick." Alexandria said unbothered.

"Pass me a sword." Ruin said to Vlad. A vampire drew a sword from the wall and threw it to me. I gazed upon the blade and smiled as I swung it around. "This will do fine." I said looking at my half-brother. "Are you ready?" I said as prepared myself. "My brother smiled as he attempted to strike me. I swiftly blocked it and our blades began to connect. I could feel all the eyes were on us as we battled. The room was still.

I kicked him through a table and prepared to finish him, but he flipped right up dodging my attack. We battled for what seemed like a lifetime until I found my opening. I dodged his last attack, and with that I sliced through his stomach. He dropped his song and wailed in agony. I placed his blade to his neck. "Now, who is your king brother?" I said. He looked at me with rage in his eyes until he closed them. "You are my brother." He said as he raised up his hand. I smiled as I pulled him up. The vampires cheered my name as we embraced one another. "I am sorry for your hand." I said to him. "It will grow back, don't worry about it." He said. "Drink!?" I asked. "Absolutely." He answered as we went the bar.

"Wait? I'm confused. Were they not about to kill each other? And now they are best friends again? What is going on?" I heard Natalia ask Alexandria. "They are brothers. Ruin would never kill his own. Evan just needs to get beat sometime to realize it. I told you it would be over soon." Alexandria said as she started to towards us. "I hate men." Natalia said as she followed behind her.

"So, brother, tell me more about this army. Have you seen it with your own eyes?" Evan asked me as he took a sip of blood from his cup. "No, I haven't, but Natalia has. She says its massive. Created by someone who can control the weather or something of that nature." I said. Evan face suddenly grew with excitement. "Finally, a battle worth fighting! I have been waiting hundreds of years for our kind to come out of hiding. The humans will have to bow to us after we fight their war for them." He said as he finished his shot. "No, brother, it's not their war to fight. This is all of ours." I simply said as I took a drink. He looked at me briefly before turning his eyes on Alexandria.

"My dear sister, how have you been?" He said as he embraced her. "I am great, but can you tell me why you insist to always cause a scene like that. You almost got yourself killed this time." She said as she hugged and kissed him on the cheek. "I was excited to see you! Plus, I have been drinking quite a lot as well." He confessed. "I knew it, your moves were slurred." I said as I finished my drink. "When is this battle and where will it take place." Evan asked. I looked at Natalia. "We are not sure where it would be at, but we do know they plan to attack in four days." Natalia asked. Evan looked at Natalia in amazement. "You must be the sister of Adam. You two look alike." Evan said as he looked at her. "You know Adam?" She asked him. "Of course, I spent some time at the castle while he was there. Cool guy, will he be joining the fight?" He asked. "Of course, he and his mate will be leading us." I said. "His mate? I thought that was going to be you Alexandria. Remember how in love you were with him?" Evan said as he laughed. Alexandria's face turned red, which never happened. "I don't recall that." She said as she walked away. "Alexandria! Wait." Natalia said as she followed behind her. "It's still a touchy subject." I simply said as I got my cup filled with blood. "Stay here for a few days. We could train in the swamps behind this structure. No humans would bother us." Evan said. "That sounds like a great idea. Show me." I asked. Evan smiled as he got up from the bar stool. "Let's have a private match first. I'm in desperate need of a rematch." He said I smiled at the offer as I followed him to a training session.

(Alexandria)

I went up the stairs until I came across an empty balcony. I looked down among the party goers and only felt sadness. The emotion came over me as a blanket would over a child. I felt as if I were a child. "Alexandria?" Natalia called from behind me. "I'm fine. I just wanted some air." I simply said. "Well, I know that you don't need air, on the count that you don't breathe. So, tell me what's going on?" She asked. I hesitated while I was consumed in my own thoughts.

"In a few days, we will fight with our lives. I am hoping that my life would be among the ones we lose." I said as I placed my head down. "What?!" Natalia said as she came close to me. "Why would you say that.?" She asked. "Natalia, I have been a vampire my entire existence. I wasn't turned like the vampires you see here. I didn't have a life. I still don't. I am just living for nothing. I have no purpose, no love. All the things I want, I cannot have. Imagine spending an eternity like that." I simply said. Natalia grabbed my hand as she looked me in my eyes. "You could do anything you want, Alexandria. You are a beautiful powerful warrior queen who deserves to live a life." She said. I walked away still enveloped within my own mind.

"After the fighting is over, everyone will go back to their natural lives. I will go back into my dungeon of a castle, because that is what a queen does. I will have no one. I will have nothing." I said. "That is not true. You don't have to go back to the life. Evan was right, the rules have changed. Go out and explore the world. I know you will love it." She said. I finally looked at her with eyes wide open.

"Thank you, Natalia. You are a good friend. Ruin is lucky to have you." I said as I smiled. "Yes, he is. Now come on let's go find your brothers before they try to kill themselves again." She said as she laughed. It was the first time I saw her laugh ever since Gabriel passed. She was more than a friend to me, she was a sister.

Joshua (Canada)

"Oh my!" Lyla said as she entered my trailer. I could see her eyes moving from one corner of the room to the other. "I think you should invest in a maid after all of this is over. This place is disgusting." She said as she tip-toed around to my living room. I grabbed a beer from my refrigerator and popped it open. "Hey, I don't appreciate you talking about my home. It was like this when you first came over." I said proudly. Lyla managed to find a clean spot to sit on. "Yes, these is true. I see you also fixed your door." She said as she smiled. "Yeah, a door that you still in fact owe me for." I responded as I finished my beer.

"Okay, what is the plan? What should we do first?" Lyla asked. I cracked my neck as I took of my shirt. "First, I will call my brothers and sisters of my pack. Then together we will go challenge the chief. I'm really not looking forward to any of this." I said. Lyla stands up and walks in front of me. "I know you don't, but it's for the good of the group. I know you can do this." She said as she smiled and walked towards my door. I looked at her briefly before following her outside.

"Stand back." I simply said as I prepared myself for transformation. Lyla smiled as she flew on top of my trailer. I turned to the wolf effortlessly and turned my sights to the woods ahead of me. I howled, calling the wolves within my pack to me. I could hear them as they ran towards me, breaking tree limbs in their wake. Within seconds they appeared from the woods in their wolf form. I transformed back to my human form as I turned my sights on Lyla. "These two are my pack. I'm pretty sure you all have met." I said as I put my pants on. "Yes, how could I forget?" She said as she hopped down from the roof of my trailer and right next to me. "Lyla, this is Luke." He said as he pointed to the larger wolf with a golden-brown coat. "Nice to meet you Luke." I said as rubbed the top of his head. "And this is Meagan." I awed at her beautiful white coat and red eyes. "Nice to meet you as well." I said only to be growled at. Meagan transformed into her human form and brushed passed me fully in the nude.

"Why is 'she' here? What is going on Joshua?" Meagan demanded. The tone of her voice was certainly angry. Joshua looked at her up and down before stating the obvious. "Here.

Put this on. I can't take you serious naked like that." Joshua said as he tossed her one of his shirts. Meagan's eyes were glued on Joshua as she placed the shirt on and immediately continued her rant. "Okay, now explain? What the hell is going on?" The last time she was here, you disappeared for weeks. Who the hell is she?" She said. "Meagan. Luke. This is Lyla. She is here because she needs our help. We are way above our heads in this one." I said as I began thinking about what I was going to tell them. Luke ran in the woods and came back shortly in his human form wearing nothing but jeans. "What are you talking about?" Meagan asked. I looked at Lyla before answering her. "A war is coming, and we must help fight it. I need you to help me fight it." I simply said. "Of course, I will fight with you, but don't you think we need a little more help if we are fighting a war?" Luke said as he approached us. "My brother and I are building an alliance as we speak, but the power and brute strengths of the wolves will be a tremendous help. "Lyla said as she entered the conversation. Meagan gave her the evilest look which caused me to chuckle to myself. "I also want to challenge the chief wolf in this area, so we can have more strength in numbers." I said as I folded my arms. Meagan looked at me in shock. "What are you talking about? You left the pack and we followed you. Now you are trying to regain power within them? What war are we fighting? Why is this so important to you? We need more answers." Meagan demanded. Her temper was what made her, and I knew she would not rest until all her questions were answered.

"Well, there is this woman with powers that could fuck everything up and she has the intentions of destroying the world. Lyla came here to recruit me and now I'm recruiting you. I've seen firsthand what we are up against and honestly, I doubt we will survive alone; but together, we have a chance. I rather die fighting for something than die for nothing. If there was a time that I would need you to trust me as your leader, today would be the time." I said as I walked pass a silent Morgan and towards Lyla. "How was that?" I whispered to her. "I think you did excellent. Now how much of that did you actually believe?" Lyla whispered back. "None of it. I just needed to sell the idea." I replied smiling. "Asshole." Lyla responded laughing.

"Okay. We are with you until the end." Morgan said. She then started walking towards me. "I apologize for being rude to you. I just don't like new people. Especially women." Morgan said to Lyla as she stuck out her hand. Lyla smiled and shook it naturally as I assumed she would. "No problem, it a pleasure to have you fight with us. You are greatly appreciated." Lyla said.

"Now that those two are friends, how do you expect to challenge the Troy? I have no idea where to find him." Luke said as he walked towards me. "I'm going to find him. How can I miss him, the prick? "I said as I continued to look at Lyla and Meagan converse. "Even if you beat him, how can you convince all of his wolves to follow you? You are not really known for you politics." He asked as he laughed. "I will figure something out." I said as began thinking of something. Luke's eyes followed mine and he saw what my attention was on. "I can't believe it. You like the angel girl, don't you?" He asked catching me off guard. I laughed at the thought, but I could feel a drop of sweat fall from the back of my neck. "Hell no. I don't 'like' anyone. This is all an attempt to save the world." I replied as I glanced over to Lyla. Her eyes caught mine which made me look away just as fast.

"So, what is the plan?" Lyla said as Morgan and herself walked towards me. "We go to Troy, follow me." I said as I transformed into my wolf form and ran into the woods. I could hear Lyla, Luke and Morgan pacing right behind me. I followed Troy's scent that led me to a large house on the edge of the water. It was beautifully, and custom made to Troy's likings. He was a rich fuck who ran this side of town not only with money, but with power. He was the leader of the entire northern sector. This meant that he had thousands of wolves in his command. He was the perfect.

I stopped abruptly in from of his home and examined our surroundings. "What is it?" Lyla asked as she landed on the ground. "Wolves. A lot of them." Luke answered as he too, began examining the house. I transformed in back into a man and began walking towards his house. "Troy! Get your ass out here!" I roar as I stood firmly in his so called front yard. Three wolves appear from behind his house growling towards me. I smiled as I didn't move an inch. "Your mutts don't intimidate me fuck face. You know why I am here!" I said. Suddenly, the front door opens and out from it was a Troy. He was wearing a nice suit and drinking what smelled like vodka. "How I could go for some vodka right now." I said to myself. "Well if it isn't the infamous Joshua Wolf. Look my friends, its

Joshua Wolf. One of the greatest most vicious wolves of our time. Your legend precedes you." He said as men from his pack exited the house and started forming a large circle around us. "I'm here to challenge you for your spot asshole." I said as I smiled at him. He looked at me and began laughing. "You come to my place of residence, in the nude, may I add, to fight me? You must be a fool. Get the fuck out of here!" He simply said as he turned away. "Or you could just give it me, I'm kind of on the clock. I have other shit to do." I said impatiently. Troy turned around angrily as he waved his hand. All the men that surrounded us immediately turned into wolves. "You want to fight for my crown I see? Well, Joshua Wolf. I hope your legend was true. He said as he began to take of his shirt. "I cannot wait to show you as I took three steps back and turned into my wolf form. Troy smiled as he transformed as well. We Immediately begin battle as he claws me in my face. Rage takes over my body as I dive into him causing us to crash to the trees in the woods.

Troy was a skilled fighter, but he was no match for me as I throw a badly injured Troy to the feet of his pack. I transform back into a human as Lyla runs to my aid. "That was quick." She said as she walked to my side. "What did you expect." I said as I hold my injured side. "I have beat your leader's ass. I am now the leader of the pack, so first things first; prepare yourselves, because we go to war in three days. Spread the word to all the others that you can. I want every wolf here by sunrise." I said as I enter the Troy's house. "Should we help?" Morgan said as I took a seat. "Hell no, we have done our part." I said. "So, is this going to be your place now? Because it's an enormous improvement to your disgusting trailer." Lyla asked. "I defeated Troy, he is banished from these parts. Well, at least until this battle is over. He can have it and his pack back." I said as I opened his refrigerator and popped open a beer. "What are you saying?" Lyla asked as she turned facing me. "I don't want to rule or be king or none of that. I want to drink and go back to the way things were." I said as I took a large gulp. "Why are you so afraid to live up to your potential? You were a legend apparently, so why not live up to it?" She continued to grill me. "I'm not afraid of anything." I simply said as I walked away. "You fear the upcoming days. It weighs heavy on your heart." She said as she placed her hands on my face. "You fear death." She continued as she looked at my face. I turned my body away from her and walked off. "What the fuck!" I scream in my head. Her words were true. I had a feeling the moment Lyla came to my doorstep that death was coming for me. It was feeling that came right along with her.

I could hear Lyla enter the empty room with just me and my thoughts. She sat next to me but didn't say anything a word for a moment. "I saw my sister sacrifice herself to destroy a being that didn't even vanquish. I am afraid just as you, but I am not afraid to die. I am afraid to lose anyone else. I will not allow you to die, Joshua." She said. I smiled as I held her hand. "Thank you." I said as I thought about her words. "One more thing?" She asked. I just looked at her as I knew she would say some more insightful stuff. "Can you please put some clothes on? I think I've seen enough of your penis today." She said as she got up from the bed laughing. "Everybody has jokes today, I swear." I said as I got up from the bed and followed Lyla out the room.

Cpt. Black (Washington D.C.)

"I need to talk the president of the united states!" I said as I entered the white house ignoring the security warnings. "This is madness! You are really going to go in the oval office tell our commander and chief that the world is going to be attack by monsters in four days? Think about what you are saying!" Commander Davis screamed as Shawn and I progressed through the building. "I don't care how it sounds. I need to inform him of what is to come. We need the united nations on this like yesterday. We don't have a lot of time." I yelled as I stood in front the presidents door. "Excuse me sir…" A security guard said as he drew his gun on us. "C.I.A. special unit. We need to talk to the president. The situation is dire, and we don't have a lot of time." I said as I showed my badge. "He looked at it then back at me. "Who is this guy?" The man said as he looked at Shawn. "He is with me, he knows more in depth of what is happening." I responded. "He continued to look at us in suspicion before looking at my commander. "This is an urgent matter. The world, not just our country is at stake." Commander Davis stated. The security man looked at us briefly once again before finally letting us in. "Okay." He said as he finally let us in.

"Mr. President, you have guest." The security said as he let us in the room. He looked up and immediately stood up to address us. "Commander Davis." He said as he shook his hand. "Mr. President. I apologize for intruding like this but there is something we must inform you." Commander Davis said. The president turned on his television instantly. "Please tell me that it is about this huge hole in the sky over London." He said as he pointed to the screen." Yes, exactly." I said interrupting the conversation. "And you are?" He asked me. "My name is Captain Ralph Black and I am here to inform you that we are at war. You need to set a meeting with the united nations immediately if we have a chance of survival." I said without thinking. "Okay, you have my attention Captain Black. Please tell me what you know?" He said surprisingly. I looked at Shawn as I opened the floor to him.

"The hole in the sky is a door way to a place called The Darkness. In it is a being of great power, her name is Lilith. I don't know what your faith is Mr. President, but at this point it doesn't matter. God Is real. The devil is real. Lilith, in my eyes is a demonic force who only wants to destroy life on earth. She is responsible for what happened in Vegas and Los Angeles and she is planning to strike again; but this time on a global scale. She has an army of millions that she will certainly release in three days top. We need to create a world army to fight against her or will not survive her onslaught. I know how this may sound, but I beg you to listen prepare ourselves for war." Shawn said. I looked at the president's response only to see something I didn't expect. "Are you positive about this?" He asked. "Yes. I have confirmed it myself. "I said. The president opened his drawer and pulled out a bible. "Even if I made the call, would it make a difference? Do we actually have a chance of victory?" He asked. "With my friends, we do. I just need soldiers willing to fight." I simply said. The president smiled. "I believe in God and I also believe in the Devil. When I saw what happened in Vegas, there was no doubt in my mind that this was the devil's work. Today, we will send him back to hell!" He said as he picked up the phone. "Commander. I want these two leading this world army. This will change everything, this war. This will change the world." He said. "Maybe it's time for the world to change." Shawn said as the president began dialing the phone.

Chapter 28
Hope

(Scarlett)

I stared out the window, only waiting and hoping my Adrian would return to me. I looked upon Lilith's monstrous army as they stood motionless in formation. I was hopeless in it all. I never could have imagined that this would be my life. I closed my eye and thought about the day Adrian proposed to me. It was supposed to be the happiest day of my life, but instead, I lost my best friend, Carmen, and an all-out war started right down my street. Adrian was all I had, and I was all he had. My mind and body were exhausted to a point of breaking, but I could not allow for it to break. I knew Adrian would need me strong for him and I couldn't be anything other.

I thought about his hands, his soft delicate hands; which were unusual, because they didn't fit his bad boy look. I loved how his hands felt against mine. I just wish we could be together, away from all of this. Away from everything.

"Scarlett?" An unfamiliar voice said from behind me. I turned to my surprise to see a young woman standing there. Her hair was vibrant and fluffy, and her green eyes were tantalizing. She looked familiar, but she didn't at the same time. "Yes, I'm Scarlett." I answered to her. Her presence didn't seem to be threatening. In fact, it felt hopeful. The first time I felt hope in a while. "My name is Ella and I'm here to get you out of here." She said as she started to walk closer to me. I felt confusion and shock on my face. "What do you mean? Who are you and how did you find me?" I asked not really caring for the answers. I was just over whelmed with what was happening. "I will answer all of your questions I promise, but right now I have to get you out of here. What I'm doing is breaking all the rules that I know." She said as she grabbed my hand.

"What is this?" Lilith said as she entered the room with Morgana. Ella stood in front of me, protecting me. "Who was this woman?" I thought to myself. Lilith eyes were not eyes of anger, but eyes of interest. "You must be a fool to enter my chambers. Do you not know who I am little girl?" She said to Ella. "I know exactly who you are." Ella simply said as we vanished into nothing.

Within a blink of an eye, we appeared in side of Adrian and my home. At was if no one has been here in months. The door was fixed to my surprise, after being kicked in by a demon. I glanced around the house, still in utter amazement and confusion on how we got back here. "What just happened?" I finally asked as I set my attention on the mysterious woman who rescued me. "I wanted to bring you somewhere, where I thought you would be most comfortable. After everything you have been through, I figured you would enjoy your home the most." Ella said with a smile as she walked towards the kitchen. She came back with two glasses of water. "Here. Drink this. Your body hasn't had the proper fluids in months." She said. I followed her directions as I took a large gulp of the water. It felt good running down my dry throat. "Thank you so much! You have no idea the debt that I owe you." I said as I could feel a tear come down my face. "I'm sorry I didn't come sooner. I can't imagine what you have been through." She said with another smile. A smile that I've seen before, but from someone else. "Who are you? You risked your life to safe me, a stranger to you. You must tell me who you are." I begged her. "There is nothing to tell. I'm just a traveler. I heard there was a prisoner in Lilith's chambers. I had to save you. That is all." She said. I looked at her, but her eyes wouldn't meet mine. "You are lying. You know who I am, don't you?" I asked. She didn't say anything. She just looked away. "Ella, it's okay. I promise that it is okay. You can tell me the truth." I said as I looked at her intently.

"Alright. I do know you. I've known you my entire life. We are going to be really close one day, so I should just let you know everything now." She said as she finally looked at me. "Okay, I am ready." I said. She finished her cup of water before she spoke. "What I am about to tell you might sound strange, but you have to promise me that you can never tell anyone. I am breaking the rules even telling you this, but I can't keep this to myself any longer." She said. "I promise. This will stay between us." I promised. She smiled at me as she placed her cup down on the table. "Okay, well. My name is…. Gabriella, but my mother calls me Ella for short. I am the daughter of Melody Marie Eve and Adam Tyler. This would in fact make you my lovable auntie." She began. I looked at her in awe, not because I didn't believe her, but because I did. I knew she looked familiar in my head. I began to realize and see all of Melody's striking features on her. I was amazed.

"Melody's daughter. My niece. But…how could this be possible?" I asked. Gabriella smiled as she looked at my shocked face. "Well, here is the confusing part. I was created with abilities that I don't even understand. Time doesn't affect me, which is why I can travel back through time. I'm sixteen years old now, so I traveled a great distance." She said. My mind was once again blown. "Wait, so you can travel back in time? That is amazing!" I said. She smiled at me with that same Melody smile.

"You are taking this quite well." She said. "You knew I would, that is why you chose to tell me." I said as I laughed. "Why won't you tell your parents? I know they would love to meet you." I asked. "I cannot tell them my identity. It could affect the outcome of the future, which is why I am here. My time and your future are bleak." She said as she looked away, towards the carpet on the floor. "This battle in the upcoming days will be known as "The Immortal War." It will be a battle unlike anything the world has ever seen. The world will fight side by side together to defeat Lilith's army. It will be a beautiful spectacle to witness because it showed me life can stand together to preserve life. The war was won, and we lived on. That was the original outcome, but now that is not case. Adrian's has changed his course of action which has changed the outcome of this war. His rage will reach a peak of no return if he continues to go down this dark road. My parents will not be able to stop him, so you will have too." She said. I thought about Adrian and how far he has gone, but I couldn't imagine him just losing it all. "So, what are you saying? What can I do?" I asked. "If Adrian reaches his limits and completely goes to the darkness, his rage will certainly consume the world and everyone with it. You are his soulmate, you have the power to save him." She said.

I thought about her words and I tried to think of any solution. "So, what can we do to stop this from happening?" I asked. "Well, I can't do anything. I have been helping my parents since the beginning; leaving clues and trails to help them get here, I even rescued you in hopes that Adrian would no longer have to serve Lilith since you were already free. I have done all I that I can do without breaking the rules of reality." She said gloomily. "What are these rules? You say there are rules to what you can do?" I asked.

"Well, not necessarily rules, but limitations of my powers. Every time I travel back or forward in time, I change the possibilities of some form of action. I traveled back as far as I could go, to see if I could destroy Lilith before she gained power, and I was stopped by a man named Mave. He told me this information because he too was a child born like me. He taught me how to use my powers effectively. Saving you from Lilith was something I wasn't supposed to do, but I had no choice." She said. "Thank you, Gabriella, for everything. I know I can bring him back. I know I can." I said as I went under the couch and pulled out two pistols. "I know you can Auntie. I believe in all of you." She said as she stood up from the couch. "Could you take me to your mother? I feel like that is where I need to be." I said as I loaded a clip into each one of my pistols. "Of course. Just remember everything I said. You mustn't say anything about who I really am to no one." She said. "Your secret is safe with me." I reply as I prepare myself. "One more thing. Make sure you tell my mother that Lilith plans on opening two more portals, one in New York City and the other in a place that continues to change. Lilith is trying to track them. These portals, including the one in London, is where her enormous armies will attack. Adrian, Morgana, and Lilith herself will appear from the one of the portals, but I'm not sure. I figured this information will give you all a slight advantage. You shouldn't be anywhere near once the fighting starts okay?" She said. "Okay. And thank you!" I said as I remember all the information told me. "Okay." Gabriella said as she embraced me. "I will see you soon auntie." She said as she held my hand and once again we vanished into nothing.

(Lilith)

I stood in Scarlett and Adrian's chamber completely interested in the young woman who vanished with my prisoner. "Who was she?" Morgana asked in confusion. "I have not the slightest clue, but I want her. I wonder what being could have the ability to do what she did?" I said. "Shall I create a search team?" She asked me. "We are so close to your objective, don't bother. Her life is insignificant to me. Adrian is well under his transformation. I don't think the girl matters anymore." I said as I exited her chamber. "Understood." Morgana said as she followed me out back to my chamber.

"But I am curious about the woman who saved her. How did she get in undetected? And how could she just vanish? What else power could she be holding?" I asked. "Maybe a witch? She didn't engage, which would let me know that she was afraid to die at the hands of you." Morgana praised. I had a feeling it was something else but was quickly regarded once I felt Adrian walk in my presence.

"I have returned." He said as he stood before me. I walked to him just to touch his face. "My powerful king, did you find what you were looking for?" I asked him. "Yes. I did. I will show no mercy towards anyone that stands in the way." He said. "Wonderful." I replied as I turned back towards my throne. "Oh, Adrian…I almost forgot to inform you that Scarlett is gone, so no need in looking for her." I said as I sat down. I could see his face begin to change. "What do you mean gone?" He said firmly. "She is gone, taken by an unknown woman with unknown powers. She could be possibly dead in a ditch somewhere, but that isn't of any importance. What you should be more focused on if the blood of our enemies." I said proudly. Adrian's face grew with fury. "What in the hell do you mean she's gone! Where is she!" He demanded. "I don't know nor care, and neither should you. You have more important matters." I simply said as I bit into my apple. Adrian drew his sword and ejected his wings. "I will find her!" He said as he attempted to fly off only to be stopped by the mere force of my hand. "Where are you going? Have you not learned anything? I thought you were ready to live your destiny?" I said confused at his actions. "I don't give a shit about you or anything else. We had a deal!" He screamed as I pinned him against the wall with just raising my hand towards him. "We did, I brought you love back to life, so you could fight for me. That was the deal. Whatever happens to her after that is completely your fault." I simply said showing no empathy at all. "You bitch! I will kill you!" He screamed as he struggled to get free. Morgana used her power to create a barrier around Adrian, causing him not to move. "I thought you were ready. I thought you could do this on your own, but I was mistaken. That's okay, I have something for you." I said as I walked to my beautiful crafted table and pulled out a bowl of black demon blood.

"This is the blood of the demon Damon, your precious father. I went to Hell myself to retrieve it. I didn't think that I would need it, but precautions had to be made." I said as I began dipping a small knife in the bowl of blood. "Let me the fuck go!" He said as he weakened the Morgana's powerful barrier. "Your powers are great Adrian, but after this. They will be unmatched, and you will finally become the monster that you are." I said as I began to walk closer to him. "What are you doing!" He screamed. "Now, I'm going to stab you right in the heart with the knife covered in demon blood. This blood is going to go through your body and veins, which will release your true demonic form and take over your angelic abilities. You will become unstoppable and over taken by your rage and your pain. This will be extremely painful and will take up to three days for it to be complete, which is just in time for you to lead my army." I said as I placed my hands on his face. "This is your destiny." I said as I stabbed him with the blade. He screamed in agony as I pierced him. I smiled as I walked away, leaving the blade still plunged inside of him. His screams were like music to my ears as I sat on my throne, watching the beginnings of his long transformation. I folded my legs and prepared myself to watch him until his transformation was complete.

(Melody)

"What is this?" I asked as we landed in a cemetery in Los Angeles. "This is where Adrian's mother is buried. I know I wasn't much of one, but this human, she was wonderful to him." Amora said as she kneeled to the grave. I looked among the tombstone and felt great guilt. "Right next to her, he buried Scarlett." Amora said. I looked among the graves only wishing that things could have been different. "We need to find a way…" I began until I felt a presence coming near to me. Amora raised her head as if she could feel it too. "Could it be?" I said as I started walking towards what I felt. "Oh my God!" I yelled as I saw Scarlett walking towards me. "Scarlett!" I yelled as I ran to her and held her tight. "Melody!" She screamed in joy. I looked at her only to see the same woman who I missed so much. "How are you here? Natalia said you were being held prisoner by Lilith. We were working on a way to free you and Adrian. I can't believe you are here!" I said happily.

"It's a long story, but I managed to get free and find you. We have a lot to talk about and not enough time to waste." She said. I had a million questions too, but I've seen this determined look on her face before and I knew right then and there that something was brewing within her mind. "We need to find Adrian." She said as she noticed her grave site. Amora looked at her as she continued to gaze upon it.

"Do you remember anything from death." Amora asked as she examined her. "No, but I think I dream about it every night. I dream about many things since I been brought back." She said as she grabbed a hand full of dirt from her grave. I sensed something was different about her, but it wasn't a bad aura. I felt power from her.

Scarlett got up from her grave and stood before Amora and I. "We need to find Adrian. I fear that he needs me." Scarlett said looking up in the sky. "Lilith has some time of power over him. It makes it impossible to track him. I've tried." Amora said. "I asked him to find you because I knew you could help us. I have seen the army that Lilith has prepared, and its massive. These creatures are something from a movie. Oh, and I know where she will attack as well. New York City, Shanghai, and London. They will enter earth through these giant portals, like the one that is in London." Scarlett informed us. I looked at Amora then back at Scarlett. "How do you know this?" I asked. "Just trust me!" She pleaded. I did in fact trust every word.

"My love, Scarlett has returned. Come to me." I said to Adam in his head. "I do." I replied to Scarlett. "So how can we find him? There must be a way. What is the plan on stopping Lilith? Fill me in." She said. "I don't think you should get involved." Amora said. "Listen, I don't know who you think I am, but I do what I want. I will not stand on the side lines while Adrian or any of you fight. I want to be front and center." She threatens Amora. She was still the same feisty woman I met months ago.

"The plan is we match her army with an army of our own. We have vampires, werewolves, and witches fighting with us. Plus, the world is putting together a world army, hopefully. I believe that all of us together cannot lose." I said to her. Before Scarlett could response, she fell to the ground as if she were in pain. "Scarlett!" I screamed as I ran to her. "What is happening?" Amora asked. "Adrian...He's in a lot of pain." She said as she got to her feet. I didn't know that the bond between Adrian and herself was this strong, but I should have known that dying and coming back would bring them closer. "I have to go to him. I know that he needs me." She said as she began looking at the sky once again.

"Adrian came to me himself." Adam said as he appeared behind us. I missed him so much, but with everything that was happening within our lives and the world, there was no time for me to express it. I could see the worry on his eyes as he looked at Amora and I. He then focused his eyes on Scarlett. I forgotten that they have never met before.

"You must be Adam? I am Scarlett. I'm sorry for this embarrassing first impression. I have heard great amazing things about you." She said. Adam smiled as he walked closer to her. "I've heard great amazing thing about you too. It is a pleasure to meet you. I just had the pleasure of meeting your fiancé as well." He said. "He told me he was coming to talk to Melody. Find a way to free us. What did he say? Is he alright?" Scarlett asked. Adam looked at me as if his next words would cut Scarlett in half. He hesitated before answering.

"He told me not to stand in his way. He is prepared to fight for Lilith and her army. His decision has been made." He said. "Ever since I was brought back, Adrian has not been the same. He is the same man I've known all my life. I know that this demon/angel shit took him over a loop. And I know that what happened in Vegas must have been hard for him. I know Adrian may not have the purest heart, but I know that there is an abundance of good in him. I see it every day." Scarlett said as she looked back at the grave Adrian dug on his own. "Adam, when the time comes, I need to be the one to confront him." She said. Adam smiled as he spoke. "Of course, you may be the only one who could get through to him." He said as he embraced her. "Let's go. I can only imagine how hungry and tired you must be." I said to Scarlett as I placed my arm around her. Adam came to my side as he gave me a kiss on the cheek. We flew back to Miss Catherine's home as we continued to plan for what was to come.

(Victoria)

"We have it!" I said as I read the final lines to the most powerful spell that I have ever done. Dawn walked to me and smiled. "Yes, it is complete. I can't believe it." She said as we both looked upon our finished work. "Well done ladies. I couldn't be prouder of you two. Along with the rest of the coven. Your powers together have increased drastically since you two first stepped in my school. The completion of this spell has put you on a level that I have never seen witches of your age accomplish. So, in this battle that will dawn upon us, I want you two to lead this coven into victory." Miss Catherine said as she handed us two powerful old wands. "Oh my?" Dawn said as she examined it. "These wands were crafted by some of the most powerful witches ever to walk this earth. The power in them are too great to fully understand now, but you will with patience. Practice while we wait for certain battle." She smiled at us as she left the room. I looked at the wand that was given to me and it was beautiful. "I think it was made from that enormous tree out in the front." I said. "It has to be. I could feel its power radiating within me." She said.

"I never thought that I would grow to like you. But I guess after almost dying next to you made my heart a lot warmer." Dawn said as we sat on the porch looking at the sun go down. "Yeah, a lot has changed." I responded. It was silent for a while before anybody spoke again. "What do you miss about your old life the most? I can only imagine how you must feel to just give up everything just to save the world." She asked me. I smiled to myself. "I miss my fiancé, Matthew. I know this is killing him and he might not even care to be with me after all of this is over. That's what I miss the most, but I miss my job, my music, my life. I miss when my sister and I were just normal girls trying to find their way through life. Everything is different mow and I have to expect it." I said as a tear ran down my face. Dawn wrapped her arm around me, consoling me. She didn't say anything, she just listened. I felt that was exactly I needed. "I just feel like I lost sight of who I was. Look at me! I have a magical arm covered in magical bandages. I don't want to be a witch for the rest of my life. I want to be normal again.

Is that wrong to say?" I asked. "No. It isn't. I understand completely. I wish I had the opportunity to live a normal life. My parents dropped me off at Miss Catherine's school after I made my Barbie dolls float to the ceiling when I was four. I never really seen anything out in the real world until I left and went on this adventure with you. I would love to be free and experience life without the magic." She confessed. I never knew that Dawn never left here before me. She was worse off than me.

"When this is all over. You and I are going to just disappear for a while. How would that sound?" I asked. "Wonderful!" She responded as she got up and glanced at the moon shine amongst us. "It's a full moon tonight." I said. Dawn smiled and entered the house. I stayed outside just a bit longer. The night's breeze felt amazing on my skin.

"Victoria!" Dawn screamed from the living room. I quickly followed her voice which led me to also follow her gaze into the television…

The Reporter: Breaking news today. As you already know, President Connor has met with the United Nations earlier today and they have come to the decision to declare war against our unworldly visitors who have been destroying major cities like Los Angeles, Las Vegas, and London. The entire world is on the same team for the first time in our planets history. The president has engulfed army and C.I.A. veteran, Captain Ralph Black to lead this world army. Thousands of troops are being deployed to London as we speak to fight the fight for our world…

"He has done it." Adam said as he entered with my sister and Scarlett. "Scarlett? Oh my God!" I said as held her in my arms. "Hey girl, what happened to your arm?" She asked. "A long story. How did you get here?" I asked. "Another long story, I'm just back and ready to help." Scarlett said. I missed her, and it was good to see that she hasn't changed. Melody came to my side and looked at me suspiciously. "Have you been crying?" She asked me. "No, I have not." I replied fast. She continued to look at me as she looked right through my lies. "I'm going to go lay down, it's been a long day." Scarlett said as she looked around. "I'll show you a bed. It's good to see you again." Dawn said as she walked her upstairs.

"I need to tell them that New York is the other planned targets of Lilith. We should spread out and have people waiting at every portal that she opens." Melody said as she continued to watch the television. "She is going to attack New York?" I asked. "Yes, in two days left, I'm positive that we can definitely can end all of this." Melody said. She sounded so sure and certain. I wish I had her strength. Adam held her hand as if he never planned to let go. Seeing my sister with him always brought joy to my heart. I couldn't wait until I was reunited with my Matthew. I smiled as I disappeared into my room quarters.

(Natalia)

I sat and watched as everyone enjoyed their time drinking and partying as if this battle would be their last. I smiled as I sat in the corner by myself. Alexandria went to feed, and Ruin was in the back training with the younger vampires. I was fine being myself, but it only fueled my rage.

I got up and stood on the balcony. The sun has longed been down and the night was fresh and warm. I continued to see visions of Gabriel every time I closed my eyes. I could not wait to take the head of Morgana. I was angry and sad at the same time and I could not manage to keep my emotions in check. "I have never seen an angel weep, my love." Ruin said as he walked among the balcony. I wiped my eyes but refused to turn at him. "What are you talking about?" I said firmly. He placed his arms around me as he kissed my neck. "You don't have to be like that with me. Stop hiding your heart from me. You can't." he said as he turned me around to face him. "I am not. I am fine." I replied sharply. I don't know why, but I refused to let Ruin in for reasons I couldn't explain. "No, you are not 'fine.' Your sister was killed yesterday. You are not fine." He said. I could feel my flames start to eject from me. "You know nothing of my pain!" I said as flames flew out of my body. Ruin did not move, he stood there as if he wasn't worried about being burned alive. "I know that you are hurting, and that's okay. It's okay to feel something. I am here with you. I love you, Natalia. And whatever that may mean to you, to me, it means that your problems are my problems. Your battles are my battles. Your tears are mine." He said as her grabbed a tear from my face. I looked at him with eyes I never knew I had. I looked at him through his soul and knew that he was genuine in every word he said. I could see that he loved me as much as he said he did. I couldn't believe that love has found me.

"I love you too." I said as my flames disappeared. I hugged him and kissed his lips like never before. He placed my body against the wall as he kissed my neck, awakening senses I never knew I had. We made love that night and for the moment, I knew I could confide in him. I trusted him with my heart, which no other has ever convinced me to do. I was his and he was mine

(Lyla)

     I sat on the porch watching Joshua and the other wolves play football. I knew the dangers that were ahead, but I was done panicking about it. With two days left, I figured we should make the best out of it. Meagan sat right next to me with two glasses of lemonade. "Here you go." She said as she passed it to me. "Thank you." I said with a smile. I took a large gulp as I continued to watch the boys play. I noticed Meagan staring at me intently. "What is it?" I finally asked to break the awkwardness. "She just smiled. "You are so beautiful, why would you be afraid to talk to him?" She asked me. I looked at her blankly and tad bit confused. "Um, talk to who?" I asked. "Really?" She said as she looked at Joshua from across the field. "Oh, no…This is for the sake of the world. I am not interested." I said as I tried to make myself believe it. Meagan looked at me as if I thought she was a fool. "It's obvious that you two like each other, I think it's cool. Joshua hasn't been seen with a woman since his wife died about eleven years ago, so I think it's good for him." She said. "I didn't know he was married." I said surprisingly. "Yup, she was beautiful as well. I'm just saying, if there is an interest, I think you two should go for it. Life is too short, even for a being that can live forever." She said as she took a sip of her lemonade and walked toward the field...

     I listened to her words thoroughly as I sat by my lonesome. She had some great points, but my mind was elsewhere. I could feel that something was happening. Some bad.

Ralph (Fort Brag, N.C.)

"Are you sure you are up to this?" Shawn asked me as our helicopter was beginning to land. "This is what I was born to do." I simply said as I took out a picture of my son just to look at it, then I placed it back. "Here we go." I said as the helicopter landed on the ground. I jumped out only to see thousands of troops from all over the world standing in attention. "This is unreal." Lynn said once she finally got off her laptop and saw the spectacle for herself. Three men immediately began to walk up towards me.

Captain Black. I am Lt. Orson. I am here to introduce you to the first world army. Everyone you see here participated their lives to join this fight. Many more will come in before the deadline day, but we are fully prepared." He said as we walked. "Good, we need all the soldiers we can get. Plus, I know the enemy's target points. London, New York, and Shanghai. We need armies on standby at these three places and have all civilians abandon these cities asap." I said as I gave him my paper work. "Yes Captain, we will get on it immediately." He said as he turned away towards a building. I turned towards the thousand s of troops and walked to greet them. Many faces stared at me, patiently awaiting my words. I got on the micro phone and smiled before I said anything…

My name is Captain Ralph Black, temporary commander and chief. I am here today to address the elephant in the room. I am here today to tell you the truth. I am here today to prepare you for the future.
Our world is facing an extinction and I know how it sounds; It sounds crazy right? It sounds like something straight out of a movie, but I can a sure you that this will be the realest battle you have ever seen. Our enemy is not each other, but something far worse than anything we could have ever encountered. If you have seen the attacks against our world already, then you have an idea of what we are against. I don't know what your faith may be, but I suggest you get right with someone, because a lot of us will not make it back to our homes. We are fighting for the sake of our planet and there will be no bigger honor than what we are fighting for today. You are no longer soldiers of your countries, you are warriors of your world. And in two days, we will rip our enemy to its core. Remember who

you are fighting for my friends. You will be legends. You will be immortal.

The troops all began to clap and cheer as I started walking away from the podium. "That was incredible." Lynn said. "Thank you, now it's all up to us." I said we all started walking away toward our living quarters.

Chapter 29
The Immortal War

(Adam)

I stood outside alone, as I took in the morning sun. There were a million things on my mind, but I managed to focus on one. I wondered where Gabriel would be and if I would ever see her again. Her death still to me feels unreal and with everything going on, I didn't have time to mourn for her. I knew killing Morgana would not bring her back, but it was a start. I felt a presence walking behind me that I could never live without.

"What is wrong, my love?" Melody asked me as she wrapped her arms around me. "Just thinking about Gabriel." I said. She dung her head within my back. "It kills me to even think about it. I miss her so much." She said as she held me tighter. I could feel the sorry within her heart, so I decided to change the subject.

"What is happening within the house? How is Scarlett?" I asked. Melody walked to the side of me as she answered. Victoria and Dawn are sleep. They finished the spell and it was ready to use. Jason is in the den with my mother, and Scarlett is sleep as well. Did you inform Ralph about the locations of where Lilith will strike?" She asked me. "Yes, he should be doing having a conference with the nations today to inform them." I replied. Melody wrapped her arms around me once again. "So much has happened since I met you. My life and all our friends and family's life has changed dramatically. Do you sometimes wish that you didn't save me when I was stuck in my car? Maybe life would have been better for you." She said as she put her head down. I grabbed her delicately and held her in my arms. "Finding you was the greatest moment in my life. Everything will be okay, I know of it. I feel it. Once this is over, we will live happy together, with our disappearing child." I said as I laughed. Melody laughed with me as she held her belly. "It's the strangest feeling I ever felt. It's like I know my baby is not in my stomach, but I could feel her elsewhere. I find that so odd." She said. "I feel her too, it's incredible." I said as I placed my hand on her stomach smiling that our child has abilities that not even I could comprehend.

Melody and I walked along the river that ran through Miss Catherine's house. The morning breeze felt amazing on my skin and the sunlight made Melody shine so beautifully. "We haven't spent much time together since this all started, I thought I would have been had my ring by now." She said jokingly. "How do you know I don't have one for you already." I simple responded. "Well, I know you have gave it to me by now. You can't keep a secret from me." She said. She was right, but in this case, she was wrong. From my pocket, I pulled out red box and displayed it for Melody. "Oh my…that cannot be what I think it is?" She said. "I wanted to wait until all of this mayhem was over, but I figured why wait. I love you more than anything and I knew I would be with you forever since the first time I saw you. Melody Marie Eve. Will you marry me?" I said as I flipped open the box and showed her a beautifully crafted ring." Melody was speechless as she gazed upon it. "Adam! This is beautiful! Of course, I would marry you! I would want nothing more than that!" She replied as she jumped up on me in joy. I smiled as I placed the ring on her finger. "It is so beautiful!" She said as she continued to star at it. "Gabriel actually crafted it for me some time ago. It was supposed to be a surprise." I said as I looked at the ring. Melody hugged me and kissed me on my check. "I know she is watching down on us." She said. I smiled because she was probably right.

We began to walk back toward the house when I began to feel a great presence appearing in the sky. "What is that?" Melody said as she stared up into the sky as well. I balled up my fist as a portal began to open blocking the clouds I was so fond of. "It's the same type of portal that opened in London. "How did they find us?" Melody said as we watched the portal grow. Victoria, Dawn, Amora, Miss Catherine, and the witches of the house ran outside to witness what was happening. "Get out of here Melody. Lilith is here." I said as I released Melody's hand. "No! I cannot leave your side!" She demanded. Before I could say anything else. Two figures appeared from the portal.

Lilith and Morgana descending to ground, landing about 30 feet away from us. I could feel Melody's anger began to grow. Lilith looked at us and smiled as she examined us one by one.

"Adam, it's good to see you again." Lilith said as she began to walk closer. "You monster!" Melody said as she stepped in front of me. Lilith smiled as she tilts her head. "Oh, Melody. You had so much potential…Wait? Is that a child within in your stomach? What an interesting species you are." She said as she examined Melody. I quickly place her behind me. Her eyes began looking amongst us all. "Scarlett? Is that you, Scarlett?" She said as her eyes remained glued on her. Scarlett placed two clips in her guns. "Where is Adrian!" Scarlett demanded. "He will be joining us shortly, but wait, how did you get here? Don't worry about it. It doesn't matter now. Oh, and I'm sorry to tell you he is not the Adrian that you know and love anymore. He is my greatest weapon. I cannot wait for you to see him" She said. "You bitch!" Scarlett said as she began to run towards her before Melody stopped her. "No, we will handle her and save Adrian." Melody said. Lilith just laughed as she raised her hands up. "It has come to my attention that an army is being built to rival mine. You just couldn't give up without a fight?" Lilith said. "Of course not." I simply said. "Lilith smiled at me. "This battle's outcome will be much different than the one in Nerite. So, I'm giving you one last chance to bow before me and I will spare your lives for my new world." Lilith proposed. Just as she said that, thousands of monstrous creatures began descending from the portal, crash landing about 50 feet away. "So, this is her army?" I said as I looked among them. Running up behind us was Natalia, Ruin, Alexandria, and hundreds of vampires. "I could sense her the moment she touched the ground." Natalia said as she looked directly at Morgana. "This is it. She won't stop so neither will we. I love every single one of you." I said as I held Natalia's hand. "I love you too Adam, thank you for bringing Melody in our lives." Natalia said. Melody smiled as I could see a tear fall from her eye. "We will end this once and for all!" Alexandria said as she held her brother's hand.

"I'm sorry Lilith, this is where we finish this." I said turning to Victoria. "You and Dawn you are up." I said smiling. They nodded as the jumped in front of us and placed a bowl filled with unknown ingredients. They both looked at each other before pouring the bowl in the ground. "What is this?" Lilith said as the ground began to shake. "Is it working?" I asked. Victoria smiled as her spell was coming to life. "Yes! Yes! It is!" She said as her and Dawn ran back towards us. "Great! Okay, I need one of you to go to Lyla and the other to Ralph. Let them know that war has started and to prepare." I said. "Of course. Be careful and take care of my sister." She said. "Of course." She gave us a final hug and disappeared with Dawn.

Coming from the cracks of the ground was the souls of thousands. Their bodies manifested in to a physical form as the touched back on the ground. They were already equipped with guns, swords, and all types of different weapons. "I can't believe it worked." Ruin said looking in awe. Lilith's eyes grew wide as she gazed upon our army. Just as we all started to move forward, something from the sky hit the ground right in front of us stopping our movement. "What is that?" Natalia said as her flames began ejecting from her body. We watched as the dust cleared only to be amazed at what was in front of us.

"It is me, my family!" Gabriel said she stood before us, wearing an all-white battle attire. Her skin was glowing as the sun shinned off her. Her hair was even different. Unlike the blonde I have been used to for my entire existence, her hair was a bold black. It gave her a different aura. "Gabriel!?" I said as I reached out to touch her. Melody's eyes were huge with disbelief. "Victoria and Dawn's spell brought back any one who wanted to fight. I cannot allow my family to fight alone." She said as she smiled and turned her focus on Morgana. "No problem, I will just have to kill you again!" Morgana said as she pointed at us causing the army to run full speed towards us. I ejected my wings, and so did Melody as prepare our self. "Baby, you can't be here! You must go!" I said to Melody only to know what she would say already. She just looked at me. "You know me Adam and you know what I'm going to say." I shook my head and handed her a sword. I opened my right hand to summon The Blade of Michael as we charged towards them. Natalia and Gabriel flew ahead of the pack with their sights on Morgana. Lilith did not move, instead she sat down and prepared to watch a war unfold before her very eyes.

(Joshua)

"It has started! Lilith is here!" Dawn said as she just appeared in front of us. "Where is she, we must go now." Lyla said as she hurried out the door. "She is in New Orleans, I don't know how she found us, but she did, and her army is here." She said. "Okay, Joshua, tell the other wolves its time." She said. I nodded as I exited the house but was quick to feel something different in the air. "You feel it too?" Luke said as he came to my side. "Yeah, what the hell is that?" I asked. "It's New York City. I just got a call from my sister saying that one of those portal things just opened in front of the Chrysler Building. I can only assume this is the fight you have been telling us about?" Meagan asked as she walked towards me. "This is it guys. Tell all the wolves we are going to New York."

Thousands of us ran through the forest, streets and mountains until we got to a New York city that was currently being invaded by this ugly ass creatures. I howled as my pack and Lyla invaded the streets with one objective. Kill every one of Lilith's monsters. We clawed our way through them only to realize, these things did not die easily.

"Come here!" I screamed as I bit the head off one of them only to find out that his legs and arms were still working. I turned back to a human as I looked at Lyla. "What the fuck are these things?" I asked as I knocked one away. "I don't know, but I know they are Morgana's creation." She answered as she beheaded one herself. "Why are these sons of bitches not dying? I asked. "I don't know, maybe we have to wait until Morgana is dead. They might break the curse she has on them." Lyla said. "Well I hope your brother moves fast." I said as I turned back into my wolf form and began tearing their bodies apart.

(Victoria)

"Excuse me miss, do you have I.D.?" A man at the gate asked me as I walked pass him effortlessly. "Call Captain Ralph, I need to talk with him asap." I simply said. "Miss!" He yelled at me as he pointed his gun at me. "Really?" I asked as I raised my arm up towards him, sending his gun to the sky with my magic. "I'm part of the super group of super powered people. I know you have heard of us?" I said as I waited for a response. "Um, no. I haven't." He said as he raised his hands. "Figures. Well, can you contact the Captain for me please? Tell him Adam sent me." I replied as I leaned against one of their military vehicles. After a few minutes, Captain Black and Shawn McQueen came running towards me.

"I sent a unit to New York, New Orleans, and London. It looks like they came earlier than expected." Captain Ralph said as loaded his weapons. "Yes, it looks like this is it. I am prepared to fight with you and your team." I said as I pulled out my wand. Ralph looked at it and smiled. "I appreciate your help. How did you get here so fast? The trip to London would take 8 hours. I would never get there in time. Can we travel with you?" He asked. I smiled as I looked at them. "Absolutely, you must already have troops down there, Captain?" I asked. "We are at war. We have troops everywhere." He said as he took his weapon of safety. "By the way, I'm Victoria. I don't think I introduced myself the first time we met, to either of you." I said as I stuck out my hands to both. They shook it just as fast as I placed it out. "Okay, now that we have that out of the way, let's get out of here." I said as I grabbed their hands and vanished to London.

"Wow!" Shawn said as we landed in London. "Yeah, it does that to people." I said as I started to look around. "Okay let's get to work!" Ralph said as we watched hundreds of figures fall out of the portal in the sky and landed on the ground unharmed. "Oh my God." I said as I watched London turn into a war zone. It seems like the army has been fighting for some time. "When did they begin to attack?" I asked as we started running to the action. "All the attacks happened within 10 minutes of one another, according to my data." Shawn said as he began loading his weapons. "Heads up!" I said as a car flew towards us. With a flick of my wand, I sent the car flying away from us. "You are quite resourceful!" Ralph said. "Okay guys, I got your 12,3,6, and 9 o'clock!" I said as I used my magic to take to the sky. I thought about Mathew as I prepared myself for battle. "Please let me come back to you." I said to myself as I dived in a large group of Lilith' monsters.

"Who is that?" Captain Ralph said as he pointed at a young woman with a samurai sword cutting through all the monsters that opposed her. "Is she one of yours?" He asked me. "No, I have not the slightest clue who she is, but she has a great ass." I said as I looked at her amazing skills with that sword. "Oh no…" Shawn said as she started walking our way. "What is it?" Ralph asked as he continued to shoot at anything that moved. "You are about to find out." He said as he began walking towards her.

"Shawn, it's been way to long." The woman said as she instantly slaps him in the face. "Damn Cara! Geez!" Shawn said as he held his face. "That was for leaving for two years. Now who are your friends?" He asked as she looked at us. "My name is Victoria and I just have to say, you are one of the coolest chicks I have ever seen. Which says a lot because I'm literally surrounded by chicks who kick quite a lot of ass." I ramble on. "Well, thanks for that. I'm Cara Nightmare. A hunter like Shawn. He deserved the slap, by the way." She said smiling. "I am Captain…" He started before being stopped. "I know who you are. Pleasure to meet you Captain. Still can't believe you got the entire world fighting as one. Very impressive." She said.

"Umm, guys?" I said as I looked up only to see a horde of these monsters coming right after us. "You guys ready?" Cara said as she lights a cigarette. "Let's end this!" I said as we charge forward.

(Natalia)

My eyes were red with fury as Gabriel and I charged through Lilith's monsters. My flames were burning bright as we battled through to get to Morgana. "Gabriel. You look amazing. It must be the hair." She said with a smirk. "I have come to destroy you Morgana." Gabriel simply said. Thunder and lightning began to fall from the sky as she began to walk towards us. This time, you die!" I said as I unleashed flames towards her. She dodged it as she thunderbolts were being aimed at me. Morgana took to the sky, surrounding herself by clouds and powerful rain. In didn't hesitate to pursue her and neither did Gabriel.

"I'm going to go around behind her. You take her forward." Gabriel suggested. I nodded as I flew through the stormy clouds only to be struck by lightning. I descended to the ground like a falling star. Before I hit the ground, I was caught by my vampire lover. "Thank you." I said as I tried to get back up to help Gabriel. Ruin held my arm as if he had something to say. "Just in case you die before I see you again." He said as he placed his hands on my cheek and kissed me so passionately, that I felt as if I was out of my body. "Now go!" He said as he released me. I looked at him with such love that I knew I couldn't die now. I had to return into his arms.

"I flew up with great speed tackling Morgana with great force. The crash was loud enough to cause an earth quake on the ground below us. I punched her into a tree and watch her crash to the ground. Gabriel flew to her and impaled her with her sword. "Stop, I am mother nature. I am what this world needs to live, to breath. You cannot kill me!" Morgana screamed. I engulfed Morgana's body with my most powerful flames, igniting her body until there was nothing left, but a shiny amulet. I picked it up and crushed it with my hand. The rain stopped, and the thunder and lightning ceased. Morgana was no more. "No!" Lilith screams as the all her monster's groan in pain. "What is happening?" I said as I looked around. "Her immortal monsters are now mortal." Gabriel simply said. "Great, lets finish the job, together." Gabriel said as she pulled her sword from Morgana's non-existent body. "After you?" I said as we dove into Lilith's weakened creatures.

(Adam)

"It's over Lilith." I said as I raised my sword at her. "Over? You are a fool to believe that. My powers are far more divine. I have been waiting for this moment for quite some time." She said as she stood up from her throne. I flapped my wing and prepared to strike Lilith with one crushing blow only for my blade to be hit by a much larger one. Standing in front of me was Adrian. He was wearing a helmet and dressed in attire fit for a warrior of The Darkness. His eyes were a dark red which only indicated that his demonic side has taken over his entire body. He was no longer Adrian.

"Did you think it would be that easy?" Lilith said as she laughed. "Adrian? What has happened to you?" Melody cried. "I am living my destiny." Adrian simply said as he pushed my blade away. "I told you that I didn't want to fight you unless you stood in my way." He said as he looked at me. "I cannot let you destroy this world." I said as I prepared myself." "Then I apologize Melody." He said as he rushed me with such speed, it was hard to follow his attacks.

His sword was massive, so I could not afford to be hit. I dodged his attacks as he dodged mine. We took to the sky creating loud bangs every time our swords touched. He was driven by such a rage that it saddens me. To see a good soul being tormented in this way was unbearable. We crashed back down to earth and stared at each other. Ruin, Alexandria, and their vampires were running through Lilith's weak soldiers as if they were paper. "Adrian! I know you are in there. Please hear me!" I called to him. He smiled. "Adrian is no more. I am the king of The Darkness. Nothing will stop me!" He screamed. "What about me!?" Scarlett screamed. She walked to the side me with tears rolling down her face. "What about me?!" She repeated.

(Melody)

I stared down Lilith with eyes of hatred and disgust "What have you done to him?" I asked. "I gave him what he needed. I gave him power. I gave him the crown. He will be what you could have, but you failed at your destiny." She said. "Serving you wasn't my destiny. Saving this world from you might be a start though." I said as I ejected my wings. "You were the chosen one. The one that was supposed to deliver this world an usher in a new. You were created to serve me! Your mother followed my teachings and opened The Darkness for us to be one. Look who you are fighting for. This isn't your fight. Join me my darling. Join me and become a God!" She said. "You are wrong! You have been in a state of revenge for so long that you don't even know what you are fighting for anymore. This world is beautiful. These people are beautiful. Despite what you may feel, you are wrong." I argued. "You are a foolish girl who knows nothing of pain and lost. You know nothing about abandonment or what lies within my deepest thoughts. Your God, casted me out for having my own mind. My own identity. You understand nothing." She protested. "I know more than you could possibly understand. You were one of God's first creations. You could have been more than what you are now, but you chose to abandon his kingdom. You chose to seek power for your own acts of malice; and you are choosing to destroy our world. You came here with the brilliant idea to destroy our world just to create a new and I cannot and will not let you do this." I said firmly. "Do you think you can stop me?" She said as she smiled. "I am sure of it." Just as I said this Amora landed in front of me.

"You are pregnant my daughter. I have failed you for your entire life. I won't fail you again. Now get out of here." She said calmly. "Amora." I said in shock. "Finally, I come face to face with you. I knew you would return to earth after your tragic death in your flawless attempt in bringing me back. I have been wondering why you haven't come to me after all this time. Now I see. It looks to me that you have had a change of heart?" Lilith asked Amora standing completely still. "Go now!" She whispered before turning towards her. "Yes, I have. There was a time where I believed in you, but watching you reminded me of true darkness. I thought you cared about something, but you don't. you only care about yourself. A good friend told me this, but I didn't listen to him" Amora said as she ejected her wings. Lilith tilted her head. "Interesting. Well, I won't argue with you Amora. If this is what you want…I just don't understand. Without you little necklace, you do not stand even the slightest chance of defeating me." Amora turned to look at me. "I love you Melody. Save your brother and tell him I love him as well. I am sorry."

She turned around and flew toward Lilith only to be cut down by a simple strike. Lilith smiled as she drove her fist through Amora's body. Her Divine was gone and so was she. "You monster!" I screamed as I charged her. We flew into four trees before she stopped me and threw me in to a building in New Orleans. The city was still being evacuated.

"Show me your strength I've heard so much about." She said as she kicked me into another building. I got up quickly and flew down towards her kicking her in to a parked car, destroying it instantly. She smiled as she got up. "I am going to enjoy killing you." She said as we both flew to one another, preparing to whatever we would hit each other with.

I could feel my built-in anger towards her as I began to overpower her. She looked at me in awe as she noticed all her attacks towards me caused me no harm. I smiled at her which only enraged her more. "I am Lilith! Queen of this world. I will not be defeated again, especially by a child! I am the reason you even exist!" She screamed. "You wanted to see my power right!?" I said as I knocked hard into the ground. Her face was twisted with disbelief. "You have cause all my family and friends so much grief and pain. Today will be the day that all of this will end bitch!" I said as I stand above her staring at her menacingly.

(Adam)

Adrian looked away from me as Scarlett spoke. His eyes began to go back to their original color. "Scarlett? What are you doing here?" He asked in confusion. "What the fuck about me, Adrian!? What have you become!" She asked. "I had to do what was necessary." He simply said without looking at her. "Necessary? Listen, baby, put the sword down and let's just go home. Let's go home and pop some popcorn, watch Hey Arnold. Let's leave all of this behind. Please." Scarlett pleaded. I watched as I could feel her heart breaking as she spoke. "I am doing this for you! Once Lilith's mission is complete, she will give us our own paradise. One where we could never die and live in eternal bliss. This is all for you!" He yelled. "I don't want it. I only want you Adrian. I only want you, nothing else." She confessed. His power was increasing dramatically. "I'm sorry Scar, I cannot do that. I want to give you more, I have too. This is what must happen. You will see, it will be beautiful. Don't you want that?" He said as he began walking closer to her. "Don't you see, there is no limitations on my power. I will be able to do whatever I please. Don't you want a life with no pain, no death? I can give this and more to you." He said as he placed his hand on her face. Scarlett closed her eyes and kissed him, pulling him closer to her. "I am sorry my love." She said as she grabbed my sword and stabbed him in his chest. "Adrian fell back and landed on his back. Scarlett cried out as she fell to her knees and sobbed over Adrian. A black light pierced itself out of Adrian's wound causing his eyes to return to their natural color. The demon within him was gone forever. "Thank you Scar…" Adrian managed to stay. "I placed my hand on his wound to try to heal him, but the power of the blade was too strong. His death was certain. "Adrian, I'm sorry. I'm so sorry." Scarlett said as she cried. "It's okay. You had to do it…I'm sorry for everything. I love you so much Scarlett. I love you…" He said. "I love you too Adrian. I always will…" Scarlett said as she kissed him once again but once her lips pulled back. Adrian was gone. "Scarlett sobbed at Adrian 's lifeless body. The sadness I felt from her, was a sadness that I never felt before. Her soul mate was gone, and she wasn't. I felt the tears roll down my face as I kneeled to her side. No words were said, and despite the war that we were fighting. Nothing was heard between.

Chapter 30
After the Storm Came Light

(Melody)

I felt it instantly and so did Lilith. "Adrian…" Lilith said as she struggled to fly to his side. Adam quickly stood up as I flew to a broken Scarlett. "He is gone." Scarlett said. Ruin and Alexandria ran to my side and all stood in front of Lilith. "I can't have believed he was killed by a foolish girl!" She said angrily. I noticed the field was empty of her monsters and all that stood was her and us. "It is over." Adam yelled. Lilith began walking backwards away from us. She was outnumbered and out powered. She stood no chance and she knew this. Her defeat was evident. I grabbed The Blade of Michael from Adam and pierced it inside her chest. Lililth looked at me in amazement as she fell to her knees. "What blade is that?" She said as her body fell to the ground. "A blade that can kill anything, even you." I said as we all watched her grasp for life, but it never came. She died effortlessly, and I could actually feel a happiness come over me. "It's done." I said as I pulled the blade from her lifeless body. Adam placed his arm around me and kissed me softly. It was over. I could no longer feel her or anything else that came with her.

Coming right behind Lilith's body was a man that I have never seen before. He was wearing a black suit with a stunning smile. "Lilith turned around and looked at him in horror. "What? What are you doing here?" Natalia asked the man. He laughed as he spoke. "Oh nothing. I came to see her demise up close and personal." The man said. We all looked at him in all as he took a bite of a red apple.

"Before any of you say anything, I want you to know that I was rooting for you all. The world is not ready to end, at least by my standards." He said as he stared at all of us. "Who are you?" I asked. He walked closer to me until Adam stepped in front of me. "Do you really have to ask?" He simply said. "Lucifer." Adam said as his eyes were glued to him. I looked at him in disbelief. "It is a wonderful treat to finally meet you Melody. You and your brother are a remarkable species." He then glanced at Adrian laying on the ground. "I am truly sorry what happened to your brother. I would have loved to see his true potential." He said. Scarlett immediately got up and slapped Lucifer across the face. Lucifer smiled as he turned back to face us. "I understand. It's still a touchy topic." He said as he rubbed his face. "What do you want?" Adam asked as he picked his sword off the ground. "I just came to congratulate you all on your victory. I think I have done all that I came to do." He said as he began working away. "He is the source of all evil, if we kill Lucifer, we may end all evil forever." He said in my mind. "Do it." I said to him. Adam rushed behind Lucifer preparing to stab him with the Blade of Michael only to be stopped by someone I didn't expect to see on this dark day.

"No, it is not the time." The familiar woman said as she stopped his blade. Adam looked at her with a face I have never seen before. "Listen to the girl. It is a smart advisory." Lucifer said as he stopped walking. "Don't worry, you will get your chance on day. I promise." He said as he vanished into nothing. I walked toward Adam and the young girl and just stared at her. We stared at her. "It's you..." Adam said. The young girl just looked at us with dazzling eyes. I knew in my heart and soul that I knew who she was, but I couldn't figure it out. Scarlett gazed upon the young girl as if she knew her. Her eyes began to water as she looked at her. "I must go, I shouldn't be here." She said as she started to walk away. "Wait..." Scarlett called out." She kissed Adrian once more before getting to her feet. The mysterious girl turned around to Scarlett's voice. "Tell them. Tell them who you are. Everyone needs to know who helped save us. Who helped saved me." Scarlett said as she wiped the tears from her face. The mysterious girl turned and looked at Scarlett. "I can't..." She said as I examined her again. "You can. It okay. I will make sure your world stays the same. Tell them." Gabriel said as she stepped forward. The girl looked at Adam and me and just smiled with tears coming down. It all hit me at once. Tears became rolling down my eyes as I walk closer to her. "I know who you are. You are me. You are Adam. You are us." I said as I embraced her. "How could I not know my own daughter?" I said to myself as she wrapped her arms around us. "My daughter?! You are so beautiful! But how could this be?" Adam said as he held us tighter. "I wanted to tell you, but I couldn't. I knew you would know..." She said as her tears turned to laugher. "But how? Why?" Adam tried to let out. "I have many abilities dad, that I don't even understand yet, but I am learning. And I came back to help you. I wanted to help you. I missed you guys so much." She said still crying. "Why do you miss us? Are we not in your time my love?" I said as my heart began to drop. Our daughter looked at us then to the ground. "It's okay beautiful, you can tell us." I said as I held her. "No. You are not in my present time." She said sadly. I looked at Adam and his face were as mine. "What happens to us?" I asked. She looks at us sadly. "You are killed when I am 14, by Lilith. That is why I did everything in my power to make sure you ended her now. I'm sorry, I shouldn't be telling you this." She said as she places her head in Adam's chest. The very thought of her words began running through my head, but I tried to be as calm as possible. "It's okay baby, we are going to be okay. Your Mom and Dad are going to be here for a long time. I promise." Adam said as he comforted her. "I tried every day to change it, but it never does. I don't think you can promise me that." She said with watery eyes. "We will figure it out baby. Lilith is gone now. There is nothing to be afraid of." I said as I kissed her on her fore head. She smiled as turned her eyes on Scarlett. "Scarlett…I'm so sorry." She said as she hugged her. "No, thank you. For everything." Scarlett said. We all held each other as if we didn't want the moment to end.

"It's time for me to go." Gabriel said as she walked towards us.

"Gabriel." I simply said as I looked at her. Her eyes were sad, but no tears came out. If only I had her strength. "I'm sorry I'm not there with you physically, but I am with you in spirit every day." She said as she kisses our daughter on the cheek. Gabriel smiles as she comes to embrace Adam and I. "Thank you for everything. I love you both very much."

"I love you Gabriel. You have always been there for me. I just wish I could find a way to make this right." I said as I continue you to hold her. "You already have. You have given me such a beautiful and amazing life. You are truly an amazing woman and I will be with you forever." She said. Unwillingly, I release her. "I love you Gabriel. We will see each other again." Adam said as he kisses her on the cheek. She smiles as she then walks in front of Ruin, Alexandria and Natalia. "I like you. You are great with my sister and she love you very much." She said to Ruin. "You are an amazing being with amazing powers. Love will find you." Gabriel said to Alexandria. She walked in front of Natalia and hugged her. "You are my sister who I love dearly. Thank you for always loving me the same." "I will see you again Gabriel." Natalia said as she struggled to control her emotions. She walks to Adrian's body. "This man has been conflicted and attacked by The Darkness for most of his life. You are his soulmate and I don't want you to be alone." She said to Scarlett as she placed her hand on Adrian's wound. Gabriel closed her eyes and a powerful white light came from her hand. "What are you doing?" Scarlett asked. "I am using the rest of my life force to revive him." She said as she focused. A demon spirit climbed out of his chest and was pulled into the earth. Gabriel got up off her knees and smile. Adrian took his first breath of new life. "Scarlett ran to his side and helped him up. "Oh my God, Adrian? You are alive!" She screamed. Adrian looked around the battle field confused and dazed. "What happened Scar?" He asked. Adam and I ran to his side instantly. "Adrian! I'm so happy you came back to us." I said as I hugged him. "Gabriel, I could never repay you. Thank you so much!" Scarlett cried. Gabriel smiled. "You are my family now, I would do anything for you." She said as her body began to evaporate. We all watched as Gabriel disappeared into the sun. Tears were everywhere, and just like that our sister was gone.

"I have to go as well. I can only be in this time for so long." Our daughter said to us. "Wipe your tears baby. You will see us again. My beautiful princess." I said as I kissed her forehead. "I believe that I will." She said as she wiped the tears from her eyes. "Good bye mom and dad, oh and Dad?" She asked. "Yes, my love?" "I know you didn't want to know, but mom named me Gabriella, after my auntie. So, can you please make sure you name me the same? I really love what it means to me." She said as she smiled. "Gabriella! I love it." I said as I held Adam's arm. "Of course, my love." Adam said. "Oh, and Dad, thank you for getting the flowers." She gave us one last smile and disappeared into nothing. He laughed as hard as I ever heard him laugh before. I didn't get the meaning, but I was make sure I ask later. We all stood there for a long time with our own thoughts and revelations. What was to happen to us in fourteen years? I ran to Scarlett and held in my arms. We didn't say anything we just held each other as if time itself. It was finally over.

We left the field in hopes of a new beginning. I walked past a lifeless Lilith and smiled to myself. I held Adam's arm and kissed him on the shoulder. He instantly picked me up and took to the sky. "I love you Adam." I simply said as I rested my head in his chest. He kissed me above the clouds. A kiss that I knew so well. "I love you too. I'll love you forever." He said. When he said that I felt in my soul that his words were true. I closed my eyes and drifted off in his forever.

Epilogue

The war was over. Melody and Adam prevailed over Lilith's vicious army of monsters and regained peace throughout the earth. They didn't do it alone though. All their allies succeeded in their efforts as well. Lyla, Dawn, Joshua, and his pack of loyal wolves saved the city of New York with their courage and fearlessness. Captain Black, Victoria, and Shawn "The Hunter" McQueen also displayed their leadership and skills in London as they fought with their lives. They even found an unlikely ally in the infamous Cara Nightmare. The four gained an alliance that made their opponents tremble in fear. It was and has become one of earth's greatest battles to be held.

Even with the incredible outcome, the earth we once knew was gone. The world watched as ferocious beast attacked the planet only to be protected by the likes of vampires, werewolves, witches, and angels. The very thought seemed like it was from a summer blockbuster movie, but this was our new reality. The governments of the world thanked our heroes for saving us and proposed a proposition to make sure nothing like this would ever happen again. Adam and Captain Black spoke for the behalf of all his fearless warriors. They promised that the threat was gone, and that the world would be safe for as long as they existed. A promise that he intended to withhold.

The world began to work together and rebuild and during that time our heroes began to rebuild. With Lilith dead, and The Darkness closed for good. The time for peace was now.

6 Months Later

(Melody)

Throughout everything in my life (the good and the bad) nothing compared like holding my child in my arms for the first time. Born July 23, Gabriella Eve Tyler was born. Adam was right all along about the sex, but I think he had an inside job of knowing. He is an angel after all.

We named her off my dear late sister Gabriel, and I wouldn't have it any other way. Life has been wonderful since the end of all the chaos. Adam and I could finally be together peacefully without someone coming to destroy the world. He is such a good father to our little princess and watching him in action is among the sexiest things he has done thus far.

For our daughter's sake, we moved out of the bustling city of Chicago to a quieter country home in Texas. Somehow, Adam got us a huge house with acres of land for Gabriella to roam around freely when she gets older. We still don't know the limitations of her powers yet, but we figured she would be away from the rest of the world once she starts using them. Of course, Victoria and my mother couldn't dare to be away from their niece and granddaughter, so they moved respectfully to their own houses within the 10 miles of where we stayed. Victoria and Matthew came almost every day. Speaking of Victoria, she gave up her witch lifestyle and became what she always wanted to do, be a wife. She finally told Matthew the truth and promised him that those days were behind her. I believed her. She only started to protect me in the first place and I would forever be thankful.

Ruin and Natalia returned to Paris. It turns out that Natalia actually may 'love' her vampire after all. I know she is a tough one to crack, but once he did, it was over for her. I really enjoy them together. He brings out a side of her that I never seen before. I like it. They come to visit often, especially because of Gabriella. She favors Natalia over everyone surprisingly.

Right after the war, Alexandria bought herself an old school convertible and drove off to unknown destinations. She said she wanted to explore the world, starting off with an America. She wanted to find her own identity and find out who she really was. Woman to woman, I understood completely. Being locked up in a castle for your entire life would make anyone just want to hop in a car and explore. Once she laid eyes on the baby, she was in love. Last time I checked, she was in Reno living her best life. She calls me every day.

Joshua returned home back to his Canadian forest with not only a half-gallon of vodka that we promised to give, but with Lyla. She claims she went with him to make sure he doesn't lose his leadership with his new pack, but Adam and I know better. Lyla flies back often to place with her niece, while Joshua returns to try to drink Adam under the table. Joshua loses every time.

Captain Black and Shawn McQueen started their own team, which I thought was the coolest thing ever. They go around saving people from the things that go bump in the night. They came to visit once, but they weren't alone. Lynn, one of the sweetest girls I had the pleasure to meet, and a woman who goes by the name of Cara Nightmare came with them. Now, this Cara Nightmare is by far the coolest woman I think I ever met. She just has a kick-ass personality. I think Shawn and Cara used to date, but I never got around to asking.

Dawn became a member of The Enchanted Ones, her lifelong dream. She was disappointed at the fact that Victoria no longer wanted to use her powers, but they are still excellent friends through it all.

And as for my brother Adrian, and his partner for life, Scarlett...they got married. Their wedding was beyond beautiful and I figuratively cried every couple of minutes. They have been lovers since they could remember. Soulmates at its finest. Gabriel returned as well, but she didn't come empty handed. Somehow, someway, she brought Carmen, their best friend, back from the dead. She was resurrected for good and Scarlett could not stop crying. Adrian and Adam have gotten so close in these past couple months that it looks *like they are best friends. Adrian and our relationship feels as if we known each other our entire lives.*

Life is great, and I wouldn't trade it for anything. Adam has been the best thing that has happened to me and I would say he would say the same about me. In the beginning we both were lost and confused about life and what our purpose was. Now we know...The purpose was for us to be standing right here in this moment...together. I was madly in love with an angel who dropped out of the sky for me. I will forever be in love with him...

"Mama." Gabriella's little voice rang down the halls. "Baby, what are you doing?" Adam asked me he kissed my neck. "I was just writing a few things." I said as I placed my pen down and folded the piece of paper I was writing on.

"Oh, I can't see?"

"Nope. Not yet, I'm not finished." I responded as I stood up and fell into his arms.

"Mama." Gabriella repeated. "Aww, my little pretty girl!" I said as I picked up off the ground. Adam smiles as he picks both of us. I look at Gabriella as she smiles so widely only showing gums. "I love you." I said as I look at both of them. Adam kissed me passionately, just like our first kiss. "I love you too." Gabriella continued to smile as we showed affection for one another. "I want to get married Adam. I want to be your wife." I said as I looked deeply in his eyes. "When do you want to have it?"

"As soon as possible." He kissed me once more to my response. "It's done." I held Gabriella closer to me as I dung my head in Adam's chest and fell into his eternal bliss...

The Eternal Saga

Thank You for Reading

Words from the Author

Wow! What an adventure it has been! Writing these words just reminds me of all the challenging work and long days it took to accomplish this beautiful piece of work. This has been an idea of mine since I was in high school and to finally have it typed is truly a feat. This novel means so much to me, words can't even come close to expressing how I feel. I free wrote the entire book with using my imagination and ideas I had throughout my writing career.

First thing, I want to thank my Lord and Savior, Jesus Christ, for giving me the strength to write when I had nothing to my name. Homeless, going from house to house, wondering what I was going to eat every day. Throughout all of it, I kept my laptop because I believe in this story. I believed it would be read by millions. The world needs love. More love.

I want to thank everyone who I bothered about this project. I promise that I will make it up to you all. I want to thank everyone who believed in my vision. I want to thank everybody who believes in love.... even in this day and age.

I based Melody and Adam's relationship on a relationship that I long to experience. Where love conquers all. I love these characters with all my heart. I love everyone else as well, but Adam and Melody were the originals, and you know how we love the originals.

I have plans and future books coming out featuring some of the support characters in their own adventures so look forward to that. I am beyond excited for the future.

And one more thing…The Eternal Saga, is not ending. It is merely hitting its surface. I cannot wait to introduce you to new characters as well as expanding on the old. This will be a journey and I want you to be a part of it. Thank you for reading and I'll see you soon…

Michael R. Finley

THE IMMORTALS

(Island of Imperium) Sits about 232 miles east from Africa. Unable to be seen or detected by mankind

(Eerous)

I stood in my royal chambers, watching my guest arrive on my island. I smiled as I placed my Chaos Gem inside my chest. "It looks like our guest have arrived." My beautiful wife said as she walked behind me. "I see. This has been long overdue, my Queen." I said as brushed my hand against her face. She kissed my hand gently and seductively as she walked away. I followed her to our grand hall and took a seat at my throne. I rested my chin on my fist as my guest entered my home. It was an emotion that I didn't think I could ever be, excited. "This is quite lovely." My Queen said as one of the servants began feeding her grapes.

"My beautiful guest! Welcome to my island. I feel you will be comfortable with our hospitalities that we have here." I said as I stood up. My five guest looked at me with joy in their eyes. "I am Eerous, God of Power and Eternal Ruler of the Cosmos. This is my queen Celine, Goddess of Eternal Life, Beauty and Eternal Ruler of the Moon. We welcome you." I said.

"Eerous. It is wonderful to see you. Where have you been?" Apep asked me. "My queen and I have been traveling among the stars, exploring galaxies far beyond this insignificant rock." I answered. "You have been gone for thousands of years. This is not the world you remember." Hera said. "What has changed sister?" My queen asked. "Everything. Humans do not worship nor believe in us anymore. Our power has suffered because of it" Kali said as she folded her arms. "How could this be? Who do they worship?" I asked angrily. "Humans are foolish beings. They worship themselves. The arrogance of it all!" Hel said as she banged her fist against the table.

"What is this world?" My queen said to me. "It gets worst. Angels walk amongst the humans once again. Raging their wars with Lucifer's demons. I hate the angel most of all." Kali said as she whipped her flawless hair back. "What about me?" Azazel said as he looked at her smiling. "Not you of course, my love." She responded. I was disgusted with everything I was hearing.

"I called this meeting amongst us Gods, to take back out world. These beings feel as if they have dominion over this world. They are greatly mistaken." I said. I waited for a response but silence the room. "What is the meaning of this silence?" I asked. "The Nephilim. They cannot be killed and their team ranges from all different type of beings. The people refer to them as 'The Immortals.'" Azazel simply said. "What is this you speak?" I roared. "In our existence, we never seen the offspring between a demon and angel, until now of course. Their power is immense. They overpowered Lilith, and every being of power within The Darkness." He replied. "You lie! Lilith is no more?" My queen asked in disbelief. "It's the truth Queen Celine. She has been vanquished." He said. I smiled to myself. "Finally, this planet has produced beings who may be strong enough to challenge me." I said within my thoughts. "The quest of power continues." My queen said in my mind so only I could hear. "Fantastic. Who are the Nephilim? I would love to meet them personally." I said with a grin. "Melody and Adrian. They are twins." Hel said. "Which one of them killed Lilith? Kill that one first." My queen announced. "Lilith was killed by the woman, Melody while engaging in battle with the Nephilim and their counterparts." Azazel said. "I want this Melody's head in my garden. I adored Lilith. Destroying this 'Nephilim' would be more than enough to demonstrate all of our power to the humans." My queen said. "I stood up and folded my arms with a smile. "I will take care of it." I said as I looked out into the oceans, smiling at my own malevolent thoughts…